Shadow of Ice Island

The King's Spies

Shadow of Ice Island
Scoundrel of Claymore Keep

Blood of Kings: Legends

Squire of Truth
Lord of Winter
Lady of Shadows
Heir of Light

Blood of Kings

By Darkness Hid
To Darkness Fled
From Darkness Won

THE KING'S SPIES
BOOK ONE

Shadow of Ice Island

Jill Williamson

Shadow of Ice Island
The King's Spies: Book 1

Copyright © 2026 Jill Williamson
Published by Sunrise Media Group, LLC

Print ISBN: 978-1-966463-26-9

All rights reserved. No part of this publication may be reproduced or transmitted in any form or by any means without written permission of the publisher.

This book is a work of fiction. Names, characters, places, and incidents are either products of the author's imagination or used fictitiously. Any similarity to actual people, organizations, and/or events is purely coincidental.

Scripture quotations are from the ESV® Bible (The Holy Bible, English Standard Version®), © 2001 by Crossway, a publishing ministry of Good News Publishers. ESV Text Edition: 2025. The ESV text may not be quoted in any publication made available to the public by a Creative Commons license. The ESV may not be translated in whole or in part into any other language. Used by permission. All rights reserved.

For more information about Jill Williamson please access her website at www.jillwilliamson.com

Published in the United States of America.

Cover Design: Emilie Haney, eahcreative.com

To Bobbi Mash, the best beta reader ever.

"But he said to me, "My grace is sufficient for you, for my power is made perfect in weakness. Therefore I will boast all the more gladly of my weaknesses, so that the power of Christ may rest upon me."

2 CORINTHIANS 12:9 ESV

"Now the Lord is the Spirit, and where the Spirit of the Lord is, there is freedom."

2 CORINTHIANS 3:17 ESV

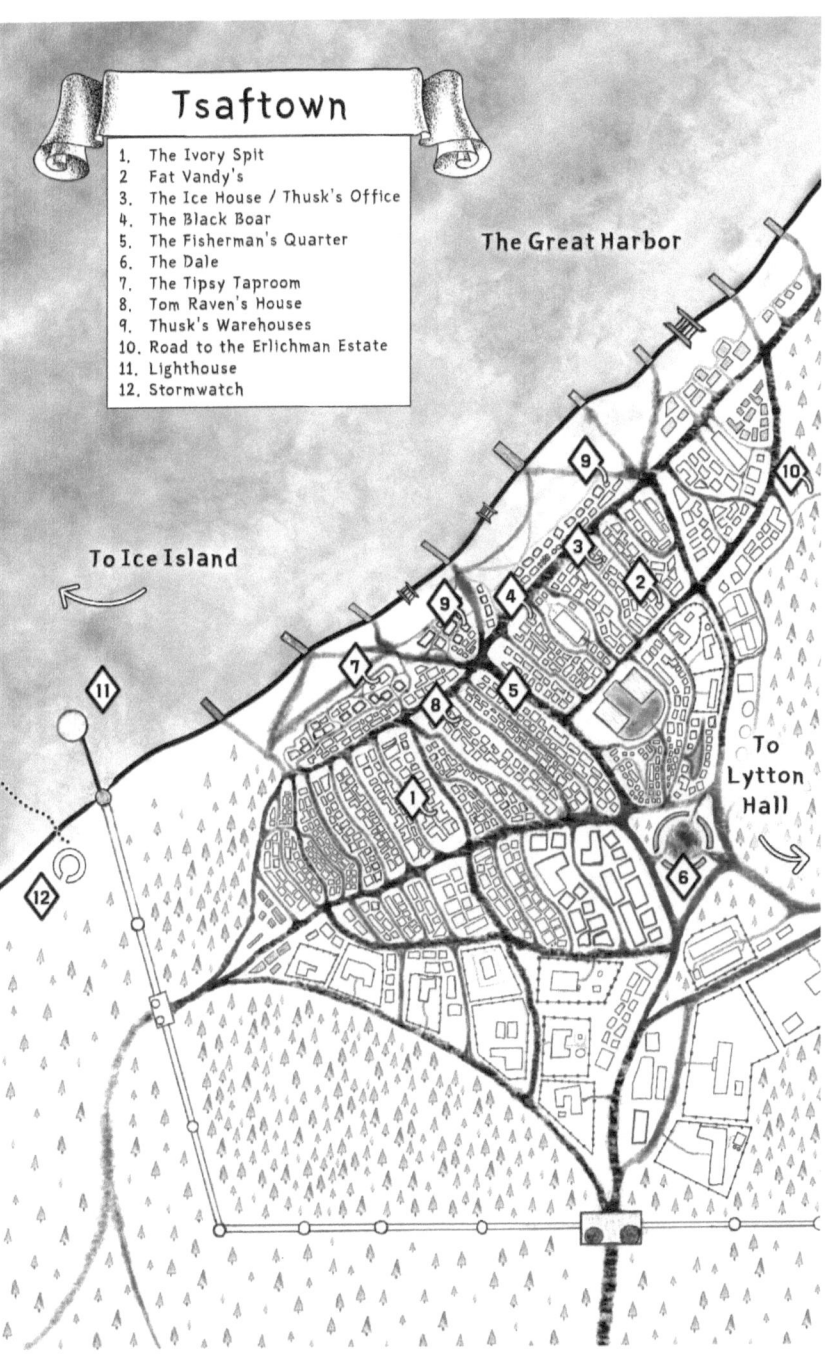

Chapter One
Cole

A SILENCED VOICE CARRIED NO TUNE. That's the thought that ran through Cole Tanniyn's mind as one of the raiders thrust a rusty sword at his chest. He leaped back and smashed against a set of shelves holding sacks of flour. One tipped off the ledge and thumped on the floor by his feet.

Blazes! Cole had better pull it together, or he'd die before he ever reached Ice Island and could question his uncle.

While the Tsaftown army had been camped to the east of Mahanaim, Lord Livna had sent out several dozen patrols to check the area. Cole had been paired off with Thakkar Oruk, a living storm; and Alden Wroxton, the silent blade—two of the Fighting Fifteen—and of course, Kurtz Chazir, Cole's friend, traveling companion, and fellow Mârad spy.

Their foursome had happened upon an outpost where two wagons sat empty, each hitched to a pair of rangy mules.

"Let's look inside," Thakkar had said, dismounting his black stallion.

"Grab your shield," Kurtz told Cole. "Sword drawn too."

Cole slid off Cherix's back, drew his sword, and grabbed his shield off the saddlebag, trying not to let his annoyance at Kurtz's continued mothering to show on his face.

He followed the others into a tiny outpost reeking of salted fish and onions. Shelves lined the walls and center of a cramped space no bigger than four peddler's carts hitched in a square. Two men's heads bobbed above the back shelves, while a burly third man stood in the front corner, stuffing candles into a sack.

Raiders.

"Ho there. It's me, Thakkar." The Berlander stood with his hands empty, palms raised. "Give me your names so I might know if you are friend or foe."

At that, seven more heads appeared as men, who had been crouched or bent over, straightened to their full height.

Not good. Cole tightened his grip on his sword and moved his shield in front of him.

"We're none of your business," said the burly man stealing candles.

Thakkar quickly drew a pair of hand axes that gleamed in the dim light. "You've had your fill. Take what you've stolen and leave. Now."

The raiders exchanged glances, their expressions defiant.

"There's plenty to share, soldier," the burly man said. "Feel free to help yourself, but you've no right to stop us."

Thakkar sighed, almost pitying. "Have it your way."

That's when the fight began.

The raiders surged forward, fierce but uncoordinated in the cramped space. Thakkar met the burly man head-on, his hand axes moving in quick, precise arcs, disarming his foe in moments. Wroxton slipped through the maze of shelves and came up behind the raiders in back, while Kurtz intercepted a bearded man on their right.

Cole found himself face-to-face with a wiry fellow wielding a rusted sword. The raider lunged, which was how Cole had knocked into the shelves of flour. He barely deflected the next blow with his shield, stirring memories of the Battle of Armonguard and the Eben he'd accidentally killed. He couldn't rely on dumb luck today. If he wanted to live—to reach Ice Island and see his uncle again—he had to fight. So he thrust out his sword.

The raider edged closer, grinning. "Don't know how to use that very well, do you?"

Behind Cole's wiry opponent, Thakkar whirled, hand axes flashing as he felled another raider, who crashed into a shelf, toppling sacks of beans and sending jars of honey spinning along the floor. A barrel of apples tipped over as well, scattering its contents past Cole's feet.

The wiry man feinted left, then swung right, knocking Cole's shield down the aisle. It hit a barrel and clattered to the floor.

Cole's breath hitched as he tightened his grip on his short sword. The raider pressed forward, and Cole parried every strike. Without the shield, keeping up felt easier than before.

Maybe he really *could* do this.

The raider struck again. Cole raised his sword, but the man twisted mid-swing and executed a vicious underhand swipe. Cole blocked the blow, but his grip was too weak, and he dropped his sword.

Blazes!

Weaponless, Cole's chest tightened as the raider lifted his rusty sword high.

And suddenly, Cole was back at the Battle of Armonguard, facing the Eben giant with nothing but the Armonguard flag.

"Lee-lee-lee-lee-lee!" the Eben sang.

Cole's stomach slid into his boots. Without a sword, he did the only thing he could think of. He turned the flagstaff and pointed the sharp end at the giant.

The Eben tossed his spear in the air and caught it with his grip reversed. Ready to throw.

Cole was going to die.

This isn't real. This isn't real.

"Cole!"

Back in the outpost, Kurtz lunged in front of Cole, intercepting the raider's attack with his longsword.

The blades clanged, and the raider stumbled back. Kurtz closed in, but the end of the raider's sword caught his shoulder. Kurtz didn't slow, though his hiss made it clear he'd been hit.

A chill flared in Cole's chest. He scanned the chaos—barrels, broken shelves, spilled food, scattered tools. Where was his sword?

He crouched, fingers searching debris, and found something heavy and rough—a fallen sack of flour. He ripped open the bag, and when he stood, he hurled it over Kurtz's shoulder.

White powder struck the raider's face, staggering him. Kurtz seized the moment and slammed his pommel against the wiry man's temple. The raider dropped to his knees, his rusted sword skittering away.

At the back of the outpost, Wroxton felled the last raider. Silence followed, broken only by labored breathing.

Thakkar, hand axes wet with blood, glanced at Cole. "Nice throw," he said dryly.

Was he being serious? Or sarcastic? Cole didn't know, but his face burned as he picked up his sword from beneath a pile of apples and threaded it into the ring on his belt.

Kurtz clapped him on the back, wincing slightly as he favored his injured shoulder. "Good thinking with the flour, eh?" he said. "You saved my neck there."

Cole's gaze fell on the battered raider, who glared at him through a mask of white dust. Just behind him, Cole's shield lay on the floor. He retrieved it, brushed off the flour, and threaded it over his arm.

Wroxton and Kurtz set about binding the prisoners' hands with strips of rope pulled from the wreckage.

"Now . . ." Thakkar crouched before the scarred raider. "Let's talk about who you work for."

"We work for ourselves," the man said. "No inbreeding lordling will tell us how to live our lives."

"Do you even know of whom you speak?" Thakkar asked.

"Donediff Hadar is no child," Wroxton added. "He ruled over Er'Rets Point these past five years. His mother is Lady Ginger of Allowntown, and he's married to Yulessa of Xulon."

"He wed a giant?" another of the raiders asked.

"To make sure his heirs don't end up as lowborn as you lot, eh?" Kurtz said.

"Let's get them into the wagon," Thakkar said. "We'll drop them off at the Mahanaim constabulary on our way back."

Cole eyed the growing brown stain on Kurtz's shoulder. "You're hurt."

"Bah!" Kurtz said. "Don't worry about it, eh?"

But that would be impossible. Traveling with Lord Livna and the Fighting Five Hundred was supposed to keep them safe on the journey to Tsaftown, but Cole was starting to wonder if surviving the journey would be harder than whatever waited for them in the frozen North.

The next morning, the Tsaftown army was on the move again. As they headed north over the snow-dusted Allown plains, Cole rode behind Kurtz, concerned by how the brawny man favored his good arm.

Last night, once they'd returned to camp, Cole had put up the horses. When he'd made it back to their tent, Kurtz had already patched up the cut on his shoulder—swore it was just a scratch.

Cole didn't believe him for a second.

Kurtz could have died, and it was Cole's fault. Sure, Cole played the lute well, was unmatched with horses, and had a knack for observation. But if he couldn't fight, how in all Er'Rets could he be a worthy spy? He simply wasn't strong enough to protect anyone.

Runt of the litter—that's what Nonda Fawst had always called him. He wanted to be strong and worthy, like the Tsaftown soldiers. Like Kurtz.

But he wasn't.

To make matters worse, Kurtz had placed them in the procession six horses behind Jeffrey Korngold, a bard also bound for Tsaftown. The golden-haired man was more talented than Minstrel Harp and bolder even than Kurtz. He was currently playing "The Ballad of the Tanniyn"—the song Cole had sung to Mistel when she'd been stormed to the Veil, the mystical barrier separating the realm of the living from that of the supernatural. Jeffrey's fingers flowed over the lute strings like river water over stone, his smooth, robust tenor twisting Cole's insides into a knot.

> "Where water meets sky, on vast ocean waves,
> A lost man adrift, above a watery grave.
> To the skies he prays, 'I have a son, a wife!'
> 'Oh Arman, how I'll serve you if you only save my life.'"

Cole hugged his lute, inferiority mounting.

Was it wrong to hate the man?

Ahead, Kurtz guided his horse, Smoke, off the path, waited for Cole to catch up, then fell in beside him on the road.

"What kind of soldier wears his sword on his back and carries a lute in his arms?" Kurtz asked. "If you're attacked, what are you going to do, bash them over the head with the instrument?"

"I would never break my lute."

Kurtz chuckled. "I've no doubt of that. What's with you, eh? Why so melancholy?"

Cole forced himself not to look at Jeffrey. "I'm fine."

"A lie as tall as a redpine," Kurtz said. "Out with it."

Cole sighed and lowered his voice. "Who will hire us with that bard in town?"

"Korngold? Bah! Don't worry about him, eh?"

"How can I not? He does everything far better than me." To further prove Cole's point, Jeffrey ended "The Ballad of the Tanniyn" with a fingerpicked run that resulted in applause and a few whistles from the surrounding soldiers. Part of their mission was to get hired at the Black Boar, a tavern in Tsaftown, but with someone like Jeffrey competing for work, Cole wasn't at all confident in their prospects. "Mistel said she and I performed better together than alone. I wish she could have come."

"Ah. So it's the ginger songbird you're sore about. Why are you still wearing that bracelet of hers, anyway?"

Cole eyed the string of beads around his left wrist. "What else is it good for?"

"Wearing it says 'Don't talk to me, ladies. I'm taken.'"

Cole wrinkled his nose. "It does not."

Kurtz gestured at the bracelet. "It's made of *beads*. It's clearly a woman's trinket. No man would wear something like that unless he's being sentimental."

"Maybe I want to be sentimental."

Kurtz groaned, the expression on his face so exaggerated that Cole couldn't help but laugh.

"What do you care, anyway?" Cole asked.

"Because you keep moping around, and it's my job to guide you through life."

"No one assigned you that task."

"I assigned it to myself," Kurtz said. "A young poet should have women tripping over themselves to speak with you. But that frown on your face scares them away."

"There are no women in the army, Kurtz. And even if there were, I have more important things on my mind." Like how they were going to get hired anywhere in Tsaftown with Jeffrey Korngold for competition.

"Bah," Kurtz said. "Talent is wasted on fools, it is. If I could spin words the way you do, I'd have more women than a king."

"You *have* had more women than the king," Cole said.

Kurtz blinked a measured beat. "Stop being so literal. I thought you were a poet, I did. Don't you know about metaphors and hyperbole and all that nonsense?"

Cole raised an eyebrow, impressed that Kurtz knew such terms. "I do, but you've missed the biggest point, my friend."

"What's that?"

"I don't want more women than a king. I'm content with my memories of Mistel."

Except for the part when she hadn't come to see him off. That still smarted, though he supposed he deserved it.

"Enough talk of women, then, if all you can do is mope," Kurtz said. "Talked to Quimby today. He wants to know our plans once we arrive in Tsaftown."

"Get hired at some alehouses and taverns," Cole said. "Unless Jeffrey gets hired everywhere first."

"He can't play every establishment in the North by himself," Kurtz said. "How do you want to handle Ice Island?"

"Don't know." Cole was still shocked that his uncle was alive when he thought the man had died years ago. Prince Oren wanted Cole to question him, see if he'd admit who framed him. "Stop by for a visit, I suppose."

"Jol seems to think we won't be able to just show up. Says the place has been locked down pretty tight lately. We'll have to get invited."

"By who?" Cole asked.

"Verdot Amal." Kurtz said the name as if it tasted bad. "He's the warden."

"And that's a problem why?" Cole asked.

"Because I spent thirteen years on Ice Island for a crime I didn't do," Kurtz said, "and Verdot Amal is the man who made it happen."

Cole's stomach dropped. He'd known getting into Ice Island would be hard. Now it felt impossible. "Wonderful. I need help from the one man who'll probably throw me in a cell just for knowing you."

"Bah!" Kurtz said. "What's thirteen years' worth of hatred when it comes to uncovering the truth, eh? I'm sure you'll think of something."

And suddenly, talking to his long-lost uncle didn't feel like a reunion to Cole. It felt like a trap.

Chapter Two
Mistel

Following the Tsaftown army was supposed to be a grand adventure, yet Mistel Wepp's great tale of daring had taken a rather tedious turn.

Bart, the horse she had *borrowed* from the Armonguard stables, shifted beneath her, his breath steaming in the dusky air as they made their way along the road, both half frozen and starved. They were somewhere between Mahanaim and Allowntown, following rolling hills of snow-covered prairie. They should be over halfway to Tsaftown by now, but Mistel had long ago lost count of how many days they'd been traveling. At least a dozen.

She wondered—for the umpteenth time—if she'd made a terrible mistake.

The idea had seemed flawless: a daring, romantic gesture to follow Cole north. He needed her. She was half of their duo, after all. That freckle-faced boy could charm every string on that lute of his, but without Mistel, his songs were just music.

Excellent music, of course, but what Cole didn't understand about an audience was that they didn't just want a song. They wanted a show. Cole gave them music, and Mistel gave them a memory. That's what made them such a perfect team.

The trees thickened into tangled brush, and Bart gave a nervous snort. Mistel glanced toward a shifting shadow, heart increasing in tempo as a pair of gray wolves darted from the undergrowth.

She cried out, and while Bart spun in a full circle on the snowy road, she clung to the saddle horn, barely keeping her seat.

One of the wolves crept low toward them, lips peeled back in a snarl. Bart whinnied and stamped, and Mistel hollered at the creature.

"Get away! Shoo!"

The wolves suddenly froze, ears flicking in the direction from which they'd come. The undergrowth rustled. Leaves shivered. Twigs snapped.

Please don't let it be more wolves.

A heartbeat later, two riders burst from the trees. The wolves flinched at the sight and, with a snarl, wheeled and darted off in the opposite direction.

Mistel stroked Bart's neck. The poor horse was trembling more than she was. "Easy," she whispered. "Easy now." Bart finally stilled, though his sides heaved and his ears pinned back.

"Identify yourself." This from a striking, iron-forged figure with a face that had been carved for admiration. His wavy golden hair was partly tied back in a half-knot above his ears while the rest hung longer than her own.

Mercy. Could this be Avenis, the god of beauty, speaking to Mistel in the middle of a snowy prairie? She hoped she hadn't frozen to death.

Beside the chiseled fortress of a man sat a bald, barrel-chested soldier with a bushy red beard so long and bright it nearly outshone Mistel's own coppery locks.

She forced her best male voice as she uttered her own surname, which seemed an appropriate title for a man. "I'm called Wepp, cap'n."

"Why are you following us, Master Wepp?" asked the god of beauty.

His accusation tugged her heart up into her throat, though she was relieved to see both wore Tsaftown uniforms. "I mean no harm, cap'n," she said. "I'm headed to Tsaftown to visit my sister. Thought it'd be safer to ride in the wake of the formidable Five Hundred than take my chances on my own."

"Who's your sister?" Avenis asked.

"Joya Wepp," Mistel said, quickly spinning the tale she'd planned on the long ride. "I suppose she no longer goes by Wepp, but she never gave me her new husband's surname. Just said she married last fall, a man called Frix, and now they're expecting their firstborn. Begged me to come visit, and when I heard the army was headed that way, seemed as good a time as any."

The stocky man reached over his shoulder and patted a longbow strapped to his back. "You're lucky we didn't shoot first and ask questions later."

Well! Mistel's fingers tightened around the reins. "Indeed, I'm fortunate there, cap'n. And that you came along when you did. Them wolves looked hungry."

"What he means," Avenis said, "is that there's been trouble in the area. Raiders."

Mistel shivered at the word. "Och! I'm glad the two of you found me and not a pack of raiders. Not that I've anything to steal."

"You have a horse," the shorter man said. "And clothes on your back. These raiders are ruthless enough to strip a man to naught but his skin."

Mistel's mouth went dry. "Doubly glad to have met you both."

"I'm Lysander Thane," the beautiful man said. "This is Cerdic Ironblade."

"Letsim Wepp," Mistel said, turning her first name inside out.

"But I go by Wepp." That way, should someone call out "Wepp," Mistel would at least be inclined to perk up and answer.

"You're welcome to travel with the army, Master Wepp," said Lysander Thane.

My, how that name sounded like a song.

"Thank you kindly, cap'n," she said.

He clicked his tongue, and his large black horse trotted forward on the road. Master Ironblade followed, giving Mistel a thorough going-over with his eyes as he went.

"I'd stick very close," he said. "A strong wind could fell the likes of you, and I'm not risking my neck to save your scrawny hide."

Before Mistel could think to hold back, she gasped. Thankfully, the hunx was already riding away with Lysander Thane, so she glared at Ironblade's bald head and nudged Bart after them.

Did travel with the army mean she could share their food and campfires? Two plus weeks into this escapade, Mistel's empty stomach clawed at her ribs, her fingers stung with numbness, and every muscle ached from Bart's hideous saddle and the nights spent curled on frozen ground with only her cloak for warmth. She hadn't thought to pack a tent—or even a bedroll—and the farther north she traveled, the colder and more miserable the nights became.

She usually bedded down under the hollow of a tree and tried to ignore the smell of something rich and meaty drifting from the Tsaftown camp—she hadn't packed enough food either. She desperately needed to purchase supplies from somewhere but worried that if she left sight of the army, she might never find them again.

And poor Bart! The horse ate constantly—grass from beneath trees or spindly branches. Yet Mistel could now see a few of his ribs through his thin brown coat. Could it be that the cold weather was making him hungrier? Or perhaps the dying grass simply wasn't enough.

She should have thought through her plan more thoroughly

before she'd stolen—ahem, *borrowed*—the horse and ridden north. But how was she to know that adventure this time of year could be so wretched?

She simply needed a hot meal, a warm bed, a stable and hay for Bart, and for Cole to take one long, stunned look at her, shake his head with that exasperated little smile, and admit that she was brilliant for coming along. Maybe kiss her hello.

Then everything would be fine.

A great deal of time passed before Mistel, Lysander Thane, and Cerdic Ironblade met up with a larger group—more than two dozen. A handful of soldiers made small talk with her, and she repeated her story about visiting her sister in Tsaftown.

Well, at least she could no longer complain about being bored, yet now her nerves tipped on the point of a needle as her gaze darted from one soldier to the next. She'd completely lost sight of Lysander Thane and his bearded companion. No sign of Cole or Kurtz Chazir either.

Up ahead, three soldiers broke into a bawdy drinking song. Mistel had to bite her tongue to keep from joining in as her voice would completely betray her.

A soldier rode up beside her and extended a bone-carved flask. "You look like you're about to freeze solid," he said. "A sip of this'll chase the chill away."

Mistel forced a tight smile. "I'd better not. If I like it, I'll drain the whole thing, and you'll hate me for it."

The man chuckled and tucked the flask away. "Suit yourself."

Mistel glanced north, where the snow-capped Chowmah Mountains loomed like a warning. Somewhere between those peaks and where she sat on Bart's back, Cole was riding his horse Cherix, maybe playing his lute and singing songs she'd helped him write.

They were still too close to civilization for her to make herself known. Lord Livna might send her back to Mahanaim or even

Allowntown. No, for now, she'd linger at the back of the line, pretending she belonged.

Pretending she wasn't afraid.

Because even if she'd told herself she didn't need anyone, she wanted to be with Cole. His kindness, his thoughtfulness, his irresistible grin, his companionship...

Something tickled above her ear. She shook her head, then winced as the tickle became a bite. She rubbed the spot, annoyed that on top of everything else she might be ill.

Achan Cham.

Her breath froze in her lungs.

Oh. Oh *no.*

The king was bloodvoicing her—using his magic to speak to her mind.

She recalled Sir Caleb's lessons on how to shield and concentrated, but the uncomfortable ache in her temple spiked.

King Gidon.

Dash it! She supposed she must answer. How could she not? What did it matter that they had been childhood friends? He was her king now.

She tugged Bart's reins and fell behind the soldiers. "Yes, Your Highness?" she whispered.

Mistel, Achan said to her mind, *you stole a horse from my stables.*

Thunder and rats. "No, Your Highness. I only *borrowed* Bart. I'll, uh, bring him back."

When might that be? he asked. *Noam tells me you've been gone well past a fortnight.*

"Well, I'm not sure," she said.

You're not sure. I can only guess you've followed Cole. Was it his idea?

"No! Of course not. He doesn't know I've come. I, uh, wanted to surprise him. He would have said no, otherwise." Had said no. Emphatically, actually.

That's a relief, Achan said. *I would have hated for Sir Caleb to hear otherwise.*

Mistel winced, knowing the stodgy chamberlain already disapproved of any relationship between her and Cole. Her current whereabouts would not help Sir Caleb's opinion of her.

"Cole is dutiful and loyal to you, Your Highness," she said. "While it was clear he *wanted* me to come along, he would not admit it. Nor would he say what he would be doing, but I surmised that part of his task is to play music. So, it was up to me to make the hard choice. He needs me to succeed."

I don't see why.

"No offense, Achan—*Your Highness,*" Mistel said. "But you're not thinking like a performer. Cole will sit on a stool, barely looking up from his lute strings while he sings to the floor. With me there, I'll have the crowd singing along in no time."

You think that's important to Cole's . . . task, as you put it? That the crowd join in?

"With me distracting the crowd, no one will be looking at Cole, and with the attention off him, he will be free to discover whatever secrets you wish to know. So, you see, I'm a necessary part of his success."

I see that you *think so,* Achan said. *Unfortunately, it's not safe.*

Ugh. Why were men always telling her that? "I can take care of myself."

That may be, but you would still be a tremendous distraction to Cole. Stop at the next major settlement. I'll see you're given some money for food and lodging until I'm able to arrange an escort back to Armonguard.

Lands! Did he honestly think he could order her around? "Forgive me, Your Highness," Mistel said, "but no."

No?

"You do not get to dictate my life. If I want to reside in Tsaftown, that's my choice."

Nor do you get to dictate Cole's life, Achan said. *Are you going to tell him you're there, or must I?*

Not yet! "I wanted to wait until we reached the mountains," Mistel said.

So that you wouldn't be sent back? I'm afraid not. You'll tell him now or I will.

"But it's almost dark," Mistel said. "I'll never find him at this hour."

Tomorrow then, Achan said.

How interfering Achan could be. "Fine. I'll tell him tomorrow."

Good. And while I won't stop you from riding to Tsaftown, if Cole doesn't want you there, I will insist that you respect his wishes. Is that clear?

What a thing to say. Of course Cole wanted her with him. He was too sweet to say so—always trying to protect her. "I understand you completely," she said.

Achan chuckled. *And I understand that your words did not at all answer my question.*

Mistel grinned and held her tongue.

If Cole tells me you're a distraction, Achan said, *you'll have to come back, whether or not you want to. If I must, I'll have you arrested. Is that clear?*

Arrest her? Mistel glanced at the sky. My, the crown had certainly given Achan Cham a newfound bossiness he'd never had before.

She couldn't resist a little mischief, so she repeated her previous reply with a bit more attitude. "I understand you completely."

The pressure left her head, so Mistel knew he'd gone. She nudged Bart into a trot to catch up with the army, yet now her skin prickled for a completely different reason.

What if Cole, in his attempts to keep her safe, insisted she go back?

What if Achan truly had her arrested?

She squeezed Bart's reins, fingers stiff, then laughed to herself. Well, if Cole said no, she'd just have to convince him he was wrong. Like she always did.

And if Achan—*the king*—tried to have her arrested, best of luck to him because he'd have to catch her first.

Chapter Three
Cole

A HORSE WHINNIED, JERKING COLE awake. He opened his eyes and squinted at the golden light from a lantern hanging at the apex of the tent. Movement by his feet made him jump, but it was only Kurtz, his back to Cole, looking out the door flap.

The man had issues with the dark, hence the lantern. Cole much preferred it to an open flame. Months ago, a candle Kurtz had left lit one night had nearly burned down their tent.

"What are you doing?" Cole asked, his voice groggy.

Kurtz didn't move. Not even a twitch. "Watching."

"Who's out there?"

"Just some travelers. Look to be merchants. They didn't see us."

That anyone could miss an entire army camped on the side of the road seemed strange to Cole, but it *was* the middle of the night.

Kurtz stepped deeper into the tent and sank onto his bedroll, draping his arms over his knees. "What woke you?"

"I heard a horse."

Kurtz grunted. "You were ten minutes too late. They'd have killed you and taken everything you own."

"I own very little."

"They'd have taken your lute."

Cole rubbed his face and scowled at Kurtz. "How can I make myself wake if I'm asleep?"

"That's another thing to practice."

Cole rolled over and put his back to Kurtz. "It's not that I don't appreciate your training. I do. I simply question the fairness of learning everything at once. In the middle of the night."

"We'll reach Tsaftown before you know it," Kurtz said. "If you're not ready, it'll be too late to learn, it will."

"How do *you* know? Have you posed as a minstrel spy before?"

"Have you ever had to keep yourself from being killed in your sleep?"

"Of course not."

"Then we both have lots to learn. Get up, eh? We'll run some drills."

Cole groaned. But his lack of skill had nearly gotten Kurtz killed. That couldn't happen again. He had to learn—whatever it took—so he pushed himself out of bed and followed his friend out into the darkness.

Steel clanged through the quiet dawn as Cole parried Derby Wenk's longsword. The impact sent a jolt up his arm, and he repeated Kurtz's mantra: *Distract, disable, don't overthink.*

But Derby's strikes were too fast, too precise. Cole couldn't keep up. The squire had two years on him and had earned his place as Lord Livna's squire through years of training—unlike Cole, who'd only had Achan's pity.

With each step Derby forced him back, the squire's grin widened.

"Hold your ground!" Kurtz yelled from the sidelines. "Push

back with the shield. When you retreat, you give your opponent control."

Cole tightened his grip on the shield, breath fogging in the cold. Derby lunged, blade arcing down. Cole blocked with his shield, but the impact rattled his teeth. Before he could recover, Derby feinted left, then deftly twisted his blade around Cole's sword.

The weapon flew from Cole's grasp and slapped into the muddy snow.

"Blazes," Kurtz muttered.

Derby stepped back, smirking as Cole scurried over and snatched up his sword.

"Again!" Kurtz crossed his arms. "And this time, hold on, because Wenk isn't going to yield long enough for you to pick it up." He shifted his gaze to Derby and nodded.

Cole squared his shoulders, raised his shield, and set the flat of his blade against the wooden edge. He had to do better, but his arms were already jelly.

Derby lunged for Cole's legs. Cole dropped his shield to block, but Derby's blade shot up. Cole barely had time to lift his shield before Derby caught the top edge with the cross guard of his sword and yanked down.

Again, Cole's shield ripped away. It rolled in a circle before thumping into the snow.

"Don't let up on him, Wenk," Kurtz said.

Cole gripped his sword with both hands, the way Derby held his longsword. When Derby attacked, Cole sidestepped, narrowly dodging the blow. Without the shield's weight, he moved quicker, more precisely, and felt stronger.

He parried another thrust, then managed a counterattack that forced Derby back a step. Now, that was more like it. Maybe he didn't need the shield after all.

Still, Derby's swift footwork left Cole scrambling. A high feint drew Cole's blade up, then Derby lunged, slamming his shoulder into Cole's chest. Off-balance, Cole barely registered the sharp crack as Derby's longsword struck his forearm.

He cried out, faltered, and Derby disarmed him.

"Better," Kurtz said gruffly.

When Cole turned to find his sword, Derby slipped up behind him, hooked an arm around his chest, and pressed his blade to his throat.

Kurtz lifted his arms, letting them fall back and slap his sides. "Well, now you're dead."

Derby chuckled and lowered his sword. "Lord Livna says never let anyone sneak up behind you."

"He's right about that, he is," Kurtz said. "If a blade is at your skin, it's over."

Cole rubbed his sore forearm. "There's no way to defend against it? Ever?"

"Nope," Kurtz said. "You do nothing and hope for mercy, eh? Of course, if your attacker is holding you there and hasn't slit your throat yet, could be he never intended to. In that case, talk your way out of it and try to get some distance between you and the blade. Let's go again."

Cole nodded toward the circle of wood on the ground. "I could move faster without the shield, and it helped to hold the sword with two hands."

"You can't wield a short sword with two hands," Kurtz said. "How will you hold your shield?"

Cole didn't want the shield. "Can I switch to a longsword?" he asked.

"You don't have the arm strength," Kurtz said.

"He could practice using the short sword like a longsword until he's stronger," Derby said. "He did fight better without the shield."

"But he needs a shield because he has no armor," Kurtz said.

Cole ran a hand through his damp hair. "But I think—"

"It's not just strength," Kurtz said. "You need control. And if you can't hold a short blade for three minutes, you can't control a longsword."

The weight of Kurtz's truth drained what little energy Cole had left.

"Pick them up," Kurtz said, nodding toward the discarded weapons. "Again."

Cole swallowed the retort burning his tongue and bent to retrieve his sword and shield. His fingers ached, his arm throbbed, and his pride? Battered to shreds. Yet he wasn't about to let Derby—or Kurtz—think he couldn't handle the training.

"Grip them both like your life depends on it," Kurtz said, "because one day, it will."

Cole had no worry for his own life. But should Kurtz be hurt worse next time because of Cole's weakness . . . He couldn't bear being a liability to anyone.

He had barely taken his position across from Derby when a small man in a farmer's hat trudged toward them.

"Finally!" the man said.

Something in the timbre of his voice gave Cole pause.

The farmer sighed deeply, as if he found them all horribly tedious, and set his hands on his hips. "Six different men said, 'They're right over there,' yet all six pointed in a different direction."

Kurtz frowned. "Are you lost?"

"I'm not *now*." The farmer swept off his hat, which revealed he was not a farmer at all, nor a man. "Hello, Cole."

The blood drained from Cole's face as he took in the woman standing before him. Ginger hair trapped in a knot atop her head, freckles as numerous as ever, pink lips twisted into a smirk, and those green eyes pinned on him.

Mistel Wepp had followed them from Armonguard, and—blazes!—even in trousers, she was stunning.

Chapter Four
Mistel

Maybe barging up on Cole while he was crossing swords hadn't been Mistel's best idea. She kept smiling, pretending all was going to plan.

His flushed cheeks and sweat-damp hair suited him. She rather liked the warrior look.

"Wha-what are you...? Where did...? How can...? Mistel?"

Mercy. The boy could barely speak. "Glad to see me, are you, my knightling?"

His brow wrinkled as his gaze traveled down her tunic to her trousered legs and stopped at the men's work boots on her feet. His freckled cheeks darkened another shade.

"No," Kurtz snapped. "This is no good, it's not. You can't be here."

Mistel arced an eyebrow at Kurtz, whose fierce expression wilted under her stare. "Master Chazir," she said. "How nice to see you again." She glanced at the third man, who looked closer to Cole's age. "Since these two have completely forgotten their manners, I suppose I must introduce myself. I'm Mistel Wepp, Cole's cousin, and a member of his band."

Cole's eyebrows shot up.

The third man bowed politely. "Pleased to know you, Miss Wepp. I'm Derby Wenk."

My, but Master Wenk had the reddest ears she'd ever seen. Or perhaps that was simply from the exercise and cold. "Apologies for interrupting this riveting exhibition of masculine prowess," she said, "but I really need to speak with Cole. Do you mind?"

"Not at all," Master Wenk said.

"Thanks for the practice, Derby," Cole said.

"I can see you have your hands full." Master Wenk bowed again. "Good day, Miss Wepp."

"Mm-hm." As the young man walked off, Mistel turned her attention to Cole. "I thought it was high time you knew I was here."

"You followed us from Armonguard," Cole said.

Mistel gave him her widest smile. "I did."

"On foot?" Cole asked.

At that, she winced. No point fibbing. He'd find out eventually. "No, I borrowed Bart."

Cole's hazel eyes flew wide. "You stole the king's horse?"

She waved one of her hands. "He knows all about it. It's fine."

"What happened to 'It was fun and all, but I'm better off without you'?" Cole asked.

Lands! Good memory on this one. He *would* bring that up. "I overreacted. Said all the wrong things. But I can admit when I'm wrong. And I was."

A little furrow wedged between his brows. So cute. "I didn't want to hurt you."

"I know. You were just trying to do the right thing. But so am I. And now I can be part of your band."

"Mistel," Cole said, "there's no band."

"You on the lute," she said, "Kurtz on the tabor, and me on vocals and tambourine. I explained it all to the king. He understands completely."

"No," Cole snapped. "You can't be here."

Well, *that* tone was unpleasant. "Oh, you're welcome, Cole, because yes, I did follow you all the way from Armonguard. Yes, I left everything behind. And no, I haven't yet frozen to death from sleeping under trees, thank you for asking."

He stepped closer, his voice dropping lower. "This isn't a game, Mistel. You can't just, just barge in here and expect to—"

"To help you?" She crossed her arms. "You're welcome for that, too, by the way."

Kurtz snorted from behind them. "You've got spine, I'll give you that, but an army is no place for a lady."

Mistel turned her smile on Kurtz. "Good thing I'm no lady, then, Master Chazir. I'm a songstress. Surely even you can appreciate the skill I'll add to your little band."

Cole groaned and ran a hand through his hair. "This isn't like playing for the king's wedding. People could die. *You* could die."

"You think I don't know that?" She softened her voice. "I've faced danger before. I know how to take care of myself."

"You've never faced *this*. You've never been surrounded by soldiers, never had to . . ." Cole broke off. Swallowed and glanced away.

He could be such a worrywart. She sighed and lightened her tone. "You're concerned. I see that. But you need me. Deep down, you know it. Who's going to distract the crowd while you're sneaking around doing . . . whatever you're supposed to be doing?"

"I don't need you to distract any crowd," he said.

"You play better when I'm with you," she said. "And admit it—you *miss* me."

"I don't miss you," he said, a little too quickly.

Mistel tilted her head and widened her grin. "See, now I *know* you're lying."

Cole released a deep breath. "If something happens to you, it'll be on *me*."

Mistel stepped closer, her voice falling to a whisper. "Nothing's going to happen to me, Cole." She tangled her fingers with his gloved ones, and even with the leather layer between their skin, tingles ran all the way up her arm. "And if it does, it won't be your fault because I chose to come here."

For a moment, they stood toe to toe, staring at each other. Oh, how she missed looking at those hazel eyes. Those freckles. Those lips.

"Miss Wepp." Kurtz's voice broke the moment. "I've just now bloodvoiced the king, I did. He said he insisted you make yourself known to us. Now that you have done so, *I* insist you sit yourself on that stump right there until Cole and I can talk with the king about all this, eh?"

"Oh, no." Mistel folded her arms. "You're not meeting about me without me there."

"Oh, yes, we are," Kurtz said. "The king has given me permission to arrest you, if need be." He grinned, his short beard dimpling around the corners of his mouth. "And if you think I won't enjoy every moment of *that*, then you don't know me at all, eh?"

Mistel huffed, slipped her hands around Cole's arm, and squeezed. "I stay with Cole."

"Do as he says." Cole tugged free from her grasp, the loss of his touch suddenly cold. He followed Kurtz through the tents, leaving her behind.

Sit on a stump? While they decided her fate? She wasn't some damsel to be managed. She was Mistel Wepp: songwriter, performer, and perfectly capable of taking care of herself.

She kicked the stump a few times, circled it until she'd made a trench in the snow, then climbed up to try and spot Cole over the tops of the tents.

That was the extent of her patience. She jumped down and strode in the direction Cole had gone, intent on finding some way to prove she belonged.

Chapter Five
Cole

COLE COULDN'T DECIDE IF HE WANTED to cheer or scream.

Mistel had followed him. Him! These past two weeks he'd thought she hated him. Clearly not. Yet her being here was also his worst nightmare. How could he want something so desperately yet dread it at the same time?

That Achan, Sir Caleb, Prince Oren, and Kurtz all knew this girl had followed him embarrassed him to no end. Did they think he had encouraged her to come?

He pondered this as he sat cross-legged with Kurtz in the tent they shared, both of their thoughts inexplicitly linked in a telepathic group meeting started by the king.

I have informed Prince Oren and Sir Caleb of the situation, Achan bloodvoiced. *They are here listening as well. Before I share our opinions on this matter, Cole, I'd like to hear yours.*

"I didn't invite her here, Your Highness," Cole said aloud. "I swear. In fact, I told her she couldn't come."

None of that matters at present, the king voiced. *What is your will?*

Cole's will? Did he truly get a say?

"Honestly, I don't know, sir. She's not wrong about her ability to woo a crowd. We'd stand a better chance of getting hired to play *with* her than on our own."

In fact, with Mistel at Cole's side, they could give Jeffrey some decent competition, get hired to play at the Black Boar.

Yet I sense some hesitation in your words, the king voiced.

Plenty. "Just that I don't feel equipped to protect her," Cole said.

When he blundered in a fight with Kurtz by his side, Kurtz's training gave the man the ability to protect himself. What training did Mistel have?

He's not equipped to protect her, Kurtz said, which smarted. *But he's right about her skill with a crowd. She's also downright cunning. If we could be certain of her allegiance . . .*

Oh, I'm certain of that, Achan said. *Uncle? Sir Caleb? What say you?*

We all know the distraction a woman can be in the wrong situation, Sir Caleb said. *This, to me, feels like the wrong situation for Cole.*

Of course Sir Caleb would say that.

Yet, if she's on his side . . . Prince Oren said. *On our side. Brought into our confidence . . . She could be invaluable. I have too few women in the Mârad.*

No offense, Your Highness, Sir Caleb voiced, *but that's for good reason. The Mârad is extremely dangerous, and Miss Wepp has no self-defense training of any kind.*

Can we stop her from following Cole and making matters worse? Prince Oren asked.

If she causes a scene or interferes in some way, then I could warrant the use of force to detain her, Achan said. *But I don't feel right telling her where she can and can't go.*

We're just over halfway to Tsaftown, Kurtz said. *We could give it a few more weeks. See how she behaves in camp.*

I don't like her being the only female there, Sir Caleb said. *I daresay Lord Livna won't like it either. He must be informed.*

I disagree, Prince Oren said. *The woman hid herself well and was only discovered because the king used his magic to seek her out. No one else will be looking for a woman. If she can keep her identity hidden, that proves her mettle.*

Derby Wenk knows, Kurtz said, *but I can talk to him.*

She introduced herself to Derby as my cousin and a member of our band, Cole said.

Cousin is a surprising twist, Sir Caleb said.

Can you do your job with her there, Cole? the king voiced. *Will she distract you from your mission?*

Cole thought about it. *Not from any task. Only that I'd be worried about her safety.*

It's only natural to worry about a friend's safety, Achan voiced. *On the battlefield or off.*

That's the story you're going with? Kurtz said. *That they're just friends?*

Apparently, we're cousins, Cole said. *She told Derby so, and I'll go along with it. That will keep things platonic between us.*

Because the mission must come first. Ice Island and his uncle. Plus, Cole cared for Mistel enough that he didn't want to risk her getting hurt because of him. Best they stay friends only.

As long as she doesn't interfere with the mission, Prince Oren said.

Or jeopardize anyone's safety, including her own, Sir Caleb added.

Cole, Achan voiced, *if problems should arise, have Kurtz bloodvoice me right away. Is that clear?*

Yes, sir. Cole tried to imagine what kind of scenario might constitute such a problem.

So, we let her stay? Kurtz asked.

It's up to Cole, Achan said. *If he isn't opposed, she can stay.*

Cole couldn't deny that he wanted Mistel around, yet he could feel the conflict inside him, fear warring with the desire to be close to her—to sing with her. To show up Jeffrey.

She consistently tells me that she can take care of herself, Cole said. *And dressed as a soldier, perhaps she can. But what about when we reach Tsaftown, and she is Mistel Wepp again? I'd feel better if she at least had a female companion.*

That'd make me feel better, too, it would, Kurtz added.

Cole raised an eyebrow at Kurtz, but the man's eyes were shut.

A prudent thought, Cole, Sir Caleb said.

I have just the person, Prince Oren voiced. *I'll check in with her. Contact me once you arrive in Tsaftown, and I'll give you instructions.*

Then it's settled, Achan voiced. *Mistel Wepp can stay and be brought in on the mission only as Prince Oren allows. She is to keep herself hidden until Tsaftown where she will have a female companion, and she will pose as Cole's cousin.*

A chorus of farewells filled Cole's mind, and then his thoughts became his own again. A heavy silence fell over the tent.

Cole met Kurtz's gaze and asked, "Since when do you think a woman needs a chaperone?"

"Since she attached herself to you."

Cole smirked, and a breath of laughter escaped. "Whatever happened to letting a woman help me forget all my troubles?"

"It's different when she's the one causing trouble, it is," Kurtz said. "Go on. Find your new *cousin* and tell her the news. And try not to look too happy, eh?"

Cole pushed to his feet, crouching beneath the low ceiling. "I'm not unhappy, but I am worried about her safety, especially once we reach Tsaftown."

"If she wants to stay, she'll fall in line, she will," Kurtz said.

As if Mistel was a string Cole could tune on his lute. Plus, some strings refused to stay in place, no matter how often he adjusted them.

He left the tent and returned to the practice field. Mistel was nowhere to be found. No surprise. As he stood, considering where she might have gone, Jeffrey Korngold's melodic notes reached him.

Hackles rising, Cole followed the sound, weaving through soldiers dismantling tents. He reached a clearing around the remains of last night's bonfire, where Jeffrey stood in a wagon bed, lute in hand, belting out the famous song Mistel had written about Achan. At least a dozen onlookers had gathered.

> *"The pawn our king, sing merry, merry, merry.*
> *The pawn our servant king.*
> *For he was once the lowest of all strays*
> *And now claims to be king."*

Mistel stood at the front, clapping, farmer's hat back in place. Less than an hour here, and she'd already found their competition. A tangle of emotions rolled through Cole—seeing her admire Jeffrey, standing among soldiers who had no idea she wasn't one of them.

He needn't fear. Right?

Mistel caught his gaze and nodded at Jeffrey, her eyes bright, her lips quirked at the corners, just enough to hint at her approval.

No surprise there. Of course she would find Jeffrey a superior musician. Cole's jaw tightened, and he turned and walked away. Deep down he knew she deserved better than him. And he wasn't about to stand in her way.

Chapter Six
Mistel

Dash it! Why did all Mistel's choices cause ruin?

She raced after Cole, trying to track him in the maze of tents, unable to fathom what she'd done wrong now. To be fair, though, what had she really expected? That shy, soft-spoken Cole Tanniyn would take one look at her, grin that boyish grin of his, and say, "Mistel, thank Arman you're here," and kiss her until her toes curled?

Well, maybe she had. Maybe, in some distant, hazy corner of her mind, she'd imagined Cole grabbing her around the waist and twirling her in circles while he declared his joy over seeing her again. Then they'd sing together—one of the songs they'd written for the king—and the entire army would applaud their amazing talent.

She could totally fix this, whatever she had done.

She passed by a group of men eating something meaty. Her stomach growled and she paused. Just . . . maybe she'd eat a little something first.

Up ahead, she caught sight of Cole helping Kurtz collapse a

tent. Food would have to wait. She approached the edge of their space slowly and stopped where she'd be out of the way.

"Any news?" she asked.

Cole shot her an unreadable look, then went back to his work. "On three," he said. "One, two, three."

In unison, Cole and Kurtz heaved the tent fabric above their heads, then walked toward each other. Cole took the corners while Kurtz grabbed the middle and drew it back. They quickly folded the tent into a small square, which Cole rolled and tied with a length of hemp rope.

Mistel shivered in the silence, certain something horrible had happened in their meeting. Was Cole upset that he had to arrest her? Or upset because he had to let her stay?

By the time they'd packed the rest of their campsite, she had lost her patience. "Well, Stoneface? Are you just going to ignore me?"

Cole's brow wrinkled. "Stoneface?"

"You're saying nothing," Mistel said. "And I can't guess anything from that blank look on your face."

"I'll carry these to the wagon." Kurtz tucked the tent under his arm and carried the two bedrolls away, leaving them alone.

Cole folded his arms and looked at her—finally. He sighed as if she were the biggest burden he'd ever encountered. "You can stay," he said. "For now."

She squealed and ran toward him.

He held out his palm, stopping her. "There are some rules. First, you must stay in your disguise until we reach Tsaftown. There you will be known as my cousin."

She smirked. "Kissing cousins?"

He arched his brow. "No. Cousins was your idea, so don't forget, all right?"

She suppressed the urge to cackle madly at her delight over getting to stay. Remaining in disguise meant no dresses or side saddle, but at least she no longer had to lurk alone in the woods.

"Second," he said, "you can't say anything to anyone about the king sending us here. As far as everyone knows, Lord Livna included, Kurtz and I have decided to leave the king's service and go our own way. Kurtz had a falling out with the king—nothing you know the particulars of—and after the war, I just want a simple life making music. We're all going to try and make a go of it as musicians in Tsaftown, where Kurtz is from."

She knew it. They were spies. Spies! A thrill coursed through her, too wild to fully contain. She bounced on her toes, pressing her lips together to stifle a squeal, and clapped lightly, the sound merely a whisper.

Cole's lips twitched, and she could see him fighting the urge to smile. Oh, she would weasel right back into his heart in no time. Just wait.

"Third, once we reach Tsaftown, you will have a female companion of Prince Oren's choosing."

"Prince Oren?" Mistel clapped again. The king's uncle had made plans for her. How thrilling. But what had he said? A companion? She sobered at the realization that the men had discussed her in relation to propriety. She had never once considered how following Cole might tarnish her reputation.

"Good idea," she said. "Thank you." Cole's arms were still crossed, like he was a bowstring ready to snap. Any hint of laughter long gone. "You seem upset."

He swallowed and looked off across the snowy prairie. "I saw you watching Jeffrey. He's a far better musician than me, and I've been worried we might not be hired to play anywhere with him in town."

The tightness faded from Mistel's stomach. Thank Arman. Cole wasn't angry with her. He was jealous of Jeffrey. That she could handle. "We don't have to be the best to play at some seedy alehouse," she said. "I doubt Jeffrey would even want to play at such a place."

Cole's brows shot up his forehead. "Because he's too good?"

"Oh, Cole." She sidled up, pried apart his crossed arms, then took hold of his hands. "You're a brilliant musician. We'll get plenty of work, I promise you."

Cole swallowed as his hazel eyes searched hers. "As long as you don't leave us and start singing with Jeffrey."

"I would never." She slid her hand over his cheek, and the feel of his scruffy face sent a thrill through her stomach. She raised onto her tiptoes and had barely brushed her lips against his when his hand clamped around her wrist and he pushed her back, scowling.

"None of that, *cousin*," he said. "Kissing me won't help you keep your disguise."

"Hmm, I suppose not." She walked away, then winked at him over her shoulder. "Until Tsaftown, then."

CHAPTER SEVEN
COLE

A STEADY HAND WAVERS WHEN BEAUTY walks by.

Cole could never help but pen lyrics in his head when it came to Mistel Wepp.

After sword fighting practice the next morning, she invited herself into their tent, humming "I Don't Belong Here," one of his favorite songs that she had written. She settled onto Kurtz's bedroll, removed her farmer's hat, and let her orange curls fall loose. Even when humming, her perfect pitch rang clear, and the beautiful, haunting melody soothed him.

He missed moments like these with her. He still couldn't believe she was here—that she'd kissed him, or tried to, at least. No denying he would have enjoyed that a great deal. Hiding his feelings for her would not be easy. Yet he could find no reason to refuse a visit from his *cousin*, and so he'd let her stay.

For now.

She wouldn't be here long. Kurtz had gone to fetch Jol Quimby, the lone member of the Mârad amongst the Five Hundred. The three of them had plans to discuss the mission, and since Prince

Oren had not yet given permission for Mistel to know all their Mârad business, once Kurtz and Jol returned, Mistel would have to go.

"What are you doing?" she asked.

Lantern light flickered off Cole's short sword as he scrubbed it with a tallow-soaked cloth, then dipped the rag into the jar for more. "Oiling the blade to keep it from rusting in all this snow," he said.

"Did you practice swordplay again this morning, my knightling?"

He glanced at her, amused by the little name she'd given him, liking it more than he should. "I'm surprised you didn't come watch." He was grateful too.

"I cannot wake as early as you." Mistel stretched out her legs and sighed. "Oh, this is nice. I didn't think to bring a tent. Or a bedroll."

Concern for her swelled in his chest. "Mistel . . . Where have you been sleeping?"

"Mostly under trees."

That would never do. "I'm sure I can scrounge up a spare tent."

"That would be fantastic."

"What about food?"

"Oh, I ran out days ago, but now that I'm here, I've been able to eat with the soldiers."

That she would take such risks to her safety frustrated him to no end. "If you ever have trouble, come find me at once. Or Kurtz."

Mistel dabbed her finger in the tallow, smelled it and frowned. "Your brow is wrinkly. You don't have to worry about me. I'm fine."

Now. But she was lucky to be alive. "It's been a long morning. Before we leave today, we're meeting with—"

The tent flap pulled aside, sending a shaft of morning light inside. Kurtz froze, partway in. "This is how you lay low? Put that hair away."

Mistel let out a soft huff through her nose and brushed a lock of her ginger curls over her shoulder. "I'm being careful."

Kurtz grunted. "I doubt that. Normally, I'm all about fun and games, I am, but the king entrusted me with both of your safety, which means you"—he pointed at Mistel—"get out."

"It's too early," she said. "Where would you have me go?"

"Wherever you slept last night," Kurtz said.

Mistel's bottom lip protruded. "On the ground under a wagon."

"Perfect," Kurtz said. "Lots of ground outside."

"I didn't think about how cold it would be when I packed for the trip," Mistel said.

"You didn't think much," Kurtz said.

Cole pushed the tallow along the blade again. "I'll scrounge up a tent for her."

"For tonight," Kurtz said. "Right now, I've got Quimby outside, I do, and we need to talk. In private."

Cole put the lid on the tallow and started to clean up. He was eager to get Jol's take on their mission.

"Can't I stay?" Mistel asked. "I want to know what's going to happen."

"We'll tell you what you need to know," Kurtz said.

"Fine." Mistel tied her hair back into a knot, shoved on her hat, and slipped outside. "Good morning," Cole heard her say in an amusingly low voice.

"Morning," came a ridiculously gravelly reply.

The door flap shook, and a broad-shouldered man ducked inside. Jol Quimby's wavy orange hair and short beard framed a face rarely without a grin. Like Kurtz, he exuded rugged confidence. Both were the kind of men who could drink heartily, fight fiercely, and talk their way out of trouble—or into it.

Quimby's eyes held a mischievous glint. "Think she knew I altered my voice?"

Cole chuckled. "The bigger question is, could you tell she altered hers?"

"Nah, she's a fine actor." Quimby dropped onto his knees just inside the door. "As long as she lays low, no one will suspect a thing."

"Enough about the girl," Kurtz said. "Let's talk about Ice Island, eh? What'll we be dealing with up there?"

"Well, the biggest concern is that prisoners have been going missing," Quimby said.

"How many?" Cole asked.

"Over thirty in the past four months."

Kurtz whistled. "You sure it's not just escapes? The guards sell everything. I've seen them *misplace* keys and look the other way. It's all for sale, for those who can afford it."

"No one is escaping," Quimby said, "nor is this related to the king pardoning prisoners. His Highness made a mess of the place when he broke out you and Sir Eagan, but eventually the guards got a firm count on who remained."

"My uncle is a prisoner on Ice Island," Cole said. "Prince Oren wants me to talk to him. Perhaps he might know something."

"Could be he does," Quimby said. "But it won't be easy for you to get in. In light of the missing, Verdot has stopped letting anyone visit."

"When they got us off the island, Gavin made me swear to be nice to that man," Kurtz said, "but it didn't sit right with me. I still don't trust him."

"I wouldn't trust him either," Quimby said.

"How's the lad supposed to visit his uncle if Verdot won't allow it?" Kurtz asked. "Think Lord Livna could help make it happen?"

"Prince Oren would rather not involve Lord Livna in any of this," Quimby said.

"Maybe we could sing at Ice Island," Cole said. "Would the warden ever have reason to entertain the prisoners?"

"That's not a bad idea," Kurtz said. "They've done such things before, they have. But I wouldn't take Miss Wepp close enough to even look on that foul place."

"Can't argue with you there," Cole said. "Surely there are bloodvoicer guards? Watching the prison through the Veil?"

"No bloodvoicers can see into Ice Island anymore," Jol said. "It's hidden by rune magic."

"Magosian witches in the king's prison?" Kurtz asked.

Cole shuddered, thinking of the Chartom mages in Armonguard who had blocked bloodvoicers from seeing into their camp. Who had attacked him.

"Aye," Jol said. "Another change after His Highness's visit. The warden felt it worth working with a Magosian to keep the prison impenetrable. And the runes work. Against bloodvoicing magic, anyway. Bribes and whatever is going on with the missing prisoners is another matter."

Getting inside Ice Island sounded impossible. "What do you know about my uncle?" Cole asked.

"Not much," Quimby said. "Crispen West was sentenced twenty years for killing a local tailor. They got into a brawl when the tailor accused West of impropriety toward his wife, and West refused to pay for the work done. West claimed he never knew the tailor or the man's wife, but there were plenty of witnesses who claimed otherwise."

"Prince Oren said he was framed," Cole said.

"That's the theory," Quimby said. "He was definitely mixed up with the wrong crowd."

"Did you know him?" Cole asked Kurtz.

"Nah, I was in Armonguard back then," Kurtz said. "Eighteen years old and squiring in the king's personal guard, so full of myself I couldn't breathe. Thought I was Arman's gift to the world, I did."

Cole had heard plenty of stories from Kurtz's days as one of King Axel's Shields. "What about the tavern?" he asked. "Prince Oren also wants us to get hired at the Black Boar."

"Didn't exist before I went to the island," Kurtz said.

"That place has a reputation," Quimby said. "The air is thick with pipe smoke and secrets. If a man has got the coin, he can buy anything—information, loyalty, an assassin. And if he's looking for the kind of dealings best left off the record, he won't find a better place, despite it being owned by an upstanding local councilman, Joonas Erlichman."

"Didn't his father used to sell hunting dogs?" Kurtz asked.

"Joonas sells them now but is better known for boar. Makes a handsome profit too," Quimby said. "Which reminds me. I suggest you also keep an eye on a man named Renshaw Thusk."

"Who's he?" Cole asked.

"Local businessman. He's also on the Tsaftown ruling council—crooked, but everyone looks the other way. Backed Esek Nathak for king, so I suspect he'd oppose our new king if given the chance. I've had no excuse to get near him or his property to investigate, but you might, being new to town."

"You want us to follow him?" Kurtz asked.

"Nothing that obvious," Quimby said. "He owns the Ice House. It's a pub. You could try and get hired there and poke around. But I'm almost positive Thusk will be at whatever banquet is thrown to honor Lord Livna's return. If I let you into Lytton Hall that night, one of you could swipe his keys. Then you'd be able to search his offices and warehouse at your leisure."

"Won't he tighten security if he thinks he lost his keys?" Cole asked.

"I'll have the keys copied while I send word to Thusk and other members of the council that keys were found," Quimby said. "If he gets them back from a member of Lord Livna's guard the same night he lost them, he won't suspect anything."

Kurtz fixed his gaze on Cole. "You're on key duty."

Goosebumps broke out over Cole's arms. "Why me?"

"Because you're not the type to cause a distraction." Kurtz punched his fist into his other hand.

"You really think that's necessary?" Cole asked.

"Definitely," Quimby said. "He'll need to draw the attention of every eye in the great hall. If you can't steal the keys, don't worry about it. I just don't know when you'd ever get another chance to be that close to Thusk in a crowd."

"We'll make the most of it, we will," Kurtz said. "Don't you worry about that, eh?"

Cole swallowed hard, glancing between Kurtz and Quimby. Steal a crooked councilman's keys in a room full of nobles and guards? Sure. No pressure there. And if he got caught, maybe they'd throw him in the Ice Island prison in a cell right beside his uncle.

One could only hope.

Chapter Eight
Mistel

A SEA OF FACES, YET NOT A SOUL TO know. Warm inside the new tent Cole had found for Mistel, she'd slept in the next morning and missed joining the procession near the boys. A long and lonely day's travel through the snowy foothills of the Chowmah Mountains left her fingers numb and her cloak stiff with ice. Bart, at least, was looking better now that he had access to the food the army horses were fed.

When the Tsaftown army finally made camp that night, Mistel wasted no time warming herself by the nearest campfire and gulping down a bowl of stew. Once her stomach was full and she was thawed enough to move, she set off in search of Cole.

She finally found him and Kurtz outside their tent, circling each other with no weapons in hand. She stopped just beyond the edge of their camp, where she could see but not be seen.

What were they doing?

"It depends how they're hooked to his belt," Kurtz was saying, holding up a metal ring adorned with trinkets. "If there's a clip, you either have to unlatch it or cut the fabric loop it's attached to."

Mistel cocked her head. A lesson in . . . stealing keys?

Kurtz pinched the top of the ring, demonstrating how the metal flexed open. He clipped it to his belt and waved Cole forward. "Come and get them, eh?"

Cole stepped closer and swiped for the keys. His fingers made them jangle.

Kurtz spun away, shaking his head. "Wrong end, featherbrain. Try again."

Biting back a grin, Mistel watched as Cole tried again. This time he gripped the right part of the clip, but when he attempted to slide it free, he yanked so hard he nearly pulled Kurtz on top of him.

"If you wanted to dance, you could've just asked, eh?" Kurtz shoved Cole off. "Gentle, lad. You've got to be light about it. You're not pulling the reins of a runaway horse."

Cole tried again, and this time he managed to remove the keys, though his hand hit Kurtz's side.

"I felt that, I did," Kurtz said.

Again and again, Cole tried. And every time, something went wrong. He stumbled or touched Kurtz, the clip snagged, or the keys slipped from his grasp at the last second. Mistel smothered a laugh behind her glove.

Then, at last, Cole managed a clean swipe. He spun away, thrust his hands above his head, victorious, and the trinket slipped from his fingers and clinked into the snow.

Kurtz sighed deeply. "So close!"

Mistel couldn't hold it in anymore. Laughter bubbled free, loud and unrestrained. She sauntered toward Cole, shaking her head. "How do you even know the man will be wearing his keys on his belt?"

Cole straightened, his face flushed as he met Mistel's gaze. "Well, uh . . . Kurtz said—"

"That's where I'd carry my keys, if I had some," Kurtz said.

Mistel smirked. Of course he would say that. "You're not wrong, most of the time, but not everyone is that predictable." She plucked the fake keys from Cole.

"Hey, give that back." He lunged after her.

Mistel darted out of reach, her grin widening. "If you don't want to get caught, there's more to this than simply fishing keys off a belt." She circled him like a prowling cat, trailed her finger lightly over his shoulder, the back of his neck, down his arm, along his waist.

Cole flinched, twisting toward her with a sharp intake of breath, hands lifted as a barrier. He fought back a laugh. "Stop that."

"If he's got sense, he'll tuck his keys here." Mistel flicked a finger against Cole's chest as she continued to circle him. "Or he might keep them in a deep pocket here." She brushed her hand over his thigh. "Or here." Her hand brushed the back of his waist.

"Hey!" Cole spun to face her and made another grab for the fake keys, but she danced back, grinning—until something on his wrist caught her eye. Her grin faltered.

A beaded bracelet. Her bracelet.

Mistel's breath hitched, the stolen keys suddenly forgotten. "Nice bracelet," she said.

Cole glanced down, then ran his hand across the beads, as if only now remembering it was there. Those gorgeous hazel eyes of his lifted to hers, and in that breathless span between heartbeats, their entire history of knowing each other passed silently between their gazes. Their first dance. Edera's death. His investigation. Him moving her into Castle Armonguard. Singing together. And that delicious kiss in the herb garden when everything had felt perfect. Safe. Real.

Kurtz crossed his arms. "I don't see how this is very helpful."

"True, Master Chazir," Mistel said, snapping back to the present. "And maybe you're right, and whoever he is will keep his keys on his belt." She hooked her finger around Cole's rope belt and gave it a tug. "Even so, you're not checking properly."

"Properly?" Cole asked.

"You have to look for them first," she said. "Not every jailer advertises his secrets on his belt."

With a dramatic flourish, she spun around, putting her back to them long enough to hide the keys in a fold of her tunic. She turned back and set her hands on her hips. "Well? Can you spot where I've stashed them?"

Cole scanned her quickly, his gaze darting down her baggy tunic, past her waist to the side pockets, then back to her waist, but when he reached for it, she danced back and laughed.

"Not so fast," she said. "You've got to be sure before you make your move, or you'll end up looking like a fool."

Cole narrowed his eyes. "I *am* sure." He reached for her lower pockets, then shifted at the last moment for the bulge at her belt.

Before he could touch her, she twisted out of reach and wagged a finger at him. "Wrong." She unfolded the bulge to reveal nothing but an extra twist of fabric. "Sometimes it's not where you think."

Cole scowled, and his gaze fixed on the opposite side of her waist. Ahh, he'd spotted them. Lunging forward, his fingers brushed the top edge of her belt and caught the wire clip. He tugged the fake keys free just as she spun around and grabbed his wrist midair.

"Much better," she whispered.

Kurtz dragged a hand over his face and groaned. "Looks like you've got it, Cole. Just try not to get pickpocketed yourself."

Mistel laughed and let her fingers slide past his wrist, over his hand, and down his fingers before she let go. "Could be you've got the hang of it." She tilted her head and grinned. "Though if you like, I don't mind giving you a little more . . . practice."

Yes, it was definitely a good idea that she'd followed Cole. No matter what the knightling thought, it had never been clearer to Mistel that he needed her. She would set up her tent here tonight so she wouldn't be separated from him again on the long day's ride.

Even if it meant falling asleep in her saddle, she'd be right where she belonged. At his side.

Chapter Nine
Cole

IF MISTEL KNEW ALL THAT HAD HAPPENED to Cole in Mitspah, would she look at him differently?

He glanced at her now, riding Bart to his left, all that glorious hair stuffed under a ridiculous hat, orange freckles scattered over her fair skin, baggy tunic sagging over what he knew to be a stunning figure.

None of that, now. There could be no pining after the girl. Cole had vowed to keep things platonic. He turned his gaze back to the road, which only submerged his thoughts right back in the haunting echoes of his childhood.

He'd never traveled the King's Road through Therion Duchy, but it wasn't far from where he'd grown up. Around him, soldiers remarked on the changed landscape—after a decade under the suffocating curse of Darkness, the forest lived again. Once-rotted trees stood tall beneath fresh snow, and faint birdsong wove through the air.

Yet all Cole could think about was how they'd just passed the road that led to Mitspah.

Kurtz Chazir.

Cole lowered his shields. *Sorry,* he thought. *Sir Caleb was on me so much to always stay shielded, it's hard now to keep myself open.*

Not open to everyone, eh? Kurtz bloodvoiced. *Just to me.*

Cole had tried many times to do what Kurtz asked, but he'd never been able to succeed for long. *It all feels the same to me,* he thought.

You went a bit pale for a minute, Kurtz voiced. *You all right?*

It's strange, Cole thought. *A place can feel like a cage when you're living there, but once you're on the outside, looking in, you see no bars. Why did I stay in Mitspah so long?*

You didn't know any better, Kurtz said.

No, he hadn't. *I spent my whole life wanting to leave, so why do I feel it tugging me back?*

The past doesn't like to let go, even when you do, Kurtz voiced.

True, Cole had a handful of good memories from Mitspah. Lunden mentoring him after he was sold to Lord Yarden, teaching him to play the lute. Some fond moments with Nya before her games became clear. And Peat, his puppy. He could still see those huge black eyes, that lolling pink tongue.

Then the dog was dead in his arms while Drustan and Fen laughed.

The switchbacks grew steep. Cole recalled helping Shung track the cham bear the prince had killed, the mix of emotions that day: the horror of the slaughtered horses and the joy of being freed from Lord Yarden by the prince, no longer a slave.

And here he was, just over a year later, on a mission for the king. Yet this was different. Cole could have said no, and Achan wouldn't have forced or judged him. When a man could walk away, there was no bit in his mouth. He was free.

As the army climbed higher into the mountains, days passed in relative quiet. Each night, Cole and Kurtz helped Mistel raise her tent, and each morning they helped her take it down. The cold nights stifled any revelry. Cole began to doubt his choice. How could anyone spy in freezing temperatures? Surely even villains would stay indoors.

One crisp morning, nearly over the last ridge of the Chowmah Mountains, two days from Tsaftown, Cole rode Cherix beside Mistel and Bart, trailing Derby Wenk and Kurtz, who was regaling the squire with a tale from his days living at Fat Vandy's tavern. Cole had heard this one before, but watching the eager faces of the listeners amused him.

"One evening, the place was packed with travelers swapping tales about ghosts and curses," Kurtz said. "Now, you've got to understand that living in a tavern was a lot of work, it was. Always something to prepare, deliver, or clean. So, I had to make my own fun, I did."

"What did you do?" Derby asked. "Put a hex on the boarders?"

"Naw, but you're on the right track, you are," Kurtz said. "Earlier that day, Serra had asked me to move an empty ale barrel out of the kitchen, and I'd placed it just inside the back door to return to the brewer come morning. But when I heard all those ghost stories, I climbed inside it, figuring I'd give them something to talk about."

The soldiers ahead of Kurtz chucked.

"I started with a low moan. Nothing too obvious, eh? Just enough to prickle the hairs on the backs of their necks. Then I added a bit of scratching, like some poor tormented soul clawing to get out." He released an exaggerated moan that had the group snickering.

Mistel glanced at Cole, her grin as wide as his.

"Well, that did the trick, it did," Kurtz said. "How they carried on! 'Did you hear that?' 'There's a ghost under the stairs!' I kept at it, I did, and eventually they started ghost hunting. When I heard footsteps growing closer, I let out the most bone-chilling wail I could muster." Kurtz paused for effect, corners of his eyes crinkling. "That's when things got ... interesting."

"What happened?" Derby asked.

Kurtz slapped his knee. "Well, as it turned out, I underestimated just how superstitious that lot was. One of them—a merchant with more gold than sense—shouted, 'It's cursed! Burn it before it brings ruin upon us all!'"

The soldiers erupted into laughter, drowning out Mistel's gasp.

"Before I knew it, they'd picked up the barrel and were hauling me toward the fireplace. I kept quiet, I did, hoping they might give up when the ghost made no more fuss, but when they started fetching kindling, I burst out of that barrel like a demon from the Lowerworld and shouted, 'Who dares disturb my rest? I'll haunt you forever!'"

The soldiers roared, Derby cackled, and up ahead, Lord Livna turned on his horse and glared back at his squire. "Master Wenk! On your post."

Derby jumped. He nudged his horse into a trot, quickly taking position behind his lord.

"That's a fierce master," Mistel said.

"Bah! Eric's all bark with very little bite," Kurtz said.

"What happened next?" Quimby asked. "What did the people do?"

Kurtz grinned so wide his eyes squinted. "I've never seen grown men scream like that. One of them dropped his mug and ran straight into another, who spilled wine all over them both. Another fainted—just crumpled to the floor like an empty tunic falling off a clothesline."

Quimby threw back his head as he laughed.

"Then Serra came out and smacked me upside the head with a loaf of bread."

The soldiers chortled.

"Of course Hargis Vandy wasn't at all amused either. He dragged me out of the tavern by my ear and said, 'Like squeezing into tight spaces, do you? Well, you can spend the next week helping the night soil man clean the privies at Lytton Hall. Let's see how you like crawling around in *those* tight spots.' And let me tell you, after a week of mucking out privies, I never looked at a barrel the same way again."

The soldiers burst into a chorus of hearty laughter.

Up ahead, the procession came to a halt at the husk of a burned-out farmhouse. Lord Livna and Derby dismounted and walked toward an iron gate that circled the property. As the place was covered in a thin layer of snow, it didn't look like a recent fire.

"My lord, what is it you mean to do?" Captain Demry called out.

Lord Livna glanced back. "I merely wish to see the scene for myself."

The iron hinges of the gate creaked as Lord Livna and Derby entered the property and began looking around.

"Wonder what happened?" Cole said.

"That *was* Glodwood Manor," Kurtz said. "Stopped there myself many times over the years. They had a well for passersby to help themselves to a drink. Strange to see it gone, it is."

"Captain Demry!" Lord Livna called. "Have archers ready."

Demry shouted the order, then drew with the rest of the line.

"What's happening?" Mistel asked.

"Don't know." Kurtz nudged Smoke forward. "You two stay back out of the way."

Cole was happy to comply. His nerves skittered as he sensed danger. The way Captain Demry sat his horse. The way some of the men had drawn their swords or bows.

Kurtz had just reached the gate when the shrill rally of war cries erupted from the forest's edge. Pale-skinned Poroo warriors, dressed in leather and fur, sprinted out of the woods, right toward Lord Livna and Derby.

"Loose!" came Captain Demry's command.

Kurtz drew his sword, yelled over his shoulder, "Get out of here!" then steered Smoke toward the fray.

Adrenaline shot up Cole's spine. He grabbed Bart's mane and turned Cherix toward the trees on the opposite side of the road. "Go. Let's go!"

Into the forest they went, but the trees had grown so close together that sharp, naked branches snagged Cole's hair, his clothes, and even the saddlebag. The little bites of pain only agitated his growing distress.

Cole released Bart's mane. "It's too tight to ride two abreast." Should he send Mistel ahead where he could see her or would that put her first in harm's way? He urged Cherix onward. "Stay right behind me."

He led Cherix along a game trail, glancing over his shoulder every four steps to make sure Mistel was with him. She'd lost her hat, and the twiggy branches caught her hair, pulling free tendrils of fiery orange curls. But she was there.

She was okay.

The past few days, he'd tried to put her out of his mind. The way she laughed or how his gaze always found her when they were traveling. He'd liked it too much when she'd watched him cross swords with Derby, called him knightling, and thanked him for putting up her tent. He didn't want to be glad she was there with them—especially now with the Poroo attacking—but he couldn't help himself.

The trail curved back toward the road, so Cole tugged on the reins, keeping Cherix behind the cover of trees. "We'll wait here," he said. "I think we'll be safe as long as—"

"Cole?"

The fear in Mistel's voice poured fire down Cole's spine. He drew his sword as he twisted around in his saddle.

A Poroo warrior stood beside Bart, staring up at Mistel, a spear in his hand.

"Hey!" Cole lifted his sword and tried to look threatening. "Get back!"

The Poroo man glanced at him, then turned his attention back to Mistel. He more than stared. He seemed to behold her in fascination and wonder, as if she were a rare sight.

"What does he want?" Mistel asked.

Cole guessed the Poroo man was just startled to find a woman—especially a pretty one—in the midst of a battle. Or maybe he'd never seen ginger hair before.

What to do? Kurtz's mantra played in his head: *Distract, disable, and don't overthink it.*

Distract, distract. Cole recalled an ancient song about the Poroo and their matriarch.

"Tuwa nakwa um," he said.

The Poroo man whipped his head toward Cole but turned right back to Mistel. He gave her one last thorough caress with his eyes, then scampered off through the trees like a jackrabbit.

Cole's heart pounded louder in his ears than the distant battle cries and rumbling hooves out on the road. Yet all was well. Mistel was safe. They both were.

Mistel stared at him. "What did you say?"

"'Mother bless you,' I think. It's an old song Lunden taught me."

"Who's Lunden?"

A shiver ran over Cole's arms. Had he really never told Mistel about Lunden? No, because he hadn't wanted her to know just how lonely and pitiful his childhood had been.

With the Poroo warrior gone, the screams and war cries from the skirmish rose in Cole's awareness. Through the bare branches, he could just make out the dark uniforms of the Tsaftown men at the old farmstead.

"Will we be all right?" Mistel asked.

"Yes," Cole said, his pulse mostly back to normal. "Most Poroo tribes are around one to two hundred, including women and children. I doubt these Poroo have more than fifty. We have just under five hundred men with us."

"Shouldn't there be more than five hundred?" Mistel asked. "Isn't that what Tsaftown's army is called?"

"The Fighting Five Hundred, yes, but they lost some in the Battle of Armonguard."

"Oh."

"Northlanders, ho!" Captain Demry yelled.

Hooves trampled over the ground, and more battle cries rang out.

"Hear that?" Cole said. "There's power in numbers. I suspect the Poroo will be retreating soon."

Sure enough, the trees on Cole's right shook as three Poroo warriors darted past, not one of them even turning their head when Mistel shrieked.

Cole waited a bit longer, listening carefully. Only when the voices from the road were calm did he decide to venture back out. He even heard some laughter.

"It's safe to return." He nudged Cherix forward. "It's a bit wider up here if you want to come alongside me."

"I'll need my hat," Mistel said.

"Oh, right." Cole stopped his horse and dismounted. "Wait here. I'll find it."

He passed Bart, patting the horse's rump as snow spilled over the tops of his boots, melting down to his ankles. Shivering, he backtracked along the game trail until he spotted Mistel's farmer's hat caught in the branches of a leafless poplar. He climbed up and retrieved it, then to spare his feet, stepped in his previous prints on the way back.

When he reached Bart, he handed the hat up, but Mistel swung her leg over Bart's backside and dropped to the ground, landing so close her heels crushed Cole's toes.

He grimaced as she turned in the cramped space, eyes wide with something unspoken—shock, gratitude? Her chest heaved as if she'd been running. Likely just adrenaline. Cole set the hat back on her head and tucked a loose tendril of hair up inside the woven straw.

"You might need to do a little fixing." He gestured to the other loose strands. "I don't think your hair likes being tamed."

She ripped off the hat, fisted Cole's shirt, and kissed him.

His breath caught, thoughts tangling as her touch set every nerve on fire. Snow might as well have melted around them. This was nothing like their lingering, curious kiss in Castle Armonguard's herb garden. Mistel kissed with force, with urgency. The feelings inside Cole were too large to contain, and the forest around them shrank to nothing. Even now, the space between them felt too great.

When she pulled away, she left him reeling, staring at her full lips, impossibly green eyes, every freckle. His mouth felt dry, yet the warmth of her mouth lingered on his, reverberating like the final chord of a song.

He could barely remember how to speak, and when he finally opened his mouth, words escaped him. He stood there, blinking at her, hoping the whole thing hadn't been some figment of his imagination.

Her gaze softened, a grin tugging at her lips, revealing her adorable overbite. She pulled the thong from her hair, letting thick curls cascade around her face, making Cole want to kiss her again. She gathered her hair up, catching all the loose strands, wrapped it in a knot, and tucked it back beneath the farmer's hat.

"Better?" she asked.

Cole nodded dumbly.

"Help me up?" She spun to face Bart and lifted one boot into the stirrup.

Cole boosted her onto the saddle, then approached Cherix, still in a bit of a daze. He climbed onto the horse and led Mistel back toward the road.

What just happened? Should he say something? Scold her?

He glanced back, caught her smiling, and for some fool reason, he spun back around like a bashful schoolboy.

A kiss like that—any kiss—it couldn't happen again. It simply couldn't. Cole had work to do. They both did.

Plus, Mistel was supposed to be his cousin!

Out on the road, the army had already continued on, but Kurtz had lingered with Quimby and some of the Fighting Fifteen, who were razzing Derby about a heroic kill he'd made.

"Poet! There you are." Kurtz mounted Smoke, and as they rode on, he regaled them with his version of all that had happened.

Cole listened avidly, eager to think about something besides the way his lips still tingled from that kiss. "Did the Poroo steal anything?" he asked. "Take the food wagon?"

Kurtz turned in the saddle and peered back through the ranks. "Nope, it's back there still."

"Then why would they attack?" It didn't make sense. Over the years Cole had lived in Mitspah, he'd had many run-ins with the Poroo. Never once had they attacked, unprovoked, in such a way. They'd stolen food, but never ambushed for the sole purpose of killing.

Cole couldn't shake the uneasy feeling that he was missing something important.

"I'm going to write a song about all this," Mistel said. "I'm certain the people of Tsaftown will love it. Let's see . . . Oh, gather 'round, good folk, and hear of Lord Livna's valiant band . . . Who rode to Glodwood's scorched remains and made a final stand."

"It wasn't a final stand," Cole said.

"But that sounds more compelling, don't you think?"

"A ballad should be as true as possible," Cole said, "and you and I didn't actually witness it."

She wiggled her eyebrows. "Oh, don't you worry. Our adventure will have its own song. Mother blessed us in those woods. But I'll get the true battle story from the men."

Cole's face flushed, and he looked away—at anything that was not Mistel Wepp.

"There was a dead body," Kurtz said, "and Walter said, 'By the Three.'"

"Then Derby went in with Lord Livna," Quimby said, "and the body was all wrapped up in rope. Derby grabbed it, but it was a Poroo trap that cinched his hand to the body."

"Then the Poroo came running out of the trees, singing their battle cry," Kurtz said. "You're right, Cole. It's unlike them to attack like that, it is."

"Then what happened?" Mistel asked.

As Kurtz and Quimby recounted the battle, Cole's thoughts drifted back to Mistel's kiss.

Ever since Nya had ripped out his heart, he'd longed for someone who truly understood him, someone who could save him from the emptiness that had haunted his life. Nya had given him a taste of companionship, but she'd been an actress. A liar. He used to wonder if there might be someone out there who could see him for who he was—and like him because of it.

Could Mistel be that person? Later, of course, long after the mission was done? Their shared love of music gave them an instant connection, and she stirred his soul in ways he couldn't deny. Yet he hated giving anyone power over him. With her brazen confidence and unparalleled beauty, Mistel could sweep him away. He wasn't sure he could trust himself around her—or trust her with his heart.

Plus Cole was, this moment, leading her into more danger. A place where she might be hurt. Even killed.

That didn't sit well with him either. Not at all.

Chapter Ten
Kurtz

HOME, JOYOUS HOME.

The sentiment rose unbidden inside Kurtz as he led Cole and Mistel through Tsaftown's narrow streets, his gloved hand tight on Smoke's reins as the cold nipped at his cheeks and his breath clouded out in front of him.

The mingling scents of roasted chestnuts, wood smoke, and manure hung thick on the air, they did. The afternoon light slanted low, casting long shadows from the timber-framed buildings that leaned precariously close overhead, frost and icicles clinging to their eaves. Up ahead, the spire of Thalassa's Temple towered over the city like an old sentinel.

Back at the Dale, they'd left the army behind and headed west through the narrow streets. Kurtz had bloodvoiced Prince Oren yesterday and received instructions. They were to go to the Ivory Spit and ask for Anna. That's all he knew.

Their horses' hooves clattered against the uneven cobblestones, a sound so familiar it almost twisted back time. How often had Kurtz roamed these streets as a gangly sapling, eh? A wooden practice sword strapped to his back, dreaming of finding glory in the Fighting Fifteen?

A fool, that lad.

It was good to see the city in Light again. The last two times Kurtz had been here during the curse of Darkness—first going into Ice Island, then over a decade later, mercifully coming out.

Thirteen years of his life, lost.

Heat burst in his chest as he recalled how, during the trial to find King Axel's killers, Kenton Garesh and his cohorts had testified—*blatantly lied*—against him and Eagan and that Verdot Amal had done nothing to stop it. Careeanne too, that blackhearted viper, telling the Council of Seven that *he* had used *her*! Of course, with Kurtz's maverick reputation, no one had had any reason to doubt the minx's word.

The injustice of so many turncloaks conspiring to help Nathak cut down a legend like King Axel—the man's own father—still boiled Kurtz blood, it did. He'd been simmering over the diabolical treachery for thirteen years, and while it pleased him that Nathak and Kenton were dead and rotting, Kurtz would not rest until everyone complicit in the king's murder was exposed and brought to justice.

Now that he was free, he finally had the time to figure out the truth, he did.

"How much longer?" Cole asked, pulling Kurtz from his reverie.

"A few more blocks," Kurtz said.

Mistel drew her hood tight around her chin. "It's so cold."

"Aye, that it is," Kurtz said. The girl wasn't dressed for it either. She'd need winter clothing and fast, or she'd turn into the prettiest icicle Tsaftown had ever seen.

They came upon the Ivory Spit suddenly. The tavern and inn sat back off the street, and you couldn't see it until you'd reached its door. Kurtz knew the place well and steered Smoke down the side of the building to the stables in back.

Prince Oren wanted them all to stay here, but Kurtz would rather find another place to shove the girl off. Only a blind man could miss the way Cole and Mistel gogged at each other, eyes all witless and full of stars. Kurtz had enough to deal with, he did, without tending a pair of lovestruck pups.

The three of them put up their horses, then went inside the tavern. A bell tinkled as Kurtz passed through the entrance and stomped his snowy boots on the mat. Ah, but the place smelled like home, and this wasn't even Fat Vandy's. All taverns had the same scent: a blend of ale, sweat, stew, and smoke—both hearth and pipe. Earthy, spicy, and savory all at once.

The Spit had a low ceiling due to all the rooms on its upper floors. The timber panel walls were covered in Merrygog's trophies: a stuffed hawk, two falcons, a boar's head, four pair of antlers of various points, and a half dozen carvings of fish, crab, or some other sea creature. Kurtz grinned, remembering how tacky Serra Vandy found Merrygog's décor.

Too early for the dinner crowd, the place was practically empty. Worn square tables sat bare, but for two: a gray-haired bloke sitting by the fire and a tall man-at-arms at a table in back. No musician or band in the corner spot now. Kurtz hoped he could talk old Merrygog McLennan into taking them on for a spell.

"Good afternoon." A dark-haired barmaid approached, wiping her hands on her apron. She wore a red skirt and sleeveless laced top that drew Kurtz's attention to her curvy torso. "You look like you've traveled far," she said. "What can I get you?"

Kurtz took in her familiar, plump cheeks, thick eyelashes, and the loose curls escaping her messy bun. "Rilla?"

The barmaid's gaze met his, and a wide smile claimed her face. "As I live and breathe. Kurtz Chazir. Darri said you'd been through here last summer—that the true prince had sprung you off the island. I told her that couldn't be. That if you got out of that horrible place, you'd have come and seen me and Loanna first thing."

Kurtz winced. "Couldn't. The prince was in danger, Edik Livna killed, and you know Gavin."

"Oh, we all know Gavin . . ." Rilla extended her arms. "Don't just stand there. Give us a kiss, you old rogue."

Kurtz grabbed her around the waist and kissed her full on the mouth, inhaling her unique fragrance of starfrost blossoms that transported him back to younger days. "Why you working here? Your parents disown you?"

"Worse," she said. "Loanna got herself hitched to a bloke with two kids. They're all but running Fat Vandy's now what with Papa's gout flaring and Mama's poor eyesight. I needed to get out of the way for a spell, so Merrygog took me on day shift."

Kurtz chest tightened at the news of Hargis and Serra's declining health. "I'll get over to see them as soon as I can, eh?"

"Yeah, why are you here instead of there?" Rilla asked. "And who are your friends?"

"This is my . . . band." How utterly ridiculous that sounded.

Rilla fell into a fit of giggles. "Kurtz Chazir, a musician? Just when I thought I'd heard it all."

"Well, to be honest, it's Cole's band, it is. I'm just the drummer, and a poor one at that. Luckily, Cole and his cousin, Mistel, are so good, no one notices my deficiencies. Cole, Mistel, meet an old friend, Rilla Vandy. Her parents took me in for the best years of my youth."

"Pleased to know you," Mistel said.

Rilla beamed at them. "Likewise, I'm sure."

"Might the Ivory Spit use some entertainment?" Cole asked. "We're looking for some places to play while we're in town."

"Oh, I'm certain Merrygog will have you," Rilla said, "if for no other reason than to see if Kurtz Chazir can really beat a drum. Want me to fetch him?"

"Aye, in a moment," Kurtz said, "but first, we're supposed to meet someone named Anna. Anyone by that name stop by?"

Rilla's eyebrows jumped up her forehead. "One surprise after another with you, isn't it?" She nodded to the man-at-arms in the corner. "Right over there."

"Oh." Kurtz straightened, a bit off-kilter at this realization. "I assumed Anna was female. Must be a foreign spelling, eh?"

"Anna *is* female, you dolt." Rilla slapped his arm. "And I suggest you tread carefully unless you want a fat lip."

Interesting. "Thanks for the warning, eh?" He took a deep breath and waved Cole and Mistel to follow. "Come on."

As they crossed the tavern toward the table in the corner, Kurtz eyed this Anna a little more carefully. Couldn't see a smidge of female in her from the back—the heavy pelt draped around her shoulders exaggerated her frame—but Berland women had always been rough around the edges. Perhaps she was from there.

Rilla's warning fresh in his mind, Kurtz decided to employ a bit of Eagan's manners. "Pardon me," he said. "We are looking to speak with Anna."

The Berlander pushed to her feet and turned, putting a pair of feminine brown eyes squarely in front of his.

Kurtz froze, his heart giving an involuntary jolt.

ZolZanna tan Quelle?

So, not a Berlander then. A half-Yâtsaq giant.

He blinked slowly. What in flames?

This striking woman had a glare that could wither a man. The memory of their challenge fifteen years ago resurfaced, her bitter, mocking words fresh in his mind. His gut clenched, and for a moment, he wished the ground would swallow him whole.

ZolZan the Barbarian. That's what most of the Kingsguard soldiers had called her back then. Outside of Berland, female soldiers were rare. Even the giant tribes didn't send women to war. Which was why Zanna had always stood out as fierce, stunning, and deadly. Of all the blasted missions, she had to be here, now?

He didn't like it.

Yet he forced his most winsome smile. "ZolZan, heh, hay! It's been a while, eh?"

"Don't call me that, you fool," she snapped. "I'm Anna Tankel here, and if you even try to greet me with a kiss, I'll stick a dagger in your throat."

And there she was. He raised his hands in surrender. "Wouldn't dream of it, eh? But keep the dagger ready. I'm sure you'll need it when the next man looks at you wrong."

"Sit down," she hissed. "All of you."

Cole and Mistel flew into their seats, but Kurtz took his time, flipping a chair backward and straddling it. He'd have to bloodvoice Prince Oren and let him know that this was not going to work. At all. No mission could succeed with ZolZan the Barbarian involved.

"The girl will stay with me," Zanna said.

Suddenly Kurtz wanted to keep Mistel close. "The girl's name is Mistel. Where do you live, eh?"

Zanna folded her arms across that ample bosom of hers. "None of your business."

"These are *my* charges," Kurtz said. "I need to know where they are at all times."

Zanna uttered a long sigh. "I have a room at Fat Vandy's."

"Really?" Kurtz lit up. "I need to go see the Vandys." He turned to Mistel. "You'll like them. They practically raised me."

Zanna glanced at Mistel. "Don't hold that against them."

"Look," Kurtz said. "I'm in charge here, I am. Better get used to that, eh?"

"I'm not taking orders from you," Zanna said. "Prince Oren told me Master Tanniyn was in charge. Didn't mention you at all. Oversight, I'm sure."

Fire and ash, he'd forgotten the tongue on this woman. "Aye, he is." Kurtz nodded at Cole to show he wasn't trying to take the leadership mantle from the lad. "But I'm in charge of the teams' safety. Won't nobody argue with you about that, they won't."

Zanna's eyes narrowed to slits. "I'd sooner put my safety in the hands of a blind mule."

"Suit yourself." Kurtz winked. "But these hands will be at your service all the same."

She leaned forward enough to invade his space. "Those hands come anywhere near me, and I'll have your head on a spike by breakfast."

He held her gaze. "You'd be pining for me by lunch."

Zanna groaned at the ceiling. "Typical Kurtz. Charm, grin, and hope the girl likes brown eyes."

"It's worked so far."

"Consider your streak broken," Zanna said. "I work five nights a week, moonlight shift. I won't always be able to join you, but I'll do my best. Which makes one of us."

Kurtz would be sure to plan all the important tasks when the woman was busy. "Where do you work?" he asked.

"Ice Island. Guard on the female levels."

It took effort not to spit on the floor. "Well, that explains your charming personality, it does. Let me guess, you're one of the nice guards, eh?" He leaned toward Cole. "They all say that."

"You don't have to like me, Chazir, but you will respect me. I'm here to do a job, same as you."

Her words lit a flame in Kurtz's stomach, and the heat curled, slow and thick. Eben's breath. Of course he found the bossy ones attractive. Of course. It was like some twisted instinct—see a woman who could run him into the ground, immediately wonder what it would be like to kiss her. Not happening.

He threw back a surly reply. "Just what I needed—another warden in my life."

A shadow darkened their table. "Look who's come back to warm his bones at my hearth." Merrygog McLennan's gravelly voice carried the weight of a life well lived. A burly man in his sixties, the tavern owner had white, unruly hair tied back in a sloppy ponytail and a thick, gray beard. "I've missed seeing your rugged mug 'round these parts, Kurtz. What brings you back from the king's service, eh? A good drink and a dance, I'd wager."

Kurtz stood and greeted Merrygog with a hug. "Good to see you, old man."

"Rilla says you're making music these days?" The old man wrinkled his nose.

"Only because of the talent of these two." Kurtz introduced Merrygog to Cole and his *cousin* Mistel and hinted that they'd like to audition for work.

"I'll hear you now, but you'd have to butcher the tune for me to turn down the likes of *the Chazir*." He patted Kurtz's shoulder.

They left Zanna to her scowling and set up in the corner spot. It amused Kurtz that the last time he'd been here was with Achan, sneaking the prince a drink and a dance. If he'd known then that he'd someday return as part of a band, he'd never have believed it.

"We'd like to play one of my cousin's most famous songs," Cole told Merrygog. "One she wrote celebrating our king, who she knew in her youth."

Cole played a quick introduction on the lute, and Mistel started singing "The Pawn Our King."

Two verses in, and Kurtz knew they'd manage their ruse just fine. One needn't be a bard to see that Merrygog was downright smitten with Mistel. That girl knew how to draw people in, she did. Not that Kurtz wanted her here, but he had to admit Mistel Wepp had, at the very least, proved her worth.

When the song ended, Merrygog and Rilla both applauded while Zanna got up and moved beside the hearth, arms folded, glowering as if music were a beast about to bite.

"Wonderful!" Merrygog said. "You must play here this very night."

"Well now, we'd like to, we would," Kurtz said, "but we've got to make an appearance at the welcome banquet in Lytton Hall."

"Afterward, then," Merrygog said. "The crowds are light this time of year, but we'll have plenty to hear you by then. And once you play and word spreads, I daresay we'll have even more here tomorrow."

"You're too kind," Mistel said.

Zanna stepped into their circle, the sound of her boots against the floor like a blacksmith's hammer on an anvil. "Time we got you settled, Mistel," she said. "Though from the look of you, I wonder if we shouldn't first stop off and get you some warmer clothes."

The suggestion put a wide smile on the girl's face. "Oh, that would be wonderful. It's so cold here, and I didn't pack the right things at all."

Imagine that. The North cold. Kurtz had to admit Zanna had a thread more sense than the girl. Maybe having her around wouldn't be so bad.

Mistel embraced Cole as she bid him farewell, and Kurtz tried very hard not to let his exasperation show. The girl would be back in a few hours, but by their lingering display, you'd have thought she was taking a voyage across the Northsea.

Finally, the females left, and Rilla showed Kurtz and Cole up to their room, one with a charmouse painted onto the door.

"I'll get the fire going for you," Rilla said, walking toward the hearth.

Cole set his things on one of the two beds. "You don't mind if I practice a little, do you?"

"Have at it," Kurtz said. "Sure you don't want to eat first?"

"Naw," Cole said. "I'll eat at the banquet. How long until then?"

"Only about an hour, I'd say."

As Cole fingered through a run of music, Rilla wandered back toward them, fiddling with her apron, fire blazing behind her. She hadn't changed all that much in the past thirteen years. Put on a little weight in all the right places.

She cast him a mischievous glance, lashes fluttering, and Kurtz had little doubt she wouldn't shy away from his touch.

"Anything else you need?" she asked.

"The lad wants to practice," Kurtz said. "I'll come down and have a drink."

"Not too many," Cole said without looking up from his lute.

Kurtz clenched his jaw. "No need to mother me, lad. I'll be good."

Yet the moment the door closed, leaving Rilla and Kurtz alone in the hallway, Kurtz slipped his hand around her waist, she grabbed his shoulders, and their lips met with a rush of heat.

Everything else seemed to vanish—the faint creak of the old wooden floors, the muted notes of Cole's lute inside the room—all swallowed by the pull between them.

"What say we steal away, for memory's sake?" Rilla whispered, jingling the keys on her belt. "Plenty of empty rooms today."

Kurtz hummed and deepened the kiss. He hadn't been with a woman since Wintara—almost four blasted months ago. Before the war. Before the Captain's Row.

Before all the shame.

Well, why not? He and Rilla had been here before. They were old friends. He pulled her closer and let his thoughts buzz with the possibility of what might come next, the thought of her soft skin, the promise of more.

Dazzling white light bloomed in the corner of his vision. Kurtz pulled back so sharply Rilla yelped. His gaze darted to the top of the stairwell. A golden-haired figure stood there, radiating light. His regal features, sharp and serene, and a pair of bright blue eyes locked onto Kurtz with an intense authority that sent a chill down his spine and tightened his chest.

"Did you see someone?" Rilla asked.

Oh, aye. Nothing *she* could see, but Kurtz knew that the watcher standing in the Veil not only knew Kurtz's motives, he'd come for a reason.

His heart pounded, not from kissing Rilla, but from the unmistakable feeling that whatever decision he'd been about to make had been the wrong one. Kurtz had seen this watcher years ago—had ignored him to his own peril. The creature's presence was a warning, one Kurtz would not ignore. Not this time.

Never again.

"Kurtz?"

Rilla's confused voice broke through his thoughts, but Kurtz was already fumbling with the latch on the door of his room, a bitter taste rising in his throat.

"Sorry, Rilla. I just remembered something I've got to do, eh?"

With that, he slipped into the room and fell face-first onto his bed.

"Short drink," Cole said.

"Tired." Kurtz took a few breaths to calm his racing heart, then reached for Eagan.

Kurtz Chazir, he bloodvoiced.

What is wrong? Eagan's voice in Kurtz's mind brought instant calm. The man was using his magical ability to affect Kurtz's emotions even from such a distance.

What makes you ask that? Kurtz thought.

I can sense your agitation. Did something happen?

Kurtz fought back the urge to laugh. *A watcher. The same one from Allowntown.*

Where did you see it?

Out in the stairwell of the Ivory Spit.

Did it say anything?

Didn't need to. Kurtz's hands were shaking, so he squeezed them into fists. *I was . . . with someone.*

A woman?

Cole started playing a new song, a melancholy tune that fit Kurtz's mood. He shot a glance at the lad, but he was lost in his music. *This watcher didn't come to Reshon Gate*, Kurtz voiced. *And not for me, anyway.*

To what are you referring? Eagan asked.

I told you I saw a different watcher the day the procession was attacked, standing beside the prince, Kurtz thought. *But none came about the prostitutes and the wagons. None warned me of the trouble that ended with the Captain's Row. So, why now?*

That is a fair question, Eagan said, *but you know well enough Arman's feelings on mischief of the flesh.*

Kurtz blew out a long breath. *And you know* me *well enough.*

You going to be all right?

I walked away.

That is good.

Kurtz fisted the wool blanket on the bed. Didn't feel very good.

Something else bothering you? Eagan voiced.

Aye. That infernal prison where he'd lived worse than a rat for thirteen years. That pitch-black abyss. *I don't want to go to that rotting island. What if Arman decides to lock me up again?*

Oh, my friend. I do not think He will do that.

But you don't know. Kurtz's chest had grown so tight, he strangled the blanket, twisting the scratchy wool in his fists. *Maybe the Captain's Row wasn't enough, eh? Could be I'm too weak to serve in this role.*

If that were true, He would not have sent you. And the king would not have insisted you go.

Kurtz considered that. *I'm not worthy.*

None of us are.

Fine. I'm less worthy than most, then.

Hmm, that is not for you to decide, Kurtz. Now, I cannot blame your reluctance to step foot on Ice Island. I would feel exactly the same. But Arman is *in this mission.*

That much is clear. If the Father God was sending watchers to admonish Kurtz, He was clearly paying very close attention.

Pray, Kurtz, Eagan voiced. *Pray often. And tell me if you see the watcher again.*

Kurtz released a shaky breath. *Will do, eh?*

He severed the connection. Cole had switched songs again—now playing "Light of the World" and humming along. So, Kurtz tried it Eagan's way and prayed, asking Arman for forgiveness for his dark intentions with Rilla and thanking Him profusely for whatever catastrophe had just now been so narrowly avoided.

Because the last time Kurtz had ignored that watcher, King Axel had been killed.

Chapter Eleven
Cole

Better a clumsy step forward than a coward's retreat, right?

As if to prove Cole's very thoughts, he tripped again over a tangle of soggy rushes in the dark, narrow passageway of Lytton Hall.

"Watch your feet," Quimby said. "The kitchen is the best way to sneak in guests. As long as you're one of the Fifteen."

Cole's stomach twisted at the task ahead: stealing Thusk's keys. He didn't think he could do it yet somehow had to succeed.

They entered an open passage where yeasty bread and roasting venison briefly replaced the dread in Cole's stomach with anticipation. To the right, a vast kitchen bustled with men and women preparing food. Ahead, beside a set of double doors, stood a pair of Livna's men: the Berlander, Thakkar Oruk; and the golden-haired lion, Lysander Thane.

"Quimby." Thakkar jerked his head in a quick nod, the jagged scar on his face catching the light. "What are you lot doing down here?"

"Giving a tour," Quimby said.

"The kitchen looks different, it does, than it did last time I was here," Kurtz said.

Thakkar narrowed his eyes. "When was that?"

"Before his time on the island," Lysander said, his long hair swaying like a curtain. "Back when he was chasing Faylyn's skirts."

"Your sister chased *me*," Kurtz said. "I couldn't have lost that girl if I tried. She made excellent pies."

Lysander pinned Kurtz with a sharp gaze. "She's married now with three boys, so just you keep your distance."

"I'll think about it," Kurtz said with a wink. "Does she still bake?"

"Her pies are even better now." Thakkar's fierce gaze smoldered beneath his matted warrior locks. "I should know, since she's *my* wife."

"Blazes, Kurtz," Cole said. "Is there a woman in Tsaftown you didn't try to charm?"

"Heh hay!" Kurtz lifted his hands, all innocence. "Can I help it if the Chazir is irresistible?" As they passed through the door, he patted Thakkar's arm. "But, well done, man. And congratulations on the sons."

They entered the great hall at the front right corner, just below the dais. The long, narrow room rose to a two-story hammer-beam roof. Rough-hewn log walls bore black-and-gold banners, every other one depicting a leaping dagfish—the sigil of Tsaftown. Opposite the dais, double doors stood atop a narrow platform, with a half flight of stairs leading down to a gold carpet running the length of the center aisle.

Over a hundred, maybe two hundred, guests filled long tables draped in black-and-gold checkered cloths. Servants wove through the aisles, filling goblets.

"They got rid of the trophies," Kurtz said, looking around at the walls. "Lord Livna used to have as many animal heads as Merrygog. Maybe more."

"Lady Viola's doing, or so I heard," Quimby said. "Don't know that Eric's seen it yet."

"Remind me never to marry," Kurtz mumbled.

Quimby led them to aisle seats near the stairs. He sat with his back to the dais, across from Kurtz and Cole, who had a clear view of the hall.

Quimby leaned across the table. "See that round fellow three tables behind me?"

Cole marked a bald man with a thin, reddish-brown mustache and no beard. He wore an orange fur cape so thick it made his head look small. "Wearing the fox fur?"

"Relative of yours?" Kurtz asked.

"Ah, no," Quimby said. "That's Renshaw Thusk, co-owner of the Thusk Shipping Exchange."

"Co-owns it with who?" Cole asked.

"His brother Magnus, who lives in Meribah Corner," Quimby said.

Kurtz frowned at Thusk. "A shipping business offers plenty of opportunities for corruption. Smuggling, overcharging merchants, skimming profits, piracy . . ."

"Not to mention a conflict of interest in local leadership," Quimby said. "And he uses it too. Prioritizes his profits, suppresses rivals, chooses all the trade routes himself. The hope is with Eric back, all that will end."

"Not without a fight," Kurtz said. "No one with power and wealth likes to give it up."

"Does the brother have the same influence in Meribah Corner?" Cole asked.

"Probably more," Quimby said. "Old man Gershom barely knows his own name these days, and I doubt anyone has brought the corruption to Lady Tara's attention."

"Perhaps we should," Cole said.

Kurtz patted Cole's arm. "Let's stick with Tsaftown to start, shall we, poet?"

A bang drew every eye to the entrance. The doors swung open, revealing a couple followed by a gray-haired guard with the thickest sideburns Cole had ever seen.

"Lord Eric Livna and Lady Viola!" the guard yelled.

All around them, people stood and applauded. Cole, Kurtz, and Quimby joined in. Roars and hoots pulled Cole's gaze to many familiar faces of the Fighting Five Hundred.

Lord Livna led his wife down the aisle. They made a striking pair, both in their thirties, finely dressed, with dark hair and eyes—his skin pale, hers deep olive. They nodded and smiled at guests on their way to the front.

Cole used the distraction to study Renshaw Thusk. The thick fur cape hid much, but when Thusk turned to speak to a man at his table, Cole spotted a leather belt with a brown suede pouch on his left hip.

He saw no key ring. No other bulges.

Could the keys be in the pouch? Maybe he didn't carry them around but left them with a steward or trusted assistant.

What would Cole do then?

The Livnas reached the dais, and Lord Livna seated his wife. The rest of his family—all women, Cole noted, including a tiny girl who could barely see over the table—were already seated. Behind them, a massive, polished carving of a dagfish hung on the wall.

When Lord Livna finally sat down, so did everyone else. Servants streamed in with trays, attending the high table first. It would be a while before the food reached them in the back.

Kurtz leaned in and whispered, "What do you make of Thusk?"

"I didn't see a key ring, but he has a good-sized belt pouch," Cole said.

"That must be it," Kurtz said.

"Or he doesn't bring keys with him," Cole said.

Kurtz raised an eyebrow. "We'll know soon enough, won't we?"

Sure. But the thought of opening that huge man's belt pouch made Cole queasy. Yet he hadn't had a good meal since Achan's wedding and intended to enjoy this one. When the food finally reached their table, he ate venison, fish, potatoes, carrots, and fresh bread.

After golden pudding was served, people lined up to greet Lord Livna on the dais—including Thusk. Cole moved down the aisle for a better look. The pouch was studded with brass facets, its front secured by a large brass latch. If he could turn it, he could reach inside.

He returned to Kurtz and Quimby and shared what he'd learned.

"Sounds good to me, it does," Kurtz said. "I know how I'm going to make my distraction."

"How?" Cole asked.

"See that man?" Kurtz nodded to a broad-shouldered blond man, hair knotted at the back of his head, who had just left the dais after speaking to Lord Livna. "That's Fenris Yarden—one of the vilest men I've known. He was in the Prodotez when the king freed us. He and I don't get along."

"He's also Lord Livna's cousin," Quimby said.

Cole frowned at the man, then at Kurtz. "Don't get yourself hurt."

"Bah! Fenris can't hurt me. Much. That bloke behind him though..."

Cole eyed the towering, muscular man trailing Fenris—shaved head, thick knotted beard, and tunic fringed with what looked like ponytails.

"Are those...scalps?" he asked, slightly horrified by the sheer number.

"Looks to be," Quimby said.

Fenris and his towering shadow approached Thusk.

"Follow my lead." Kurtz started down the aisle. "If you get the prize, hand it off fast, eh?"

Cole nodded, breathing deeply to keep his dinner down. He was part of the Mârad now. He had to do his best.

Kurtz slowed, letting Fenris and the big man reach Thusk's table. Cole's stomach twisted. Fenris Yarden reminded him of his uncle Crispen, even the green eyes.

"Eben's breath!" Kurtz exclaimed to a thin man across from Thusk. "Has anyone told Lord Livna he has a rat problem? Someone should—oh! Fenris"—he chuckled—"it's only you."

Fenris's lip curled into a wicked grin. "Kurtz Chazir. I don't know about rats, but isn't a *chazir* a pig?"

Fenris's lackey guffawed. "A *big* pig."

"Right you are, Ikârd," Fenris said. "And big, fat pigs don't belong in Lytton Hall. Unless they're on a spit."

"A chazir isn't a pig, eh?" Kurtz said calmly. "It's a wild boar. Surprised a learned man like you didn't know that."

Cole edged around to Thusk's right. He could see the pouch but had no clue how to touch it, let alone open it. Then Thusk leaned forward, fixated on the tension between Kurtz and Fenris, and the pouch vanished from sight.

Fabulous. What was he to do now?

"I suppose it makes sense," Kurtz said, loud enough for those nearby to hear. "Fenris Yarden, traitor to his bloodline, dungeon dweller, bane of intelligence."

Fenris sneered, cracking his knuckles. "Big words from a man I could snap like a twig."

"At least they're words and not grunts," Kurtz shot back.

That did it. Fenris lunged, shoving Kurtz into Thusk's table. A goblet tipped, spilling wine onto Thusk's lap. The man yelped and jumped up. Quimby stuck out a leg, tripping him, and down Thusk went with a cry.

Cole crouched, pulse pounding. "Sir, are you all right?" He

gripped Thusk's arm while his other hand found the brass clasp. He flipped it open and reached inside. Cold metal met his fingers, and his heart leaped.

Thusk muttered, "Unacceptable rudeness . . . uncouth soldiers . . . no manners." He shoved Cole away. "Get off me, boy."

Cole straightened, keys fisted at his side. Spotting Quimby behind Thusk, he stepped closer and, without looking, slipped the keys into Quimby's hand—smooth as golden pudding.

The weight left his chest. He'd done it!

"Careful now, Fenris." Kurtz laughed. "Only us old Prodotez friends know the truth. Should I tell Lord Livna your secret fondness for eating lice?"

"Go ahead," Fenris sneered. "And I'll tell everyone how the dark made you weep."

Kurtz swung, landing a punch to Fenris's jaw that sent him stumbling.

Thusk flailed his arms. "Someone help me."

Two men from his table jumped in and hauled him upright. Cole hoped Thusk didn't notice his empty coin purse, but if he did, maybe now he'd have some more memorable faces to suspect.

Glass shattered, and a heavy grunt turned every head back to Kurtz and Fenris.

Fenris locked Kurtz in a headlock, growling something unintelligible and grinning all the while. Ikârd slammed a fist into Kurtz's gut.

Women screamed and scattered.

Red-faced, Kurtz clawed at Fenris's arm, still managing to gasp, "That all . . . you've got?"

Soldiers swarmed in from all directions. Ikârd stepped in front of them.

"Let go of him!" Thakkar yelled to Fenris.

"You feckless oaf!" Torin Oxbow yelled. "Get out of the way."

"I think not," Ikârd said.

Lord Livna shoved through the crowd. "Enough! Enough!" He seized Fenris, yanking him back.

"Briny maggot!" Fenris swung an elbow, but Lord Livna caught his arm and wrenched it behind his waist.

Kurtz, now free, reared back to punch, but a burly soldier stepped in and grabbed his arm.

"Restrain him!" Lord Livna shouted.

As soldiers swarmed Kurtz, Cole drifted aside, unsure what to do. They had the keys, but as guards dragged Kurtz out of the hall, Cole couldn't shake the feeling that their mission had failed.

Despair was a fool's companion. Cole reminded himself of that as he paced outside Lord Livna's office, unsure what Kurtz was facing inside. Should he knock? Enter? Break down the door? Acting in haste was folly, but doing nothing felt like surrender.

Three of the Fifteen approached—Thakkar the Berland warrior, golden-haired Lysander, and Wroxton the refined. They stopped beside Cole, each so fierce and deadly he felt dwarfed.

"They still in there?" Thakkar asked.

"Yes," Cole said.

"Those detestable Howlers deserve their fate," Wroxton said. "My sister, Rixie, harbors no trust in them, but many in town do. In our absence, they've fashioned themselves as heroes."

Lysander's golden hair shifted as he tilted his head. "I don't much like their way of being heroes. Wearing scalps like trophies."

"How in flames are we to assert authority when—" Thakkar straightened and lowered his voice. "My lady."

Lysander and Wroxton darted aside, clearing the way as Lady Viola approached the door. Despite her petite stature, she carried herself with such grace and authority that the soldiers stood down as if commanded.

"Is the brawler inside?" she asked.

"Yes, my lady," Thakkar said.

Her sharp gaze fell on Cole. "Who are you?"

"His friend, madam," he said, grateful to be a few inches taller—though if looks could wound, he'd be in trouble.

One sculpted eyebrow rose. "Friend of the brawler? Did you fight in my great hall too?"

"No, madam."

She pursed her lips, managing to look down her nose at Cole.

The door opened, and the burly man who'd dragged Kurtz into Lord Livna's office escorted him out. Praise Arman! Now they could get back to the Ivory Spit.

Kurtz grinned at the crowd. "Quite the reception," he said. "Good evening, my lady."

"Master Dunn, what recourse has Lord Livna placed upon this man?" Lady Viola asked.

"Just that he stay out of trouble, m'lady," said the burly bear—Dunn apparently.

Lady Viola's expression remained unreadable, though Cole swore her eyes frosted over. "Detain them both," she said.

"But we're leaving," Cole said. "We don't want to make trouble."

"You should have thought of that before starting a brawl at my banquet," she said. "As lady of this house, I believe a night in the dungeon will help the lesson take root."

Seriously? She was contradicting Lord Livna?

Cole glanced around. Thakkar scowled at the floor, Wroxton grimaced, and Lysander Thane frowned over Lady Viola's head. Only Master Dunn bowed obediently.

"Yes, my lady. Master Thane, would you take the boy?"

Cole's face burned as Lysander gripped his arm. "This way, *boy*." He winked, leading Cole down the hall.

Behind them, Kurtz chuckled, as if a night in the dungeon

were an old joke. "Lady Viola, allow me to explain. You see, Fenris Yarden—Get off, Dunn!"

Cole glanced back. Dunn had pulled Kurtz along, while Lady Viola's withering stare followed them.

"I trust your hospitality includes clean straw?" Kurtz yelled.

At that, the lady of House Livna turned away.

Kurtz grumbled as they descended a narrow stairwell. Cole's mind raced. The weight of what he'd done—handing Thusk's stolen keys to Quimby just before Lord Livna intervened—pressed against his chest like a loaded crossbow. If anyone had seen and told Lady Viola, a night in the dungeon would be the least of his problems.

Chapter Twelve
Zanna

H ELPING THE HELPLESS WAS ZANNA'S calling. She'd dedicated her life to it.
Helping the hopelessly arrogant, however . . .
"This is even smaller than the room I had in Castle Armonguard," Mistel said as she stood frowning just inside the doorway of Zanna's room above Fat Vandy's tavern.

Zanna dropped the clutch of dresses onto the spare bed. Mistel had shopped for hours. The girl was pickier than a princess. "Hope the hardship won't be too painful."

Mistel must have caught Zanna's tone because she quickly said, "Oh, I didn't mean to complain." Yet she still wrinkled her nose at Zanna's spare boots by the door. "I just think we'll have to announce our intentions when crossing the room so the other can move aside."

Zanna eyed the narrow space between the beds. "This is a single," she said. "I asked Hargis to bring up a second bed because leaving you alone isn't safe. Arman knows what riffraff you'll attract with Master Chazir's scheme to play every tavern in Tsaftown."

No one pleasant, that was certain.

Zanna hadn't seen Kurtz Chazir in over a decade, but the moment she'd spotted his broad shoulders, sandy-blond hair, and reddish beard, something had flickered inside her—something she'd immediately wanted to crush. Then he'd met her gaze with those mischievous deep-brown eyes, and her stomach had twisted like a smitten girl. Such base urges were beneath her duty as a soldier, and her reaction annoyed her deeply.

"It wasn't his idea," Mistel said. "The king and Prince Oren hatched this plan. Cole told me so."

Hmph. Kurtz was no musician. The young king must have talked Prince Oren into supporting this reckless mission. "I'll bet Master Chazir went along with it eagerly," Zanna said.

"I wouldn't know," Mistel said. "I wasn't there." She sat on the bed and gave it a little bounce. "You seem to dislike Kurtz."

"Oh, I despise him."

Mistel's eyebrows rose into two perfect arcs. "Did he break your heart?"

"Absolutely not. I'd sooner throw myself in the Northsea."

"Then why do you hate him?"

Zanna wouldn't pass up a chance to cast judgment upon the likes of Kurtz Chazir. "He misused my charge and humiliated me." Even now, the memory of his challenge made her chest burn. "The man's an insufferable peacock, strutting around as though every maiden's heart were his by right, but he's a torch in a hay barn. He thinks rules are for others, responsibility is a joke, and his wit is sharp enough to cut steel. If arrogance were a weapon, kingdoms would crumble at his feet. And the worst part? Half the time, he actually pulls off the impossible, which only makes him bolder."

"Lands! Remind me not to cross you." Mistel stood and peeked through the shutter slats that covered the window. "How long have you known him?"

Too long. "Met him training for the Kingsguard. Must have been fifteen or sixteen years ago."

Chapter Twelve
Zanna

Helping the helpless was Zanna's calling. She'd dedicated her life to it.

Helping the hopelessly arrogant, however . . .

"This is even smaller than the room I had in Castle Armonguard," Mistel said as she stood frowning just inside the doorway of Zanna's room above Fat Vandy's tavern.

Zanna dropped the clutch of dresses onto the spare bed. Mistel had shopped for hours. The girl was pickier than a princess. "Hope the hardship won't be too painful."

Mistel must have caught Zanna's tone because she quickly said, "Oh, I didn't mean to complain." Yet she still wrinkled her nose at Zanna's spare boots by the door. "I just think we'll have to announce our intentions when crossing the room so the other can move aside."

Zanna eyed the narrow space between the beds. "This is a single," she said. "I asked Hargis to bring up a second bed because leaving you alone isn't safe. Arman knows what riffraff you'll attract with Master Chazir's scheme to play every tavern in Tsaftown."

No one pleasant, that was certain.

Zanna hadn't seen Kurtz Chazir in over a decade, but the moment she'd spotted his broad shoulders, sandy-blond hair, and reddish beard, something had flickered inside her—something she'd immediately wanted to crush. Then he'd met her gaze with those mischievous deep-brown eyes, and her stomach had twisted like a smitten girl. Such base urges were beneath her duty as a soldier, and her reaction annoyed her deeply.

"It wasn't his idea," Mistel said. "The king and Prince Oren hatched this plan. Cole told me so."

Hmph. Kurtz was no musician. The young king must have talked Prince Oren into supporting this reckless mission. "I'll bet Master Chazir went along with it eagerly," Zanna said.

"I wouldn't know," Mistel said. "I wasn't there." She sat on the bed and gave it a little bounce. "You seem to dislike Kurtz."

"Oh, I despise him."

Mistel's eyebrows rose into two perfect arcs. "Did he break your heart?"

"Absolutely not. I'd sooner throw myself in the Northsea."

"Then why do you hate him?"

Zanna wouldn't pass up a chance to cast judgment upon the likes of Kurtz Chazir. "He misused my charge and humiliated me." Even now, the memory of his challenge made her chest burn. "The man's an insufferable peacock, strutting around as though every maiden's heart were his by right, but he's a torch in a hay barn. He thinks rules are for others, responsibility is a joke, and his wit is sharp enough to cut steel. If arrogance were a weapon, kingdoms would crumble at his feet. And the worst part? Half the time, he actually pulls off the impossible, which only makes him bolder."

"Lands! Remind me not to cross you." Mistel stood and peeked through the shutter slats that covered the window. "How long have you known him?"

Too long. "Met him training for the Kingsguard. Must have been fifteen or sixteen years ago."

"That's practically forever," Mistel said. "People change."

Didn't seem so to Zanna. The fact that Prince Oren found him worthy of the Mârad was beyond her comprehension. "If you're going to change before tonight's performance, you should do that now."

"All right." Mistel spread out the dresses on her bed. "Which one should I wear? Whimsical blue, enchanting green, or passionate red?"

Zanna resisted an eye roll. What did it matter which dress she wore? Tiny thing like her with that hair . . . She'd draw a crowd wearing a burlap sack.

"Whichever you think best," she said. "Find me in the stables when you're done. I'll have your new side saddle ready."

Truth be told, Zanna needed a break from Mistel's prattling. And Tyndor, her black-and-white piebald mare, had no opinions on dresses.

Or Kurtz Chazir.

Chapter Thirteen
Cole

A *CAGED DOVE SINGS NOT OF GUILT, but of the open sky beyond its reach.*
Cole rather liked that idea. He sat cross-legged on his cot, head against the cold brick wall, arms knotted over his chest as if holding himself together. He hadn't moved since Lysander and Dunn had left them in this cell.

Kurtz, on the other hand, had not stopped moving. He paced the cell like a caged wolf, boots cracking against the stone floor. He fiddled with anything: a loose brick in the wall, a floor splinter, a tiny down feather from his pillow.

"This is *ridiculous*, eh?" Kurtz muttered, for the fifth—or was it sixth?—time.

Mistel must be worried. What if Anna, Zanna, whatever her name was... What if she couldn't keep Mistel safe? What if something happened to her because Cole was here, in this cell that reeked of damp stone, mildew, and the metallic tang of rust?

"Lady Viola defies her husband's order?" Kurtz said. "On his first day home as lord? Well, I don't envy Eric's position, I don't. He should have known better than to marry a Jaelportian female.

They can't stand anyone having authority over them, eh? Eric will have his hands full, he will, trying to settle into his place as lord with her in the way."

Cole winced and hoped Torin Oxbow and Gunnar Gedmund, the guards on duty, wouldn't take offense at Kurtz insulting the Livnas.

Kurtz slammed his palm against the bars, the sound reverberating through the corridor. He angled his face in a gap between two rods and eyed the guards. "Let us out, Ox," he asked for the third time.

"You know I can't," the bald man replied.

Kurtz shook the bars until they rattled. "What's the going rate for keeping secrets from Lord Livna, eh? He frees me, yet his wife defies him. I assume the lady pays well for his men's loyalty."

"She didn't pay us!" Gedmund yelled.

"Don't encourage him, Gun," Oxbow said. "This isn't our fault, Kurtz. Take it up with Lord Livna when you next see him."

Kurtz tap-tap-tapped his fingernail on one of the bars. "And when might that be, exactly?"

"No idea," Oxbow said.

Kurtz growled, shoved off the bars, and paced to the wall where he wiggled the loose brick. *Clink-clink, clink-clink.* He sighed and leaned against the wall. "And you—" He jerked his chin at Cole. "Say something."

Cole exhaled slowly. He disliked Kurtz's temperamental side. "You didn't like my idea."

Because, Kurtz bloodvoiced through their open connection, *even if I voiced Prince Oren, he wouldn't ask Eric to release us. That would expose our alliance, and Oren wants no one—not even Eric—to know.*

Then bloodvoice Lord Livna, Cole thought.

If it were Eagan or Nitsa or even Lord Pitney, I would. But Eric and I . . . we have a history, we do, and I've already mucked it up enough today.

You said you wanted to complain to him about his wife, Cole thought.

I want someone to tell him what happened so he'll get mad at his wife, manipulative female that she is. But I don't want to be the one to do it.

That made no sense. Cole clenched his jaw but stayed silent. Would Mistel worry if she knew they were locked up?

He recalled their kiss after the Poroo attack. What if she never kissed him again? Not that it mattered—it was too dangerous to get involved.

Right?

Kurtz moved back to the door and rattled it. "Shoddiest cell I've ever seen. If I had my sword, we'd be out in five minutes. Less, eh?"

Kurtz had insisted they leave their swords at the Ivory Spit. Even if they hadn't, Oxbow and Gedmund would have confiscated them.

"Cruel woman didn't even let me argue," Kurtz said. "'Detain them both,' she said."

Cole smothered a grin at Kurtz's impression of Lady Viola. He shut his eyes, trying to block out the sound of Kurtz's pacing, but as another set of footsteps approached, his heart began to pound.

He met Kurtz's eager gaze and said, "Someone's coming."

Chapter Fourteen
Mistel

A CROSS MOOD COULD ALWAYS BE mended with the right dress.

Not that Mistel was cross. Just cold. And ready to sing. But as they stood in the smelly stable, ready to ride back to the Ivory Spit to meet Cole and Kurtz, Mistel had a short detour in mind.

"Take me to that Ice House place," she said.

Zanna, frost-dusted and stone-faced, glared as she boosted Mistel onto Bart's new side saddle and handed up the reins. "Whatever for?"

Mistel fumbled with her skirts, tugging and twisting them until they lay properly. "I heard Jol Quimby say Renshaw Thusk owns it and has an office upstairs. If I can get us hired to play there, we'll have a reason to be on the premises once Cole gets the keys."

He could be stealing them this very moment. The least Mistel could do while Cole risked everything was figure out a convenient way to use them.

Zanna mounted her black-and-white horse and nudged it forward. The woman had to have some giant blood in her. She'd stood nose to nose with Kurtz in the Ivory Spit, sinew and steel in every line of her body, and a glare that could curdle milk.

Mistel nudged Bart to follow. After a month riding astride, her body welcomed the change in position the side saddle afforded, but she keenly felt the loss of control, like she could, at any moment, slip clean off.

"Is the Ice House far out of the way?" she asked.

"Not really."

Chatty woman, this Zanna-called-Anna. Mistel steered Bart after her.

Mistel had chosen the enchanting green dress for tonight, though none of her new gowns resembled the ones Cole had commissioned in Armonguard. This clothing was practical—thick wool dresses, scratchy stockings, a flannel petticoat, and a hooded wool cloak—enough to keep her from freezing when outside.

Thankfully, it wasn't long until they were tying their horses to a hitching post outside the Ice House.

They entered a cramped, dimly lit den, its low beams and soot-streaked walls pressing in like a crypt. The sour tang of stale ale and unwashed bodies hung thick in the air, though the warmth was a welcome reprieve from the cold. Two withered patrons hunched over their drinks, barely glancing up as Mistel and Zanna approached a narrow counter where a balding man wiped a grimy tankard with an equally filthy rag.

Mistel squared her shoulders and said, "I'm looking for Master Thusk."

The man looked up, eyes widening. "He's gone to Lytton Hall for the festivities."

Just as Mistel thought. "Oh dear," she said. "I'd hoped to get permission to sing here with my band tomorrow night."

The man grinned, gaze drinking her in. "Well now, I handle the hiring. No need to bother Thusk. What's the band called?"

Called? Mistel had no idea. "What luck! Mistel Wepp is my name, sir, and we're called the ... uh ... Wandering Songweavers."

"I'm Bower Renwall, miss. You can play here tomorrow. We pay by occupancy, so I can't promise you a lot of coin, it being the middle of the week. But you keep your tips. Some regulars are real generous, especially if they take a liking to you."

"Don't you want to hear them play first?" Zanna asked.

Master Renwall shrank under Zanna's glare. "No need. A pretty lass like this could crow and still draw a crowd." His gaze peeled away Mistel's woolen layers.

She clenched her teeth at the grimy hunx and forced a smile. "That's very kind of you to say, Master Renwall, but I assure you, our band is quite good."

"Glad to hear it," he said. "Tomorrow, then."

"Yes," Mistel said, eager to get upstairs into Thusk's office. "I look forward to it."

The sun had set by the time they reached the Ivory Spit, which was so crowded it felt like a different place than before.

Someone whistled. "Fancy a dance, lassie?"

Mistel searched the crowd for her new admirer but couldn't tell who had spoken.

"Men," Zanna muttered. "Stick close."

Lands! This towering woman was all work and zero fun. "I can handle myself in a crowd," Mistel said, "and I'm not afraid of men."

"Then you're a fool," Zanna said. "The Spit isn't bad, but you're playing the Ice House tomorrow, and that place attracts miscreants."

Was the woman deaf? "Like I said, I can handle ..."

Zanna started toward an empty table in the back. Mistel

huffed and followed. She'd barely taken a seat when a barmaid approached—older than Rilla, with a long brown braid.

"Evening, Darri. Two plates of whatever's hot." Zanna set two rutahs on the table. "Any sign of Masters Chazir or Tanniyn?"

"No." Darri picked up the coins. "Rilla said they went to the banquet."

Zanna nodded to an elderly fisherman. "Shouldn't Haldor Deppner be at the banquet?"

Darri eyed the man. "Certainly, and he's been here over half an hour. Could be the banquet is over but some stayed to revel."

"Cole wouldn't have dawdled," Mistel said. "Not when we're playing here tonight."

Darri shrugged. "I'll send them over the moment they come in."

But when Darri returned with two bowls of steaming chicken and dumplings, she said, "Merrygog's asking after the band, but still no sign of your men. Can you play without them? If not, Arbin Roxley's here. He's a fiddler."

Did Mistel *want* to play without them? No. But she certainly *could*. "I can sing on my own," she said.

"No," Zanna said. "Not without the others."

Mistel glared at her. "Why do you get to decide every—?"

"Give the job to Arbin tonight," Zanna said to Darri. "Master Chazir will apologize to Merrygog when he gets back."

"Will do," Darri said.

Mistel pushed her plate aside and leaned across the table. "Something's happened. We should go see."

"You need a reason to go to Lytton Hall," Zanna said. "Otherwise, you risk exposing us."

Mistel folded her arms. "I do have a reason. We can't just sit here and do nothing."

"*I* certainly can." Zanna took a bite of her food, then added a bit of salt. "But if you can't, then we have a problem."

Mistel bristled. "What do you mean by that?"

"Aren't you here on trial?" the woman asked. "If I tell Prince Oren you gave me a lot of trouble, it won't help you."

That her chaperone felt she could threaten her... "You don't have many friends, do you?"

Zanna's brow creased.

Oops. Had that been too mean?

Zanna quickly masked any hurt with indifference. "In my line of work, friends are a liability."

"That's tragic," Mistel said. "Perhaps you should find another line of work."

"This is what Arman created me to do."

Mistel widened her eyes at the table in a discrete eye roll. She wasn't sure she could take much more of this woman's intensity.

The bell clanged as new patrons entered the Ivory Spit. Mistel craned her neck, trying to see. Scattered greetings rose up near the door.

"It's the Ox!"

"Evening, Torin."

"The army's returned, has it?"

"We arrived just today," said a beardless bald man in a Tsaftown army uniform. The only hair on his face was a long black mustache. "I'll take a pint, Darri."

"Me too." This from the bald man's younger companion, also in uniform.

Mistel didn't recognize the bald man from the journey here, though the younger one had spoken often with Derby Wenk. He had messy brown curly hair and patches of scruff on his cheeks. Either he shaved very poorly or was failing in his attempt to grow a beard.

"Do you know those men?" she asked Zanna.

The woman glanced over Mistel's head. "Older one is Torin Oxbow. He's with Gunnar Gedmund. Both in the Fighting Fifteen."

"Heard there was trouble at the hall tonight, Ox," said a white-haired man near the hearth. "Howlers are in an uproar."

"Let them roar," Oxbow said. "They had no business at Lord Livna's homecoming banquet, let alone starting a brawl."

"What were they fighting about?" asked a man with a pockmarked face.

"No idea," Oxbow said. "But they were fighting with Kurtz Chazir, so it was likely over a woman."

A chorus of laughter rang out.

Mistel perked up. Kurtz had been planning some diversion so Cole could steal Thusk's keys. He must have picked a fight.

Darri carried two frothing mugs of ale to the men's table. Oxbow swept his up and took a long drink.

"Thought Kurtz was on Ice Island for treason," said the pockmarked man.

"The king freed him," Darri said. "It was all lies. Kurtz and Sir Eagan both falsely accused."

"I knew that much the day it happened," the old man said. "Those boys would never have betrayed King Axel. Where they been?"

"Went south with the real prince and Sir Gavin and Lord Livna and the army—all of us," Oxbow said. "We fought alongside them in Armonguard. Sir Eagan is down there still—pledged to marry Nitsa Amal, if you can believe that. But Kurtz came back with us. Hasn't passed one night here and already locked up again, the unlucky fool."

Mistel grabbed Zanna's arm.

"Locked up with the Howler?" the old man asked.

"Nah." Oxbow took another drink. "Lady Viola sent Kurtz and his friend to the dungeon for the night." He started to laugh. "Dunn and Lysander Thane brought them down when me and Gunnar were on duty. Kurtz verbally skinned me bare, so when it was time to leave, I didn't bother telling the next shift how long the new prisoners were meant to stay. Who knows? Lady Viola might forget about them, and they'll be there a week. Maybe more."

The crowd chuckled.

"Now we know where they are." Zanna ate another bite of chicken dumplings and spoke over a full mouth. "Safe and sound in the dungeon of Lytton Hall."

How awful. Mistel leaned over the table and whispered, "We have to get them out."

"Just how will we do that?" Zanna snapped. "You going to reason with Lady Viola? You're a bigger fool than I thought."

"You don't have to be mean," Mistel said. "I'm sure she'll be reasonable when we tell her . . ." Her voice trailed off as her gaze locked onto the keys clipped to Ox's belt.

"No, do go on," Zanna said. "Love to hear your plan."

Mistel folded her arms and sank back in her chair. If she shared her idea, Zanna would surely try to stop her.

A fiddle's tune drew her gaze to the corner where she, Cole, and Kurtz had played earlier. Arbin Roxley perched on a stool, tapping his foot to his music. Wiry, with thick black hair and rolled-up sleeves, his fingers danced across the strings while his bow hand coaxed a lively melody.

Clapping started. Boots stomped. The rhythm quickened, and two couples leaped up to dance.

"Be right back." Mistel rose as more pairs crowded the fiddler. She wove to Torin Oxbow's table, where the bald soldier sat laughing, ale in hand. "Torin Oxbow, is it?"

He raised a brow, eyeing her. "That'd be me. And you are?"

"Eager to dance," Mistel said with a curtsy. "Care to prove if the Fighting Fifteen are as quick on their feet as they are with a sword?"

Cheers erupted. Oxbow chuckled, setting down his mug. "Think you can keep up, lass?"

"That's what I intend to find out." Mistel seized his calloused hand and led him to the dance floor.

Despite Master Oxbow's burly frame, he moved with surprising agility, boots stomping to the beat. Mistel matched his pace, skirts flaring as they circled. He twirled her under his arm, and her gaze flicked to the keys on his belt. Timing her movement carefully, she brushed close, fingers poised to snatch them and—

"Mind if I cut in?" Gunnar Gedmund stood there, his crooked grin and scruffy cheeks far too confident for his young face.

"Go ahead." Master Oxbow winked at Mistel as he stepped back. "But don't let her wear you out, Gun. She's got more energy than you can handle."

Before she could protest, Master Gedmund grabbed both her hands and spun her. "You're light on your feet," he said, twirling her again.

"And you're a windstorm." Mistel's vision blurred as the room tilted, and she stumbled. "Less spinning, more dancing—unless you're trying to send me through the rafters."

He laughed, unfazed, and spun her again. Mistel's mind raced. Oxbow, back in his seat, clapped along, his keys still in plain view. She needed to reach him.

The next time Gedmund spun her, she misstepped just enough to stagger into an olive-skinned man by the fire.

"Oh, pardon me!" she exclaimed, disentangling herself.

Before Gedmund could reclaim her or she could slip away, the olive-skinned man caught her hands. "If you insist," he said, pulling her into a quick step.

Thunder and rats. She recovered quickly, matching her partner's movements, until a pockmarked man cut in. Soon Mistel found herself at the center of a rotating line of eager partners.

Mercy. Were there not enough women in Tsaftown? She laughed and twirled, but her focus stayed sharp. The moment she was able to break away, she spun back to Oxbow's table.

"Back so soon?" he asked, his brows raised.

Mistel reached for his hand. "Some men can't keep up."

Around the room they went, and when Oxbow finally twirled her, Mistel leaned in, feigning dizziness. Her hand brushed his waist and slipped the keys free. She tucked them into her sleeve and kept dancing, grinning until the song ended.

By the time Mistel reached Zanna, her cheeks were flushed, and she was breathing hard. She dropped into her chair, the keys safe in her lap.

"Got his keys," she said.

Zanna leveled her with a flat stare. "Must you make a performance of everything?"

Mistel fanned herself. "Where's the fun in doing it any other way?"

"Eat," Zanna said. "Then we'll fetch the men."

Mistel bounced on her chair. "Thank you." She took a bite. Rich gravy filled her mouth, and she gasped. "Oh! That's very good." She dug in like a starving woman.

Zanna watched, brows low.

"What?" Mistel asked.

"I was just thinking—if Kurtz Chazir had a sister . . ."

Mistel laughed. "I'll take that as a compliment, even though I know you meant otherwise."

Chapter Fifteen
Cole

Disappointment. A gift Cole had never asked for.

The footsteps had only been the changing of guards. Oxbow and Gunnar replaced by two men Cole didn't recognize. Kurtz tried the same tactics to win them over, but when that failed—and the sun set, cutting off the last light through the barred half window near the ceiling—he flopped onto his stomach on his cot, feet on the pillow, chin on folded arms, and glared out the bars at the distant torch.

The darkness grated on Kurtz, and Cole could only help by staying silent.

Lying on his cot, Cole examined the timber ceiling, thoughts circling Mistel and whether letting her stay had been a mistake. Clearly, he was doing a shoddy job of protecting her.

His head itched, and before he could scratch it, the king bloodvoiced a knock. *Achan Cham.*

Cole lowered his shields. *Yes, sir?*

Kurtz tells me he got you both arrested.

Unfortunately. We were trying to steal some keys—

He said you got them. Prince Oren doesn't want me to interfere, so . . . I'm afraid you're stuck for now. Hopefully, you won't be there long.

Cole wanted to ask the king to check on Mistel—at the very least, tell her what had happened to them—but the mere thought of voicing such a request embarrassed him.

Still seeing Ebens? Achan asked.

No, actually. Not since the raiders in Mahanaim.

That's good. What about Mistel?

Zanna took her shopping, so she's likely very happy.

Achan laughed. *I'm sure she is. Are the two of you, uh . . . Caleb is worried you've formed an attachment.*

Caleb is worried. Of course, he was.

He's afraid she'll distract you with her feminine wiles.

Wiles?

Is there an echo?

Why doesn't Sir Caleb bloodvoice me if he wants to give a lecture?

Because I told him to leave you alone unless you asked to talk to him. You've already got me nosing into all your business. Arman knows you don't need him too. Speaking of which, would you say that you and Mistel are romantically involved?

Cole's face flamed. *Excuse me?*

I know. That's an impertinent question. And while Sir Caleb tells me I am king and can ask people whatever I want, it's not my way. Usually. Truth is, Vrell wants to know. She's been begging me to ask you ever since the two of you first sang for us. I told her it was none of our business, and I wasn't going to bother you with such nonsense. But since you've got nothing better to do at present . . . Unless you'd rather tell the rest of the story about the Battle of Armonguard and the Eben.

I vowed we'd remain friends, Cole thought, the way she called him *knightling* and the kiss they'd shared in the forest near

Glodwood Manor filling his mind with his blatant failure. *The mission is more important. And we're cousins, now, after all.*

Yes, and my wife was once my squire, so . . .

Cole opened his mouth, his thoughts completely tangled. *I don't—*

A distant snap broke the silence. The scuffle of feet. A grunt. Something fell at the end of the corridor, followed by a muffled groan.

Cole's heart skipped. He rolled onto his side. *Just a moment, Your Highness. Someone is coming.*

Let's hope it's Lady Viola to set you free. I'll leave you to it, then. The king ended their connection.

Kurtz was already on his feet, gripping the bars, staring into the dark corridor. "You hear that?"

Cole sat up and nodded, his pulse beating hard.

Seconds, then minutes passed without another sound. Kurtz stepped back. "Nothing."

Cole stared through the bars, willing them to open. He felt like they were no longer alone, yet there was no evidence to prove it. "Must have been the guards." He finally lay back on his cot.

"Cole?" came a whisper.

His head snapped up, and he glanced across the dark cell at Kurtz. "What?"

Kurtz frowned back at him. "I didn't say anything."

"Cole?" The voice came again.

Cole leaped to his feet. "Mistel?"

At the end of the corridor, a faint light swelled, revealing a shadowy, feminine figure with a lantern.

"Who else?" she said.

How in all Er'Rets? Cole kept his voice low. "We're over here."

Kurtz's scowl melted into a grin. "About time. Figured Zanna was hoping I'd been killed."

"She might be," Mistel said. "Lucky for you both, you have me."

She appeared then, a goddess of light, lifting a set of keys. The soft jingle was the sweetest sound Cole had heard all day. "Ready to leave, my knightling?"

Cole stepped to the door, only the bars between them. "What about the guards?"

"Zanna took care of them," Mistel said. "But we need to hurry."

Cole's stomach knotted at the thought of Lady Viola finding more violence in Lytton Hall. "You shouldn't have come. It's too dangerous."

"Don't be so dramatic," Mistel said, working the lock.

From behind Cole, Kurtz let out a laugh. "Remind me to buy you a drink at the tavern."

"Make it two." Mistel glanced at him while she worked. "One for freeing you, the other for getting us a gig at the Ice House."

"Where?" Cole asked.

"Thusk's alehouse," Mistel said. "I went over there and got us hired for tomorrow n/ight."

Cole went cold all over. "How could you put yourself in harm's way like that?"

She rolled her eyes, lips twisted to one side. "I'm not a child, Cole, and I don't need your permission to take risks. Now hush and let me concentrate."

Three more seconds, and when the lock clicked, Cole felt a shift. Mistel had freed them and secured a performance at Thusk's alehouse. She was part of the Mârad now, not just a tagalong needing protection, but a valuable contributor.

The realization hit harder than he expected. If she belonged with them, he had to stop worrying about her. But how could he do that when his heart was so deeply tangled with hers?

The next morning, a knock at Cole and Kurtz's door in the Ivory Spit revealed Jol Quimby and Lovell Dunn.

A chill ran over Cole at the sight of the man who had jailed them last night. Struggling for words, he managed only, "What...?"

Quimby chuckled, clapping Cole's shoulder as he stepped inside. "You've frightened the lad, Dunn."

"It's my face, isn't it?" Dunn said. "Terrifies anyone who sees it. Best I wear a helm in public."

Right. Only someone who looked like he belonged on a coin could say something like that with a straight face. Cole had little doubt women lined up to speak with Lovell Dunn.

Quimby shut the door. "Dunn's worked for the Mârad before. He can be trusted."

"Trusted, my holey boot," Kurtz said.

Cole had to agree. "He put us in the dungeon."

Kurtz stepped up to Dunn, nose to nose. "You dragged me from the hall, manhandled me in Eric's office, stayed silent when Lady Viola undermined Eric, then locked me up like a common criminal."

Dunn's grin parted his thick beard. "I follow orders. Always have, always will. And Viola didn't undermine Eric. He let you go. Then she arrested you again."

Kurtz folded his arms. "Eben's breath, you're her pet, aren't you?"

"Eric left me in charge when you rode south to war," Dunn said. "After I failed to keep Esek out of Lytton Hall."

Kurtz sobered, and a grimace passed over his face. "That was partly my fault, it was."

"No, it was mine. Kenton nearly killed me. I tried to resign. Eric had other plans, charged me with keeping his family safe. So I've done. But I'll help you where I can."

"I'll take that as an apology, I will," Kurtz said.

Dunn barked a deep laugh. "If it helps you sleep."

Quimby handed Cole a set of keys. "One copy, ready for use."

Cole pocketed them. "You don't think Thusk suspects?"

"Nope," Dunn said. "I gave him his real keys last night. All he had were complaints about unruly convicts."

"Thusk's a morality monger, is he?" Kurtz scoffed. "Let's dig up his dirt, see how he likes Ice Island, eh?"

"Want to sit?" Cole gestured to the table by the hearth.

"Don't mind if I do." Dunn dropped onto a chair, which groaned under his weight.

Quimby and Kurtz took the others, leaving Cole to lean against the hearth.

"Tell them about the Howlers, Dunn," Quimby said.

"Howlers work for Fenris Yarden," Dunn said. "The council hired them to protect against Poroo raids."

"Poroo don't raid this far north, they don't," Kurtz said. "The tribes here are peaceful, eh?"

"Well, they *are* raiding," Dunn said. "I've seen it myself. Could be displacement from the end of Darkness, hunger . . . Who knows?"

"Why would the end of Darkness be a problem?" Cole asked. "There's more land now, more food."

"The lad's right," Kurtz said. "That don't add up, it don't."

"That's why we want you playing at the Black Boar," Quimby said. "It's Tsaftown's biggest haunt of thieves and outlaws."

"Joonas Erlichman owns it," Dunn added. "And Fenris Yarden made it his base."

Cole recalled the mad glint in Fenris's eyes when he'd been choking Kurtz. "Does Thusk have ties to Fenris or the Black Boar?"

"None that I know of," Quimby said.

"Because he has his own alehouse?" Kurtz asked.

"The Ice House," Dunn said. "Maybe. Thusk is greedy. Why send his lackeys elsewhere when he can take their coin himself?"

"We'll let you know what we find," Cole said.

"What's your plan?" Dunn asked. "Just going to nose around?"

"Cole searches Thusk's office. I stand guard," Kurtz said.

"Plus, Mistel got us hired to play there tonight," Cole added. "So if anyone asks, I'll say I'm scouting the venue."

"That place is a dump," Quimby said.

"A dump below Thusk's office," Kurtz added.

"Don't get caught," Dunn said. "Thusk's guards hurt first, ask questions later."

Cole didn't like the sound of that but said, "We'll be careful."

Chapter Sixteen
Cole

Cole's boots crunched over the frosty ground as he left Cherix at Fat Vandy's and made his way down the street. The early morning sky blushed pink and blue. The cold had turned his cheeks numb and his breath to vapor. There wasn't a soul in sight, and the empty streets only deepened the chill.

The Ice House loomed ahead on the corner, a two-story structure of dark wood, its roof heavy with snow. Icicles hung from the eaves like jagged teeth, gleaming in the morning light. Intricate dagfish carvings framed the door and shutters, proof someone valued both craftsmanship *and* luxury.

A hollow call rang out—soft and sorrowful—ending in three clear trills.

The whistle was their signal, another part of Cole's training. He followed the sound to a figure across the street from the Ice House. Kurtz, leaning against a building, arms folded, gaze sharp beneath the brim of his dark cloak. As Cole neared, two more figures stepped from the shadows: Zanna and Mistel.

What were they doing here?

"You're late," Kurtz muttered as he pushed off the wall. "And you didn't tell me you'd invited the women."

"I didn't invite them." Cole eyed Mistel's rosy cheeks. "Why are you here?"

"Because we're a team," Mistel said. "Because I got us hired here for tonight. And because you need me."

"We don't—"

Shut your yap, lad, Kurtz bloodvoiced. *If you don't want the girl to hate you, don't say things you'll regret.* Then he said aloud, "Thusk went hunting this morning with Joonas Erlichman."

"Erlichman is a local businessman," Zanna said. "Sells boar for the rich to hunt. He's also the head of the ruling council."

Kurtz didn't bother softening his tone. "I know who he is."

"If you're going to stay here, I'll post myself around back," Zanna said.

"I didn't ask for your help," Kurtz said.

"And I didn't ask for permission." Zanna took off across the street. Mistel followed her.

Cole smirked at Kurtz. "Don't say mean things, huh?"

Kurtz grunted. "Difference is, I don't want that one to like me. Let's get this done."

Kurtz took position catty-cornered from the alehouse. Cole hesitated before heading down the alley to join Mistel and Zanna around back where an exterior staircase led up to a narrow door.

Zanna nodded across the alley. "I'll wait just there."

Cole inhaled deeply and glanced at Mistel. "I suppose you're coming with me?"

"Of course." She grinned, flashing her winsome overbite.

Arman, help me, Cole prayed.

They climbed the stairs. On the square platform at the top, Cole tried the keys. The fourth one clicked, and they crept into a dark, dusty room. Dim light squeezed through slats in the shutters, revealing a cluttered desk, shelves lined with ledgers, and bottles of what looked like alcohol.

"It's cold in here," Mistel said.

Cole stepped lightly, trying to avoid creaking floorboards. He reached the desk and flipped through a ledger. They needed proof—smuggling, piracy, anything illegal. It had to be here.

Mistel lifted a bottle from a shelf and examined it. "Excited for tonight? It's our first show."

"Not really."

"Why not?"

He considered the question. "My music has always been personal. Playing for a rowdy crowd makes me . . ." He trailed off.

Mistel tilted her head, a knowing glint in her eye. "The first time I sang for a crowd, I thought I'd faint."

"You? Nervous?"

"Terrified. I was eight, visiting Sitna's midsummer festival. I begged my mother to let me sing a song, but when I stepped on stage and saw all those people staring..." She shuddered. "I froze."

Cole fought back a smirk. The idea of Mistel suffering stage fright felt absurd. "What happened?"

Mistel's expression softened. "My mother knelt beside me and whispered, 'Pretend you're singing to the stars. They're always listening, and they never judge.'"

"The stars? That worked?"

"Not at first." Mistel chuckled, her eyes glossy. "It was midday, and I stood there like a fool, staring up at a blue sky. But then I closed my eyes and imagined it was only me and the stars. And I just . . . sang. When I looked up again, the crowd was clapping."

Cole crossed his arms. "Doubt that'll help when half the alehouse is drunk."

"Well, if it doesn't, find one friendly face in the crowd, and play for them."

Cole rubbed the back of his neck. "What if I can't find one?"

"Then focus on me." Mistel traced her finger over the back of his hand. "I'll be right there, cheering you on."

Warmth stirred in Cole's chest. He glanced down at their hands, wanting to grab hold, knowing he shouldn't, wondering if their differences were too great to overcome.

"Better keep looking." He pulled his hand away, and for a split second, hurt flashed across her face. It was gone in a breath, though, and she set about searching a bookshelf.

Cole opened a desk drawer and pulled out a stack of invoices. Spotted the name Erlichman on the top one.

"Thusk ships boar for Erlichman," he said, paging through the invoices. "He sold to Abidan Levy in Sitna, Julian Coble in Land's End, Angaro Boar in Meneton. Ships all over Er'Rets, it looks like."

Mistel moved beside him and peered at the paper. Her hair brushed against his ear, and he couldn't help feeling a little warmer, despite the chilled room.

The invoices were detailed, listing recipients of goods, amounts shipped, and destinations. A name on the third invoice twisted Cole's stomach.

"Jaira Hamartano," he muttered. "She hunts for sport?"

"Who?" Mistel asked.

Cole exhaled. Who, indeed. "Daughter of Jaelport's ruling lady. She fancies herself a princess. Not exactly the hunting type."

Mistel pointed at another name. "This one was shipped by Verdot Amal. Isn't he the one who runs Ice Island?"

"Yes . . ." Cole frowned. "I could see Amal buying livestock to feed prisoners, but selling it doesn't make sense." He flipped through more invoices. Dozens listed Verdot Amal as the shipper.

A sharp whistle sliced through the air, sending a jolt through Cole.

"That's Zanna's signal," Mistel whispered.

"Zanna has a signal of her own?" Cole asked.

"Why shouldn't she?"

Didn't matter. Cole shoved the invoice into his pocket and the rest back into the drawer. He hurried to the window and spotted Zanna speaking to a man who was ascending the stairs.

"It's one of Thusk's men," Cole whispered. "I saw him at the banquet."

His heart pounded as he spun, searching for a place to hide.

"In here!" Mistel yanked open a narrow door. A broom closet. Cole noted its lock and slipped inside. Mistel followed, her skirts brushing his leg as she pulled the door shut.

In the dark, Cole fumbled with Thusk's keys, hands trembling as he tried one after another. The jingle of metal seemed deafening in the cramped space. Finally, the lock clicked. He tucked the keys into his pocket and stilled.

Someone's coming, Kurtz bloodvoiced.

We saw. We're hiding.

If it comes to it, don't confront him. Invent a story.

Right. A story for why he and Mistel were hiding in a closet. He could only think of one.

Cole heard nothing but their breathing and his pulse pounding in his ears. The closet barely fit one person, let alone two. Mistel's shoulder pressed against his chest, her warm breath tickling his ear. The faint scent of mint, lemon, and parchment clung to her. He turned his head, and his nose brushed hers. He swallowed hard, locking his gaze on the inky darkness above her head. His body betrayed him, every nerve on high alert. He wanted to kiss her—oh, how he wanted to—but he couldn't. Shouldn't. Cousins and all.

A door creaked. Bootsteps.

The intruder clomped across the floor, pausing at the desk. Papers rustled. Drawers slammed. Cole shifted, his boot scuffing Mistel's. She grabbed his wrist, stilling him, then ran her fingers along the beads of the bracelet she'd given him months ago. The trinket he couldn't bear to part with, even as he pretended, daily, not to care for her.

The footsteps were moving again, growing louder. Outside the closet.

The latch rattled.

Cole held his breath. *Arman, keep us safe.*

Mistel's fingers tightened around Cole's wrist. The intruder cursed, shook the latch again before stepping back.

Then the footsteps retreated. The front door creaked and finally clicked shut.

The office fell silent.

Mistel released a long sigh.

Cole didn't move. He strained his ears, waiting for any sound that might signal the man's return—or that he'd only pretended to leave and was waiting right outside the closet.

You're in the clear, Kurtz bloodvoiced. *He's coming down.*

Cole released a slow, shaky breath. *Thank you, Arman.* "Kurtz said he's gone."

Mistel shifted, her nose grazing his chin, the lemony smell of her hair intoxicating.

"Well, this is cozy," she said, her voice a husky whisper.

Cole huffed a nervous laugh, very aware of how close her body was to his and how it made his heart race. "Terrifying is a better word."

"I wouldn't mind if it happened again." She laced her fingers with his.

Time to move or Mistel's suggestion of kissing cousins was going to become a prophecy fulfilled. Cole squeezed her hand, then let go and pulled out the keys. "Good thing I locked it."

"If it had opened, I was going to kiss you. Best excuse for being in a closet together."

Cole chuckled, his cheeks warm. "That was my only idea too."

He unlocked the door, and cool air rushed in. Cole walked into the now-empty office.

Mistel came alongside him and tugged his rope belt. "Why a rope? You used to wear a leather one."

"Kurtz's idea. Says it's always handy to have rope."

"And the bracelet?" She ran her finger along the beads.

"You gave it to me."

"You must really like it."

Fishing for compliments again. He didn't mind. He wanted to say "I really like *you*," but all that came out was "I . . . do like it."

She smiled so brightly it lit up her entire face and brought out the charming quirk in her teeth. Before Cole knew it, he grinned back, caught off guard by just how stunning she was. He ached to kiss her, to reprise that dazzling moment in the forest after their encounter with the Poroo. No one would see. No one would know but them.

He slid his thumb along her cheek, cradled her neck, pulled her toward him.

He's not leaving, Kurtz bloodvoiced. *We'll distract him so you can get out of there.*

The interruption brought a wash of shame over Cole. Where was his head? Not on the mission. Not on protecting Mistel but taking advantage.

He'd agreed to be her cousin for a reason.

Cole forced himself to release Mistel, feeling as if he'd stepped outside into the bitter cold. "Kurtz says we need to go. Come on." He crossed to the door, thinking he should search the desk again, but the invoice in his pocket would have to do.

He found the key he'd used to open the door, then glanced outside and saw Zanna talking with Thusk's man at the foot of the stairs.

Cole twisted the knob carefully and opened the door. He inserted the key into the lock and motioned Mistel out. She slipped past, and he followed, pulling the door closed behind him. With the key already in place, he quickly twisted it, then tucked the keys into his pocket.

On the ground below, Zanna said, "I don't have to explain myself to you."

"Go," Cole whispered, gesturing Mistel down the stairs.

She went, and Cole followed, careful not to make a sound.

Halfway down, Mistel called out, "Did you find a way in, Anna?"

The guard turned, frowning. "What are you two doing up there?"

Mistel smiled sweetly. "Looking for the dressing room. You do have one, don't you?"

The guard blinked. "Why would we need one?"

Mistel glided down the steps. "We're musicians, playing here tonight. I wanted to see if there was a dressing room. If not, I'll wear my best costume and leave the others behind."

The guard blinked again, eyeing Cole warily. "No dressing room, miss. But wear whatever you like."

Mistel's grin faltered. "That's a shame. I'll be sure to choose carefully. See you tonight?"

The guard nodded, clearly flustered as Mistel trailed a finger over his shoulder as she walked past.

Cole rushed after her, admiration warring with irritation. When they reached Kurtz across the street, he asked, "Was that really necessary?"

"She covered for us well," Kurtz said. "When the guard sees us play tonight, he won't think on this morning again."

"Yet there's a whole day before tonight for him to talk," Zanna said.

"Exactly," Cole said. "You should think before you speak, Mistel."

"I did," Mistel said, frowning. "The whole point in coming this morning was so that we could use the excuse of playing here tonight. I did exactly that."

"I need you to be more careful," Cole said.

"And I need you to be less bossy," she said.

"I'm not trying to—the king put me in charge of this mission. So, I should get some say in how much unnecessary risk we take."

"Risk is part of the game, Cole. You knew that when you let me stay."

He gritted his teeth. "Let's just go," he said. "I want to show Kurtz and Zanna what we found."

The four of them made their way to Fat Vandy's, entering through the back. Zanna led them into the dim main room to a table by a window.

"Still standing," Kurtz said, looking around. "Didn't think I'd see this place again."

"They don't get up as early as they used to," Zanna said.

"I'll come by later to say hello," Kurtz said.

They sat down, and Cole pulled out the invoice he'd taken.

"Thusk is tangled up with more than just Erlichman." He traced his finger under Jaira Hamartano's name, then Verdot Amal's. "This must prove something, but I don't know what."

Kurtz squinted at the writing. "Verdot Amal shipping boar to Jaira Hamartano? I don't think so. Where would he get them, eh? And why?"

"Verdot runs Ice Island," Zanna said, "and he—"

"We know," Kurtz cut in.

She glared at Kurtz. "I was going to say, he doesn't ship anything from the prison."

Cole eyed the invoice. "How much does a boar sell for?"

"Anywhere between five to ten golds," Kurtz said.

"Lands!" Mistel said. "That's a fortune."

"These boar cost even more," Cole said, pointing at the prices. "Lowest one sold to Jaira was thirty golds."

"No one would pay thirty golds for a boar," Kurtz said.

"Who even has thirty golds to spend on anything?" Mistel asked.

"Not many," Kurtz said, "but the Hamartanos do."

Cole frowned. "They must be smuggling something."

"Oh, definitely," Kurtz said. "The question is, what?"

"Prisoners from Ice Island?" Cole said.

Silence fell.

"Now, that could be," Kurtz said. "You're on to something, poet."

"We need to search Thusk's warehouse," Cole said.

"I've passed it a few times," Zanna said, "but it's always swarming with workers."

"Then let's look at Verdot Amal," Cole said. "He must be involved."

"I'm sure he is," Kurtz said. "But tread lightly. He put me in Ice Island for thirteen years. He's dangerous."

Cole felt that in his bones. Prince Oren hadn't sent them here for nothing. He didn't want Mistel near a man who trafficked people, but today had again proved she had skills the rest of them lacked. She would risk herself again and again, and he had to allow it, learn to work with it somehow.

Trust Arman to do what he could not.

Chapter Seventeen
Mistel

Smile and nod, Mistel. Smile and nod.

Bower Renwall smelled like ale and onions and stood far too close. "You sing like a songbird," he said, his grin revealing teeth crusted with bits of food. "When you're done, let's find a more private space. Some of my regulars like an *intimate* encore."

Mistel held her grin but clenched her fists at her sides. "I perform onstage, Master Renwall. Nowhere else."

"We'll see." The grimy hunx chuckled, slow and knowing, as if certain that time would change her answer.

Before she had to decide between smacking him or walking away, Kurtz stepped in and clapped a hand on the man's shoulder like they were old friends. "Master Renwall, is that your storeroom I passed on the way in? I noticed the latch is cracked, I did. Might want to check on that before someone walks off with your best ale, eh?"

Bower cursed under his breath and shuffled off, muttering about thieves and lazy help.

"Thank you, Kurtz. I wanted to check on Cole, but Master Renwall would not stop talking."

Kurtz gestured to where Cole sat on a chair by the kitchen door. "You're free now, you are."

Mistel hurried over to Cole. "This is a terrible spot," she said. "Will you be able to play with that door swinging open?"

Cole glanced up at her as he continued to tune one of his strings. "I'll be fine."

She looked over the tiny space, counted fifteen tables, only five of them occupied. "This is shocking," she said. "I've never sung in a venue this empty."

"Might be because of the attack on the city today," Zanna said, coming to stand beside her. "Poroo raiders ambushed a caravan at the southern gatehouse—killed several merchants and at least one Howler."

A chill ran over Mistel's arms. "That's horrible. I'm not surprised people don't feel like going out."

"We already accomplished what we needed to this morning," Cole said. "Tonight is just about playing well enough to get people talking."

Mistel frowned at the measly crowd. "All nine of them."

"Let's start with 'Hear the Pretty Maiden,'" Cole said. "Then do, 'I Bless My King,' followed by 'The Pawn Our King,' then slow things down with 'Mountain Song.'"

"Perfect!" Mistel said.

"Best avoid singing about the king," Kurtz said. "This is more of an epic ballads crowd."

"But Mistel wrote 'The Pawn Our King,'" Cole said. "And the king asked us to sing it along with 'Sparrow' wherever we went."

"Well, he wasn't thinking about our necks when he said that, was he?" Kurtz stroked his short beard. "Give 'Pawn' a try. Introduce it however you like, but wait and see what the reaction is before you sing any other royalist songs."

Cole frowned, chewing on the term royalist, and said, "All right. Let's switch 'I Bless My King' to 'Chamswrath.'"

"Oh, they'll like that one, they will," Kurtz said.

Master Renwall returned and, once all was set, made his introduction. "Ladies and gentlemen," he called, though there were only men in the alehouse, save Mistel and Zanna. "Tonight, we have the great honor of welcoming a truly special performance. Give your ears—and your hearts—to the Wandering Songweavers!"

Kurtz started the beat on his tabor, and Cole plucked out the jaunty intro to "Hear the Pretty Maiden." Mistel's lips twitched, trying to hold back a grin as Cole shot her a sideways look.

Songweavers? he mouthed as his fingers struck the first chord.

Mercy. In all that had gone on since she'd invented that name, she'd completely forgotten to tell anyone. She winked at Cole, turned her attention to the sparse crowd, and began to sing.

> *"Hail the piper, fiddle, fife,*
> *The night is young and full of life.*
> *The Corner teems with ale and song.*
> *And we will dance the whole night long."*

Mistel danced in the very small space she'd been given. Master Renwall tapped his foot, his gaze clinging to her like a burr to a wool cloak. Zanna watched the man with narrowed eyes, and Mistel was grateful for her statuesque protector. ZolZanna tan Quelle was not one to cross.

But the crowd barely looked up. A man at the farthest table slouched in his chair, mug to his lips. Nearby, two men talked, oblivious to the music. Only one man at a table in front glanced their way, then promptly went back to gnawing a chicken leg.

When the song ended and Mistel curtsied, no one clapped. "Hunxes, anyway," she muttered, just loud enough for Cole to hear.

He shot her a sympathetic look but dove into "The Ballad of Bryndor and Chamswrath," its melody dark and heavy. Mistel adjusted her tone, her voice ringing out like a bard in a great hall.

This song at least drew some attention. Gazes lifted briefly before returning to conversations. Mistel tried to coax them into clapping along, but they remained indifferent, clutching their drinks close as if that was all that mattered in the world.

After "Chamswrath," Cole instantly strummed his way into "The Pawn Our King." As he played through the first bars, Mistel addressed the room. "This is a special song to me," she said. "I was born and raised in Sitna, and I knew our king when he was young. His story inspired me to write this. I hope you enjoy it." She began to sing.

> *"He grew up here in Sitna town,*
> *The hand his life was dealt.*
> *He milked the goats and fetched the wood,*
> *Or Poril gave him the belt."*
> *"The pawn our king, sing merry, merry, merry.*
> *The pawn our servant king.*
> *For he was once the lowest of all strays*
> *And now he is our king."*

As Cole strummed into the second verse, a man in back yelled, "That stray ain't no king of mine. This is the North!"

Mistel faltered for a heartbeat, caught Cole's eye, and went right into the next verse.

> *"Then the Great Whitewolf took him up,*
> *Taught him to use a sword.*
> *He fought quite well, his blade struck true*
> *And blood from Esek poured."*

Before she could return to the chorus, something soft smacked her ear, and a half-eaten roll of bread tumbled to the floor. She yelped and combed breadcrumbs from her hair.

Cole stood, his chair scraping back to the lone sound of Kurtz's tabor. "Who did that?"

Kurtz stopped playing. "Sit down," he said sharply.

"I will not," Cole snapped. He set down his lute, then turned back to the patrons. "Who threw that?"

A massive man at the back of the room pushed to his feet, chest and arms like boulders beneath his tunic. "I did," he growled. "We don't want any songs about kings up in the North."

Another man leaped to his feet. "A hex upon him!"

"Fool boy got our lord killed, now, didn't he?" a third man chimed in, his words slurred.

The big man spat on the floor and walked toward Cole. "Only fools sing praises for a king who cowers behind walls while better men die for his mistakes."

Oh, knightling, take care, Mistel thought as Cole clenched his fists.

"Now, see here," he said. "You know nothing about our—"

But Kurtz slipped up to Cole and looped an arm around his shoulders in what appeared to be a friendly gesture. He turned their backs to the crowd, which stalled the big man's forward movement. When Kurtz said nothing more, Mistel knew he was speaking to Cole with his bloodvoicing magic.

"Lost your voice, have you?" the big man said, drawing laughter from the patrons.

Zanna came to stand beside Mistel, who was grateful for the woman's commanding presence.

Kurtz finally released Cole, who gritted his teeth, sat down, and picked up his lute.

"I can't laugh," he muttered.

"What?" Mistel asked.

Kurtz, back at his tabor, started a steady *thump, thump, thump,* and Cole's fingers picked out the lilting intro to "Mountain Song."

Well! Apparently, the show would continue. Mistel entered on cue, her voice softer now. Her heart ached as she sang, but she forced a smile, even as heat simmered beneath her skin.

Never had she been so disrespected by an audience. The thrown bread had rattled her, and when that man had stood and walked toward Cole... She shuddered.

But at least this motley crowd was seated again, their attention back on their drinks, and the food stayed on the tables. Ignoring the band completely but... Fine by her.

After their performance, Mistel and Zanna found Cole outside on the street, lute in hand.

"What did Kurtz say when he bloodvoiced you?" Mistel asked.

Cole glanced around them and spoke softly. "Not to forget that we supposedly left the king's service, so we don't get to defend him when drunkards throw insults. We're to laugh instead—at the very least, hold our tongues."

Mistel's heart went out to Cole, who loved the king like a brother. "I'm sorry," she said. "That entire experience was awful."

"I'm just glad things didn't escalate further," Zanna said.

Kurtz exited then. "Bah! That was nothing," he said, holding out his palm. "Plus, we made fourteen rutahs."

Mistel gasped. "Even though they hated us?"

"One for each patron," Kurtz said, "and five from Master Renwall, who said you held the entire room in rapture." He waggled his eyebrows.

Mistel's cheeks warmed. "Thanks for dealing with that hunx. It was wrong of me to run out when he was speaking to me, but I couldn't stomach another word."

"That's what I'm here for, lass," Kurtz said.

"Actually, that's what *I'm* here for," Zanna said, "but had I spoken to him, he might have lost some teeth. So perhaps I owe you a thanks as well, Master Chazir."

"Well, this is a special moment, it is." Kurtz tipped his head back to the stars. "Watchers, bear witness to this miracle!"

Cole and Mistel laughed. Zanna shook her head, clearly annoyed. Mercy, the woman still couldn't lighten up about Kurtz.

"What's the plan for tomorrow?" Cole asked.

"We need to play the Ivory Spit, or Merrygog will throttle me, eh?" Kurtz said.

Playing at the Ivory Spit would be lovely, but this place... "How will we ever get hired at the Black Boar?" she asked. "This audience will have nothing good to say about us."

"Master Renwall will, thanks to you." Kurtz winked.

Mistel grimaced and edged closer to Zanna. "I don't like his sort of compliments."

"Joonas Erlichman owns the Boar," Cole said. "If we can connect with him, maybe he'll ask us to play."

"Cough up ten golds and go boar hunting," Kurtz said.

"I couldn't even get half that for my lute," Cole said.

"Why don't I just go to the Black Boar and ask," Mistel said. "That's how I got hired here. They might have a Master Renwall-type who does the hiring."

"You can't just walk into the Black Boar," Zanna said. "Even with me at your side, those men will get the wrong idea. But—" She held up her finger to Mistel, whose mouth was open to argue. "Why don't you set up in the Dale tomorrow? For the festival?"

"Will they have it after the attack today?" Cole asked.

"They'll insist on it, they will," Kurtz said. "This is the North. We don't let something like that affect us."

Playing outdoors sounded miserably cold. "Will they have us on such short notice?" Mistel asked.

"You won't be onstage," Zanna said, "but playing a street corner at the festival is enough to get noticed and invited elsewhere."

"Don't hate that idea, I don't," Kurtz said. "The Boar is the goal, but give it a little time, eh?"

"Let's meet at the Dale tomorrow afternoon," Cole said. "That way we can sleep in."

"Now you're speaking my language, you are," Kurtz said.

"I'll have to work," Zanna said, "but I'll drop Mistel by the Spit on my way."

Mistel reached out and touched Cole's arm. "You did wonderful tonight. I'm sorry the crowd was horrible. They won't all be that way, I promise."

"Guess I'd better listen to Kurtz next time," Cole said. "He was right about royalist songs."

Kurtz growled and crowed, "This is the North!"

Mistel laughed. She and Zanna left the boys and walked toward Fat Vandy's in silence.

They made it two blocks before Zanna spoke. "You're quiet. I find it alarming."

Zanna was a perceptive woman. How to answer that? "I was just thinking . . . What have I got myself into?"

Zanna chuckled. "That's the first sensible thing I've heard you say."

Mistel wasn't sure how to take that. "When I got hit with that roll, it surprised me and hurt my feelings a little. But it was fine. All part of singing in a place like that. I've performed for rowdier crowds, honestly. But when Cole stood up to defend me . . . He was so angry and determined. Then that man stepped forward . . ."

"And looked like he could use Cole for a toothpick?"

Mistel gaped at Zanna. "That's not funny."

"It's a little funny."

"I thought Cole needed me here," Mistel said. "But if I wasn't here, then he wouldn't have to put himself in foolish situations like that to protect me. And if Thusk is really selling people out of the prison . . . that's only going to worry Cole more."

"That you said all that makes me like you," Zanna said. "Just a little."

Really? This fierce woman valued transparency? Mistel would never have guessed that. "I care about Cole. I think we're better together than apart—singing, I mean."

"You *are* good together."

"Then he does need me?" Mistel asked. "And if I leave, he might not do as well. Right?"

Zanna lifted her hands. "Don't ask me for advice about romance. I know nothing."

"I wasn't talking about romance. Not really. Cole is my friend. I care about him."

"Platonically."

Mistel thought about that. "Well, not exactly."

Zanna growled at the sky. "I take it back. I hate you again."

"I just want to make things better," Mistel said. "But sometimes, I make things worse. Maybe I'm just too much? Too loud. Too reckless, like he said. I want to dive in and help, but what if I'm the reason he gets hurt? The reason we fail?"

Zanna gave Mistel a sharp look. "You're not too much, Mistel. But you are a lot. And sometimes, a lot is what people need to wake up and see things differently. Don't second-guess yourself. People who wait around for permission to live aren't worth much in the end."

Chapter Eighteen
Cole

Some men had no shame.

Cole's stiff fingers moved instinctively over his lute strings, but his focus drifted. Mistel danced and sang before him and Kurtz, her hair unbound and spiraling freely, her new red dress swirling around her legs. She was radiant—utterly in her element—and the way some onlookers gawked made Cole's jaw tighten.

They had set up to play in the Dale, the city's sprawling festival grounds where the community gathered to celebrate and compete. Though the vast amphitheater had a main stage and stone rings for feats of strength, the band kept to the open yard, near one of the many firepits that blazed against the afternoon chill. The flames in the pit crackled, sending glowing embers spiraling into the clear sky.

Distant laughter, music, clashes of steel, and the occasional burst of cheering did not distract their small audience. Coins clinked steadily into Mistel's wide-brimmed farmer's hat, which she'd tossed on the ground near the fire. They'd already earned more than the previous night at the Ice House—something to be thankful for—yet Cole couldn't shake the unease gnawing at his bones.

Mistel was a firebrand, wild and untamable. He'd told her not to come to the Ice House, and she'd shown up anyway, as if his warnings had been mere suggestions. Keeping her out of trouble felt like trying to hold onto a lark determined to fly. Yes, he'd trusted her to Arman, but to what extent? Did Arman expect Cole to do nothing? Or had he put Cole here to act as Mistel's protector? If the latter, Cole couldn't afford to fail such a purpose.

The moment they'd stepped foot in the Dale, Kurtz had muttered, "Keep your eyes on her," and Cole knew the advice had been sound. With the way Mistel flitted from one admirer to the next, gracing them all with her dazzling smile, some fool might get the wrong idea.

Snow fell, flurries at first, then flakes the size of rutahs, so they finally packed up and returned to the Ivory Spit. Zanna was working Ice Island today, so the trio played Citadel in the common room to pass the time. This allowed Rilla, who worked days, to chaperone Mistel until Zanna finished from her shift.

That night, their performance at the Ivory Spit earned them four times what they'd made at the Ice House. Merrygog was so pleased, he invited them back.

The next day, they went back to the Dale. The snow had lightened, as had the crowds, but they still earned twelve rutah just from passersby, which thrilled Mistel until Cole reminded her they weren't here to build a career as musicians. They needed to get hired at the Black Boar. And he still had no idea how they'd get to Ice Island to speak with his uncle. Cole had sent two letters to Verdot Amal. So far, no response. And Zanna told him that guards weren't permitted to bring visitors.

That afternoon, their merry band visited local taverns to offer their services. Markim at the Jig and the Jug had a regular musician and refused them. No answer at the door of the Gathering or at the

Driftwood Pub. The owners of the Tipsy Taproom and Belanna's Barrelhouse insisted they perform on-the-spot auditions, which resulted in invitations to play both venues.

If they could get someone to listen, they were as good as hired. That—and the fact that they hadn't seen Jeffrey Korngold anywhere—reassured Cole that they were on track.

So it went. Days in the Dale, nights in alehouses.

One clear afternoon in the Dale, Zanna, off duty from Ice Island, went scouting. The milder weather drew such a thick crowd that after an hour, Kurtz emptied Mistel's hat into a satchel, wary of leaving such a bounty in plain sight and tempting thieves.

While they were taking a break, Zanna crouched between Cole and Mistel, her dark eyes scanning their surroundings.

"Joonas Erlichman is here selling horses," she said. "I saw him in the east stables."

Mistel brightened and gazed across the yard. "Maybe he'll hear us."

This might be the North, as Kurtz was fond of saying, but Master Erlichman was one merchant who hadn't returned to the Dale following the Poroo attack. Some said he'd been busy with the ruling council. Others said he was afraid. Cole was simply glad he was here.

"Maybe we should set up near the stables tomorrow," he suggested.

"Not a bad idea," Kurtz said. "What shall we play next?"

"Let's do the set that starts with 'Mountain Song' and ends with 'Chamswrath.'" Cole started them off, and the moment Mistel began to sing, a handful of people in the crowd applauded.

Cole grinned. Mistel was so talented, he sometimes forgot what it must be like to hear her for the first time.

After the final note of "Chamswrath," a young man stepped forward, his focus on Mistel.

"Simply fantastic." He bowed. "I'm Nash Erlichman. This is—"

Mistel's face lit up. "Erlichman? Are you any relation to—"

"Joonas Erlichman? He's my father." Nash flashed a grin and gestured to the tall man beside him. "This is my friend, Drustan Fawst."

Cole's stomach dropped like a stone, for this was one person he'd hoped to never see again in his life. Drustan, his former stepbrother, had grown taller, stronger. The moment their eyes met, recognition flashed across Drustan's face.

Mistel dipped a polite curtsy. "Pleased to meet you. I'm Mistel Wepp, and this is Cole Tanniyn and Kurtz Chazir."

Drustan's grin widened, making Cole's skin crawl. "By the depths, I thought you'd died. That's what Mother told us. Said you caught something from one of those mangy dogs you used to coddle."

Cole grip tightened on the neck of his lute. "Drustan."

His stepbrother laughed, sharp and mocking. "You always did have the luck of a cockroach."

Mistel stepped between them. "Is there a problem?"

Drustan's gaze lingered on Mistel like a cat sizing up a mouse. "None at all."

Nash, oblivious to the tension, said, "We're having dinner tonight at my father's estate. You should come."

A private performance for Joonas Erlichman? Cole couldn't believe their luck. This could be a major step toward getting hired at the Black Boar.

Mistel looked at Cole. "Don't we have something tonight?"

He thought it over and winced. "Oh, unfortunately, yes. Belanna's Barrelhouse."

"Perhaps tomorrow?" Nash offered.

"You would reschedule your dinner for us?" Mistel asked.

"Dinner does tend to come along daily." Nash gave directions to the estate, then left with Drustan, who shot Cole a final glare before they disappeared into the crowd.

Kurtz's bloodvoice sounded in Cole's mind. *You all right?*

Cole remembered to think his reply. *Fine.*

I know the look of a man whose nightmares just came to life, Kurtz voiced. *Who is he?*

Former stepbrother, Cole thought. *He and his brother used to... They weren't kind.*

We don't have to take the job, Kurtz said. *Or you* don't. *Mistel can play chords now. We can manage.*

No. Cole would not let Mistel out of his sight, especially around Drustan Fawst. He glanced at her, then, and found she was already chatting with another admirer. Blazes, she was a handful.

But the king had put Cole in charge of this mission, and Arman trusted Achan as king. So when Cole had agreed to let Mistel stay, keeping her safe—and alive—had become his responsibility, even if that meant he had to face Drustan and the ghosts of his past.

Chapter Nineteen
Mistel

If Mistel focused on the view, she could almost forget her numb toes. Almost.

The Erlichman estate perched on a rise east of the city, commanding a breathtaking view of the frozen harbor. Mistel rode Bart between Zanna and Cole along the snowy road. On the horizon, the brilliant blue sky blurred into the sea. Absolutely gorgeous.

She pulled her cloak tighter. Tsaftown could freeze the joy right out of a person, but at least their destination looked warm. Ahead, just past a set of large iron gates and framed by frostbitten pines, stood a sprawling, snow-blanketed estate, larger than any Mistel had seen in Armonguard's Hamisha Hills. The three-story manor's pale gray stone walls contrasted with dark wood beams. Smoke curled from a dozen or more chimneys spaced along steep, snow-laden roofs. Icicles hung from their ledges, gleaming like crystal daggers.

Mistel counted seven outbuildings, not including all the tiny doghouses—some occupied by dogs lounging atop their roofs—and a vast stable adorned with decorative iron horseshoes.

They left their horses with the stablemaster and approached the manor's grand double oak doors. Mistel spun in place, imagining the parties she could throw in such a location.

"Everything is so clean and tidy," she said. "I half expect a royal procession to arrive."

"Undeniable wealth," Cole said.

"And excellent taste," Mistel added. "If they have warm pastries, I might stay forever."

A steward ushered them into the spacious manor, and warmth immediately swept over Mistel. They passed by a small hall with a high-beamed ceiling and four long wooden tables. The perfect place to throw a ball. The elevated platform at the end could serve as a stage for their band to perform. Yet the hall sat empty. Too bad.

The steward led them to a modest chamber warmed by a crackling fire. Dark wood paneling, velvet-upholstered chairs, and a silver tray of steaming mulled wine gave the place a luxurious feel.

"Make yourselves comfortable," the steward said. "I'll inform the master of your arrival."

"Don't mind if I do." Kurtz poured them each a cup.

Mistel wrapped her hands around the warm ceramic, inhaling the scent of cinnamon, cloves, and nutmeg.

She had drained her mug by the time the steward returned. He escorted them down a hall lined with towering tapestries and crystal candelabra. The mouthwatering aroma of roasted meat curled around her. How was she supposed to sing with such a feast taunting her?

They entered an elegant dining room where a hearth blazed. Four people sat at one end of a long table adorned with fine linens and silver platters heaped with food. Mistel recognized Nash Erlichman and Drustan Fawst, the rude one Cole admitted on the ride up that he'd known in his childhood. The older man and woman must be Nash's parents.

The steward cleared his throat. "Sirs and madam, may I present the esteemed musicians who have graciously accepted your invitation: Master Cole Tanniyn, Master Kurtz Chazir, Mistress Mistel Wepp, and Mistress Anna Tankel."

"At last!" Nash stood, his smile broad. "I bid you welcome. Please, have a seat."

Mistel's heart leaped. Sit at the table?

"You don't want us to play?" Cole asked, raising his lute.

Nash winced. "A misunderstanding. I simply wanted to get to know you all better."

Mistel couldn't believe it. They were guests!

They took their seats, men on one side, ladies on the other. At the head of the table sat Joonas Erlichman, Mistel assumed. Only when they were settled did Nash resume his place on his father's right. "Father says you've come from Armonguard and might even know our new king and queen."

"I grew up in Sitna," Mistel said. "Achan—er, the king—and I weren't close, but I saw him often enough. Cole squired for him."

Drustan, who sat between Nash and Kurtz, let out a chuckle. "Not sure I like what that says about the king."

Master Erlichman cut in sharply from the head of the table. "Don't be rude."

Indeed. Drustan Fawst was a complete and utter hunx.

The conversation shifted to the estate, its history, and the family's thriving business.

"This place has been passed down through generations," Master Erlichman said. "One day, Nash will take over. He's already running parts of it."

Cole leaned forward. "We saw the kennels on our way in. What do you do with so many dogs?"

"He sells them," Drustan said.

"Well, not those," Nash said.

His father's face brightened. "The dogs you saw are our sled dogs. But I do sell hunting dogs, boar, and most recently, horses.

Boar are my specialty, though. Started with just one boar and sow, and now my stock is famous across Er'Rets."

Mistel admired the man. Ambition, drive, and success—qualities she knew well.

Kurtz inquired about Erlichman's clients while Zanna discussed falconry with Madam Erlichman.

"What got you into singing, Miss Wepp?" Nash asked from across the table.

"Oh, I've always loved it," she said. "Cole is my cousin. When he invited me to join him and Kurtz, I couldn't pass up the adventure."

"Your *cousin*?" Drustan glanced between Mistel and Cole and chuckled darkly.

How odd. Mistel took a sip of her wine to put something between her and Drustan's piercing gaze.

"Do you plan to wander forever?" Nash asked. "Or might you one day be convinced to marry and settle down?"

My, what a question. Mistel swirled her goblet, considering how to answer. "Perhaps someday, but not now. There's too much of Er'Rets left to explore."

After they'd eaten a delicious feast, Master Erlichman stood and helped his wife to her feet. "It's been a pleasure, but we must retire. Please, enjoy yourselves. I'm sure Nash and Drustan will be good hosts." He offered his wife his arm. "Come, my dear."

As they left, Mistel shot Cole a glance and found him wide-eyed. They'd missed their chance to ask about the Black Boar.

Nash retrieved a dark bottle from a cabinet and poured a generous amount of amber liquid into his goblet. "Anyone for a drink?" He grinned as he made the rounds.

Drustan held out his goblet first.

Kurtz followed with a casual, "I'll have one."

"No, thank you," Zanna said.

Nash turned to Cole. "A drink for the road?"

Cole's expression was unreadable. "I'll pass."

Mistel shook her head. "I'll stick to mulled wine. Best to keep my wits when riding a horse side saddle."

"More for us then." Nash winked and raised his goblet. "To friendship."

"To friendship," Mistel echoed, sipping her now-cool wine.

"We've been performing all over Tsaftown," Cole said, the statement awkward and out of place.

Drustan snorted. "More like begging for scraps."

Mistel shot the lousy hunx a glare, then dove in to help steer the conversation. "We heard your family owns the Black Boar. Someone told us to speak with a man named Fenris about playing there. Do you know him?"

"He's our best customer," Drustan said. "We rent rooms to him and all his men. It's perfect because now we never have vacancies."

Nash's grip tightened around his goblet, his smile polite but strained. He cast Drustan a brief glance before answering. "Technically, I own the Boar. My father passed control to me last year. I've left the day-to-day to Drustan, but with it being Fenris's base of operations, most assume he runs the place."

"Sir Fenris has been protecting this town since the army went south," Drustan said. "That's why people think he's in charge."

"Protecting it?" Mistel raised an eyebrow. "How noble."

"Not noble—practical," Drustan said. "He's rich and has his own army."

From what Zanna had told Mistel, the Howlers hardly counted as an army but more of a band of lowborn mercenaries who broke skulls first and never asked questions.

"Rich yet he lives in a tavern?" Kurtz asked.

"Wealthy men don't do their own dirty work," Drustan said. "They hire it out, like Nash did with me."

"Fenris used to have an estate," Nash said, "but years ago he helped his father try to take over House Livna. The former lord threw them in Ice Island for treason."

Kurtz grunted and drained his drink.

Mistel raised her eyebrows. "Mercy! That sounds like the start of a ballad."

"Depends whose side you're on," Drustan said.

Cole leaned forward to see Nash around Kurtz and Drustan. "How does a man who lost his estate afford to rent rooms and pay mercenaries?"

"A fair question, that is," Kurtz said.

Nash poured himself another glass. "Not through honest work, that's for certain. While we built our fortune breeding the finest animals in the kingdom, Fenris had another approach—burn down a house and steal its gold."

Drustan lounged back in his chair. "He didn't steal it. That gold was his father's. Rightfully his."

Zanna tilted her head. "What gold?"

Nash exhaled. "Frederick Yarden's estate was seized after the coup, but before that happened, the old man hid his wealth with friends so he could get it later. He never got out, though. Rotted away in prison. But Fenris? The moment your young king pardoned him, he went straight for his father's gold."

"Where was it?" Cole asked.

"Buried in an estate south of the city," Nash said, sipping his drink. "A place called—"

Drustan tossed his wadded napkin at Nash. "Don't tell them that."

"—Glodwood Manor," Nash said.

Mistel perked up. She knew that name.

Drustan groaned and fell back in his chair. "Remind me not to tell you my darkest secrets."

"And they just gave the money back?" Zanna asked. "After so many years?"

Nash barked a laugh. "Of course not. They *claimed* it was gone. Said they'd never seen it." He leaned forward, voice dropping.

"But Fenris didn't buy that. Oh no. He tortured the lot of them until they talked, then killed them, took the gold, and burned their house to ash."

Mistel's hand flew to her mouth. "He didn't!"

"Oh, he most certainly did," Nash said, jerking his head in a quick nod. "It was his legacy money. He wasn't about to let it slip away."

Drustan straightened, his expression dark. "It wasn't just about the money. It was about reclaiming what was stolen. The Glodwoods betrayed him. And they paid for it."

"With their lives?" Mistel said. "That's a rather brutal way to settle a debt."

Drustan's lips curled into a slow smile. "Justice isn't always clean, Miss Wepp. Sometimes it takes blood to balance the scales."

Nash grunted, his gaze flat. "Spoken like a man on Fenris's payroll."

"Spoken like a boy who hides behind his father's name," Drustan countered.

Mistel glanced between them, heart racing. Were these two friends or enemies?

"We passed the remains of that place on the way here," Cole said. "It's completely gone."

"A warning to anyone who crosses Sir Fenris Yarden," Drustan said.

Mistel's stomach churned. Glodwood Manor... That was where the Poroo had attacked, where Cole had spirited her into the trees. Time for a lighter subject. She turned to Nash. "Why do so many people buy boar?"

Nash chuckled. "They're delicious, but people buy them to hunt."

How peculiar. "Why hunt something you already own?"

Drustan fixed his dark gaze on Mistel. "For the thrill of the chase."

She fought back a shiver and looked away from that callous hunx.

"Ever go hunting?" Nash asked.

Mistel shook her head, searching for a way to steer the conversation back to the Black Boar—or maybe Ice Island. "I could never kill an animal. The three of us"—she gestured to Cole and Kurtz—"we're focused on making a living . . . and visiting Ice Island."

Nash's grin faded. "That's a prison, not a tourist destination."

"Oh, I know." Mistel kept her tone breezy. "But Cole needs to see his uncle."

"Your uncle works there?" Nash asked.

Cole's jaw tightened. "No. He's a prisoner."

Drustan cackled, his eyes glittering in the candlelight. "Your only living relative is incarcerated? Perfect." He winked at Mistel.

Gracious! That was rude. And why would he wink about Cole's uncle being in prison? Or was he simply winking at Mistel? She shot him a glare and turned back to Nash. "There must be a way we could visit."

"Ice Island doesn't allow visitors," Drustan said.

"That's not entirely true." Nash draped his elbow over the back of his chair, angling his body to face Mistel. "I can get you in. I'll speak to Verdot Amal about it."

Mistel fought the urge to squeal and gave Nash a bright smile. "That's so kind of you."

They lingered another hour, Mistel feigning interest in Nash's boasts while steering attention away from Drustan's jabs at Cole. When they finally left, she welcomed the cold night air. Its bite was a relief from the suffocating tension of that dining room.

As they rode away from the manor, Mistel and Cole followed Kurtz and Zanna. The setting sun cast a dusky golden glow over everything.

"You were amazing tonight," Cole told her. "You asked all the right questions."

"So did you," Mistel said.

He laughed. "I tried. You succeeded. You're important to this mission, Mistel. I'm really glad you came."

A grin spread across her face. "I do think I'm getting the hang of this. Maybe I should visit the Black Boar and talk to Drustan about playing there. Or twist Nash's arm."

Silence stretched between them, the horses' hooves crunching in the snow.

"Stay away from them, Mistel," Cole said.

Her grip on Bart's reins tightened. "We've been over this, *my knightling*. I can handle myself."

"Not with them. Not with Drustan."

Of all the . . . Mistel pressed her lips together. Who did Cole think he was to—

"Mistel, please!" he practically yelled.

She blinked at his intensity. Lands, what had gotten him so worked up? "All right," she said, more to calm him than to agree.

He nodded stiffly. "Thank you."

She knew he had more to say and likely wouldn't. Time to pull it out of him in a roundabout way. "Why do you have so little faith in me? I've proved myself."

He opened his mouth to speak, then exhaled. "You have. You're amazing. But Drustan is a merciless fiend."

She couldn't help laugh, which only deepened that wrinkle between Cole's brows. "Mercy. That's harsh. I've met hunxes like Drustan before. He's rude but harmless."

"No, Mistel. Drustan was . . . sort of my stepbrother. Though he'd probably say I was their stray. Their slave."

Mistel's thoughts spun. Stray? But that meant Cole was an orphan. The tension between him and Drustan suddenly made sense.

Cole had never mentioned his parents. Was this why? He'd lived with Drustan's family? "What did he do to you?"

Silence.

Mistel couldn't take it. "Cole...?"

"When I lived with the Fawsts," he said, "Drustan and his brother Fen were much older. They didn't just fight me. They enjoyed hurting me. I was never without a bruise, cut, or burn. They stole my food too, so I was always hungry."

Mistel's chest ached for him. She could almost see the small, battered boy he'd been, and wanted to reach for his hand. But she didn't dare on this side saddle. She merely listened, captivated by this rare glimpse into his past.

"I had a puppy, runt of the litter. Nonda—that's Drustan and Fen's mother—she threw it outside, left for dead. I found him, fed him, named him Peat since he was the color of peat moss. He was my... my best friend."

"Oh, Cole." Mistel squeezed the reins. She knew, deep down, that this story was going to end badly.

"One day, I got Drustan in trouble, and he and Fen came after me. They killed Peat. Made me watch."

Mistel's breath hitched. She rubbed her gloved fingers to her throat. "What did their mother do?"

"Nothing."

"What? Why?"

"She didn't like me either," Cole said. "Or the dog."

"They sound like monsters," Mistel whispered.

"They were. And I don't think Drustan has changed."

Mistel recalled the glint in Drustan's eyes. He did seem to be waiting for the right moment to strike. "I'll be careful around him. I promise."

"Thank you."

She let the silence stretch, the sound of their horses' hooves over the mushy snow filling the void until, "You never told me you were an orphan."

"My surname is Tanniyn. I figured it was obvious."

Should have been. Children in Er'Rets who had no parents were given an animal surname to mark them as strays, though sometimes it also happened when a child was abandoned or . . . "But some have animal surnames because their parents disowned them, like Sir Eagan."

"I'm an orphan," Cole said. "My earliest memories are with my uncle. He was a soldier, and whenever he got called out, he'd leave me with Nonda, who he was seeing at the time. She hated me. As did her sons. They hated having to share food with me. Hated sharing air in their tiny house. One day, Uncle Crispen never came back, and eventually Nonda sold me to Lord Yarden. Lucky for me, life got better then."

Mistel let the weight of his words settle in her heart. She'd always known Cole carried scars, but hearing the plain and unembellished truth twisted her stomach. It wasn't just the cruelty of his past but how he'd survived it. He wasn't bitter, didn't let it define him. Instead, he'd carved out a life, clever and resilient, without needing to be the loudest voice in the room.

She studied him in the golden light—sandy brown hair, freckled cheeks, calm composure, quiet strength. She now saw the effort it took him, and she admired him more than she could say.

Drustan, on the other hand . . . Mistel had half a mind to let loose on that hunx the next time he opened his obnoxious mouth.

She nudged Bart closer to Cherix and lowered her voice. "You know, Cole, I think you're incredible."

His brow furrowed. "What?"

"The way you live. The way you are. You don't need to boast like Nash or wound like Drustan. You're just . . . you. It's admirable. And it makes me want to be a better person."

Cole turned to her, a smile tugging at his mouth. "Good, because you're stuck with me."

Mistel chuckled, adjusting her reins. "It *is* good. Thank you for letting me stay."

Cole let out a breath that was almost a laugh. "Thank *you* for following me."

"Anytime," she said.

She would have liked to have kissed him then. For now, the quiet closeness of the long ride back to Fat Vandy's was enough. There would be time for more later.

Chapter Twenty
Kurtz

Kurtz worked methodically, the steady rasp of the currycomb against Smoke's dark coat falling into the background as he focused on his bloodvoiced conversation with Prince Oren.

We found a link, we did, between Verdot Amal and the Hamartano family, Kurtz relayed silently. *An invoice Cole swiped from Thusk's office confirms it. Thusk also ships boar for Erlichman. It's all connected, it is.* He knocked the comb against the wall to free the accumulated horsehair. *And tonight, we learned Fenris Yarden murdered the entire Glodwood family, he did. Burned their house to the ground.*

Prince Oren's voice came sharp in his mind. *Are you certain?*

Certain enough, eh? Fenris took their gold—what he saw as his—then torched the evidence.

I'll inform Lord Livna at once, Prince Oren voiced. *He should know what his cousin has done.*

The gelded courser flicked an ear back, shifting his weight as Kurtz leaned in to brush beneath his mane. *We also have a lead on Ice Island and playing at the Boar, we do. I'll keep you updated.*

Arman be with you, Prince Oren said.

The connection faded, and Kurtz sighed, running a hand over Smoke's neck. "Guess we just keep at it, eh?"

The horse snorted, flicking his tail in what Kurtz took as agreement.

He tucked the comb away. Ah, how he loved Fat Vandy's. His skin buzzed, just being back. He'd spent countless hours as a young man dozing in an empty stall when he should have been shoveling.

Grinning at the memory, Kurtz left the stables. Outside, the sun had nearly set, a sight he'd never again take for granted after thirteen years in that Ice Island pit.

He was tired, had stayed up too late last night trying to enter the Veil. He knew better. He wasn't suddenly going to develop a magical ability he'd never had. Yet he desperately wanted to track Careeanne—find out where she lived, what she was doing.

He couldn't even sense her mind.

Maybe she'd learned to shield her thoughts. Maybe she was dead.

That thought didn't bother him. That woman deserved death and more for what she'd done. He needed to stop fixating on her and focus on something possible, like finding Kosotta Brovau. Rilla had said the former nursemaid moved back to Tsaftown after King Axel's death and was now working at a tavern, but she hadn't known which one. Their band had played six or seven already, and no one had heard of her. Maybe Rilla was mistaken, eh? There weren't many watering holes in Tsaftown left to check.

Kurtz stepped into Fat Vandy's tavern. Warmth hit him first, then the scent of roasted meat and fresh bread, followed by the low hum of conversation. Unlike the Ice House, the Tipsy Taproom, or Belanna's Barrelhouse, this wasn't a raucous den of drunkards. Fat Vandy's was for travelers and families, it was. A place where a hearty meal and a warm hearth mattered more than tankards of ale.

Just inside the door, he paused to let nostalgia wash over him. Home. At least the closest thing he'd ever had to one. Four years here had been a lifetime compared to the dozen he'd spent bouncing between that nightmare of a brothel and the chaos of life on the road with his father. Fat Vandy's had been his refuge, a flicker of light in an otherwise bleak childhood. Arman knew the few months he'd spent with Gavin had been colder than the streets.

"Kurtz!"

Hargis Vandy rose stiffly from a table by the hearth, beaming as he crept toward Kurtz. Rilla had warned about his gout. "Fat" Hargis was as round as ever, his white beard too big for his head, his clouded eyes full of warmth.

Kurtz met him halfway, letting the old man pull him into an embrace that smelled of woodsmoke and pipe tobacco.

"You blasted fool," Hargis said, cuffing his shoulder. "Why didn't you come see us the moment you got off that cursed island?"

"Gavin said no," Kurtz said. "Then Lord Livna was killed, and we had to move south."

"The king really freed you?"

"That he did."

"What's he like?"

"Spitting image of his papa. Smarter. More just."

"Arman's chosen."

"Without a doubt."

Hargis chuckled, the sound rich. "Why come so late? Serra's already in bed."

"I'm with a band now. We had dinner up in the hills."

"I know better. Eagan's got you wrapped up in some mission, hasn't he?"

Before Kurtz could answer, the door opened, letting in a gust of cold air. Zanna stepped inside, commanding without effort.

"Evening, Anna." Hargis greeted her with the fake name she

used around town. "Have you met Kurtz Chazir? Kingsguard Knight."

"I'm not a knight, Hargis," Kurtz muttered.

"Bah!" The old man waved him off. "Kurtz lived here four years before joining the army. He's like one of our own, he is."

"Yes, we've met," Zanna said flatly. "When you have a moment, Kurtz, I'd like a word. I'll be quick."

"Certainly," he replied, watching as she moved to a corner table.

Hargis leaned in. "That one would make you a fine wife, she would."

Kurtz barked a laugh. "I'm not looking for a wife. And if I was, she'd be last on the list." Though if he were honest, that temper and steel spine of hers had started to grow on him. Like mold. Or fire. Or something equally problematic.

"You were never practical. You know, Rilla's still single. Though I don't fancy you two together. Both of you, always chasing a warmer wind."

Kurtz chuckled. "So I'm fickle?"

"Naw, just haven't found the right woman to make you stay." Hargis patted his shoulder. "Thirsty? I'll get Loanna to bring you a mug of blackbrew."

Kurtz's mouth watered at the thought of Hargis's famous dark ale. "I'd like that, thanks."

Hargis limped off toward the kitchen.

Kurtz exhaled, scanning the small space. Zanna sat alone at her table, back to the corner, a bowl of soup before her, untouched. She leaned forward, arms braced against the table's surface, assessing the other patrons beneath that ever-present scowl.

Objectively, she was a striking woman. Tall and toned, every muscle exquisitely perfected. Thick, jet-black hair, braided into a single plait, framed skin darkened by the sun. A few faint scars that only added to her appeal. And something in her face, in those eyes, softened the vicious strength she projected.

Kurtz liked all kinds of women, but he preferred the ones with a backbone. He wondered, briefly, what she'd look like in a dress, hair undone, scowl replaced by... well, anything else.

The thought made him snort. ZolZan the Barbarian in a dress? Ridiculous. She'd throttle anyone who suggested it—him especially.

She caught him watching her, and that scowl zeroed in on him like an arrow finding its mark.

Definitely ridiculous.

Still, she wanted to talk, so he made his way over. He flipped the chair across from hers and straddled it.

She wasted no time. "You've been good for this mission," she said.

Well, that was new. "Thank you?"

She frowned, leaning in until he could feel the heat of her breath. "You cheated that day."

Kurtz released a low chuckle. This again? "And you still hate me, I see."

"Tell me why, when you went to such trouble to avoid fighting me."

Kurtz let his gaze trace her face like he was mapping enemy territory. "You knew I was trying to avoid a fight?"

"You couldn't stand the thought of a woman defeating you publicly."

"Oh ho! Certain you'd have won, are you?"

"Certain I wouldn't have?"

He laughed louder this time. "What would have happened, then? Me losing to you before a crowd, or them watching me beat you bloody? Neither would have done us any favors."

She exhaled sharply, shaking her head. "You're insufferable."

"Hear me out, woman. Whether you won or I did, both outcomes meant ruin. A challenge of wits was our only chance to walk away unscathed."

"So you wouldn't be humiliated when I bested you."

"Aye," he said, feeling a smile tug at the corner of his mouth, "but also so I wouldn't look like a brute if you didn't."

Zanna's nostrils flared. She slammed her fist on the table, the bowl between them jumping with a dull clang. "So that's it, then? As long as you kept your coin and your cushy post, it didn't matter who else got trampled? You just had to keep the game going by making your jokes, chasing your pleasures, charming your way into every room. And when someone else paid the price for your antics, you shrugged and moved on?"

"What else was I supposed to do?" Kurtz said. "You'd made far too big a spectacle out of the matter, same as now."

She shook her head, eyes flashing like parchment catching fire. "Then you admit you cheated."

He met her glare, the space between them dangerous ground. "I made a calculated move. I did what I had to do to keep my position."

"At my expense." Her voice cracked, just slightly. "Lady Tanana's mother was so embarrassed by the ordeal, I lost *my* position. Said I was a disgrace. That I'd sullied her daughter's name by even being challenged."

Fire and ash. Kurtz's heart stilled as silence bloomed between them. "I didn't know."

"Of course you didn't. And why would you have cared? You've always only ever thought about yourself."

The accusation hit harder than he expected. He glanced down, exhaled slowly, and rubbed the back of his neck. "Aye," he said. "You're not wrong about that."

She said nothing, but held her stare, unblinking.

Why had he always been such a selfish cad? "I'm sorry, Zanna. Truly. I never meant for you to lose your position, eh? Only wanted to protect mine. Doesn't make it right. I see that now. I've got no excuse for any of it but my rotting pride, which I promise you is weaker today than it once was."

Zanna studied him, her dark gaze flitting over his face, and somehow, he felt the fire between them dim. It hadn't gone out, but she'd banked it. And the heat left her eyes. Finally, she nodded once. "I can see that," she said. "A little."

Thank Arman for that. "Thirteen years in a reeking pit does a lot to kill a man's pride."

Kurtz had slept through the morning of King Axel's assassination, drugged by tainted stew, only to wake in a world of Darkness. Falsely accused, convicted, and thrown into the Prodotez: the special hole where Ice Island kept its worst offenders.

"A quarter of the men on Ice Island are innocent," he said. "Did you know that?"

"Ice Island is nothing if not corrupt," Zanna said.

He supposed she would know. One couldn't work there and stay ignorant for long.

"I don't want to go back there," Kurtz admitted. "Verdot deserves to be put on trial for his part in King Axel's death, and I don't relish groveling to him for a favor."

Zanna's scowl softened. One of the little scars on her face ran through the top curve of her lip. He wondered how that had happened. A sword? Knife?

"What they did to you and Eagan," she said quietly, "was injustice."

This woman who'd held a vendetta against him all these years, suddenly acknowledging the wrong done to him? A lump lodged in his throat. Time to lighten things up. "Hold on. Was that sympathy? From you?"

Zanna looked away. "Don't get used to it," she snapped. "I said it because it's true, not because I like you."

"Ah, there's the venom I know and love." But he was being a jerk, so he softened. "Thank you. Grudging pity suits you."

Before she could respond, Loanna arrived, carrying a pitcher and tankard. She resembled her sister Rilla in the way a still lake resembled a rushing brook. Both had dark curls, thick lashes, and curvy figures, but where Rilla was flirtatious, Loanna carried quiet strength. Kurtz had loved "Lo," as he'd called her, more than anyone—Rilla included. If he lingered on the thought too long, it still made him ache.

"Kurtz Chazir," she said.

"Lo!" He stood and pulled her into a warm embrace. "Rilla said you married."

"I did." She poured him a tankard of blackbrew. "Edric Tamsin. His wife died three years back. His children are ten and twelve now. Briony's the younger—already in bed. Edric and Dain went to Hargis' cabin to hunt for an eider duck for my ageday dinner."

Kurtz grinned. "It's that time of year, isn't it? A blessed ageday to you, Loanna. Wish I had something to give you."

"I don't need another shell necklace."

"You kept it?" He'd crafted the trinket himself when he was fifteen.

"Gave it to Briony last year. She found it in an old chest and admired it."

Kurtz rather liked the thought of a child wearing it. He turned his chair the right way and sat down again, inhaled the scent of malted barley, molasses, cinnamon, and figs.

"You seem happy," he said.

"I am. We've a good life here."

"I'm glad of that. Congratulations, Lo."

"You hungry?"

"Nope. Ate before I came."

Lo turned to Zanna. "Can I get you anything else, Miss Anna?"

"No, thank you."

Kurtz took a sip of his blackbrew, warmth flooding his belly. "Ah, that's good, it is."

"I should get back to the kitchen," Lo said. "I do hope you won't be causing trouble with Rilla."

Kurtz looked up from his ale. "What kind of trouble?"

"What kind, indeed?" Lo raised an eyebrow. "She's waited for you all these years. Always hoped you'd get off the island and marry her."

"Marry *Rilla*?" Kurtz had never been the marrying type, but if anyone could have talked him into it, it would have been Loanna, not Rilla.

"You heard me. The day you got back, she stormed over here, furious. Wanted to talk to Mother."

Kurtz shrank on his chair. He never should have kissed Rilla. No question. Yet things could've been worse. He thanked Arman for sending the watcher before disaster had struck.

His fingers drummed against the table. "Rilla and I had a moment. Nothing more. Truth is, I'm not sure how long I'll be in town, and I wasn't about to start something I couldn't finish."

Liar. That wasn't at all the way things had gone.

Lo blinked. "Doesn't sound like you," she said, "but good. Rilla won't like it, but she'll get over it once you're gone. Enjoy your drink, Kurtz."

He watched her walk away, feeling raw. He turned back to his drink, only to find Zanna glaring.

"A *moment*, huh?" she said. "Then I guess Rilla has nothing to blame you for."

"There's nothing to blame," Kurtz shot back. "It was a kiss. She started it as much as I did."

Zanna pushed her chair back, the scrape sharp in the quiet room. "You play with fire, Kurtz Chazir. Don't be surprised when you get burned."

He couldn't allow this woman to lecture him. "You have lots of rules, Zanna. Too bad none of them teach you to mind your own business."

"Let's just agree to finish this mission, then never speak again."

"Perfect."

Kurtz grabbed his blackbrew and moved to join Hargis by the fire. The old man greeted him with a warm smile.

"How's the brew?"

"Delicious, as always." Kurtz took a long drink, hoping to cool his anger.

Infernal woman. She could gut a man with words—with a look.

Yet when she headed upstairs, he couldn't stop his gaze from following.

There was something about her.

A man had to be careful with poisonous creatures, he did. Didn't want to get himself killed, eh?

Chapter Twenty-One
Cole

Cole had sung plenty of ballads about Ice Island and the villains trapped within—never once imagining he'd one day ask to be let inside.

He and Kurtz rode toward Cliffwatch, the larger of the two watchtowers guarding the prison. The stone sentinel loomed above, its walls weathered by salt and wind. Beyond it, the frozen sea stretched beneath restless drifts of snow toward Ice Island: a gray stone fortress, half shrouded in fog. No waves lapped the shore, no ships cut through the harbor, only silence and the bitter wind gnawing at Cole's exposed skin.

"Try and lose the fear behind your eyes, eh?" Kurtz said. "That'll give you away, it will. You have to believe you're just a minstrel looking to visit your uncle."

Cole swallowed hard and nodded. He'd always been a decent playactor, but the sight of the infamous prison had turned him inside out. A minstrel here to see his uncle. That's who he was. Should be a simple request. Yet the weight of the sword at his hip felt foreign. He should be carrying his lute.

"What if he wants to hear me play?" Cole asked.

"We're here on Nash's recommendation," Kurtz said. "That should be enough."

Again, Cole nodded, as if doing so might convince him.

Their horses' hooves crunched over the snowy road as they neared the gatehouse. The rhythmic clang of hammers on stone and distant voices carried on the wind.

"What's going on?" Cole asked.

"Who knows?" Kurtz said. "Verdot is always stirring up trouble."

The gatehouse abutted a smaller, square mural tower jutting out from the larger, circular one. After giving their names, they were let inside a tiny bailey where laborers swarmed over stacks of timber and stone, hammering, hauling, and shouting. Cole followed Kurtz past carts of mortar and tools and up a narrow stone staircase to Verdot Amal's office.

"Look there." Kurtz gestured above the door to a series of faint gray markings on the stone.

Something like a letter Y, what looked like waves, and a diamond with two circles that resembled an eye. Cole hadn't seen their like before. Not even in the Magosian priestess's apartment back in Armonguard.

"Runes," Cole said.

"Not just any runes," Kurtz said. "They repel bloodvoicing magic."

"Verdot doesn't want anyone spying on him," Cole said.

"Which means he's up to something." Kurtz pushed open the door.

Inside, a thin, white-haired man stood behind a desk cluttered with scrolls, ink pots, and a tarnished brass lamp. Verdot Amal, Cole presumed, and he wasn't alone.

In front of the desk, his back to the door, stood a short, plump man with a flushed face. He clutched a ledger to his chest. His coat, once fine, was travel-stained and rumpled.

"... not my decision," Verdot was saying. "That order comes from above."

"But you could fix this," the man said. "You run this prison."

"And just you remember who runs you," Amal shot back.

Cole froze just inside the doorway. He glanced at Kurtz, who merely leaned against the doorframe, watching with mild curiosity.

"Drop it, Tom," Verdot said. "I don't want to hear about it again."

The man—Tom, apparently—shifted on his feet. He reminded Cole of an abused puppy, starved and begging for food.

Kurtz cleared his throat. "Are we interrupting something?"

Both men turned toward the door.

"Not at all." Clutching his ledger, Tom scurried past, and Cole caught a whiff of pickled herring and brine as the man disappeared down the staircase.

"Friendly fellow," Kurtz muttered, closing the door.

Verdot sighed deeply. "Kurtz Chazir." His gaze fell on Cole. "And you must be young Master Tanniyn. I'm honored, truly. Though I confess, I have little time for unexpected visitors." He paced behind his desk, shuffling scrolls, as though their presence was an unbearable inconvenience. Finally, he waved toward two chairs. "Sit if you must."

Cole exchanged a glance with Kurtz before they both sat.

"Who was that?" Cole asked, nodding toward the door.

"Tom Raven. My clerk," Verdot said.

Kurtz hummed, as if that explained a great deal. "What's with all the construction? Expanding the gatehouse?"

Verdot unrolled a scroll. "A remodel," he said absently. "I tested the idea at Stormwatch—three apartments there. Cliffwatch is larger, so it will hold six."

"Apartments for guards?" Cole asked.

"Mercy no." Verdot chuckled. "High-end accommodations for prisoners willing to pay for an upgrade."

Cole's stomach churned. "You're extorting incarcerated men?"

Verdot finally looked at him, his smile thin. "It's called a business model, boy."

Kurtz shifted in his chair. "Eric know about this?"

"He's Lord Livna to you now," Verdot snapped. "And no, I don't believe he concerns himself with prison operations."

"Which suits you just fine, I'll bet," Kurtz said. "You do your best scheming when no one's looking over your shoulder, eh, old friend?"

Verdot slammed down the scroll and finally faced them directly. "What do you want?"

Cole's stomach twisted. "Didn't you get my letters? I wrote twice. And Nash Erlichman said he spoke to you about me."

"Letters?" Verdot said, as though the question was absurd. "I have no idea. I'm terribly busy. Dozens of letters pass through my clerk's hands each week, most from people begging favors." He waved a dismissive hand, the rings on his thin fingers catching the light. "Tom knows I hardly have time to read them, let alone reply."

Cole's jaw tightened. "This was a simple question."

Verdot sniffed, brushing something off his sleeve. "Then how fortunate you've come in person to ask it where I can hear you." He arched an eyebrow. "Go on."

Cole straightened, glanced at Kurtz. "I'd like to visit my uncle, Crispen West."

Verdot stepped closer, looking down his nose at Cole. Something in his sneer brought to mind Drustan Fawst, Osrik Nath, the Eben warrior—all looming while he was too small to fight back.

Cole jumped to his feet, refusing to let Verdot tower over him. Even so, the man had a few inches on him, which only fueled his irritation.

Verdot's smirk deepened. "We don't allow visits."

"Nash implied there were ways," Cole said.

"Nash Erlichman does not work here." Verdot waved his hand.

"Truth is, nothing is free, boy. You might think you have friends in high places, but I have a business to run. You want to see your uncle? You make a donation."

Cole's eyes narrowed. "How much?"

Verdot shrugged as if the number meant nothing to him. "The going rate for an hour-long visit is two golds."

"You filthy crook." Kurtz shot to his feet, knocking his chair over. "Let's go, Cole. We'll see what Eric Livna has to say about this, we will—and about that construction."

"Wait," Verdot said, raising his hands. "Calm down, and I'm sure we can come to an agreement. I'll waive the fee if Master Tanniyn and his pretty cousin play a concert at Ice Island."

Heat flared in Cole's chest. So the man did know about them? And Mistel? "No," he said flatly. "I don't want Mistel out there."

"There's no danger, I promise you," Verdot said. "Not when you're with me."

Cole shook his head. "I don't think—"

"I'll personally vouch for her safety. And yours."

Cole glanced at Kurtz, who grimaced and flexed one shoulder. Yeah, he didn't like it either, but he didn't see any other option. "One performance."

"One hour-long performance for an hour-long visit," Verdot clarified. "And if you want to visit again, you perform again."

Cole took a deep breath. "Agreed. Shall we play tonight?"

Verdot laughed. "Mercy, no. I need time to arrange things. Plus, I'll need to hear you first. Nash said you'll be at the Black Boar soon. If I like what I hear, I can arrange something next week." He flashed an oily smile. "I'll send word."

Cole clenched his fists, breathing deeply. "Fine. When you're ready, we'll return."

"Almost lost your temper back there, eh?" Kurtz said.

The road wound through a sparse forest of spruce and pine, branches heavy with frost. Cold air stung Cole's cheeks, his breath puffing in small clouds.

"You did good," Kurtz added. "It was the best offer we were going to get without involving Eric, and it's best we don't involve him."

"I didn't like that man," Cole muttered, still wound up by Verdot Amal.

"He's a weasel."

"A weasel who was taller than me."

Kurtz snorted. "Still dwelling over your height? Listen. Men who care too much about what others think tend to be so paranoid they're unstable. Constantly blow things out of proportion, worry, whine. That kind of man makes a terrible leader, he does. And no woman feels safe around a man like that. Be content with who you are, eh? Know your strengths and use them well. That'll make you stand out, no matter how tall you are."

Cole glanced at Kurtz, his words lingering. "What if I *am* paranoid and unstable?"

Kurtz blinked, then grinned, his dimples tucking in. "You're funny, poet. I love it, I do."

Cole hadn't been joking. He let Kurtz's laughter fill the silence while his thoughts churned—runt of the litter, unworthy to live, too small to protect anyone.

Peat's final breaths haunted him, as did the Eben warrior. His childhood had left him battered inside and out, and the war had only deepened the scars. No matter how much time passed, the pain remained, branded deep inside him, tattoos he couldn't scrub away.

"Do you ever think about Ice Island?" Cole asked.

"I try not to."

"But you can't help it, right? It's part of you."

Kurtz sighed. "I suppose. Lots of things remind me of it."

"What do you do when you remember?"

"I thank Arman and our king for getting me out." Kurtz shot him a sidelong glance. "What's on your mind, eh, poet? I can tell when you're stewing, I can."

Cole fidgeted with the reins. "It's just... When something happens—like with Verdot Amal back there—memories rush back. Bad ones. I feel small, angry, trapped. I either cower or lose my temper. I don't know why, but I can't stop it from happening."

"Takes time, it does, to get over certain things. Shadows from my past sometimes return in a rush of heat and shame."

Shadows. Good word for it. "What do you do?"

"I remember other things." Kurtz grinned, dimples tucking above his beard. "Anything pleasant to get my mind off the ugly, but Eagan warned me, some happy thoughts lead to trouble. Instead, he said to remember what Arman has done."

Arman? "You mean like sending his son?"

"Aye, but also the good Arman has done in *our* lives. For me, I remember Achan springing me and Eagan from Ice Island. It's easy to dwell on the ugly. Gets us all riled up and ready to fight scrappy for our worth, it does. But if a man lets himself get swept up in the ugly, he becomes ugly inside. Angry. Spiteful. A victim. Eagan says when I start dwelling on the ugly, I should remember the good instead. And while I don't know all you've been through, poet, I've seen plenty of good."

Cole thought of Nonda selling him to Lord Yarden, who put him in the stables with Lunden, who taught him about dogs and horses and playing the lute—gave him music. He thought about Lord Yarden giving him to Achan, who set him free, put him in charge of his horses and later made him a squire. He thought of Sir Caleb's wisdom and kindness, how he'd given Cole parchment and charcoal to use to write songs, and how Cole had used them to teach Matthias to write his name. And he thought of Mistel, solving the mystery of her friend's death, singing with her, kissing her.

Yes, there had been plenty of good in his life.

So why did he believe the voices of Nonda, Drustan, and Fen more than those of Achan, Sir Caleb, Kurtz, and Mistel? People who mattered.

Why did cruelty echo louder than kindness? Was he letting those memories make him a victim all over again?

Cherix huffed, and Cole patted the horse's neck. Beside them on the road, Kurtz hummed under his breath, oblivious to the storm still raging in Cole's mind.

Maybe Kurtz was right. Maybe Cole should focus less on how others measured him and more on how he measured himself. And when the ugly memories came, remember the good instead.

As they neared the city, Cole took a deep breath. He wasn't sure it would work, but if he listened to the people who cared about him instead of the ghosts that didn't—if he dwelled on the good instead of the ugly—maybe he'd find a way to mend what was broken inside him.

Chapter Twenty-Two
Mistel

"Keep your back to the wall and your mouth out of trouble."

That was Kurtz's only advice to Mistel before they entered the Black Boar. With Zanna on prison duty, Mistel would have to be doubly careful.

The stench nearly knocked her off her feet. A roaring hearth and a few flickering lanterns barely cut through the smoke-filled air, revealing a packed room that reeked of sweat, cloudweed, wet fur, and rancid fat. The latter, Nanette Swain had once told Mistel, came from overusing cooking oil in a kitchen that prioritized quantity over quality.

Kurtz led them to a small platform in the corner. Cole pulled a chair from a table, sat, and began tuning his lute. Mistel withdrew her tambourine from her satchel and surveyed the lively crowd.

Beneath the watchful glare of a massive stuffed boar's head above the bar, patrons laughed, talked, and clinked tankards.

"So many people," Mistel murmured.

"It's a base for Fenris Yarden and his Howlers," Cole said. "See the man in the back with his feet up? That's him."

Mistel searched the crowd. "The one Kurtz fought in Lytton Hall?"

"Yeah," Kurtz said. "Let's steer clear of him tonight, eh? But if anything happens, distract, disable, and get out."

Mistel finally spotted the notorious man, lounging in a high-backed chair at the back of the room, feet propped on a barrel like he owned the place. He looked close to Kurtz's age, maybe older—too much curly blond hair, too loud a laugh, too gaudy a tunic, too many rings. A preening rooster.

"That's Ikârd beside him," Cole added. "He helped Fenris fight Kurtz."

"Man has no manners, eh? Barging into another man's brawl like that."

Mistel eyed Ikârd, whose shaved head gleamed in the lantern light as he toyed with an ax on his belt. He reminded her of Osrik Nath, her former slumlord.

On the other side of Fenris sat an old blind man with a linen cloth over his eyes.

"Who is—?" Mistel started.

"You made it!" A cheerful voice cut her off. Nash approached the stage, grinning, snow dusting his slicked-back hair and coat. "Can't wait to hear you sing."

Recalling Cole's warning, Mistel offered a polite smile. "Thank you. We're excited too."

"Did Drustan show you the storage room?"

"We haven't seen Master Fawst," Mistel said, which was a very good thing, or she might have throttled the man for what he'd done to Cole.

Lines pinched on Nash's forehead as he scanned the room. "He's probably in the office. Let me show you the room, in case you need a private place to rest between performances."

Cole set down his lute. "I'll come with you."

Nash led them down a hallway toward a back door. "That leads to the alley," he said. "But this . . ." He pushed open a door across from the kitchen. "It's not much, but it's yours whenever you perform. I'll have the lamp lit."

The storage room was cramped and dark, the air heavy with ale-soaked barrels and dried herbs strung from low beams. A battered table sat against the wall, its top cluttered with three upside-down mismatched stools and an unlit oil lamp.

"Oh, this is perfect," Mistel said. And it smelled ten times better than the main room. "Thank you."

Nash leaned in, bracing a hand against the wall beside her head. "I've been looking forward to this since I heard you sing at the Dale. Tsaftown's been a wasteland of talent until you came along."

Cole cleared his throat. "We need to run through a few last-minute things before we start."

"What things?" Mistel asked.

Cole shrugged, not meeting her eyes. "Just . . . band things."

Mistel hid a grin. Last-minute, indeed. He just wanted Nash gone.

Nash laughed good-naturedly. "All right, all right, I'll get out of your way." Before he left, though, he hesitated, letting his gaze linger on Mistel.

She had long been used to such attention from men, but Cole glared at Nash's back as they followed him out to the main room. She touched Cole's arm lightly, a silent thank-you for his rescue, but if he felt it, he pretended not to notice.

Nash joined Drustan Fawst at a nearby table. Sitting with them was a thin, white-haired man, whose many rings gleamed in the low light.

Mistel leaned toward Cole. "Who's that old man with Drustan and Nash?"

"Verdot Amal," Cole murmured as he sat down and began tuning his lute. "We need him to like our performance so he'll invite us to play at the prison—and let me visit my uncle."

So that was the man who'd put Cole in such a foul mood the other day. Honestly, Cole didn't look much better now. Mistel moved behind his chair and hesitantly placed her hands on his shoulders.

He tensed up. "What are you doing?"

"Relax," she said, rubbing the knots in his shoulders. "It's going to be great. You'll see."

Cole nodded. Her touch had calmed his stiff posture, yet his brow stayed pinched adorably. Mistel leaned over his shoulder and pressed her finger to the wrinkle between his eyes. "Relax!" she teased.

He turned and grinned up at her. Good. He'd been carrying the weight of their mission for too long.

Kurtz's boots thudded against the wooden floor as he approached. "If anything goes wrong, that hallway leads to the alley. Run and don't stop until you reach the stables."

Mercy. Kurtz was wound up too. "We know about the back exit," she said, "but nothing's going to go wrong. It's a great crowd."

"It's a drunk crowd," Kurtz muttered, tapping his drumstick against his thigh. "Which makes it anyone's guess how things will go."

"It's time," Cole said. "Kurtz, count us off for 'Stars Above.'"

Mistel blinked, confused why Cole had changed things. "Not starting with 'Hear the Pretty Maiden'?"

"No offense," Cole whispered, "but I'm not leading with a song that calls attention to how pretty the maiden is. Not with this crowd."

Mistel clicked her tongue. "Cole . . ."

"I'll sing lead for the first two songs," he said. "Then you can start us out on 'The Messenger.'"

"I think you're overreacting, but fine." She'd rather not relive the Ice House.

Kurtz struck the tabor drum, launching them into "Stars

Above." The melody rose, steady and strong, with Cole's voice carrying the lead.

> *"Oh, stars above, eternal bright,*
> *Keep vigil through the darkest night.*
> *Protect us all from evil's sway,*
> *Against the storm, we make our way."*

The crowd responded instantly—clapping, stomping. Two men linked arms and danced in a circle. Mistel's heart soared. See? Cole and Kurtz had nothing to worry about. The audience loved them already.

But when she took the lead on "The Messenger," the mood shifted. Whistles and crude remarks erupted. Mistel's practiced smile faltered, though she did her best to ignore the drunken hunxes.

She sought a friendly face to focus on—the trick she'd taught Cole for playing the Ice House—but even Nash's eager gaze made her uneasy. She finally settled on the old blind man beside Fenris. He sat still, except for his fingers tapping rhythmically on the table. She sang to him, relieved, until—

Never seen a blind man before? A voice boomed inside her mind.

Mistel's breath hitched. A sharp ache seized her skull. She began to tremble as she recalled how Atul Shakran, the evil bloodvoicer, had taken control of her mind months ago in Armonguard—had tried to kill her. Could it be him? Back from the dead?

She couldn't move. Couldn't speak.

"Mistel?" Cole's voice cut through the haze.

She opened her mouth to respond. Nothing. No! Not again.

She fought against the bloodvoicer in her head, but invisible strings pulled her forward, as if she were a puppet. She began to dance—against her will. Then her lips parted, and she continued singing.

> "On weary steed, he braves the night,
> Through shadows cast by fading light.
> No sword he wields, for peace he keeps,
> Yet bears the words that others reap."

Her feet moved unbidden, carrying her into the crowd.

No, she thought. *I don't want to leave the stage.*

But she did, and hands reached for her, grabbed at her arms, her hair. Laughter and jeers swelled around her.

Who's doing this? she thought.

Her gaze snapped to the blind man. He smirked, head tilted as if he could see her perfectly.

Very good, he said inside her mind. *You catch on quickly.*

Stop! she thought. *Leave me alone.*

Tears streaked her face as she fought the unseen force, but her body continued to betray her. She sashayed to Nash's table, trailing her fingers over Verdot Amal's shoulders and the back of Drustan's neck.

Then, to the roaring delight of the crowd, she sank onto Nash's lap and launched into the chorus.

> "Stay your rage against the messenger,
> For his duty is but to relay."

Around them, spectators turned their heads between Mistel and the old man in back, laughing, and the realization hit her hard. They knew! But how?

Cole pushed to his feet, still strumming, and maneuvered through the crowd as Mistel belted out the final verse, trying in vain to move herself off Nash's lap.

"The herald's road is paved with fear,
Each hoofbeat loud, yet none to cheer.
Condemned for truths he cannot sway,
A pawn upon the board in play."

Halfway through, Cole reached Nash's table. He strummed a slow chord, letting the sound ring out, then seized the break to bow to Mistel and offer his hand. When she didn't react—she couldn't!—he took hold of her hand, tugged her to her feet, and twirled her under his arm, somehow breaking the spell. Mistel stumbled, her body finally her own again. Just as Cole, her knightling hero, resumed playing the lute and joined Mistel in the final chorus, Nash grabbed her hand and pulled her back to his side, tucking his arm around her waist.

"Stay your rage against the messenger,
For his duty is but to relay."

Three quick strums, and Cole ended the song. The crowd erupted in applause as Cole pulled Mistel away from Nash and told him, "We're done."

Laughter rippled through the tavern.

Tears blurred Mistel's vision, but she still had control of her body. She yanked free from Cole and fled to the storage room.

Cole followed her inside and shut the door. "Mistel? Talk to me. Are you all right?"

The enormity of what had happened crashed over her. "The blind man," she choked out. "He's a bloodvoicer. He controlled me. Just like Atul."

Then she burst into tears.

Cole set his lute on the table and reached for her. She stepped into his embrace, pressed her forehead to his chest. His arms slid around her back and held her tightly.

"I wondered if it was him," he said, resting his cheek against her hair. "I saw him staring at you and everyone looking back and forth between you. They all know he's a bloodvoicer. Nash knows."

She cried harder.

"You have to shield your mind from now on," Cole said, one hand making slow circles on her back. "Do you remember how?"

Her stomach twisted. What if the bloodvoicer pried into her thoughts, overheard their plans, and ruined everything?

Cole gripped her shoulders and pulled back, his hazel eyes intense, his freckled face so entirely endearing that tears blurred her vision. "Mistel?"

"I need to shield my mind," she whispered, blinking hard.

"You do," he said. "Do you remember how?"

She nodded, forcing herself to block out the terror and focus. A tiny voice whispered that she wasn't strong enough, and that terrified her more than anything.

"Do it now." Cole pulled her close again and pressed a kiss to her forehead.

Mistel concentrated, almost certain she'd succeeded. She sagged against Cole and let him hold her. She'd always dreamed of someday being a famous minstrel, never needing to depend on anyone. That the old man had controlled her with his magic was one thing, but that Cole had to save her? That was another. What if he hadn't been there? She could have been trapped forever, at the mercy of another madman.

Kurtz entered the room. "She all right?"

"She will be," Cole said, smoothing his hand down her back. "Can you get our cloaks? It's time to go."

"What about Verdot Amal?" Mistel asked. "I thought you wanted to talk to him."

"Not anymore," Cole said. "If he didn't like us, he's a fool. We'll find another way into Ice Island."

"The only other way is getting arrested," Kurtz said. "I don't recommend it. Wait here."

While they waited, Mistel cried a bit more. Cole hummed in her ear, rocking her gently. Kurtz returned with their cloaks, and the rest was a blur until Mistel found herself on Bart's back. The horse carried her through the freezing night, away from the Black Boar and the evil within.

Chapter Twenty-Three
Cole

Miss Wepp,

I could not let another day pass without expressing my admiration for the performance you and the "Wandering Songweavers gave the other night. It was truly stellar. Your voice was so clear and beautiful that it silenced even the noisiest in the room. A rare feat, I assure you, in such a place as the Black Boar.

Might I dare hope that you would consider singing again? I am certain that the patrons of the Boar would be eager for your return, though none more so than I. Your presence lingers in my thoughts, Miss Wepp, as does the memory of your *voice.*

"Would you consider another engagement tomorrow night? It would bring great cheer to many, myself most of all.

"With high esteem,

Nash Erlichman

COLE READ THE LETTER AGAIN, EACH word rubbing him raw. Nash's tone, all smooth admiration and compliments, set his teeth on edge. He tossed the letter into the center of the table at the Ivory Spit, where he sat with Mistel, Kurtz, and Zanna.

"They want us back," Mistel said. "That's good right?"

"Only if you're up for it," Cole said. Her well-being must come first. "And if we're all certain we can fully shield our minds."

"I can," Mistel said, meeting his gaze. "I've been practicing every moment."

"And you don't mind facing Nash again?" Cole asked. "He knew Crow was a bloodvoicer."

She lowered her gaze and fingered a groove in the table. "It's not Nash. I can't stop thinking about that old man. But if I don't go back, he wins. And I'm done losing to men like that."

Cole wanted to pull her close, tell her she didn't have to prove anything, but her strength was part of what drew him to her.

Kurtz speared a piece of roast from the platter. "It's a rough location, it is," he said. "And if all we do is perform, I don't see how we'll ever learn anything useful. So far, all we know is that Fenris has a friend who can bloodvoice."

"You think we should spend time there just . . . mingling?" Cole asked.

Kurtz shrugged. "Maybe have dinner beforehand. Gives us a chance to eavesdrop a bit, maybe catch something important, eh?"

"We wouldn't all have to go." Zanna leaned forward, resting her elbows on the table. "Mistel and I could arrive just before the performance. Less risk that way."

"I can eat dinner there too." Mistel gave a casual wave toward the letter, which had curled into a loose scroll. "Nash seems to like me, so I may as well make use of that."

Cole's jaw tightened. "You can make use of his interest as a *friend*," he said, "which means you never meet with him alone."

"Yes, Father." Mistel rolled her eyes, a teasing smirk on her lips.

Cole glanced down at his plate, stabbing his eating knife into a carrot with more force than necessary. He didn't like the way she had called him *Father*. He was nothing like that. Right?

Before he could decide how to respond, Rilla approached, her apron dusted with flour and her sleeves rolled to her elbows. "More ale?" she asked, already reaching for their mugs.

The group fell silent as Rilla refilled their drinks, the clink of the pitcher and the soft hum of the tavern filling the air.

"Why don't you tell me where you're playing next?" Rilla said to Kurtz. "I'll come watch."

"Looks like the Black Boar," Mistel said.

Kurtz cleared his throat and pinned Mistel with a glare. "We don't yet know for sure," he said.

"Then play here," Rilla said. "Or better yet, come dance with me at the Jig and the Jug."

Kurtz glanced at her, then back to his tankard. "Can't," he said. "We've got business."

Rilla set the pitcher down harder than necessary, the liquid sloshing inside. She let out a sharp breath, then gave Kurtz a tight, bitter smile. "Right. Business," she said. "Wouldn't want to get in the way of *that*."

She wiped her hands on her apron and stalked away.

"Lands!" Mistel said. "She clearly likes you. Why not go dancing with her?"

"Because that's not why I'm here, eh?" Kurtz said. "Can we focus?"

Now that Mistel had pointed it out, Cole realized he hadn't seen Kurtz chase any woman since they'd left Armonguard, which, to be honest, was downright odd. He wanted to ask about it, but now was not the time. He turned his attention back to Mistel.

"I suppose you'll need to write Nash back," he said, carefully measuring his tone. "Accept the offer to play again."

Mistel picked up the letter and spread it flat on the table in front of her. "I can do that."

Cole watched her closely, his chest winding tight. He didn't like Nash's interest in Mistel. Didn't like the thought of her being vulnerable in a place like the Black Boar, with its unruly crowds and rogue bloodvoicer. And he *definitely* didn't like the idea of Nash Erlichman writing her romantic letters.

As the conversation shifted to song choices for their next performance, Cole made a silent decision. If Nash didn't get the hint to back off, Cole would have a little chat with him, make it very clear that if anyone was going to write Mistel romantic letters, it was going to be Cole.

Her cousin.

He sighed heavily, remembering his vow to keep things friendly between them. Stupid vow, that. Stupid ruse, too, pretending to be her cousin.

Lots of stupid here in Tsaftown, starting with Cole for pretending not to care, but if he had to blow his cover to keep Mistel safe, he wouldn't hesitate. And if that meant punching Nash Erlichman in his smug, letter-writing face, so be it.

So you killed the Eben, Achan bloodvoiced. *You triumphed in battle. Why didn't you say?*

Why would I? Cole thought. He lay in bed, talking with the king, who had bloodvoiced and insisted on hearing the full story of the Eben Cole had killed during the Battle of Armonguard. *It was an accident. Not skill.*

Ahh, but that's where you're wrong, Achan said. *You assessed your options in a moment, used the only tool at your disposal—a flagpole!—and made it work. You survived. That's incredible.*

Didn't feel incredible, Cole thought. *It was horrifying.*

Do you feel as bad about Atul's death?

What did Atul have to do with the Eben? I don't feel bad about either. Atul was trying to kill you. The Eben was trying to kill me.

Interesting. No recurring memories of Atul's death, but you went after him. The Eben came at you. Maybe it felt like reliving the past.

What past?

When you were little. I don't mean to presume, but we were both strays . . . I have some dark memories of Poril beating me with his belt. Was there someone from your past who felt like a giant to you?

A sharp breath caught in Cole's throat. He started coughing, had to sit up for a drink of water.

Cole? the king called. *You all right?*

Just a cough. He took a deep breath. *There was someone like that.* A couple someones. Did that make Drustan and Fen the cause of Cole remembering the Eben? That seemed ridiculous.

Feeling helpless as a child—feeling defenseless, desperate to survive—it stays with you, Achan voiced. *Maybe with the Eben, you weren't just fighting for your life. Maybe you were fighting that giant someone from the past.*

Cole swallowed hard, his hands curling into fists. *Maybe. I don't know. I don't remember thinking about anyone else when I fought the Eben.*

Doesn't mean they weren't there. Memories don't always come as thoughts. Sometimes they're feelings: terror, rage, helplessness. But listen, Cole. You're not that boy anymore. You were never as weak as that someone made you believe.

Cole's throat tightened.

Runt of the litter.

Unworthy to live.

Too small to protect Peat.

Kurtz had warned him, said dwelling on dark memories would make him a victim all over again. The idea that Cole might have fought the Eben from such a perspective angered him. That all these years later, Drustan and Fen's cruelty might have cost him his life.

How do I make myself believe I'm strong? he thought to the king.

You are *strong. You might have felt powerless that day with the Eben, but you weren't. When it mattered, you fought. You won. That wasn't weakness, Cole. That was strength.* Achan paused, then added, *The only way to believe it is to live like it's true.*

He made it sound so easy. *How?*

Remember what I said before? Stop lying to yourself. And remind yourself of the truth. Frequently, if needed. Arman's Word tells you who you are. Strong and courageous. More than a conqueror. Bold as a cham. Confident. Armed with strength for battle.

I don't have a copy of the Book of Arman.

We'll get you one. Does Kurtz know about the Eben?

No.

Tell him. I mean it. Telling the story helps. I still can't believe you killed an Eben with a flagpole. I should call you Lancecloth.

That's really not necessary, Cole thought.

Bannerbane. Maybe Stormstaff. Achan laughed. *I like Stormstaff. Write that song about yourself, will you, Cole? I want to hear it.*

And with that shift in topic, Cole had reached his limit. *Goodnight, Your Highness.*

Night, Cole.

Several days passed before the band returned to the Black Boar. Cole still had no idea why Prince Oren wanted them here. Fenris? Erlichman and his ties to Thusk? They'd found nothing last time, but he hoped tonight would be different. The sooner they uncovered the mystery, the sooner they could move on and Cole could stop being Mistel's cousin.

They arrived early for dinner and settled at a corner table. Cole sat beside Mistel, across from Kurtz and Zanna, trying to appear relaxed as his fingers tapped a restless rhythm on the table. The grimy, smoke-filled tavern buzzed with its usual rowdy energy.

The barmaid approached—a different one from before—and Kurtz shot to his feet, nearly toppling his chair.

"Kosotta?"

Her eyes widened, and she curled her lip. "I thought you were in prison."

He snorted, crossed his arms. "I'll bet you did. The young king pardoned me. Wasn't hard since he knew I was innocent."

"Care to introduce us to your friend, Kurtz?" Cole asked.

"She's no friend of mine. This is Kosotta Brovau, it is. She and Verdot Amal used to be quite the pair."

"That ended a decade ago," she said.

"I wouldn't know, would I?" Kurtz shot back. "Kosotta was once a nursemaid to the infant king."

"To Achan?" Cole asked, shocked.

Kosotta turned to Mistel. "What'll you have?"

"Dinner for all of us, please," Mistel said.

"I'll bring it right out." Kosotta strode away.

"Bring some answers with the meal, eh?" Kurtz called after her.

Kosotta glared over her shoulder before passing into the kitchen.

"She'll spit in your food," Mistel said. "Frix always did that when someone annoyed him."

"Why does she hate you?" Cole asked.

Kurtz sank onto his chair. "She was there when King Axel was killed. Testified against me to the Council."

"She didn't seem eager to talk," Zanna said.

"No, she wouldn't, would she?" Kurtz said. "But I'd like to talk to her."

Yet Kosotta didn't return. Another barmaid served their meal.

"Rotting coward." Kurtz pushed to his feet and marched toward the kitchen.

Cole didn't know what to think of Kurtz and his side mission to exonerate himself. He hoped the man's agenda didn't end up blowing their cover. They weren't supposed to be royalists, after all.

He had just taken a bite of stew when the door swung open, ushering in a gust of icy wind and Cernell Crow. The old man shuffled forward, cane tapping out a steady rhythm as he navigated around tables. For some reason, he was without the band of cloth over his eyes today. At first, he seemed to be passing through, but then he altered course, heading straight for their table.

Cole rose sharply, his chair scraping against the floor. He intercepted the man before he got too close. "Looking for someone, Master Crow?"

Crow tilted his head, milky-white gaze eerily perceptive. "Just wanted to thank the band. You're the lute player, aren't you?"

Something in the blind man's stare put every instinct on alert. "How do you know that?"

Crow chuckled, dry and brittle. "I'm blind, boy, not deaf. I recognize your voice."

Cole's shoulders tensed. "I'll share your compliment with the band, but let's be clear—you stay out of our heads."

Crow's forehead creased. "Wasn't my idea," he muttered. "It's not easy being old and blind and at the mercy of powerful men. If I'm not useful, I'm on the street. It's happened before."

Someone had orchestrated the attack on Mistel? Cole's hands formed fists at his sides. "Who asked you to do it?"

Crow hesitated, then sighed. "Young Master Erlichman. Master Fawst put him up to it, and the boy can't resist a dare."

Cole should have known. He leaned in, voice a harsh whisper. "If anyone asks you to use your magic against us again, you'll regret it."

"Big words," Crow said with a faint, bitter smile. "But no need to worry. The girl's shielded now. She's safe from me."

Cole returned to the table, appetite soured. Mistel watched him, brow furrowed.

Zanna stood up, glaring after Crow. "What did *he* want?"

"To compliment the band," Cole replied. "I told him to leave us alone."

Mistel's gaze flicked to Crow. "Do you think he will?"

"He doesn't have a choice," Cole said. "Your mind is shielded."

She nodded but fidgeted with the edge of her scarf. Zanna sat again, but none of them could eat after that. Cole studied the room, cataloging faces, looking for threats. What did Prince Oren hope they'd find here?

Kurtz returned like a thundercloud and fell into his chair. "She's gone. I literally scared the woman away, I did. If that doesn't prove she's guilty of something, I don't know what does."

Well, they were off to a fine start tonight. By the time they took the stage, the crowd had thickened. Cole led them through three songs, and the familiar rhythms eased his nerves.

Sir Fenris arrived with Ikârd, their presence commanding attention even in the packed tavern. Cole tracked them to the back where Fenris took his regular seat. Cernell Crow soon slid in beside him.

Midway through the fifth song, Cole spotted Derby Wenk enter with a group of soldiers, including Lord Livna and Lovell Dunn.

They wove through the crowd to Fenris's table in back. Stood in conversation for a full two verses.

Cole had barely finished the final chord of "Confidence" when an empty tankard clattered onto the stage near Mistel's feet along with scattered applause. She yelped, leaping back, and her smile faltered.

Cole stood up, holding the neck of his lute in one hand. "Time for a break."

"I need to visit the privy," Mistel murmured.

Zanna, who'd been sitting at a table in front, rose and joined Mistel. "I'll go with you."

As the women disappeared down the hall, Cole and Kurtz settled at Zanna's vacated table, Cole still watching the crowd to try and figure out who had thrown the tankard.

Suddenly, Fenris was on the move. Cole's gaze followed him as he led Lord Livna and another man across the room and into a side office, leaving Ikârd and Lovell outside the door.

"What's Lord Livna doing here?" Cole asked.

Kurtz pushed to his feet. "Dunno. I'll ask Dunn." He disappeared into the throng.

Cole's attention returned to Fenris's table where Derby handed Master Crow a satchel. The old man fumbled inside and pulled out a pair of fur-lined boots. Bribes for the bloodvoicer?

Derby left Crow and headed across the room toward Dunn and the door he and Ikârd were guarding.

As Derby approached Cole's table, Cole nodded toward Crow and asked, "Running a charity ward?"

"Those aren't from me. Lady Viola sent them." Derby's gaze flicked to the stage. "You're playing here? Why?"

Cole shrugged, forcing a casualness he didn't feel. "The pay's good."

Derby's frown deepened. "I kept quiet on the journey home because you were always with Kurtz, but . . . what are you doing here? You were squire to the king. Don't you care what happens to him?"

Cole set down his mug harder than intended. "Of course I care."

"You have a funny way of showing it," Derby said. "Why abandon him his first month in Armonguard to play bard in a place like this?"

Cole shifted, wishing he could say the king had sent him. Movement near the kitchen caught his eye. Mistel and Zanna emerged from the hallway, laughing softly. Good. Mistel was smiling.

"I don't know," he finally said. "I'm just not a killer, I guess."

Derby's brows pinched. "None of us would call ourselves killers. But sometimes that's what it takes to keep people safe."

"I meant no offense," Cole said. "But I have to be who I am, and Arman made me a musician."

The tavern door swung open, letting in a gust of snow as Nash and Drustan entered. Nash scanned the room, quickly spotting Mistel as she moved toward the stage.

Cole's jaw tightened. Drustan took a seat at a table, but Nash continued on. Cole tracked his movement, pulse quickening as the man headed straight for Mistel.

"I think you'd fight for what you care about," Derby said.

Cole blinked, taking in Derby's words. The challenge behind them.

Then it clicked. Yes, he would. And he cared about Mistel. More than he wanted to admit.

He pushed back his chair and stood. "Excuse me a moment, Derby."

He strode toward Nash, cutting him off before he could reach Mistel.

"Question for you," Cole said softly. "Did you put Crow up to controlling Mistel with his magic?"

Nash hesitated, and his face flushed. "Just having a bit of fun."

"She was terrified, and using bloodvoicing like that is unethical. Just... stay away from Mistel."

Nash raised his hands. "Sorry! Didn't mean any harm. I'll back off."

Really? Just like that? Maybe Cole didn't need to be a strapping warrior. Maybe he just needed to speak up—fight for what mattered.

"Cole!" Mistel waved him over to the stage.

"Thank you," Cole told Nash, then turned to go.

But Nash called after him, voice just loud enough to carry. "Bit protective of your *cousin*, aren't you?"

Cole froze.

A few nearby patrons turned their heads. Mistel tilted hers, brows knitting as she watched him.

"Shut it, Erlichman," Cole said through gritted teeth, but his gut twisted.

Had anyone heard?

Again Nash held up his hands, innocent as ever. "No offense. Drustan mentioned you didn't have any family left, besides your uncle on Ice Island. Knew the man didn't have a daughter. But hey"—he leaned in slightly, voice lowering—"I understand. Sometimes people make up stories to protect the ones they care about."

Cole said nothing, fists clenching at his sides.

"If word got out Mistel wasn't really your cousin..." Nash gave a sympathetic shrug. "Then she's just a single woman traveling with two men. And that's simply not done. Right?"

Cole stared at him, trying to read between the lines. Was Nash offering to keep their secret? Or threatening that he wouldn't?

"I've got a song to play," Cole said, then turned and walked back to the stage, heart hammering.

Mistel handed him his lute, her gaze searching his face. "Everything all right?"

"Brilliant," he lied. "Let's give them a show."

But as his fingers moved automatically over the lute strings, he couldn't stop scanning the room. Not for threats, but for evidence of cracks. In their cover. In his control. In the satisfied smirk on Drustan's face.

And he couldn't help thinking *I've ruined everything.*

Chapter Twenty-Four
Mistel

THIS WAS WHAT FREEDOM LOOKED LIKE to Mistel, coin by coin, stacked high and gleaming.

The storage room was quieter now that the tavern's chatter had faded. She sat at the battered table, savoring the scent of dried herbs and the metallic tang of money. The warmth of the lamplight and the soft clink of coins settled over her like a blessing. "We made a lot tonight. Best performance yet."

"It did go well," Cole admitted, leaning against the wall beside his lute. "Verdot Amal wants us to play at Ice Island."

"Perfect," Mistel said. "If we keep this up, we'll make a fortune."

"Why does it matter?" Cole asked.

She hesitated, fingers hovering over a rutah. "Because if we make enough, we can keep singing—make a living doing what we love. No one could control us."

Cole tilted his head. "Who's controlling us? We signed up for this."

"I don't mean now." For once, the ache in her chest was quiet. She felt safe, wrapped in something larger than herself, as if she were exactly where Arman meant for her to be. Maybe that's why the words spilled out before she could stop them. "Remember when you asked me why I'm always happy?"

His dark lashes looked thicker in the lamplight's glow. "You said if you weren't happy, the darkness would catch you."

Mistel smiled faintly, no pleasure in it. She dropped her gaze. "When I was little, my mother got sick. My father worked, so I had to care for her. One day, she started coughing up blood. It scared me. And while I loved her, I didn't want to be around her."

She flicked through a stack of coins, grounding herself in the present.

"One day, she kept calling for me. When I finally came, she said, 'Mistel, you're such a beautiful girl. Promise me, no matter what happens, never lose your smile.' So, I smiled really big. And that made her smile back. She asked for tea, and I went to fetch some. When I came back, she was gone." Lying dead on the bed, eyes wide. No amount of shaking her or pleading with her to wake had made any difference.

"Oh, Mistel." Cole caught her hands in his, smoothed his thumb over her knuckles.

"I was nine." Her eyes glazed with tears. "Father came home and got angry, like I'd done something wrong. But I had smiled. I had made the tea. I did what she asked."

Cole's brow furrowed. "That's terrible, Mistel. I'm so sorry."

"I wanted to get away from that house, go outside, breathe fresh air, see flowers, but my father made me stay home. He was afraid I'd get sick too. Over the years, he never let up. I wasn't allowed anywhere. Not even to the Corner to hear the music—not that it stopped me from sneaking out."

Cole's grip tightened. "He kept you locked away?"

Mistel jerked her head once, a short nod of assent. "I felt betrayed," she whispered. "By my mother, who left me alone and told me to be happy about it. And by my father, who took my freedom and made me stay in that horrible, lifeless house. We weren't allowed to talk about her death, either, but it was everywhere, in every breath, every frown, every cup of tea."

Cole laced his fingers with hers. "That sounds awful."

No one had stirred sugar into the tea anymore. She and Father had both drank it bitter. "After Father died, I couldn't wait to leave Sitna—to get away—and Emory was going places. But then he betrayed me, and I had no one. I had to figure out how to survive on my own." She glanced at Cole, loved the intense look on his face, those freckles. "Until I met you. You made me feel safe. Brought me into the castle, had dresses made, played with my band. You cared what I thought, made me feel important. I didn't know I needed all that until I met you."

Cole's lips tugged into a grin. "Because you're so capable."

Mistel shrugged. "I've had to be."

"As you're always so quick to point out," Cole said, "you can take care of yourself."

"I can." Mistel released his hand to sift through the coins again. She picked one up and studied it. "But it's more fun when you have money *and* you're not alone." She dropped the coin on the top of the stack. "Money sure makes life easier."

"Can't argue with you there." Cole clasped his hands between his knees. He wasn't brushing off her words to strategize about Ice Island, practice chords, or write a new song. He was just listening. Present.

He cared.

The weight of that truth struck her. Cole wasn't just a singing partner or even a friend. He was someone who made her feel like she could be herself, chase her dreams, and not be alone.

What if she wanted wealth, success . . . and someone to share it with?

She ran her fingers through the coins one last time, her heart racing at the possibility of making space for Cole in her dreams. They might live happily together all their days.

But if she truly wanted a future with him, Mistel couldn't keep hiding behind her smile. She had to let him see the real her.

And maybe . . . just maybe . . . she was ready to try.

Chapter Twenty-Five
Zanna

Zanna rolled the stiffness from her shoulders, but the day's weight lingered as she descended the spiraling stone steps. Her shift had ended. Exhaustion clung to her like a wet cloak, yet her mind refused to rest. She'd sworn not to get attached, but every night, she carried these women's stories with her. She always did what she could, but it never felt like enough.

She rounded a bend and nearly collided with a man in the shadows. No uniform. No jangling keys. No weapon.

Her pulse jumped. "Who are you?" Her voice came out sharper than intended, echoing along the stone stairwell.

"Bahram Rakkel." The dim light obscured his features but not his flaxen hair and gleaming blue eyes as he said, "*Enayim lema'ala*," in the ancient tongue.

The Mârad passcode. Zanna's breath hitched. A spy? Inside the prison? It didn't make sense. Who let him in? And why?

"Follow me," he said.

Rakkel descended with a measured pace that made her skin prickle. She hesitated. Had he no fear of getting caught?

Instinct told her to report this breach, yet something deeper pulled her forward as she followed at a cautious distance, one hand brushing the damp wall as the air grew colder.

They passed the ground floor, the kitchen, the larder, the pantry, went deeper than the supply rooms, the armory, even the interrogation chambers. Lower than she'd ever been.

The staircase gave way to a twisting corridor lit by sputtering torches in iron brackets.

Every step echoed.

The corridor ended at a massive stone door. Rusted iron hinges. A thick wooden beam across its center. Cold air seeped through cracks, carrying the scent of damp earth and freedom.

Rakkel lifted the beam, set it aside, and pulled the door open. It groaned, revealing the mouth of a dark tunnel that swallowed the torchlight.

"What is this place?" Zanna asked.

Rakkel handed her a torch. "You must continue. I have looked ahead. It's safe. I'll close the door behind you and stand watch."

"Stand watch where?"

"On the shore. Go with Arman."

The shore? Zanna's gaze snapped to the tunnel's abyss. This ran beneath the ocean? A shiver crawled up her spine. She stepped over the threshold onto gravel. "How will you—?"

Behind her, the door slammed shut. The bracket slid into place.

She had meant to ask how he would reach the shore before her. Why not come with her?

Because he had to close the door from inside. He'd said as much.

She exhaled. How did Prince Oren pick Mârad recruits, anyway? First Kurtz Chazir and the minstrel boy, now this enigma.

Holding the torch high, she moved forward, boots crunching over gravel. The slick stone walls glistened with condensation in the flickering light. The frigid air carried the tang of salt.

"I shouldn't be here," she muttered, breath misting.

Yet she couldn't go back. He had locked her out of the prison.

The only option was forward.

So she walked into the abyss, trusting that something important lay ahead.

Zanna could hardly wait to tell Kurtz about the tunnel off Ice Island.

It was nearly closing time when she stepped inside the Black Boar. The tavern buzzed with the usual mix of clinking mugs and raucous laughter, but she barely noticed. Her gaze swept the room until she spotted Kurtz, leaning against the bar, whispering to a giggling barmaid.

Fiora Lingel.

Unbelievable.

Zanna strode up, boots thudding against the floorboards. "Where's Mistel?"

Kurtz straightened, his smile fading. "Storage room with Cole."

"You left them alone? You're supposed to be their chaperone."

"They're fine." He waved her off. "The place is practically empty."

"But who'll guard her from him? I hope you haven't taught him your ways."

Kurtz sighed. "Beg pardon, Miss Lingel." He motioned for Zanna to follow. "Let's check on them, eh?"

She followed him down the hall to the storage room where he gently cracked the door open. Mistel sat at the table, coins piled before her. Cole held her hand while she spoke, too softly for Zanna to hear.

She reached to push the door wider, but Kurtz shut it with a soft click and leaned against the frame. "Let them talk," he said. "Tonight's show went well, but Ice Island's next, and Cole's worried."

"Verdot finally picked a date?"

"Three days from now."

Zanna couldn't hold back. "I found a tunnel tonight. Runs underground from Ice Island to a cave near Cliffwatch."

Kurtz barely blinked. "Not surprising. Moving goods over snow's no easy task."

"This isn't for goods. There's no way into the fortress from the outside. Someone has to let you in. And on the other end, it's just a cave hidden in scrub brush with little more than a game trail for an entrance. No gate. No guards. It's been used, but not often. And there are runes just inside the cave—same as those on Ice Island's gates."

Kurtz's deep-brown eyes locked on hers. "That's how they're moving prisoners. How'd you find it?"

"That's the weirdest part." Zanna told him about the mysterious man with the Mârad passcode.

"I don't know a Bahram Rakkel," Kurtz said. "What'd he look like?"

"Blonder than you, bright blue eyes. Felt like he could see right through me."

Kurtz frowned, then glanced away as Fiora exited the kitchen, tray in hand. His gaze followed her. Typical, though not surprising. The woman was barely contained in that uniform.

Zanna crossed her arms. "I'll wait for Mistel. You can go back to your carousing."

Kurtz smirked, though it lacked humor. "I wasn't carousing. I haven't caroused in..." He paused, rolling his eyes upward. "Since we got to town."

Zanna laughed dryly. "Three whole weeks? You must be miserable."

"I prefer disciplined."

"That doesn't sound like you."

"You don't know me."

"I know enough." But there was warmth behind his glare.

Maybe he really was just doing his job. "What did you learn from her? Anything on Sir Fenris?"

Kurtz stroked his beard. "Didn't ask about Fenris. Asked about a family she worked for in Mahanaim."

"What family?"

"Garran and Delia Nariel."

The names meant nothing to Zanna, but Kurtz was clearly working an angle. "What'd she say?"

"Not much. She worked for them after King Axel's death, then came home when her mother fell ill."

Ahh. This was about Kurtz unraveling the mystery of the former king's murder. "Prince Oren put you on this?"

Kurtz stared at her, his lashes so thick and hooded in the dim hallway, she almost couldn't see his eyes. "Let's talk about you for a change, eh? What's your life been like these past few years?"

Zanna crossed her arms. "Why do you care?"

"That bad, is it?" His smirk baited her, but his eyes lingered as if he genuinely wanted to know.

Zanna hesitated, giving him nothing but the rigid set of her jaw. Yet she had nothing to hide—except the way her fingers clenched the seams of her tunic. "I've been in the Kingsguard all my adult life."

Kurtz's gaze dropped to her hands, igniting a smile. Of course he'd noticed. "Don't hold back on me," he said.

Zanna lifted her chin. "I'm not."

He leaned a fraction closer. "You always react like this," he said softly, "like the world might crumble if I look at you the wrong way."

What? "I do not."

Kurtz's mouth curved into a dangerous smile. "Do too. And I like it."

Zanna's pulse spiked. She swallowed, the heat in her cheeks

matching the fire in his eyes. "You're infuriating," she whispered, looking over his shoulder.

"And *you* like that," he said.

Their eyes met again, and she recognized the dare in them. She rarely backed down from a challenge.

"Four months ago," she said, "I was reassigned here. Three women had vanished from Ice Island, and no one knew why. Prince Oren sent me, thinking a female guard might get further. But I've failed. Since I got here, six more have disappeared." Her voice dropped to a whisper. "And I feel responsible."

Those brown eyes held her gaze. "Oren doesn't expect you to solve it overnight. He sent you because you wouldn't quit. Do you honestly think someone else could've done better? Because I don't. You're exactly who they need in there."

Zanna looked away, uncomfortable with the praise.

"Can you be on the island when we perform?" Kurtz asked. "Cole won't take Mistel there without a chaperone, and I agree. The girl doesn't know how *not* to smile."

"I'll be there," she said. "I promise."

"Good. Thank you."

Zanna studied him, searching for any hint of the rogue she used to know. But Mistel was right. Kurtz Chazir had changed. He wasn't the same man he used to be.

And that wasn't a bad thing.

Chapter Twenty-Six
Cole

"If any guard so much as reaches for shackles," Kurtz said, "I'm putting them in the ground, eh?"

Cole sat beside him in a dogsled driven by Verdot Amal, while Mistel rode in a sled steered by Zanna. Apparently, horses weren't suited for the icy terrain, so Verdot had supplied dogsleds for the journey to Ice Island.

As they raced over the frozen harbor, bitter wind stung Cole's eyes and made them water. His breath seeped through the gap in his scarf, turning the fabric damp and frosty. How could the sun blaze in a cloudless sky and do nothing to warm the day?

Kurtz had been grumbling since they left, clutching an unlit oil lantern like a child with a favorite doll. "We'll be coming back after dark," he'd said, "and I'm not crossing a barren wasteland blind."

Had Zanna's underground tunnel been this cold? They hadn't mentioned it to Verdot—Kurtz's call. He'd bloodvoiced Prince Oren, who had never heard of Bahram Rakkel. This had set everyone on edge, Kurtz most of all.

"Spent thirteen years trying to leave this place," he muttered. "Seems it had other plans."

Ice Island loomed ahead, a diamond-shaped monolith of gray stone rising twelve stories high. Jagged icicles clung to its crevices, glinting in the pale light. They were headed for Smokegate, the prison's southern entrance, where the five-level curtain wall was half buried in snowdrifts. The dogs skidded to a stop before the gate: two watchtowers flanking a narrow iron portcullis.

As Verdot barked orders at a fur-clad guard, Kurtz muttered, "Looks worse in daylight. Swore I'd never set foot here again. Should've sworn louder."

Cole elbowed him, nodding at white runes painted on either side of the gate. "Same as Cliffwatch."

Kurtz's eyes narrowed. "Won't be able to bloodvoice here either. Zanna saw the same runes inside the tunnel's cave."

The portcullis groaned upward, and the dogs surged forward, pulling them into a snow-blanketed bailey. Trenches had been shoveled between wooden outbuildings and the Pillar, which was the towering heart of the prison that loomed overhead like a tanniyn ready to strike. Crates stamped "Thusk Shipping Exchange" had been stacked outside several structures. So, Master Thusk delivered goods to the prison, did he?

Cole would have to wait to discuss that with Kurtz since the sleds halted at the Pillar's entrance, and he didn't want Verdot to hear.

Kurtz sighed, tipping his head back to take it all in. "Last time I entered this place kicking and screaming. Let's hope history doesn't repeat itself, eh?"

Into the Pillar they went, and the cold seeped into Cole's bones. The only way to reach the prisoners was up a one-way stairwell to the roof, then descend back down into the yard in the center of the diamond.

So, up they went.

No number of torches could heat the twisting stairwell, but the effort of climbing soon warmed Cole's body. Still he wondered if his fingers would thaw enough to play his lute.

When they reached the roof, a gust of wind nearly sent him stumbling. Kurtz steadied him. Mistel shrieked as wind caught her skirts like a flag. Zanna wrapped an arm around her, and they hurried after Verdot toward the entrance where the steps went down.

Relief came inside the second tower, but as they descended, the prison's weight pressed in. Kurtz had lost his usual swagger, nervously tapping his lantern like a drum.

The spiral stairwell fed into a corridor that echoed with clanking chains and disembodied whispers. Fingers clawed under doors. Voices garbled together. Cole didn't need to understand the words. The sound alone was chilling enough.

Finally, they emerged into the yard, a vast, diamond-shaped atrium stretching twelve levels high. Cells stacked upon cells, iron bars like a thousand unblinking eyes. Dozens of prisoners shuffled through the yard or sat around crates that bore the same "Thusk Shipping Exchange" mark. Shackles clinked as prisoners walked or gambled.

Cole nudged Kurtz, then tapped his temple.

"Can't in here," Kurtz reminded him. "The runes, remember?"

Right. The warden couldn't allow bloodvoicers to communicate with prisoners or spy on the place. Cole leaned in. "See the crates?"

Kurtz glanced at them and frowned. "Thusk must be a regular patron. Wonder how much he makes off this place?"

Verdot led them to a wooden platform positioned at one end of a large grate in the ground. Prisoners lurked on the far side, jostling for a better view. Beneath the grate, faint movements hinted at something—or someone—below.

That must be the Prodotez where Kurtz had lived for so many years. Cole gestured toward it. "That what I think it is?"

"The Pit." Kurtz retreated to the back of the platform. "Let's do the show and get out of here, eh? I don't like how—"

"Hey, Kurtz!"

Kurtz's head snapped up, eyes wide and unblinking.

"It's the Chazir!" someone else hollered.

Kurtz set his lantern by his feet. "Of all the places to send a spy," he muttered, "they pick the one place that already knows my face."

Cole's fingers were stiff as he tuned his lute. "Hopefully, we'll learn enough from my uncle that we won't need to come back."

Kurtz grunted.

Out in the yard, Verdot shouted, "Circle up! On this side of the Pit if you want to see the show. Move it."

Cole didn't wait for Verdot to walk over and introduce them. He struck up "Woe to the Five," hoping the ancient ballad might calm the crowd. Mistel stepped forward, poised despite the leers and crude remarks flying her way. The moment she sang, silence fell.

"Woe, woe, woe to the Five.
Woe, woe as they flee for their lives.
As the Father God grieves how they fail to believe,
Woe, woe to the Five."

Her haunting voice cut through the noise like sunlight through frost. Cole grinned. He'd read the crowd right. But by the second verse, the jeers returned. Mistel held firm, though the tightness of her jaw and her clenched hands betrayed her unease.

Cole went straight into "The Messenger" next, hoping an upbeat tune would shift the mood. Some clapped or danced, but the rowdy ones only grew bolder with their remarks to Mistel. Zanna stalked forward, hands on her hips, and looked ready to beat some sense into them. That only provoked the men, who diverted their jeers to her.

A few shouted for silence, but a fight broke out, and guards started dragging prisoners away.

By the fourth song, some of the taunts from the Pit turned vile. One man clung to the grate, hanging by his fingers while somehow rattling the metal. Cole stopped mid-strum and glared down at the man, only then realizing the prisoner was perched on another man's shoulders.

"If you don't settle down, we're going to leave," Cole shouted.

"What do we care?" the man sneered. "If you want to give us a gift, pass down the girl."

Howls of laughter erupted. Mistel's smile trembled, but she held steady while singing the chorus of "Stars Above."

Cole backed up from the grate until he could no longer see the men in the Pit. He scowled at Verdot. "This is our last song."

Verdot crossed his arms. "You promised me an hour."

Blazes. How were they supposed to last that long? Grinding his teeth, Cole played on. They didn't have enough songs to fill an hour without singing those with royalist or religious themes, so he eventually played "I Bless my King," "The Pawn Our King," and "The Sparrow that Was a She." He honestly didn't notice a change in the rowdy crowd.

Ending with "Light of the World" turned out to be a mistake though. The verses dragged on, and the jeers gnawed at Cole's nerves. When the last chord finally rang out, he stormed off the stage.

"We're done," he told Verdot. "Take us to my uncle now."

Verdot hesitated, but at the band's hard stares, he finally motioned for them to follow him toward a narrow doorway on the far side of the yard.

A few paces before they reached it, a shabbily dressed nobleman limped up and seized Kurtz's arm. "Master Chazir, do you know me?"

Kurtz frowned. "Should I?"

"Let him go, Your Grace," Verdot said. "This is Yagil Hamartano, imprisoned for treason after the Battle of Armonguard. He fought for Nathak."

Cole had never seen the former Duke of Cela Duchy, but he had watched his son Silvo die, killed by Lord Nathak's black magic. The duke's tattered silk tunic and leather jerkin hinted at his former wealth, but his gaunt face and trembling frame showed the toll of starvation.

"Can't the duke afford one of your special apartments?" Kurtz asked. "Or at least a decent meal?"

"Not everyone qualifies," Verdot said. "Leave him."

"They killed my son," the duke whispered. "Now they're trying to kill me. Look!" He held out a fistful of white petals. "I found these in my bed."

"That's because your daughter, Princess Jaira, sent money for flowers," Verdot said. "A generous amount."

The duke's eyes bulged. He clutched Kurtz's sleeve. "They're working with the women now, don't you see? The black knights and the mages together. Tell your king. Get me out, or no one will be able to stop them."

"All right, Your Grace. That's enough." Verdot gestured to a pair of guards.

They seized the duke, who thrashed against them. "No! If you don't listen, I'll die! They're working together. Trying to kill me. Have mercy and help me!"

Mistel clutched Cole's arm and tucked her face behind his shoulder. He covered her hand with his.

"He's not well," Verdot muttered, leading them forward.

"What kind of flowers did you buy him?" Kurtz asked.

"If you must know, I had Tom purchase a starfrost plant," Verdot said. "Rare, expensive, and fitting for winter."

"Very fitting," Zanna said.

"And not at all poisonous," Verdot added.

He led them through a series of dimly lit corridors. The air reeked of mildew and decay. Their boots scuffed over frosty stone, and chains clanked in the distance.

Cole's heart pounded. He was about to see Uncle Crispen, whom he'd long thought dead. Would the man even remember him?

Verdot halted before a scarred iron door where two guards stood watch.

"He in there?" Verdot asked.

"Yes, sir," one of the guards said.

"Open it, and keep it open. You go inside. Benton stays out here with the rest."

"Yes, sir." The first guard pulled a ring of keys from his belt and swiftly found the right one.

"Just you, Master Tanniyn," Verdot said as the guard unlocked the door. "The rest wait here with Benton."

"And you?" Kurtz asked.

"I'll be in my office. When you're done, Benton will bring you to me. One hour."

Mistel squeezed Cole's hand. Kurtz nodded as Cole passed over his lute.

Time to face a ghost.

Chapter Twenty-Seven
Cole

The guard opened the door, and Cole stepped inside. The stench hit him first—unwashed bodies, urine, and damp stone. The small cell contained a wooden table with two benches.

Sitting across from him was Crispen West.

Cole had been a child last time he saw his uncle, but there was no mistaking him. Uncle Crispen's once-blond hair hung in greasy brown tangles. His pale, freckled skin stretched over sharp cheekbones, and a stringy beard draped off his chin like witch's-hair lichen. His clothes swallowed an emaciated frame, and those green eyes were a window to the past.

"Who are you?" Uncle Crispen rasped.

His weak, broken voice made Cole's throat tighten. "It's me. Cole."

Crispen stared, unblinking, then his face lit with recognition. "Coley, m-m-my son? Is it . . . is it r-really?" He gasped in a shaky breath. "You . . . you look g-good. Well-fed."

Cole stiffened at the word *son*. Had the years in prison scrambled the man's mind? "You don't look good at all."

Crispen chuckled and fell into a hacking cough. "I-I suppose... not. How did you... find out I was here?"

"Drustan told me," Cole lied, his stomach twisting as the words left his mouth. "He said you killed someone."

"Yes, yes." Uncle Crispen dismissed this with a frail wave.

A strange reaction. "Who did you kill?"

"Does it m-m-matter?"

"Of course." Cole hesitated, then added, "A guard said you're innocent."

Uncle Crispen let out a bitter laugh. "Innocent? Wh-what's that even m-m-mean here?"

"They said someone wanted to silence you." Cole leaned in. "Is it true?"

Uncle Crispen's expression remained blank. "Wh-what would it m-m-matter?"

"Who wanted to silence you, Uncle?"

Uncle Crispen blinked slowly. "Uncle?"

Mistel paced by the door, slowing to peek inside. Uncle Crispen saw her, and his lips curled up.

"Wh-who's that?"

"That's Mistel," Cole said. "She sings with me in our band. I play the lute. Um... Who tried to silence you?"

Uncle Crispen's smile grew. "That's your g-girl, is it? She's a... a pretty one."

"We're a good band," Cole said, seeking a way back on topic. "We've played several taverns in town, including the Black Boar. Drustan Fawst runs it for Nash Erlichman."

"Wish I could hear you... hear you play."

Cole had left his lute out with Kurtz, and he didn't see how playing anything would help him get information from his uncle. "We also performed at the Ice House."

Uncle Crispen sobered. "No. Stay away from... Thusk. The Ice House too. You'll only find... trouble."

So his uncle knew Thusk. "Did *you* find trouble there? Were you working for him?"

Uncle Crispen's gaze flicked to the open doorway. "You keep . . . keep that g-girl of yours . . . keep her away from Thusk. You hear m-m-me?"

A chill ran down Cole's spine. "I heard some prisoners disappeared. Does that have anything to do with Thusk?"

Uncle Crispen shook his head. "Don't know about . . . about the m-m-missing."

"Served their time?" Cole asked.

"No."

"Bought their way out?"

"Oh, a . . . a handful, sure," Uncle Crispen said. "That's different. Too m-m-many nobodies have vanished. People with no m-m-money and no . . . no hope. Ain't no one paying their debts."

Outside, Mistel passed the door again.

Uncle Crispen's gaze followed her. "You going to m-m-marry that g-girl?"

Cole flushed, caught off guard. "I don't know."

"Don't play g-games with her, son. Life's too . . . too short."

There it was again—*son*. Cole's jaw tightened. Maybe Crispen meant it kindly, but it sat wrong. "I saw crates here with Thusk's name. Maybe he's sneaking people out. Selling them as slaves. Maybe if I check out his warehouse, I'll see exactly what he's shipping."

Uncle Crispen stood and reached for Cole. "Don't, son. Stay . . . out of it."

This time, the word hit like a stone. "Why do you keep calling me that? I'm not your son."

Uncle Crispen's frown deepened. "Of course you're m-m-my son. Are you saying that because I . . . because I left?"

The room tilted, the air stuck in Cole's throat. "You're my *uncle*. That's what Nonda said."

Uncle Crispen muttered a curse under his breath.

Cole barely heard it. His gaze snagged on the man's thick freckles, the same scatter that covered his own nose and cheeks. It couldn't be. His heart thudded like a tabor drum in his ears. "You left me," he said, trembling.

"I-I had to."

The excuse burned. Everything burned. "Why didn't you take me with you? Why would you leave me with the Fawsts?"

"Didn't know wh-what else to do."

"That's a lie." The words tore out sharp, raw. "You left me because I was too small."

Uncle Crispen flinched. "I-I left you because you always did the right thing."

"I was a child."

"You were a talker. Always spoke up. I knew if I . . . if I brought you with m-m-me, you'd g-get hurt."

Talker? Cole searched the shadows of his memory but found nothing, only the sting of Nonda's cane, Drustan's and Fen's fists. If he'd ever been a talker, the Fawsts had beaten it out of him.

He barely whispered, "She said my father didn't want a runt like me."

"That woman!" Crispen's hands balled into fists. "I should have . . . should have taken you with m-m-me. I thought I . . . I'd be back soon, but I . . . I loved you too m-m-much to risk it."

Cole's chest squeezed so tight it hurt to breathe. His voice cracked. "You loved me?"

"I'm your father. I never thought . . . you believed otherwise. I'm sorry for Nonda, m-m-my boy. So sorry."

Sorry for Nonda? As if that fixed years of abuse, neglect, silence from the one man who should have been there. Cole's mind spun. *Father.* The word didn't fit. Didn't belong to this man.

"I-I never should've . . . taken that job," Crispen said.

The word "job" cut through Cole's haze like a blade, and his head snapped up. "What job?"

"Working for Frederick Yarden."

Sir Fenris's father. Cole chased the crumb. "What did he ask you to do?"

"Look the other way. I was in . . . the Tsaftown army. He stationed m-m-me near the . . . the docks so I wouldn't r-report anything . . . suspicious."

At last, a glimmer of progress. "But you saw something? And they framed you?"

Crispen chuckled. "I-I saw plenty . . . but that job . . . it has no connection to wh-why I'm here. If I tell you about that . . . I'm dead."

The words rubbed against each other and didn't fit. "So you're innocent?"

Crispen stared for so long, Cole thought he might not answer. But then he nodded once. A confession.

The air left Cole's lungs. Innocent. All these years, Cole had been so sure his father was a deserter, a coward, the kind of man who ran off without looking back. But this—this was something else. A man rotting in chains for someone else's crime.

"Then I'll figure it out," Cole said, his voice raw. "And I'll get you out. You've got a lot of years to make up for."

"Coley, m-m-my boy. It's too dangerous."

Dangerous? Cole almost laughed. What did danger matter when his father's whole life had been stolen? "I need to know about the missing," Cole said, fighting to steady his voice. "And Thusk."

"And I-I need you to . . . stay alive."

Cole bit down on the swell in his throat. *Stay alive.* The kind of thing a father said. Meaningless coming from Crispen, yet the words sank deep. "Arman will keep me alive. Help me, or I'll figure it out myself. That means taking Mistel to Thusk's warehouse so we can—"

"All r-right." Crispen bounced one knee, rattling the chains around his ankles. "Years ago . . . the Thusk brothers befriended a-a Barthian noble . . . He had them spy on . . . Lord Livna, Lord Orson, Lord G-Gershom, Duke Amal, Lord Yarden. Passed information south. It's how they g-got into . . . smuggling. Wh-when they tried to . . . break free . . . he threatened to-to go to the king."

Cole's stomach turned. So this was what had stolen his father away and put him in chains all these years. "Who's the Barthian?" he asked.

"Name's Falkson . . . Dovev Falkson. Son of the Duke of Barth. Far as I know . . . he's still . . . pulling their strings today."

"I knew Falkson was dirty, I did," Kurtz said. "He should be on Ice Island with Duke Hamartano, eh? He tried to sacrifice Achan to Barthos, yet he's still free, in charge, *and* on the Council of Six."

"How?" Cole asked.

The four sat at a corner table in the Ivory Spit, bellies full after their harrowing concert on Ice Island and Cole's life-changing conversation with his . . . father. He shoved the thought away and scribbled Falkson's name on a piece of parchment.

"Same tricks he's using on the Thusk brothers," Kurtz said. "Blackmail."

"He's blackmailing the king?" Cole couldn't believe it. "Achan would never allow that."

"Oh, the king's furious, he is." Kurtz absentmindedly swirled the ale in his mug. "Put a warrant out for Falkson, but when he sent Inko to arrest him and take over, the Barthians captured Inko and refused to give up the duke. With assassination attempts and Jaelport to handle, the king made a deal. Falkson stays as lord, but Inko serves as a land warden."

"He got his man inside," Zanna said. "It's a start."

Kurtz hummed. "That's how he sees it, but Falkson's his enemy. And I know he was involved in King Axel's murder. I just can't prove it."

Cole steered the conversation back. "So, what did we learn? We already knew Thusk was dirty."

"But now we can link him to Falkson," Kurtz said, "which gives us reason to investigate."

Cole drew a line on the parchment from Falkson's name and wrote *Thusk*. "But we still don't know their motives. Or why people are disappearing from Ice Island."

"Their goal is money," Kurtz said. "Smuggling and getting rich without paying taxes."

"Agreed," Zanna said. "And they must be sneaking prisoners out through that tunnel."

"Should we monitor the cave?" Mistel asked.

"It's too cold to sit out there day and night," Kurtz said.

"I saw Thusk Shipping Exchange crates all over Ice Island," Mistel said.

"Me too," Cole said. "We need to search his warehouse."

"I don't see how," Zanna said. "It's always busy."

"Hold on a second," Kurtz said. "Let's not jump past Verdot, eh? He's exploiting the prisoners, he is. Probably selling them overpriced goods and pocketing the extra coin."

Zanna tapped her mug. "Families send money to Verdot, thinking it'll help their loved ones. Verdot buys goods from Nash Erlichman, who uses Thusk to ship them in. Prices are exorbitant, and they split the profits while prisoners who can't pay starve."

Cole turned to Kurtz. "Can prisoners in the Prodotez purchase perks?"

"Depends. Ice Island is a marketplace for corruption. Guards sell everything: softer beds, better food, contraband. If you have coin, you can buy your way out of hard labor, pay for protection, make your enemies suffer. If you can't pay, you're nothing to them.

I couldn't afford it. I also think Verdot saw to it that Eagan and I received no leniency or privileges."

"You didn't qualify." Mistel quirked one eyebrow.

"Nope," Kurtz said.

Cole's stomach churned at the thought of Crispen rotting away there. "Did you ever get out of the Pit? For walks or fresh air?"

Kurtz laughed bitterly. "No, and neither did Eagan. Gavin tried bribing Verdot, but Verdot always claimed his hands were tied by someone higher up."

"Who's above Verdot?" Cole asked.

"That's what we'd all like to know," Zanna said.

"It used to be the Council of Seven," Kurtz said. "They're who voted to put me there, but none of them are the same people today."

"Could it be Falkson?" Cole asked.

Kurtz snapped his fingers. "I like that, I do. If Falkson controls Thusk, he likely has Verdot too."

"I noticed Verdot Amal called Jaira Hamartano Princess Jaira," Cole said.

Kurtz grimaced. "I caught that too. Verdot seems to have all the wrong friends."

"Is there a list of the missing?" Mistel asked.

"No official one," Zanna said. "Ice Island holds just over a thousand cells, not counting the Pit. Floors ten and eleven are for women. Nine of the 152 women on the island have vanished. When women disappear, we notice."

"Oren has a list from people who filed complaints about not being able to communicate with their incarcerated family or friends," Kurtz said. "Some petitioned priests, others sought Lady Revada's help. Since Lord Edik's death, concerns have been raised for thirty-eight prisoners."

"Which means the number is likely higher," Zanna added. "Many prisoners have no one to ask after them."

"If Verdot and Thusk are moving prisoners," Mistel said, "why? What's the purpose?"

"Boar sold to Jaelport," Cole said.

"But why send prisoners there?" Mistel asked.

"Slavery is rampant in Cela Duchy," Zanna said.

"But even if they take prisoners through that tunnel," Mistel said, "how do they move them to a ship? Someone must have seen something."

"We need to check Thusk's warehouse," Cole said. "Unless Kurtz can see through the Veil."

Kurtz shook his head and took a long sip from his mug. "Never mastered that magic. We'll have to do it the hard way."

"I work the next two nights," Zanna said. "You'll have to wait until I'm free."

"We'll wait," Kurtz said. "What about West? How do we prove his innocence?"

Mistel tapped her finger on the table. "There must be court records," she said.

Kurtz chuckled. "Think Ice Island keeps good records, do you?"

"To be sentenced to twenty years, there must have been evidence." Zanna leaned back in her chair and crossed her arms. "Did Prince Oren mention witnesses?"

Kurtz set down his mug and leaned forward. "The dead man's wife saw the whole thing, he did. But Crispen swore he never met the tailor or his wife."

Cole scribbled the words "not guilty" on his parchment. "He was framed. Admitted as much to me."

"Then someone must have seen something," Zanna said. "We'll start asking around."

Cole nodded, his mind racing. What would life be like if his father were free? He pictured him clapping along as Cole and Mistel performed "The Sparrow that Was a She," and his heart ached. He wanted such a future for Uncle Crispen—his father. He still couldn't believe it.

Somewhere in Tsaftown, the truth was waiting. And Cole would find it, no matter how many lies he had to unravel.

That night, Cole lay in bed at the Ivory Spit, thinking about his father and how Prince Oren had known they were related. Only Sir Caleb could have told the prince that, as he was the first person who had interviewed Cole in Mitspah after Achan had taken him on to help with the horses. "Kurtz, can you ask Sir Caleb to bloodvoice me?"

"Certainly," Kurtz said. "Give me a second, eh?"

Cole tucked his hands behind his head and stared at the ceiling. A moment later, he heard Sir Caleb's voice in his head.

Sir Caleb Agros.

Cole lowered his shields and thought, *Thank you for voicing me.*

Happy to. How have you been?

Cold. Today I found out that Crispen West is my father. Did you know?

Gracious me, I did not. Lord Yarden told me that the woman who sold you to him said Crispen West was your uncle, that he'd been arrested and couldn't care for you.

Why didn't you tell me he was alive?

It never occurred to me that you might not know. He's your father?

So he says. And he has a lot of freckles.

Sir Caleb laughed. *Well, that settles it.*

He was falsely accused, like Kurtz and Sir Eagan. I have to prove it. I have to get him out.

Someone went to great lengths to frame him and likely won't want the truth uncovered.

But that's why we're here, Cole thought.

You'll get to the bottom of it, Sir Caleb voiced. *I'm glad your father is alive, Cole. I'll pray Arman leads you to the answers you seek.*

Thank you, Sir Caleb. Goodnight.

Goodnight, Cole.

Cole raised his shields, picturing Crispen West's freckled, gaunt face. He thought of Duke Hamartano's accusations of being poisoned. The many Thusk Shipping Exchange crates at Ice Island. The underground tunnel. The missing people.

The words Tom Raven had said to Verdot Amal in his office surfaced, how Verdot could fix something but refused to.

Cole needed to know what "it" was. Tom Raven likely had answers about the Ice Island prison. Maybe about his father too. If Cole could talk with that clerk, he just might find out what was going on.

Chapter Twenty-Eight
Mistel

Mistel should be focusing on their mission, not the adorable wrinkle between Cole's eyes that always formed when he was worried or concentrating, which was the first thing she noticed when she entered the Ivory Spit.

"What are we talking about?" she asked as Cole pulled out a chair for her at the table he was sharing with Kurtz.

Adorable *and* chivalric manners. The boy didn't even know he was racking up points.

"Questioning Merrygog about the happenings in Tsaftown fifteen years ago," he said. "Trying to see if we can figure out who might have framed Crispen."

Good idea. Mistel sat down and let the heat from the hearth fire seep into her bones. It was early afternoon, and Zanna had just dropped her off on her way to work at the prison.

Mistel was grateful not to be going back to that horrible place and hoped Cole had learned all he needed on their visit. She studied him as he sank back onto his chair. He looked to be holding up well, considering he'd found out only yesterday that the man he'd always thought was the uncle who abandoned him was actually his father.

Poor Cole.

His hair was an absolute mess today—staticky from the dry heat of the fire. She hated how much she loved it.

"Andric Gershom, for sure," Merrygog said, his bushy white eyebrows all wrinkly. "Lord Gershom's younger brother. A right rascal, he was. Smuggler through and through. Wouldn't be surprised if some of his blood still stains the docks."

Rilla approached and set a steaming mug in front of Mistel. "Some mulled wine for you."

"Thank you." Mistel palmed the mug, letting it warm her hands. Ever since their visit to the Erlichman's estate, she'd developed a taste for the spicy, heated drink.

"Could I get a refill?" Kurtz asked, lifting his tankard.

"Drink slower," Rilla said as she walked away. "Problem solved."

"Ouch," Mistel said. "What'd you do to upset her?"

"It's more like what he didn't do," Cole said.

"Still no dancing, huh?" Mistel asked.

Cole shook his head.

"Anyway . . ." Kurtz, frowning, turned his attention back to Merrygog. "Did he have any accomplices?"

"None worth noting," the old man said. "Even his son, Tom Raven, refused to take his father's name when he offered it. Always trying to prove he was cut from another cloth, that Tom."

"Verdot Amal's clerk?" Cole asked.

"That's right," Merrygog said.

"On the straight and narrow now, is he?" Kurtz asked.

"He certainly tries," Merrygog said. "Arman knows it can't be easy, working for Verdot."

Mistel hadn't liked Verdot Amal. He reminded her of Vasaa Hoff, a merchant from Sitna who'd known her father. The man thought very highly of himself, until he was around someone above his station, then he became a simpering, fawning toady. Mistel bet Verdot Amal would do the same should Lord Livna come to call.

Rilla returned and poured ale into Kurtz's tankard so fast, it sloshed over the side. "It was only about eight years back when Andric Gershom died," she said. "That's too recent for what they're asking about."

"Thank you, Rilla," Kurtz said, pulling his drink close.

"Try not to choke on it," she said as she strode away.

Cole and Mistel exchanged smothered grins. Cole had told Mistel stories about women vexed with Kurtz, usually because he'd wandered into the arms of another. But this was different. Rilla's indignation didn't stem from betrayal, but from the sting of his continued rejection.

"Andric got himself killed by some Hamonayan pirates, he did," Merrygog said.

"Pirates this far north?" Mistel asked.

"Sure," Merrygog said. "Pirates'll go anywhere there's money to be made."

"Or stolen," Kurtz added.

"Did you know a man called Crispen West?" Cole asked.

Merrygog stroked his beard. "Can't say I recall the name."

Kurtz took a drink. "What about any other unsavory sorts back then? Smugglers, scoundrels, someone who might've been mixed up in shady dealings?"

"Well, let's see . . . Would that have been when you were in Armonguard?" Merrygog asked.

"That's right," Kurtz said. "Before I left, all I remember was guarding the harbor from pirates."

"A lot of pirates back before Darkness came," Merrygog said.

The door banged open, and Gunnar Gedmund rushed inside, his brown curls wilder than usual.

"There's to be a duel!" he shouted.

The tavern wasn't very full at the moment with only three tables occupied, but everyone stopped what they were doing and turned their attention to the young soldier.

"What duel?" Merrygog asked.

Gunnar strode over to their table. "Lord Livna challenged Fenris Yarden to a duel."

"Is this about Lady Viola?" Kurtz asked.

"No," Gunnar said. "Sir Fenris has been stirring up trouble ever since we returned. Got half the town thinking his lordship is unfit to rule. Just now, the council was down at the Dale, all set to vote Lord Livna out and put Sir Fenris in charge."

Merrygog snorted. "That's just what we need. Howlers running everything again."

"This happened at the Dale?" Kurtz asked. "I thought council meetings were held in Lytton Hall."

"They're supposed to be," Gunnar said. "But Councilor Erlichman has been hosting some publicly."

"In these temperatures?" Mistel shivered.

Merrygog tapped the table in front of Kurtz. "Now that's a man who caused trouble back in the day and is still causing trouble now."

"Joonas?" Kurtz said.

"Fenris," Merrygog said. "You know what he was like back then."

Gunnar put his hands on the table and leaned between Kurtz and the old man. "You should have seen it, Merrygog. His lordship rode up to a chorus of oxhorns. He said since Sir Fenris is his blood, the Northlander Charter gives him the right to challenge the Council's vote of no confidence. And he chose to settle the dispute through combat."

"When?" Kurtz asked. "What are the terms?"

"High sun tomorrow at the amphitheater in the Dale," Gunnar said. "To the death."

"Oh!" Mistel clapped her hand over her mouth.

"What'll we do?" Cole asked Kurtz.

"Do?" Kurtz took a deep breath. "I suppose we'll go watch. Show our support for Lord Livna, eh?"

Mistel didn't think she could watch two men try to kill each other and one of them succeed.

Cole grabbed Kurtz's arm. "Unless we go to the harbor instead."

"Why would we go—ah!" Kurtz slapped Cole on the back. "I bet it'll be real quiet at the harbor tomorrow at high sun."

Cole winked at Mistel, which made her stomach flutter. "Exactly."

The next day, as Mistel rode Bart alongside Cole and Kurtz down an empty street near the harbor, the wind carried the reek of brine and fish guts.

"It's so quiet," Cole said.

The city had gone still, as if holding its breath. Mistel knew why.

"Do you think Lord Livna will win?" she asked.

"Most certainly," Kurtz said.

Mistel hoped so. "We haven't been here long, but I've seen enough of Sir Fenris and his Howlers to know that things would be bad if he wins."

"He won't win," Kurtz said.

"From what Merrygog said, the Howlers are more conquerors than soldiers," Mistel said, "taking whatever they want, leaving fear behind them. He said they would hold this city hostage more than protect it."

"They're a bunch of biters, they are," Kurtz said, "but Fenris is not going to win, eh?"

"How do you know?" Cole asked.

Mistel waited anxiously for Kurtz to answer.

"Because while Fenris spent all those years on Ice Island, Eric was training. He's been training since he could lift a sword. There are few who fight better, and while Fenris was taught by the best, too, the years he spent in prison will have weakened him."

"It didn't weaken you," Cole said.

Kurtz yanked down the neckline of his tunic, bearing a slashing scar across his collarbone. "This is proof of my weakness," he snapped. "If I'd been the top of my game in the Battle of Armonguard, I wouldn't have gotten hit."

Mistel glanced at Cole. The war had left him battle bruised. Perhaps it had left its mark on Kurtz as well. She nudged Bart after them.

When they reached Thusk's warehouse, Mistel found the building unremarkable—long, low, and rectangular, with a sagging thatch roof. No guards. No workers.

"Looks like even Thusk's men abandoned their posts to watch the duel," Kurtz said.

Just as they had hoped. The place was theirs.

Still, as Kurtz led them down the side of the building, Mistel couldn't shake the feeling that someone might see them and tell Thusk. Thankfully, the nearby houses showed no sign of life.

They tied their horses to a fence that separated the warehouse from a row of small family homes and approached the building.

Cole squinted at the walls, hands on his hips. "No runes," he said.

Mistel frowned. "That's strange. Why wouldn't Thusk want to shield this place from bloodvoicers?"

Kurtz crouched by a side door, drew his boot knife, and slid the blade into the lock. A few deft twists, and the latch gave way with a quiet click.

They slipped inside.

The place smelled like a barn. Sunlight filtered through high slats near the ceiling and cast long, pale stripes across rows of wooden crates.

Mistel crept forward and peered inside one of the crates.

Snort! The cage shook, and she yelped.

Boars.

She widened her gaze. Dozens of boars—some brown, some black, and some with bristling white coats and gleaming tusks—in cages of varying size, snorting and rooting in the hay.

She glanced at Kurtz, a few rows over. "Thusk's main trade is in flesh," she said, "just not the kind we feared."

"Don't go acquitting him yet, eh?" Kurtz said. "There's a lot of warehouse left to search."

Mistel followed Cole deeper into the building, past the rows of animals, to an area where shelves stretched up to the rafters. Stacks of goods filled the space—dried fish, furs, barrels of salt, and bags of grain.

They searched every aisle, checked every crate. But there were no hidden compartments. No secret shipments. No signs of trafficked prisoners.

Kurtz exhaled through his nose. "She's right. Thusk is clean."

"He can't be," Cole said.

Mistel bit her lip. If Thusk wasn't shipping the prisoners, then who was? And if they were wrong about Thusk . . . what else had they missed?

"Let's head over to the Dale," Kurtz said.

"Do you mind if we make a stop first?" Cole asked.

"Where?" Kurtz said.

"Tom Raven's house," Cole said. "Merrygog McLennan told me where he lives. I think he knows something about what's going on at the prison."

Mistel grinned. Now there was the investigator who'd so intrigued her back in Armonguard.

Kurtz scratched his chin. "All right. Let's go talk to him, though he might be at the duel too."

They set off on their horses again and had just turned down one of the wider, main roads when a woman on horseback entered the road up ahead. She sat side saddle and wore a long, hooded cloak, which hid her face from view until she glanced down a side street, giving them a good look at her profile.

"That's Lady Viola," Kurtz said.

"Why wouldn't she be watching the duel?" Mistel asked.

"I'll get the truth of it." Kurtz nudged his horse on ahead.

"You want us to come or wait here?" Cole asked.

Kurtz glanced back. "You two head over to Raven's house. I'll meet you there."

Cole turned Cherix up the next street and motioned Mistel to follow.

Mistel steered Bart after Cole, hoping Kurtz would take care with Lord Livna's wife.

Chapter Twenty-Nine
Mistel

In Mistel's opinion, Tom Raven's house looked like it had given up on standing yet didn't know how to fall. The squat, weathered structure of salt-stained wood and crumbling plaster reeked of the fish-scented air of the harbor.

Cole knocked on the door, and a thin, middle-aged woman with brown hair tucked beneath a faded scarf answered.

"Good afternoon," Cole said. "We're looking for Tom Raven."

"Certainly." She opened the door wide. "I'm his wife. Do come in."

They stepped through a low doorway, and Mistel wrinkled her nose at the way the briny smell of the Fisherman's Quarter clung to the place.

The house was little more than one open room, divided into living spaces by the careful placement of furniture. A scarred wooden table stood at the center, surrounded by mismatched chairs—one missing a leg and propped up with a brick. Against the far wall sat a narrow bed with a lumpy straw mattress, its threadbare quilt tucked neat and tight.

In a narrow hearth, a low fire struggled against the draft creeping through the shuttered windows. What must be Tom Raven's three daughters sat on the floor, darning socks, while their younger brother carved driftwood with a dull knife. Four children in all, the youngest Mistel guessed to be four years old. At their entrance, the eldest—a girl of maybe thirteen?—straightened and smoothed her faded skirts, while the boy popped to his feet and gawked.

Tom Raven stood from the head of the table and clasped his hands in front of his round belly. "What's this?" he asked.

"Travelers on a cold day," Madam Raven said, already moving to ladle liquid from the pot over the fire. "You must be chilled through. Please, have something warm to eat."

Mistel opened her mouth to refuse, but Cole shook his head at her. So Mistel bit her tongue and watched as bowls of thin fish stew were placed before them at the table. It smelled strong. Too strong to be edible.

"We appreciate your kindness," Cole said to Tom. "I'm Cole Tanniyn, and this is Mistel Wepp. We came to ask about your relationship with Verdot Amal. How long have you known him?"

Raven's brow barely flickered. "Oh, many years," he said.

"I suppose that's why he speaks so freely around you," Cole said. "I couldn't help overhearing your disagreement the other day."

The children stilled. Mrs. Raven dropped the ladle, and it glubbed beneath the liquid in the pot. She turned suddenly and crossed the room to a shelf in the corner.

"I think he's hiding something at the prison," Cole added.

Mistel kept her head down. Cole certainly could be blunt when he had something to investigate.

Tom Raven shook his head. "I wouldn't know anything about that."

Cole took a bite of fishy soup, hummed, and nodded to Madam Raven, who seemed to be writing something on a table beside the bed. "Delicious." He glanced back at Tom. "My father is a prisoner there, but I believe he's innocent. Have you ever known an innocent man on Ice Island?"

"No." The answer came too quickly.

Cole tilted his head. "Not even Kurtz Chazir or Sir Eagan Elk?"

Raven opened his mouth, and his fingers curled into the neckline of his tunic. "They were exceptions."

Mistel fought the urge to roll her eyes. What a strange thing to lie about.

"The other day in Verdot's office, you suggested that Verdot fix something, but he said to leave it alone." Cole leaned forward. "What needs fixing?"

The eldest Raven girl sucked in a sharp breath and glanced at her father.

"The roof leaks," Raven said.

Cole rubbed his jaw. "And who's above Verdot? Isn't he the warden?"

"The Tsaftown Ruling Council oversees the prison," Tom said stiffly. "And Lord Livna, of course."

"Of course," Cole said.

Mercy. Tom Raven wasn't giving away anything.

Cole rose from the table and bowed. "You've been very helpful, sir. I thank you."

Tom stood as well. He withdrew a handkerchief from his pocket and dabbed his forehead.

Madam Raven scurried toward them and gestured to the door. "Thank you for stopping by."

"My pleasure," Cole said. "Thank you again for the soup."

"Yes, thank you," Mistel echoed.

Just as she stepped over the threshold, she felt something slip into her palm. She looked down and saw a small piece of parchment held there by Madam Raven's thin fingers.

"It was lovely to meet you both." The woman's gaze briefly met Mistel's just before she shut the door between them.

Mistel stumbled down the icy walk to the hitching post where they'd tied their horses. She didn't look at the parchment until she had reached Bart's side. There she unfolded it, and the words sent a chill down her spine.

Master Fawst has threatened my daughter.

Mistel looked up. "Cole."

He turned back, and she handed him the parchment. "Madam Raven gave that to me on the way out." She watched as he read and his jaw tightened.

"Drustan always did like picking on those who couldn't fight back," he said. "They're either trying to keep Raven quiet or force him to act."

"Maybe both," Mistel said. "What should we do now?"

Cole sighed at the house, then down the road. "No sign of Kurtz. I suppose I should take you to Fat Vandy's."

Had he lost his sense of adventure already? They'd just found a clue! "Shouldn't we go find Drustan Fawst? Ask him about threatening Tom Raven's daughter?"

"We are *not* looking for Drustan without Kurtz. And maybe Quimby and Zanna too."

Mistel supposed that was fair, considering Cole's past with the brute. So, what else could they do? "You know," she said casually, "we're already near the harbor. We should ride past on our way to Fat Vandy's and take a quick look at the docks."

Cole frowned at the sky. "It's starting to get dark."

"But it's not dark yet. And you've got your sword. No one's going to bother us."

He grimaced. "You don't know that. The docks aren't likely full of friendly faces."

"Which makes this the perfect time to look around without anyone noticing us," Mistel said. "The duel? Anyone who has to work will still be working, and villains won't come out this early. We might find one of Thusk's ships."

Cole hesitated, twisting his lips. She could see the gears turning in his head, weighing the risk. She knew he wanted to go, wanted answers as much as she did.

"Fine," he said at last, boosting her up onto Bart's side saddle. "But we're just looking. No sneaking onto ships, no drawing attention. Agreed?"

"Agreed."

Cole mounted Cherix, and Mistel steered Bart after him, grinning as they made their way toward the waterfront.

They neared a tangle of piers where the filthy slush of the road gave way to the wooden planks of a wharf. The entire place felt deserted. Where were the workers?

Ahead of Mistel and Bart, Cherix's hooves skidded. He tossed his head and snorted, ears pinned back.

"I don't like this," Cole said. "If there's a gap under all this snow, we won't know until a hoof goes through. The Tipsy Taproom isn't far. Let's stable the horses there and walk a bit."

Walk hand in hand alone with Cole at twilight? "I love that idea."

Cole paid a few rutahs each at the Tipsy Taproom, and soon they had put up their horses and were walking back toward the wharf. Cole slipped his gloved hand through hers. He wasn't one to make such a bold move, and it made her stomach tighten. Spying all the time made it terribly difficult for her to have alone time with Cole, and this moment felt like a victory.

The sun faded quickly, and the moon hung strangely bright in the twilit sky, its light mingling with the breathtaking glow of red and orange skyfire rippling across the heavens. Their boots thudded softly against the wooden planks as they approached the darkening expanse of the harbor.

"I don't see any ships," Cole said.

Mistel was about to agree when she caught sight of the shadowy outline of a mast against the dusky sky. "There's one." She released Cole's hand and hurried toward the boat. "Let's get a closer look."

Cole muttered under his breath, but his steps pounded after her.

As the ship came into view more clearly, Mistel's steps slowed. The vessel sat pitched at an odd angle, half submerged and rotting. Completely frozen in the ice, its masts had splintered, its deck sagging. On the other side of the berth, the skeletal remains of a ship jutted from the ice like the broken ribs of a tanniyn.

"Thusk can't ship from here," Cole said. "No one can."

Because the harbor had been frozen for years, which was why they'd ridden to Ice Island on the dogsleds. Why would things be any different here in town?

Mistel turned back to Cole. She had grown up in Sitna, far from any ocean. She knew nothing about ships. "But I heard soldiers talking about the *Brierstar* sailing back to Tsaftown. So, how does a ship sail here?"

"Ships are too big to sail straight into a shallow berth like this," Cole said. "The *Brierstar* would have to anchor out in the bay where the water is too deep to freeze. They'd use longboats to haul cargo back and forth. My guess is, they take dogsleds across the ice, or there might be a longer pier out here somewhere from which they can launch longboats. Best head back. I'll ask Kurtz about it."

Mistel supposed there was nothing else to be done. "Well, that was disappointing," she said, allowing Cole to lead her back toward the city streets.

A block from the Tipsy Taproom, Mistel caught the rattle of an approaching horse and wagon just before Cole yanked her into the shadowed alcove of a thatcher's shop. His body pressed against hers, warm and unyielding, and sent a tingle racing through her belly.

A moment later, a wagoner steered two horses around the corner of the next block, heading down the street toward them. As the wagon passed by, Mistel caught sight of a series of runes painted in white along its side.

She sucked in an icy breath and tugged Cole's hand. "Did you see those runes? They were the same ones we saw at the prison."

"Are you sure?" Cole asked.

The wagon slowed at the next intersection, then turned left. Mistel ran after it.

"Mistel!" Cole whisper-yelled.

"One minute," she called back, eager to get a better look at those runes. When she reached the corner and peeked around, she saw that the wagon had stopped halfway down the next street. The driver was nowhere to be seen.

Perfect.

She crept forward, her heart pounding so hard she could hear it between her ears. When she reached the wagon, she ran her finger along the runes. The first was a line with three shorter ones coming out its top. The second, two parallel wavy lines. And the third, a square balanced on one point with two concentric circles inside.

Yep. Same ones from the prison.

A snort made her jump, and she peered into the back of the wagon where three large cages sat in a row. Inside were boars—two regular brown ones and one white ice boar. She frowned, her excitement fading. Just more meat.

"Mistel!" Cole's hissing whisper pulled her gaze to the corner. And here came her knightling, striding toward her, hand on the hilt of the sword at his belt.

My, he looked handsome and brave, all focused and determined to make sure she was all right. She started toward him, but a figure stepped between them, his back to Cole. A gruff man with a scar slashed across his face. His eyes locked onto hers, and something about that angry scar rendered her immobile. Mistel couldn't breathe—forgot all about her skills in charming strange men. For a moment, neither of them moved.

"Hey!" Cole's voice cut through the air, sharp and urgent.

The man turned his head toward Cole, and Mistel ran the other way.

Chapter Thirty
Cole

When the stranger swung his attention to Cole, Mistel scampered toward the opposite street corner.

Cole thought quickly and gave his best impression of Kurtz in a fury. He increased his speed, striding past the stranger with an urgency he hoped would prove nonthreatening. "Little minx stole my coin purse, she did."

The man's chuckle rang out behind him. "Best of luck getting it back, mate."

The tension melted off Cole's shoulders as he held his brisk pace. Until a sharp scream rang out.

Cole's stomach dropped, and he sprinted toward the intersection, his boots hammering against the icy cobblestones. He rounded the corner and skidded to a stop where Mistel stood facing a shadowed figure.

Cole drew his sword and yelled, "Leave her alone!"

Mistel jumped, clearly startled by Cole's sudden presence, but she didn't step aside or run toward him. "It's all right," she said breathlessly. "It's only Master Crow."

Which didn't exactly set Cole at ease. He eyed the blind blood-voicer warily. The man's milky, unfocused eyes were without their bandage tonight. Cole sheathed his sword, willing his breathing to slow as he checked the shields around his mind. He hoped Mistel had done the same.

"Ah," Crow said, his head tilting as though he were studying them. "I'm not surprised to find Master Tanniyn so nearby the lovely Miss Wepp. He does take your safety quite seriously, does he not?"

Mistel beamed at Cole. "He does indeed."

"What an unexpected delight finding the two of you prowling about the Fisherman's Quarter at this hour," Crow said.

Cole jumped in with a quick defense. "We weren't—"

"Skyfire," Mistel said. "We came to see the skyfire as we were told it's quite romantic. I'm sorry you cannot see it, Master Crow. The reds and oranges are breathtaking."

Romantic? Cole's face burned. Thankfully, Mistel kept her gaze fixed upon the old man.

Crow chuckled, the sound low and phlegmy. "Romantic, is it? I wouldn't know. I've only seen skyfire through the eyes of others, and that's been over a dozen years ago now. I don't suppose either of you would share your vision with an old, blind man?"

Cole stiffened. "I'm afraid not, Master Crow."

"No, thank you," Mistel added, a slight tremor to her voice.

Crow hummed, leaning on the cane he carried. "Curious how this *romantic* skyfire led to such a loud scream. What happened, girl? Did you find the romance overwhelming?"

The flush in Cole's face crept down his neck. Overwhelmed by romance... What did the old man think Cole had done? If Kurtz had heard that comment, he'd tease Cole for months.

"We were headed back to fetch our horses from the stables at the Tipsy Taproom when Cole realized he dropped a glove,"

Mistel said. "I was waiting here for him when something scurried by. A rat, I think."

"It's my fault, really," Cole added.

The blind man chuckled again. "You best head back before the romance—or the rats—get the better of you. The Fisherman's Quarter is no place for young folk after dark."

Cole and Mistel exchanged a look, then muttered their goodnights to Master Crow.

Once they were out of earshot, Mistel looped her hand around Cole's arm and said, "That was terrifying."

"Proof we shouldn't have come down here without Kurtz," Cole said. "I wonder what happened to him and Lady Viola?"

"Oh, I think we did all right for ourselves," Mistel said. "I heard you tell that man I stole your coin purse. That was quick thinking."

"Why did you run after that wagon, anyway?" Cole asked.

"Because of the runes." Mistel told him of the symbols painted on the side of the wagon holding the boars.

"Runes of concealment," Cole said. "Which means no bloodvoicer can see what's in Thusk's wagons. Good eye, Mistel. That's a fascinating discovery."

Mistel beamed and bumped her shoulder against his arm. "Thank you."

"It could be that Thusk is transporting prisoners from Cliffwatch in one of his wagons. But is he helping them escape? Or is he selling them?"

"The latter is too horrible to think about," Mistel said.

It certainly was. They reached the Tipsy Taproom and headed into the stables. "Let's not talk about it until we reach Fat Vandy's," Cole said. "These streets have ears."

They rode in silence all the way to Fat Vandy's, and only when Cole had unsaddled Bart and was brushing him down, did he circle back to the topic.

"I wonder if there's a rune that counteracts the concealment ones," he said. "Or if we were to erase the concealment runes or paint over them, would that end their magic?"

"Who could know?" Mistel said.

"Madam Vinzen would," Cole said, thinking of the old Magosian priestess who'd helped him catch an assassin. "Maybe Achan could send Trizo to ask her."

When Cole had left Armonguard, Madam Vinzen's son, Dewin Sessit, had finally awakened after having been stormed by Atul Shakran, the man who'd killed Mistel's roommate and tried to assassinate the king and queen.

"I think she'd help us after all we did to help her." Cole gave Bart one last swipe with the currycomb, knocked the hair from it, and put it away. "All done. Want me to walk you inside before I go?"

Mistel grabbed his hand and tugged. "I don't want you to go at all. Stay and have some dinner."

"We had lunch before we left, and I had several bites of Madam Raven's fish soup."

Mistel wrinkled her nose. "That smelled awful."

"It wasn't bad."

She laced her fingers with his, and he liked how small and slender her hands were, even through both layers of their gloves.

"Tell me about that girl," she said. "The one you wrote about in your song."

Cole thought back to the songs he'd played most recently. "What girl?"

"I saw her," Mistel sang, "at the fountain in front of the castle. She wore red. Had a flower in her hair."

A shiver ran up Cole's spine. "Oh. *That* girl." Back in Armonguard, Mistel had once asked Cole to play her something he'd written. He'd sang the first verse of a song about a girl he'd known in Mitspah.

"You said she wasn't who you thought she was," Mistel prompted.

He couldn't help but frown, wondering what had made Mistel

think of such a thing. "Nya was the marshal's daughter, back in Mitspah." His lungs felt tight, like he wasn't bringing in enough air.

Mistel rubbed her thumb on the back of his hand. "Tell me about her."

Why would she ask that? "There's not much to tell," he said. "We weren't a good match."

"Why not?"

Because she'd been ashamed of him. "She ran ahead of me on everything. And she never asked permission."

"What do you mean?"

He rolled his shoulder. "She made up stories. Once insisted I walk with her to a gathering at a house outside the stronghold. She introduced me by saying, *'This is Master Harlen. Isn't he dashing? He's training to be a knight, will likely join Father's men soon.'* Then all night she called me Master Harlen. I was completely bewildered. When I asked her about it, she laughed and said it was only a game."

"How odd," Mistel said.

Odd wasn't the half of it, but Cole wasn't about to admit the full truth about Nya. She'd insulted him. *"You look ridiculous in those rags."* Forced him to wear her father's clothing. *"Here, put on this tunic."* Bossed him. *"Stand straighter. No one will take you seriously if you slouch like a servant."* And perhaps worst of all, she'd complimented and berated him in the same sentence. *"I picked you because you're handsome. When you say such stupid things, you make me regret choosing you."*

"I don't think she liked me at all. Just wanted someone to order around."

"Was she pretty?"

"Yes," Cole admitted.

Mistel huffed. "You're supposed to say no."

He chuckled, liking the way her lips twisted in that little pout. "She wasn't nearly as pretty as you."

"I should hope not." Mistel tucked his hand behind her back, then reached around his neck. His pulse shot up at her nearness. "She sounds like a fool."

"You think so?"

"I know so," Mistel said, scratching her fingers through his hair. "You're a fascinating, creative, thoughtful person. I've never heard anyone write words so deep and raw and honest. When you sing, Cole Tanniyn, you take me back in time, to the future, to the top of mountains and the bottom of the sea. Your words call out to something deep and ancient, a longing for more in this broken world. You move me. Inspire me."

Cole grinned. When Mistel started complimenting him, he knew exactly what she was after. A kiss. Why that amused him so much, he couldn't say.

But no one was here. No one would know. And he wasn't about to make her beg.

He pressed a soft, lingering kiss to her lips. "Goodnight, Mistel."

"Goodnight, Cole." She beamed, her smile revealing her overbite.

He walked her inside, then headed back to the Ivory Spit. As he rode Cherix through the cold night, his thoughts churned. The boars in that wagon hadn't been the evidence they'd hoped for. If anything, it made their suspicions harder to prove. But the runes had been a good clue, as had the note from Madam Raven about Drustan threatening her daughter. And Cernell Crow...his presence at the docks was more unsettling than Cole cared to admit.

Yet it was Mistel's scream that returned to him over and over. The fear that had ripped through him when he'd heard it, the desperate relief he'd felt when he'd found her unharmed.

He pulled his cloak tighter around himself as the truth settled in his chest like a weight.

He loved Mistel Wepp.

He shouldn't be surprised. She was a goddess, a firebrand, a friend, and an incredible musician. Who wouldn't love her?

And yet, love felt dangerous.

The first time Cole had kissed Mistel, he'd thought he'd made a mistake. He'd feared that once she truly got to know him, she'd grow bored, find him lacking, just as Nya had. But Mistel wasn't like Nya. She only seemed to like him more with each passing day.

Still, if Nya had taught him anything, it was that loving someone meant giving them the power to wound him, to humiliate him. He wasn't sure he could survive being cast aside by Mistel.

Yet he also knew he couldn't live without her.

Her laughter, her boldness, the way her presence brightened a room, it had all slipped past his defenses before he'd even realized he'd lowered them. He probably shouldn't have kissed her tonight. Why was it so easy to forget himself where she was concerned? And what if he gave in to this thing with her and she ultimately decided he wasn't enough? Worse yet, what if his feelings for her compromised the mission? Drustan and Nash already knew they'd lied about being cousins. If others found out, too, everything would unravel. Could he afford that risk?

Cole's grip tightened on the reins as Cherix plodded through the quiet streets. Failing Mistel—failing the team—that's what truly terrified him.

Chapter Thirty-One
Cole

ONE COULDN'T CROSS A SEA BY SIMPLY staring at the water. And that's exactly what Cole felt they were doing.

The day after their visits to Thusk's warehouse, Tom Raven's house, and the frozen harbor, he sat at a table in the Ivory Spit with Kurtz and Mistel, listening to Arbin Roxley play his fiddle by the fire. The goal had been to try and figure out what to do next, but Mistel had rushed inside with big news that had completely sidetracked their conversation.

"Lady Viola was taken last night!" she said.

"Taken by who?" Cole asked.

"Master Vandy didn't know that," Mistel said. "He just heard that Lord Livna won the duel but that his daughter and wife were abducted during the fight."

"That's impossible," Kurtz said. "I tracked Lady Viola all the way back to Lytton Hall."

Mistel's posture wilted. "Oh dear. I was hoping you might have a clue. It must have happened after she got back."

Cole pictured that tiny little girl sitting up on the dais the night of the banquet in Lytton Hall. "That's horrible," he said. "Is there anything we can do to help find them?"

"I don't know what," Kurtz said. "I've never been able to bloodvoice people I don't know well, and Lady Viola and I didn't exactly become fast friends when she threw us in the dungeon, eh?"

"Where did Lady Viola go when you followed her?" Mistel asked.

"The Black Boar," Cole said.

Mistel looked from Cole to Kurtz. "Are you positive?"

"As sure as my sword is sharp," Kurtz said. "The woman tied up her horse at the hitching post, she did, then went inside the Boar."

Cole had heard all of this last night, but Mistel hadn't gotten the story yet.

"Who let her in?" she asked.

Kurtz took a sip of his ale. "Cernel Crow."

Mistel's eyes flashed wide. "Why would she visit him?"

"That's a very good question, that is," Kurtz said.

"How long was she in there?"

"About ten minutes."

"Did you speak to her when she came out?"

"I did, and let's just say, she didn't like my questions. And I didn't want to spend another night in Lytton Hall's dungeons, eh?"

"Then you followed her back to Lytton Hall?" Mistel asked.

"From a distance, aye. She rode through the gates, she did. And that's as far as I went."

"They must have been waiting for her." Mistel slouched in her seat. "Oh, I wish you'd followed her all the way to the door."

"Had no business doing that," Kurtz said.

"But why would she visit that old bloodvoicer?" Mistel asked.

"My best guess?" Kurtz said. "To bribe the man to use his magic to help Eric win the fight."

"Lord Livna cheat?" Mistel's tone made her feelings on that idea plain.

"Never," Kurtz said. "Lady Viola, however . . . I'd put nothing past a Jaelportian."

"That's not fair," Cole said. "She's only half Jaelportian, and she grew up in Zerah Rock with Sir Rigil."

"Bah!" Kurtz said.

Cole though it over. "My guess is Fenris Yarden has something to do with this. Maybe he wanted to take Lord Livna's family in case he lost the duel."

"What if he's working with Verdot Amal and sells them?" Mistel asked.

"We should go to Lytton Hall and offer our help to Lord Livna," Cole said.

"You think you and I are going to add muscle to the Fighting Fifteen?" Kurtz asked.

Kurtz would, but Cole would only be a burden. "Can't you at least try to bloodvoice her?"

Kurtz pinned him with a heavy stare. "All right." He closed his eyes.

Cole stared at Kurtz: blond eyebrows and dark eyelashes, reddish beard, the thin scar on the right side of his beard where no hair grew. He stared a moment longer, then let his eyes drift to Mistel. Her ginger curls and easy smile somehow lightened the tension in the room.

Kurtz sucked in a deep breath and blinked. "Sorry, lad. If she heard me, she didn't answer."

"Maybe she couldn't," Mistel said.

Near the fireplace, Arbin finished one song to a smattering of applause, then began another. Cole supposed there was little else their trio could do to help a man like Lord Livna, who had his own army. He steered their discussion back to their mission.

"We know Thusk ships goods to Jaelport, but his warehouse was clean," Cole said. "We're fairly certain prisoners are being taken from Ice Island through that tunnel, but we don't know who's doing it or where they're taking them. We know Verdot is hiding something—"

"Many somethings," Kurtz added.

"And we know Drustan is somehow connected," Cole said, "because he threatened Tom Raven's daughter."

"We also know there are runes on some of Thusk's wagons that match those at the prison," Mistel said. "But there are none on his warehouse."

"He must have another warehouse," Cole said. "We should search the town until we spot more of those runes."

Kurtz leaned back in his chair. "That's not a bad idea, but it'll take a while. Tsaftown is not exactly small."

"We also know Cole's father doesn't trust Thusk," Mistel said, "and that Thusk is being blackmailed by Lord Falkson."

"Right," Kurtz said, "and we still have no idea who framed West or why."

"Or how the Black Boar ties into any of it," Cole said. "Apart from Drustan running the place."

"And Fenris living there," Kurtz added. "And Crow and all the Howlers too."

"And Lady Viola's visit," Mistel said.

The tavern door swung open, letting in a chilly gust of air. Lovell Dunn and Jol Quimby entered.

Merrygog, who was sitting with a group of old timers over by the fireplace, gestured toward Dunn with his mug, sloshing a bit of ale over the side. "What's all this ruckus I've been hearing about, then? Half the town's buzzing like a kicked beehive that Lady Viola is in trouble."

"Yes, Master Dunn," Rilla piped in as she filled a man's tankard with ale, "do tell us what's happened."

Dunn spread his arms wide and let out a booming proclamation. "Good people of the Ivory Spit, rest assured that the trouble has been resolved! Lady Viola is home safe, as is Miss Nevandra. Alas, Fenris Yarden and Joonas Erlichman are dead."

A ripple of shock ran through the room. Arbin Roxley stopped playing his fiddle, which made the silence in the tavern even more pronounced. Cole tensed, his gaze snapping to Kurtz, who leaned an elbow on the table, his eyes narrowed.

"Was Sir Fenris the one who waylaid her ladyship?" Rilla asked.

Dunn sank onto a chair at the table beside theirs. "As you all know, Lord Livna and Sir Fenris fought a duel yesterday in the Dale. While that was happening, some of Sir Fenris's Howlers sneaked into Lytton Hall and abducted little Nevandra." He paused for effect, and the collective gasp he drew from the crowd seemed to spur him on. "The fiend wanted a way to blackmail his lordship into handing over rule of the city."

Mistel grinned at Cole and whispered. "You were right."

"Not a chance." Merrygog slammed his mug on the table. "Our lord bested that scoundrel fair and true. I saw it myself!"

Dunn leaned forward. "Picture this, my friends," he said, his voice low and dramatic. "While his lordship was locked in a duel with Fenris Yarden, that villain had already ordered his men to sneak into Lytton Hall like shadows on a moonless night. They snatched young Nevandra, intending to use the wee lass, should Fenris lose the duel, to twist Lord Livna's arm into surrendering the city."

"Hunxes, all of them," Mistel mumbled.

Dunn paused, waiting, it seemed, for the crowd to finish reacting. "Fenris underestimated the courage of the women of Lytton Hall. Lady Viola discovered the abduction before her lord returned, and with Lady Lathia by her side, the pair rode out to confront the blackguard. They stormed Fenris's camp—two noblewomen against a den of wolves! And when it came to saving her daughter, Lady Viola didn't hesitate. She traded herself for Nevandra's freedom."

Cole's heart hammered as he imagined such a thing. He could almost hear music building as Dunn told the story. What a song this would make!

Dunn raised his hand. "This dawn, Lord Livna, Captain Demry, and the Fighting Fifteen marched up the mountain to rescue her."

"Dunn and me with them," Quimby piped in.

"But Fenris was a clever fox," Dunn said. "He'd set traps to slow us down. An avalanche, my friends. Snow and ice came crashing down the slopes, nearly swallowing us whole." He mimed the roaring cascade with a sweep of his arm, earning a few startled flinches.

"But the Fifteen pressed on," he continued, "their hearts as fierce as their blades. And because of our lord's and lady's diplomacy skills, the Poroo joined them in the fight, and together, we outwitted Fenris's men. Yet the fiend didn't go quietly. Oh no. Sir Fenris fled with Councilor Erlichman across the frozen lake, taking Lady Viola with them, thinking the ice would hold. But ah, the warmer days of late had thinned it, and as they neared the center, the ice gave way. Erlichman and his festrier fell."

"He was killed?" Merrygog asked.

"Aye, that he was. But our lordship..." Dunn stood and spread his arms as if to embody Lord Livna himself. "He raced onto the precarious ice to save Lady Viola from going under. Fenris tried to stop him. And to save his beloved bride, Lord Livna, brave and true, tackled Fenris into the icy waters."

Mistel gasped.

"His vile cousin tried to drag him down, but our lord's love for his wife gave him strength beyond measure. He prevailed against that villain, and Lady Viola herself pulled his lordship from the icy depths. They say her hands were trembling, but her heart was as steady as the mountains."

"Lady Viola rescued Lord Livna?" Mistel asked, her eyes shimmering.

"Aye, lass," Dunn said, nodding gravely. "She saved him as much as he saved her. A true love story, if ever there was one."

He let his words linger before sitting down, a satisfied grin on his bearded face. "And that, my friends, is how courage and love overcame treachery and cold steel. Lord Livna, Lady Viola, and little Nevandra are safe, while Fenris, Erlichman, and their many schemes lie frozen at the bottom of the lake."

"Where none will miss them," Quimby added.

Silence hung heavy in the room.

Cole could hardly believe it.

"What a story," Mistel said.

"Indeed, Miss Wepp, indeed," Dunn said. "His lordship is in bed now, warming his bones, which I can tell you were frozen clear through."

"What part did Councilor Erlichman play in all this?" Merrygog asked.

"Ahh," Dunn said. "Poor Joonas never had much of a spine, I'm afraid. Personality as strong as Fenris clipped the bit right into his mouth. He'd been steering the man for months."

The tavern erupted into murmurs of reflection. Rilla served Dunn and Quimby bowls of steaming stew and tankards of ale.

"Poor Nash," Mistel said. "He must be heartbroken. Councilor Erlichman seemed like such a nice man."

"He was," Kurtz said. "You know what they say about bad company, though."

"I wish I knew what this meant for our investigation," Cole whispered.

"As do I." Kurtz took a drink. "Actually, that gives me an idea." He raised his voice. "Hey, Dunn," Kurtz said, "did you ever know a man named Crispen West?"

Dunn tapped his chin, then nodded slowly. "Aye, I knew him. That was years ago. He wasn't in the army long before he went bad. Was like a colt fresh out of the stable, all legs and no sense. Ran with Fenris, actually. They played their pranks, though I never got involved. Roxburg warned me off."

"Do you remember his arrest?" Kurtz asked.

Dunn shook his head. "Wasn't here for it, but I heard he killed a man. Shame, really. On his own, he wasn't a bad fellow. Just got mixed up with the wrong crowd. A bit like Erlichman, I'd guess, though West was always dead broke."

"We think he was framed," Cole said, surprising himself with the bluntness of his comment.

Dunn's eyebrows lifted. "Do you now? Wouldn't surprise me. Fenris had a way of steering people into trouble, now, didn't he?"

Arbin struck up a new tune on his fiddle, and the conversation around them returned to its usual hum.

Kurtz leaned across the table and kept his voice low. "That was a big clue, about West and Fenris."

"It connects Fenris to Thusk," Cole said. "At least back then. You think Fenris had something to do with framing Uncle Crisp—uh, my father?"

"Wouldn't doubt it," Kurtz said. "Can't believe that blighter is dead."

Cole stared into the flames, his thoughts spiraling. He might still stumble over the word *father* when speaking of Crispen, but he believed wholeheartedly that the man was innocent.

He knocked on the tabletop, and when Kurtz met his gaze, Cole tapped his temple.

What you got? Kurtz bloodvoiced.

"Oh, don't leave me out." Mistel pushed out her bottom lip.

Cole winked at her. "I'll tell you later." Then he thought to Kurtz, *What if my father wasn't framed at all? What if he took the fall to protect Fenris and his men from something bigger being exposed?*

Wouldn't surprise me, Kurtz voiced. *Fenris kept Crispen alive because killing him would've pointed back to him. But now that Fenris is gone, Crispen talking could expose Ikârd and the rest.* Kurtz shook his head. *That rotting brute won't let your father live.*

Cole shivered at the memory of the scalps on Ikârd's belt. *He'll silence him to keep the past buried.*

Your father's expendable now.

We need to get him out of there.

Kurtz grunted. *Even with what we know about the tunnel, it's not that easy.*

But we also have Zanna.

True, that. I'll think on it.

Cole nodded his thanks. He couldn't let his father end up like Councilor Erlichman, a pawn in the schemes of miscreants. No matter what it took, Cole would clear his father's name and get him out of Ice Island, whichever came first.

Crispen West deserved a chance to start over.

And Cole would make sure he got it.

Chapter Thirty-Two
Mistel

THE HIGHER THE RISK, THE SWEETER the song. That's what Cole had said when he'd told Mistel he wanted to rescue his father from Ice Island. Mistel had replied with: only for those who live to sing it.

She sat between Cole and Zanna at a table in the Black Boar, straining to hear Zanna over the buzz of voices and clinking tankards. The guardswoman was explaining the plan she'd formed with Kurtz to break Crispen West out of Ice Island. Kurtz, who was currently across the room, talking to that Lingel barmaid woman instead of sitting here, convincing Mistel all would be well.

"It has to be tomorrow night," Zanna said. "Things should be nice and quiet."

Mistel didn't see how they could be so certain. "What if Verdot Amal doesn't attend the funeral?"

"He will," Zanna said. "Everyone will be cozying up to Nash Erlichman, trying to get on his good side. He's in charge of a dynasty now. Worth a fortune. Verdot won't waste a heartbeat trying to tuck that boy into his pocket."

Mistel's stomach churned at the thought of people taking

advantage of poor Nash, who had just lost his father. "It sounds awfully dangerous." She looked at Cole, and her heart squeezed at the thought of him getting stuck forever in that horrible place. "If you get caught, they might lock you up."

"I'll be fine," Cole said. "If anyone asks why I'm there, I'll say I've come to visit my father. Worst case scenario, they'll throw me out."

Worst case scenario, they'd lock him up beneath that grate covering the pit.

Under the table, Mistel took hold of Cole's hand. His eyes had shone when he'd said the word *father*, and it made her heart ache. "He was falsely imprisoned," she said. "Wouldn't it be so much easier if the king just pardoned him?"

"We don't have any proof that he's innocent," Cole replied. "And Achan may not want to get involved, especially considering why we came."

"Kurtz should bloodvoice him and ask," Mistel said. "Then we'll know."

Zanna's brows shot up. "Don't you dare ask Kurtz to bloodvoice the king."

Mistel waved her hand dismissively. "Kurtz and Cole are friends with Achan. He talks to them often, doesn't he?"

Cole shrugged. "He checks in."

"Will you go ask Kurtz, Zanna?" Mistel batted her eyelashes playfully.

Zanna frowned, clearly unimpressed with Mistel's antics. "Why me?"

"Because he likes you best," Mistel said.

Zanna barked a laugh. "He most certainly does not."

Cole raised his eyebrows and smirked at Zanna. The look on his face was so disarmingly adorable that Mistel couldn't help but giggle.

Zanna sighed and lifted her hands in defeat. "Fine. I'll ask him. But I'm certain he'll say no." She got up and walked away.

"I can tell you're worried." Mistel reached up and pressed the wrinkle between Cole's eyes. "You show it right here."

He twisted his neck and chuckled. "A little," he admitted. "Zanna has keys, and they both can use a sword much better than me. But what if we can't get him out?"

"You will," Mistel said, squeezing his hand. "Cole Tanniyn, I've never seen you fail at anything."

His brow furrowed adorably, and the vulnerability in his expression nearly broke her. "Guess you haven't been around me long enough, then."

Always so negative, especially in regard to himself. "A situation I'm happy to remedy." She wished she could kiss him right there in that greasy old tavern, but that would only embarrass him. Plus, someone would likely see and make a fuss. And Mistel was tired of drunken men whistling or shouting at her. What she and Cole shared was private.

"Hello, you two. What'll you have?" Rilla Vandy set four tankards on their table and started filling them with ale.

"What are you doing here?" Mistel asked.

"The Boar had an opening for night shifts," she said, "and since I work days for Merrygog, I figured I could pick up some extra money. You four eating tonight?"

"We ate before we came," Cole said. "But thank you for the drinks." He set his hand over the last empty tankard to keep Rilla from filling it. "Anna isn't staying. She has to work tonight."

"No Anna." Rilla snatched up the empty tankard.

"Which server quit?" Mistel asked. "I've gotten to know them, so I'm curious."

"Don't know," Rilla said. "Best of luck on your performance tonight."

Cole watched her walk away. "Bet it was Kosotta Brovau who quit."

"The woman Kurtz talked to?"

"He spooked her."

It certainly seemed that way. Mistel wondered what the woman knew about King Axel's death and if she'd really left town or was simply hiding.

A gust of icy wind swept through the room, and the noise dimmed. Mistel looked up to see Nash Erlichman walk inside, flanked by Drustan Fawst. A few men called out somber greetings to Nash, and a pang throbbed in Mistel's chest. She had liked Joonas Erlichman. She still couldn't believe he and Sir Fenris had abducted a little girl, the hunxes.

Nash and Drustan approached their table.

"Cole," Nash said. "Miss Wepp."

Cole stood and patted Nash's arm. "I'm sorry about your father."

Mistel met Nash's eyes, which were bloodshot. "Our deepest condolences on your loss."

Nash's tight smile looked forced. "Thank you." His gaze swept to Cole's lute propped up on the small stage. "Would your band consider playing at the funeral tomorrow night? It would mean a lot to my family. My father loved music."

"Of course," Mistel said immediately, her heart going out to him. "We'd be honored." She gestured toward the empty chairs. "Please join us."

The men took seats as Rilla approached to take their orders.

Cole spoke low in Mistel's ear. "Can I see you for a moment in the storage room?"

Uh-oh. His tone sounded serious. "Certainly. We'll be right back."

As Cole stood and walked away, a knot twisted in Mistel's stomach. She pushed her chair back and followed.

Had she done something wrong? Said something inappropriate? If so, what?

Chapter Thirty-Three
Cole

THE STORAGE ROOM WAS CURRENTLY dark, lit only by the sliver of light sneaking in under the door. The scent of old wood and ale mingled with the musty smell of burlap sacks and spices.

Cole paced, his boots scuffing against the floor. His chest was tight, his thoughts tumbling over themselves like an avalanche.

She'd done it again. Swept the rug right out from under him.

Why did she always do that?

The door creaked open, and Mistel came inside. Cole slipped past and pushed the door shut a little too hard.

"What were you thinking?" he hissed. "Saying we'll play at the funeral? We can't possibly play at the funeral. We're supposed to rescue my father tomorrow!"

Mistel crossed her arms and raised an eyebrow. "You don't have to yell."

"I'm not yelling." But he was. His voice filled the tiny space, and he forced himself to take a breath. To calm down. "I just... Why do you make decisions without consulting the rest of us? Without consulting me?"

Mistel had the decency to look sheepish. "I don't know. I just get an idea in my head and act. But don't worry. The rescue will still happen. And it will be even better now."

Cole fisted his hands in his hair and stared at her. "How is that possible? I'm not leaving you alone with Nash and Drustan to sing by yourself."

"You won't have to." Her lips curled at the corners. "Because you'll be there with me."

He blinked, his thoughts stumbling to keep up. "How?"

She stepped closer and reached up, her fingers brushing the collar of his tunic in that infuriatingly casual way she had of dismantling his defenses. He jerked back and pushed her hand aside. "Don't play. This is serious."

"I know that." Her gaze, so full of mischief moments ago, now held something deeper. A rebuke, if Cole wasn't mistaken. "I wish you would trust me."

Her words hit a nerve. "How can I? You're always making split-second decisions. I never know what you're going to do."

She took his hands in hers, her touch steady, grounding. "This isn't just about me, is it?" she asked. "It's about your father. And the Fawsts. And Nya. But I'm not abandoning you or betraying you. I promise."

He looked down, his throat tight. She saw right through him, as always.

"It's going to be okay, my knightling," she said. "You and I will be singing at the funeral while Kurtz and Zanna rescue your father. Verdot Amal will be at the funeral, as will Renshaw Thusk. This way, you and I can keep an eye on them while the others get your father out."

Her plan clicked into place in his mind, easing the tension from his shoulders. Knowing where Verdot Amal and Renshaw Thusk were when Kurtz and Zanna went into Ice Island felt like less of a risk. "That's actually better," he admitted.

Mistel's laugh bubbled out, light and triumphant. "I know."

Cole couldn't help smiling. Mistel was exasperating and unpredictable, but she was also brilliant. He slipped his arms around her waist and pulled her close. "Thank you." His lips brushed her ear as he spoke, and her familiar scent of lemon and mint curled in his chest. He drew back long enough to glimpse those wide green eyes, then kissed her lips, finding them soft, warm, and familiar. His hands tangled in her curls, and the world outside the storage room disappeared.

A ribbon slipped free from her hair, fluttering to the floor, and her hair spilled down her back. She was gorgeous and smart and talented and funny and had a way of completely consuming him. He knew he shouldn't keep this up—kissing her two days in a row—yet he shoved all caution aside and slid his arms around her waist, pulling her closer just as she pushed back.

"Cole!" she said, breathlessly, half scolding, half laughing. "You messed up my hair."

The tension in his chest had been replaced with warmth. He grinned and combed his fingers through her wild curls, arranging them around her face. "I think it looks better down."

She bent to pick up the ribbon and muttered, "Men," though the corner of her mouth twitched. "Go tell Nash we'll play for him. Poor fellow is probably heartbroken. I'll be out after I fix this mess."

"All right." Yet he hesitated, his feet rooted to the floor. With so much uncertainty about tomorrow night, the funeral, and rescuing his father, Cole wanted this moment with Mistel to last. Here with her was exactly where he belonged.

He wanted to tell her he loved her.

The words swelled inside his chest, aching to be said. *Just tell her,* he thought. *Say it.*

She caught him staring and her lips curled invitingly. "What are you looking at?"

"You." It was all he could manage.

She rolled her eyes, though her cheeks flushed, and she gave him a little push. "Go, silly. Nash will be wondering what's going on."

As much as he wanted to stay, to hold onto this moment, he reached for the door.

Later. He'd tell her later.

Chapter Thirty-Four
Kurtz

"Haven't seen Kosotta since the night you talked to her," Fiora said, twirling her finger in her hair. "Master Fawst hired Rilla to replace her."

Kurtz leaned against the wall, one ankle crossed over the other as he listened to Fiora fill him in on the latest gossip. "Rilla Vandy?" he asked.

Fiora nodded behind him. He turned and saw Rilla carrying a platter across the room. Why was *she* working here?

"Kosotta hasn't answered at her house either," Fiora said. "I went over there, like you said, but it's all locked up."

Kurtz dragged his attention away from Rilla and back to the conversation. "What about Verdot? Did you talk to him?"

"Yes, and you were right." Fiora nudged his arm. "He was *very* happy to see me. I thought I'd feel bad about tricking him, but turns out I don't mind it at all. That one deserves what he gets."

"What'd you find out?" Kurtz asked.

"I only had to mention your band," Fiora said, "and he started bragging about how he got you to play at the prison. He thinks you're trying to learn something from the boy's father that will make him look bad, though, so he said he's moving him."

Alarm flared in Kurtz's chest. "Moving him when? And where?"

"Tomorrow morning," Fiora replied. "He said south. I guessed Mitspah, but he laughed and said somewhere warm."

Kurtz's jaw clenched as movement across the room drew his gaze to Zanna, who was headed toward them.

He'd bet anything Verdot would put Crispen West on one of Thusk's ships, likely to rotting Jaelport. He wished he could prove that Verdot Amal was dirty, that the man had had something to do with King Axel's murder, but if he couldn't pin that on him—*yet*—getting Verdot behind bars for trafficking prisoners would do nicely. Anything to put the man where he belonged.

But first, they were going to have to spring Crispen West from Ice Island. Tonight. No time to plan, no margin for error. Kurtz wasn't about to let Cole's father slip through their fingers. Or be made a eunuch in Jaelport.

Drustan Fawst strode past, his boots striking the floorboards like anvils. "I don't pay you to flirt, Lingel," he barked. "The tables in back are waiting for refills."

Fiora sneered at Drustan's retreating back. "Yes, sir." Her gaze returned to Kurtz, lips twisted into a smirk. "As if I'd flirt with the likes of you, Kurtz Chazir." She winked and sauntered off toward the back tables.

Kurtz chuckled just as Zanna arrived. They were almost the exact same height, but the few inches he had on her forced her to tilt her head to look at him. As the brown depths of her eyes focused on him, he lost his trail of thought.

"What's so funny?" she asked.

"Nothing." He swallowed and glanced away. "We've got trouble. I'm going to bloodvoice you."

Those gorgeous eyes widened, and Kurtz ignored the way his belly flipped at the sight of this woman taken off guard.

Then she blinked, and her stoic mask returned. "All right," she said. "I'm ready."

He chuckled again—couldn't help it—and sent his knock. *Kurtz Chazir.*

I hear you, Zanna thought.

Verdot is going to ship out Crispen West, Kurtz voiced. *Tomorrow morning.*

Her brows sank. *How do you know?*

Fiora found out. Which means, it has to be tonight.

Then we'll do it tonight.

You'll need to open the tunnel door from the inside so Cole and I can get in.

How will I know when to come down?

When was your break again?

Two in the morning.

Meet us then. He hesitated, then spoke aloud. "Be careful."

"I'm always careful," Zanna said. "You'll take Mistel back to Fat Vandy's first, right?"

This woman. Nag, nag, nag. "Already said I would the first two times you asked."

"I was just checking."

Sure she was. "You were just meddling."

A brief silence followed, filled with the low hum of the tavern. Rilla strode by and winked at Kurtz, leaving a gust of air in her wake that carried with it the smell of starfrost flowers.

"Can you do this?" Zanna asked. "Go into the prison?"

"Why wouldn't I be able to?"

"That tunnel is dark," she said. "Very dark."

Fire filled every pore on Kurtz's body to hear this woman speak publicly of his weakness. "Of course I can," he snapped, though his hands squeezed into fists.

The mere thought of that cursed place clawed at him, but he'd take his lantern, and all would be well. It wasn't like they were staying. In and out, quickly. They'd be done in no time.

Cole walked out from the back hallway and approached Nash's table.

At least the lad would be with him tonight. Because if Kurtz were going alone . . . even *with* his lantern . . . he wasn't sure he could do it.

Chapter Thirty-Five
Cole

How did you tell someone you were sorry for their loss yet warn them that most people wouldn't be?

Cole's boots scuffed against the wooden floor as he approached Nash's table. The noise of the tavern buzzed in his ears, but all he could focus on was the weight of the conversation he was about to have. He stopped a pace short of the table and looked down on Nash.

"We've worked it out," he said. "We'll play at the funeral."

"Thank you." Nash's shoulders sagged under invisible weight. "It's... overwhelming that he's gone. Drustan has been a big help. Verdot Amal too."

Exactly what Cole was afraid of. He panned his gaze around the room, but didn't see Drustan anywhere. The absence of the brute made his heart beat faster. This was his chance.

He took a deep breath. "Listen. I know this is none of my business, but you should take care. A lot of people are going to suddenly want to be your closest friend."

Nash frowned and leaned back in his chair. "Why do you say that?"

"I've seen it happen before." Cole lowered his voice. "When Achan was discovered to be the Crown Prince, everyone wanted a piece of him. And most weren't offering friendship—they were chasing power. Money changes people, Nash. And you suddenly have a lot of it."

"That's awfully cynical."

"Maybe," Cole said. "But I'm telling you because it's true. Be careful who you trust. Most of the people who show up to help—people who never cared before—they're only interested in what they can get for themselves."

"I'm not a fool." Nash crossed his arms. "No one is going to take advantage of me. I'm too smart for that."

Cole resisted the urge to call the man naïve. "I hope you're right, but if you'll hear one more piece of unsolicited advice... Your father's legacy doesn't have to be yours. You have an opportunity to make a clean break. Start fresh. Make your own future. A spotless one. Just be careful who you let get close."

Nash's brow pinched. He pushed to his feet and slapped Cole on the shoulder. "I'll think about it." Then he crossed the room and entered the office.

Cole exhaled and ran a hand through his hair. Bold words for someone who usually kept his head down. He hoped Nash wouldn't repeat them to Drustan. The last thing Cole needed was a fight with that walking nightmare.

Feeling a bit lighter, he went and sat in his chair where his lute waited. He began tuning the strings, letting the familiar motion ease his nerves. Just as he adjusted the last peg, a sharp ache stabbed through his temples.

Cernell Crow.

Cole's breath caught at the force of that man's knock. He set down his lute and lowered the shields around his thoughts. *Yes?*

I hear you're asking about Crispen West, Crow bloodvoiced.

Cole's arms tingled. *You know him?*

In an age long past.

Do you know who framed him for murder? Cole asked.

What makes you think he was framed?

Interesting choice of words. Did he know the story? *Because he said so.*

A low chuckle echoed in Cole's mind. *Talked to him, did you?*

At Ice Island. Last week.

Well, then. Yes, West was framed.

Cole's pulse pounded in his ears. *Then who's to blame?*

Fenris Yarden, Crow said. *Back when he was training for the army, he had a habit of sneaking off during his shifts. He and West looked a lot alike, so Fenris often used West's name to keep himself out of trouble.*

So the tailor and his wife only knew Fenris by the name Crispen West? Cole asked.

By no other, Crow voiced. *His father didn't much appreciate his son's obsession with fashion.*

Cole's fists clenched. Fenris had killed that tailor, and Cole's father had taken the blame. *Why are you telling me this?*

Fenris is dead. No need to carry his secrets anymore.

Ahh. All this time Cole had thought his father had gone to prison to protect Fenris and his men, but if Fenris had framed him from the start, then his father had never been a shield. He'd been a sacrifice. *Thank you,* he thought to Crow. *I appreciate that more than I can ever say.*

Remember me with a coin next time we meet.

I'll do that.

The pressure in Cole's mind vanished as Crow ended their connection.

A grin spread across his face. He had answers. Real ones. He leaped off his chair and rushed to the storage room, eager to share the news with Mistel. When he pushed the door open, he found the room empty.

Odd.

Cole frowned and walked back into the tavern. His gaze panned the room, searching for those ginger curls.

Nothing.

He strode to the table where Kurtz sat. "Have you seen Mistel?"

"Not since the two of you headed into the hallway," Kurtz said.

A chill ran up Cole's spine.

"So guess what?" Kurtz said. "We have to—"

"Where could she have gone?" Cole asked.

Kurtz stood up. "Calm your ruffled feathers. I'll check the outhouse and stables. You wait here in case she returns."

While Kurtz rushed off, Cole made a lap around the tavern, eyeing every table carefully to make sure Mistel hadn't joined some new friends for a chat. When that yielded nothing, he checked the storage room again, then went into the kitchen, as Mistel occasionally talked with the barmaids while they filled pitchers and plates.

No one had seen her.

His stomach slid down into his boots.

Nash emerged from the office, and Cole stalked toward him. "Have you seen Mistel?"

"She was talking to Drustan a few minutes ago," Nash said.

Cole's blood ran cold. "Where?"

Nash hesitated, then showed Cole a narrow passage between the office and kitchen. "That door at the end leads outside."

Cole's feet were already moving. He shoved open the heavy oak door, which scraped an arc through a layer of fresh snow. Large flakes drifted from above, quickly covering his head and shoulders.

"Mistel?" Cole yelled, forming fresh boot prints as he made his way around to the back door. He caught sight of Kurtz in the distance, headed back in from the stables.

Kurtz Chazir.

Cole lowered his shields. *Anything?*
Kurtz shook his head and bloodvoiced, *No sign of her.*
Mistel was gone.

Chapter Thirty-Six
MISTEL

MOVE, MISTEL. MOVE!

Her head lolled against a broad shoulder, her body swaying with each step her captor took. Beneath them, a wooden staircase creaked, the sound muffled by the fog in her mind. Cold air nipped at her exposed hands, sharp enough to sting. Her thoughts spilled like ink on wet parchment, leaving her unable to grasp where she was or how she'd gotten there.

Someone had grabbed her. That much she remembered. Rough hands pinning her arms, prying open her mouth, shoving something inside. The bitter, woodsy taste had made her gag. Then an iron grip over her mouth and nose and a low warning growl in her ear.

"Swallow it."

She'd made the motion, and he must have believed it because he released her face and swung her over his shoulder. She'd spit out most of the vile substance behind his back, the liquid running hot along her cheek and into her ear. Yet some of it had managed to pass down her throat, enough to send dizziness spiraling through her.

The faint light flickered past her drooping eyes, casting shadows across splintered walls. The air grew damp and heavy, the earthy smell of wet dirt everywhere. A chill snaked through her, and she groaned, the sound overly loud in the darkness.

"Awake, are you?" Her captor's gruff voice chilled her more than the air. "Don't bother trying to move. That soporific works wonders, doesn't it? You'll feel like yourself again soon enough. Though by then, you won't want to feel anything."

The words stirred fear inside her. *Get up. Move!* She managed to shift her lips, but the sound came out garbled, like a child trying to form their first words. Her fingers twitched, the only other rebellion her body could muster.

"Don't bother trying to resist," her captor said casually, as if discussing the weather. "You'll only hurt yourself."

All of a sudden, she knew him. Drustan Fawst. Cole's former stepbrother, the one he'd warned her to stay away from. The one who had beat Cole and killed his dog.

Moisture blurred her vison, but she blinked it away, wanting to see everything she could, to figure out where they might be.

They reached the bottom of a staircase, and Drustan turned sharply, making Mistel's head roll. The space around them seemed to shift. Narrow walls lined with beams gave way to an open tunnel. Above, the ribs of a stone ceiling arched like the carcass of a giant beast.

"You're going out on the next ship," Drustan said, "though I might buy you for myself. Either way, no one's going to find you."

Buy her? Mistel managed to whisper Cole's name.

"Oh, yes. I'm sure he'll try to find you, but he has no idea how to get here. Few do. And I'll grab him, too, after you're taken care of. Sell him to Jaelport." He chuckled darkly. "Can't have the likes of you two trying to set Nash on the straight and narrow. I've put up with far too much from him and his father over the years, waiting for a moment like this. That business should be mine."

The weight of Drustan's words pulled Mistel into an abyss. No one was coming for her. Not now, not ever. Her breathing came shallow, frantic. Her fingers trembled, useless at her sides. The soporific had dulled her body, but not her senses. This was everything she'd always dreaded: losing her freedom, being helpless, *controlled*.

Images from her past flickered through her mind, unbidden and merciless. Sitting at her mother's side as she died. All the times her father had dismissed her, forbidden her to leave the house, stripped away her independence.

Father's words rose up in her memory, angry and vivid as when he'd first uttered them.

"One step outside that door, and you'll see how cruel this world really is. You'll thank me one day for keeping you here."

"You think I'm being unfair? Life is unfair, Mistel."

"Think I don't know what happens to girls who wander? You'll end up hurt—or worse—so stay put."

So she'd stayed, for years, trapped in that tiny house where her mother had died. She endured the loneliness, survived in silence. Now here she was again, trapped, powerless, and spiraling deeper into the chasm of her darkest memories.

And the worst part? The pitch-black corners of her mind that taunted her with things she couldn't fight, couldn't escape. She had no way to sing over them, no way to exaggerate or flirt her way out this time.

Drustan's boots scuffed along over cold dirt, each step carrying her farther from the light, farther from hope. The darkness grew thicker, colder, swallowing her whole. She was trapped, powerless, with nothing but the weight of her dark memories for company. She could no longer be the bold songstress who could brighten even the bleakest moments. In the darkness, she was just Mistel. Small and forgotten. Alone.

And that was the deepest wound of all.

Chapter Thirty-Seven
Cole

Cole's legs burned as he tore through the falling snow, his breath clouding in erratic bursts. He met Kurtz at the back door to the Black Boar. Snow fell thickly around them, covering the ground with a powdery blanket.

"If she left any tracks, they're gone now, they are," Kurtz said, fiddling with the wick of his lantern, coaxing more light from its feeble flame.

Cole glanced down at his boots, already half covered in fresh snow. There was nothing around them—no scuffs, no drag marks, no footprints. "Think Nash was distracting me?" he muttered, more to himself than Kurtz. "Then why show me the passageway?"

"Maybe Drustan was acting on his own," Kurtz said, "and Nash knows nothing about it, eh?"

Cole fisted his hands as he paced back toward the tavern. "He took her right under my nose. I didn't even see her come out of the storage room. I was sitting there, tuning my lute. I'm such a fool!"

"We'll find her, we will," Kurtz said.

Cole spun back. "You can't know that!"

"Hey," Kurtz barked, his tone sharp. "Keep it down, will you?"

Cole barely heard him. "What was I thinking? A good soldier pays attention."

"And what did you see?" Kurtz asked, his voice gentler this time.

Cole rubbed a hand over his face. "Nothing. She was in the storage room. We talked about playing the funeral so we could keep an eye on Verdot and Thusk while you and Zanna..." Movement pulled his attention to two barmaids and a man standing outside the tavern's back door, their gazes fixed on him. Cole lowered his voice, suddenly wary. "I went out and talked to Nash. Then Crow voiced me and—"

"There's your problem," Kurtz said. "What did *he* want?"

Pressure coiled around Cole's throat, threatening to strangle him. "He heard I was asking about Crispen West. Said Fenris used that name back in the day when he went to the tailor's shop, so his father wouldn't know he'd snuck off."

Kurtz grunted. "Sounds about right."

"I ran into the storage room to tell Mistel, but she was gone." Cole's voice broke slightly as he added, "What am I going to do? I was supposed to keep her safe. I failed her and the mission and I—"

Kurtz fisted Cole's tunic and shook him, snapped him out of his spiral. "Enough! Look at me, lad. Into my eyes."

Cole reluctantly fixed his gaze on Kurtz. It felt too raw, too exposing, and he glanced away.

"Look at me," Kurtz sang.

Cole shifted his gaze back, his heart pounding in his ears.

"Breathe," Kurtz commanded.

Cole sucked in an icy breath through his nose.

"I'm done listening to you lie to yourself, I am," Kurtz said. "You're not a failure or you wouldn't be here. Even the best of men get the hood pulled over their eyes every so often, they do. But they don't stand out in the snow whining about it, eh? They act. You're going to go get her, you are. And right now."

Cole wiped the melting snow off his face. "How?"

"You're a smart lad. Think! He couldn't have gone far."

"The road?" Cole suggested, his voice gaining strength. "One of Thusk's wagons?"

"I like that, I do," Kurtz said, releasing him. "Let's go look."

Cole sprinted past Kurtz toward the stables, his boots crunching over the snow. Cherix would carry him faster than his feet, and he'd find Mistel.

He had to.

What was breath without Mistel? What was life if she was lost?

Cherix's hooves thudded against the snow-packed cobblestone streets of the Fisherman's Quarter, his steps steady despite the slick surface. Thick, heavy flakes spiraled from the dark sky, coating Cole's cloak and stinging his cheeks. The wind bit into the tops of his ears, but he didn't care. Not now. Not with Mistel gone.

Beside him, Kurtz rode Smoke, his lantern held aloft, its flickering yellow glow casting long, dancing shadows over the frosted eaves and snow-covered ground. The darkness pressed back heavily, swallowing details in every direction.

Cole scanned the streets, his gaze darting down alleyways and through the rare glass window. The snow seemed to smother even the faintest sound. No voices, no creaking wagons, not even the distant howl of the wind. It was too quiet. Too still. Either Drustan hadn't come this way, or he and Mistel were already gone.

"If Drustan harms her in any way, his blood will clean my sword," Cole said.

Kurtz raised an eyebrow. "That's the spirit." He pulled Smoke to a halt at a crossroads. "I'll take the east side. You check west."

Cole turned Cherix westward. He pushed him into a canter and strained to see through the falling snow. His heart sank deeper with every empty street. All lay deserted, the fresh snow untouched by man, beast, wheel, or sleigh. If Drustan had come this way, the evidence had been buried.

By the time he met Kurtz back at the crossroads, Cole's chest felt like it might erupt. "Anything?" he asked.

Kurtz shook his head. "Nothing."

Cole clenched his reins, his knuckles white. An idea sprang to mind. "Bloodvoice Crow," he demanded, his voice harsher than intended. "See if he knows anything."

Kurtz didn't argue, merely closed his eyes. The seconds stretched unbearably long as Cole waited, frustration building into something raw and desperate. He wanted to shout at Kurtz to hurry. Instead, he rubbed Cherix's neck, trying to calm his trembling hands.

Kurtz finally came back to himself. "Crow thinks there's a vault or cavern beneath the Black Boar. He's never been in it and doesn't know where the door is, but he swears he's heard footsteps descending under the floorboards."

Cole didn't wait for more. He jerked Cherix's reins and galloped back toward the Black Boar, snow spraying up around him as they tore through the night.

When they reached the tavern, Kurtz took Cherix's reins. "I'll put them up. Go on inside."

Cole dismounted and rushed into the tavern, which was nearly empty now. The scattered chairs and few lit lanterns made the place feel strangely hollow.

He found Nash in the office, holding open a scroll, a candle guttering beside him.

"There's an underground chamber here," Cole said. "How do I get to it?"

Nash frowned, and the scroll he'd been reading curled on the desk in front of him. "There's no underground chamber."

"Crow thinks there is." Cole eyed the walls. "He told Kurtz he's heard footsteps going down stairs."

"Crow's crazy," Nash said.

"What if he's not?"

"I take it you didn't find Miss Wepp outside."

Cole clenched his teeth. "We did not."

Nash sighed and pushed his chair back with a scrape. "I'm telling you, there's no lower level. Look for yourself."

In the distance, a door slammed, and bootsteps preceded Kurtz's arrival in the office doorway, hair dusted with snow. "Well?"

"There's no downstairs," Nash repeated. "Check if you want."

"A trapdoor, perhaps?" Kurtz asked.

Cole eyed the office floor, studying it for cutout lines.

Nash shrugged. "I've never seen one. Maybe in Fenris's office?"

Cole's pulse quickened. He exchanged a glance with Kurtz. "Show us," he said, already moving out into the tavern.

Nash led them to the door just down from his. He opened it, revealing a long, narrow room that felt like it might have been built for storage. It held only a scarred table and three mismatched chairs. Along the back wall, a thin crack under an exterior door allowed fresh snow to drift inside.

The floorboards groaned underfoot as Cole crossed the room. "It's got its own exit." He swung open the door to the snow-covered night, but the storm had erased any hope of tracks. "Drustan wouldn't have risked this exit," he said. "He'd have taken her out some hidden way, where no one would have seen them."

Nash pulled back a braided rug, revealing nothing but bare, splintered wood. "No trapdoor here."

Cole swallowed hard, his gaze scanning the floor, the walls, everywhere. There had to be something. There *had* to be.

Kurtz's voice touched his mind. *Open up.*

I hear you, Cole thought.

There's something I've got to tell you, Kurtz voiced, *and it can't wait. Verdot is moving your father tomorrow morning. Looks like he's going to sell him down Thusk's trafficking river. If we're going to break him out, it's got to be tonight.*

Cole's heart dropped. "We'd have to go now," he whispered.

Nash, still standing by the rug, glanced at him. "Go where?"

Cole clenched his jaw. "Nothing. Kurtz and I will search the floor in the tavern. Will you check the kitchen?"

"Sure," Nash said, brushing past them.

Cole followed him out, then waited for Kurtz to join him. Once Nash was out of sight, he leaned toward Kurtz. "What am I supposed to do?" His voice cracked, and he hated himself for it. "I can't save them both."

Kurtz gripped his shoulder. "One of us goes to Ice Island. The other stays here and finds the way down."

A strange hollowness spread through Cole's chest. "How can I choose between them?" He was supposed to be stronger than this. Strong enough to protect the people he loved. But he'd let his guard down, and now Mistel was gone, and his father, a man he'd never even gotten to know, was about to disappear forever.

Kurtz's gaze didn't waver. "Who did you make a promise to?"

"Mistel," Cole said hoarsely. "I told her I'd keep her safe. But I also told Crispen I'd get him out."

"You stay here and find Mistel. I'll go get your father. Keep your mind open to me, and let me know what's happening. I'll do the same."

"But we'll lose the connection," Cole said. "Once you step into that tunnel, the runes will cut off your magic."

"Right. Forgot that, I did. I'll message the king. He can help you."

Cole blinked. "It's the middle of the night."

"Bah! He won't mind." Kurtz beamed, and it felt almost out of place in the tense moment. "I'm glad I thought of it, I am. The king is good at this sort of thing."

The knot in Cole's chest loosened. Yes, Achan could enter the

Veil and find any underground chambers in moments. "Good idea."

"I have to go," Kurtz said. "Zanna will be waiting for me."

"Go," Cole said. "Thank you."

"We can't let the enemy win this one." Kurtz clapped him twice on the shoulder. "I'll message the king from the road. Don't forget to pray."

"You either," Cole murmured.

Kurtz started away, then paused and turned back. "One more thing, poet. If you come against something ugly, don't get stuck there. Remember the good, eh? What Arman has done."

Cole nodded. "I will."

With that, Kurtz left Cole standing alone in the empty room, the weight of Mistel's absence pressing down on him. He stared at the floor, searching for any sign of a trapdoor, but all he could see was Mistel bound and gagged in the hold of a ship bound for Jaelport.

If he was a hero, he wouldn't need the king's help to save her. If he was strong enough, she never would have been taken in the first place.

He shook the thoughts away, forcing himself to move, to keep looking. He could do this. Mistel was out there, somewhere. Arman would send the king to help. And Cole would not fail her again.

Chapter Thirty-Eight
Mistel

How had it come to this?

Mistel sat huddled in a cage meant for animals, iron bars cold against her back. A coarse layer of straw lined the bottom, scratching her legs and reeking of urine and damp rot. She curled her fingers into the folds of her skirt, trying to steady her trembling hands. She wasn't sure if it was the cold or her nerves making them shake. Maybe both.

The bitter chill of the room turned her breath into pale clouds that vanished in the dim light of the warehouse. A different warehouse. Cole had been right about Thusk having a second. This one stretched higher and had alcoves, rather than long shelves.

Memories came back to her in jagged flashes. Drustan Fawst's cruel sneer as he shoved her into this cage, his heavy footsteps retreating, leaving her alone in the suffocating darkness.

But she wasn't entirely alone.

She squinted through the murky room. To her left, several cages held boars. One pale ice boar with massive tusks rooted at the hay, its snout wet and glistening. Across from her cage, a man lay in another, his head tilted against the bars in what looked like fitful sleep, flaxen hair leaking out the gaps.

Drustan's parting words repeated in her memory. He'd said he was going to *buy* her, as if she were no more than a sack of grain. Her throat tightened at the thought. *This will not be my life,* she told herself. She would belong to no man, especially not that brute.

Mistel set her jaw. She couldn't stay here and wait for him to return. She wouldn't live as someone's captive, caged like an animal, her every move controlled, her freedom ripped away.

Her memories—her worst memories—pressed in on her. She'd been here before, after her mother's death, in a different kind of cage. She shoved those thoughts away and fought to focus on the present.

Her gaze swept the room. A single oil lantern hung from a beam overhead, its weak flame barely lighting the cavernous space. Crates stamped with the Thusk Shipping Exchange insignia were stacked in uneven towers, their wooden sides stained and splintered. Chains dangled from the rafters, some tipped with hooks. She caught sight of a guard leaning against the far wall on her left, a piece of straw between his teeth, his hand resting lazily on a belt that held a ring of keys.

"Excuse me?" Mistel called, her voice cutting through the stillness.

The guard flinched, the straw falling from his lips.

"Quiet down!" came a sharp voice on her right.

Mistel twisted toward the sound. Over the stack of boar cages, she spotted two more men, their heads bent close in conversation. She narrowed her eyes. How many guards were in here?

She tried again with the first one. "Oh, sir? The one who dropped the straw?"

The man straightened, his brow pinched. "What you want?"

"Can you let me out, please?" she asked sweetly.

"'Course not," he snapped. "You're going on the next boat."

Mistel's stomach dropped, but she masked it with a tilt of her head. "You must be mistaken. Master Fawst said he was going to buy me for himself."

Behind her, someone snorted. "You'd like that, wouldn't you?"

She glanced back and saw three men standing around a stack of crates, a lantern between them illuminating a dice game.

"Certainly not," she replied.

"Well, Fawst ain't in charge." The first guard pushed off the wall and took a step closer. "And Thusk already sold you, so you're shipping out."

Sold her. She shivered. "Sold me to who?"

"What do I look like, a ledger?" The man's lip curled. "Now quiet down, or I'll make yeh."

"Well!" Mistel straightened, mustering a haughty tone. "There's no need to make threats."

"Bite your tongue!"

Ah ha. That this hunx of a guard had a temper gave Mistel an idea. She cleared her throat and began to sing.

"Woe, woe, woe to the Five. Woe, woe as they flee for their lives."

One of the dice players groaned. "Woman, spare us your clamor."

Another said, "Let her sing. She's got a right fine voice."

Mistel sang louder, filling the cavernous space. "As the Father God grieves how they fail to believe. Woe, woe to the Five."

The animals stirred, blinking in the darkness. The ice boar snorted and pawed at the hay. The man in the cage two down from hers lifted his head and fixed a pair of shimmering blue eyes her way.

A boot kicked the back of her cage. "Pipe down."

Mistel kept going. "Woe to the realms as they turn from the light. Following darkness and evil delight."

The straw-chewing guard stormed over, his boots sharp on the floor. "Stop that!"

She met his glare and sang louder. "Their emperors scheme and sorcerers teem. Woe, woe to the Five."

He pounded his fist against the top of her cage, rattling the bars. "I said stop!"

She paused long enough to say, "Don't like my voice?"

"Get her, Veek," said a voice behind her.

"Yeah, teach her a lesson," said another.

Veek reached between the bars, clawing for her.

"No!" Mistel shrank back and gave her very best performance. "Don't hurt me!"

His fingers caught her hair and yanked her forward until her face struck the bars. Pain shot through her cheekbone, but Mistel gritted her teeth and reached for his belt. Her hand found his keys, and with a flick of her wrist, she slipped them off his belt, holding them tightly to keep them from clinking. She drew them into her cage and tucked them beneath the folds of her skirt.

"All right," she said. "I'll be quiet."

Veek released her. "You'd better. Where you're going, if you pull stunts like that, you'll get worse than I just gave you."

As he stalked away, Mistel slumped back into the straw, her heart racing. She wondered again who had purchased her and where she was headed.

It didn't matter. The keys were hers now. As soon as she found the right moment, she was getting out of here.

She glanced around the warehouse again. The guards. The exits. The stacks of crates and cages. She didn't know the layout of this place or how many obstacles stood between her and freedom, but she knew one thing. She wouldn't leave here as someone else's property.

Not tonight. Not ever.

Chapter Thirty-Nine
Cole

What am I looking for again? the king bloodvoiced.

Cole stood alone in the empty seating area of the Black Boar tavern. The king had bloodvoiced him, as Kurtz had requested, and Cole had done his best to explain the situation. "We think there's a secret passage to an underground chamber," he said.

"I know that." Nash exited the kitchen, wiping his hands on his trousers. "Not so much as a loose stone in the kitchen."

"Sorry," Cole said, lowering his voice. "I wasn't talking to you. The king's here. He's . . . helping."

Nash froze mid-motion. "The king of Er'Rets? Here?"

"In the Veil," Cole said, as if that explained everything.

Nash's brows shot up. "The Veil? That's sheer madness."

Tell him I said all things are possible with Arman, Achan voiced, his tone light.

Cole relayed the message, and Nash squinted at Cole as if he had sprouted a second head. "Really? I'm supposed to believe the king is talking to me?"

Tell him I like his doublet. It looks formal but not uncomfortable.

Cole passed along the compliment, then thought, *Could you focus on the task, please, Your Highness?*

As long as you stop calling me 'Your Highness' when there's no one to overhear. You're making me itch.

Cole sighed and forged ahead. *We think it's under the office—or close to it.*

Can you carry some lights in there? And the passageway too? I'll need to see.

Certainly, Cole thought, then said to Nash, "We need to light the office and the passage between it and the kitchen."

Nash shrugged and headed toward the office. "Why not?"

They had barely finished arranging lanterns when Achan voiced, *Found it.*

A thrill ran up Cole's arms. *Where?* he thought.

In the passageway, about two paces past the kitchen door on that same wall. There's a latch on the inside, chest high for me. Hold on. Let me come to the other side.

"He's found it." Cole led Nash out of the office and into the passage.

Ah, Achan voiced. *See if you can fiddle with that big knot in the wood. About the size of a coin and chest high. See it?*

"He says there's a knot in the wood," Cole told Nash, scanning the grain. His gaze caught on a golden-brown knot, and he pressed it cautiously.

The knot sank into the wall with a soft click, and a hidden door swung inward.

"Well, mark me," Nash said.

Cole exhaled a long breath and crouched to grab a lantern. "I'm going down."

"I'll go with you," Nash said.

Cole hesitated. That would never do. "Actually, I need you to fetch the guard."

"Whatever for?"

"In case I don't come back."

"You don't know that these stairs even lead anywhere," Nash countered. "Besides, you've got the king. Apparently."

Cole gave him a dry smile. "The king doesn't know his way around Tsaftown. If you come down with me and something happens to us both, there'll be no one to rescue us."

"Ah." Nash tipped his head back, clearly reluctant. "How will I convince them to come?"

"Go to Lytton Hall," Cole said. "Ask for Jol Quimby or Lovell Dunn. Tell them I'm in trouble and bring them here."

Nash sighed. "All right. But it's not my fault if they think I'm mad."

"They won't," Cole said.

"Luck go with you," Nash said.

Cole raised the lantern as he stepped into a square passage. Narrow stairs started down right away and creaked underfoot as he descended into darkness. The walls closed in, raw and cold, and the smell of damp earth thickened with each step.

At the bottom, he found himself in a storage room. Crates of wine were stacked along one wall, and shelves crammed with various weapons lined another.

Grab a sword, Achan voiced.

Good idea. Cole hadn't brought his today. He lifted a few, testing their weight, and settled on a short sword with a leather-wrapped hilt that felt balanced in his hand. He threaded it into the ring on his rope belt, grateful Kurtz had insisted such a thing would come in handy.

Opposite the stairs, a gap in the timber frame led to a dirt tunnel. Cole ducked between the exposed studs, his boots scuffing over the frosty soil. Wooden beams and braces supported the rough shaft. Icicles clung to cracks in the ceiling and low-hanging joints like jagged teeth, glinting in the lantern's light.

How you holding up? Achan bloodvoiced. *About Mistel, I mean.*

Cole's jaw tightened as he trudged through the darkness. He saw no reason to think his replies and answered aloud. "I'd rather not talk about it."

Achan's tone softened. *She means a lot to you, doesn't she?*

The silence stretched out. Cole's throat grew tight, his mind a twist of dark possibilities of where Mistel might be this very moment. Finally, he said, "I'm afraid for her. But more than that... I love her."

His words seemed so much louder, spoken into the dark void of the tunnel.

Have you told her?

Cole frowned. "No."

All the more reason to find her quickly, Achan voiced. *Those words are far more important to women than they tend to be to us men.*

"Really?"

Oh yes. I learned that the hard way, so be sure and tell her as soon as you can.

"All right, I will."

Achan chuckled. *Vrell will be delight—*

The pressure abruptly left Cole's head.

Cole spun around. "Your Highness?"

The silence pressed in, heavy and suffocating. Cole raised the lantern higher, but the tunnel was empty. As the light spilled over the walls, he noticed something painted there. He stretched his arm out, bringing the lantern closer. White markings, their shapes jagged and illegible, shimmered faintly in the light.

His skin prickled.

Runes.

Just like the ones on the gates of Ice Island.

On a whim, Cole backtracked a few steps toward the Black Boar, then called out, "Your Highness?"

Here! Achan's voice returned, the sharp twist at Cole's temples a relief. *I lost sight of you. Where'd you go?*

"There are runes painted on the wall."

Show me.

Cole inched closer to the markings, careful to stay on the southern side of them, and lifted the light close.

Achan was silent for a moment. *They look Magosian. Never thought I'd see runes used so far north.*

"They're the same ones that keep bloodvoicing magic out of Ice Island," Cole said. "Did you know about those?"

Not until Kurtz told me. Seems I'm learning all sorts of dark magics lately. First, the effigy killing. Then the cursed smoke around the Magosian camp. Now this. I don't like it.

"What shall I do?" Cole really didn't want to go on without the king's company.

Wait here a moment.

Alone with nothing but the faint crackle of the lantern flame, Cole's thoughts turned to Mistel. Was she cold? Hurt? Frightened? The images that flickered through his mind were sharper than he wanted, and his chest ached at the thought of anyone causing her harm. *Arman, keep her safe. Please.*

Straight above us is a road. Achan's voice came like a firm hand on Cole's shoulder. *We've come about two blocks north of that tavern and appear to be heading toward the harbor. My guess is this tunnel leads to one of the warehouses. I'll bloodvoice Lord Livna and have him send a squadron to the waterfront. When you reach the end, come outside. I'll be watching the area for you.*

Look for the runes, Cole thought. *If you see any, that's likely the place.*

Will do, Achan said. *Keep your shields down. I'll keep trying to voice you.*

Cole exhaled slowly, letting the plan steel his resolve. "All right."

Arman be with you, Cole. Now, get going.

"Yes, sir."

Lifting the lantern high, Cole walked past the runes again. The hairs on his neck tickled as he continued into the unknown.

He walked for what felt like an eternity. The tunnel narrowed and widened unpredictably, until suddenly the walls fell away entirely, and Cole found himself in the bowels of a building. A forest of wooden beams and posts supported a low ceiling. The faint smell of mildew and animal musk filled the air. His lantern light revealed crates stacked haphazardly against the walls. He heard the occasional rustle of movement—rats or perhaps something larger. Nearby, a low grunt echoed, unmistakably animal.

He came to a staircase and climbed cautiously. At the top, he emerged into a warehouse, its vast interior shadowed and cluttered. Crates of varying sizes formed mazelike rows, and the occasional glint of glass hinted at bottles or jars. A pair of goats in a cage beside a stack of barrels chewed idly, their eyes reflecting the lantern light with an eerie gleam. This wasn't the warehouse they'd searched before.

Cole moved slowly, heading toward the wall in hopes of finding an exit. As he neared it, he spotted a door. A guard stood there, his stance casual but alert.

Blazes! Cole ducked behind a stack of crates and turned the lantern flame so low it was almost out. Hopefully, it would still be lit if he needed to come back for it.

The loss of light heightened his hearing, and every creak of the building, every animal noise, every scuff of his boots on the floor sounded louder than before.

Achan hadn't bloodvoiced him. The runes, then—they must be painted somewhere on this warehouse, blocking his magic.

Cole peeked around the crates at the guard, the door, the wall until—sure enough—he spotted the runes, painted just above the doorframe, a place they couldn't be seen from the street.

Well, that explained that.

His pulse quickened. No help was coming. Not until he made it outside.

How was he going to get past that guard? Should he attack the man? Look for a different door? What if he couldn't get out?

He'd find Mistel and go back through the tunnel to the Black Boar.

Cole left the lantern behind and worked his way around the warehouse, searching for Mistel, for another door. The only thing he found was more guards—five, by his count, stationed in various places, though he couldn't see that they were guarding anything in particular.

No sign of Mistel.

She could be anywhere. Or she might not be here at all. He didn't want to waste time wandering. He needed to get outside so Achan could send in Lord Livna's soldiers. They'd make quick work of this place, subdue the guards, and search it much faster than he could alone.

Doubts clawed at him, twisting in his chest until it was hard to breathe. *Please, Arman, help me get through this. Thank you for the good in my life, for the king and Kurtz and Mistel and Matthias. Watch over my father. I pray that Kurtz and Zanna have already found a way to get him out of there. Help me find Mistel. Don't let me fail.*

He returned to where he'd stashed his lantern and studied the door, breath slowing as his racing thoughts settled. This seemed to be his only way out. The guard on duty yawned and shifted his weight but otherwise showed no sign of leaving. Cole thought back to Kurtz's lessons.

Distract, disable, and don't overthink it.

How to distract the guard? Create a noise to draw him away? Push the crates on his head? Try and talk his way past, pretending to belong?

All those options would make noise, which might call the attention of the other guards. He needed a silent option.

Cole fingered the rope belt around his waist. If he succeeded, Kurtz would love this.

He withdrew the sword and leaned it beside the lantern. Then he untied the knot in the rope belt and slipped it from around his waist. He gripped each end loosely, then crept to a position just behind the guard. The moment the man turned his head, Cole darted forward. He looped the rope around the guard's neck and pulled tight. The guard stumbled, his hands clawing at the thick hemp. Cole kicked in the backs of the man's knees, and when the guard collapsed, Cole wrestled him to the floor.

It wasn't graceful, but it worked. He held tight until the guard went unconscious.

Cole tied the rope back around his waist and started to rise. Pain exploded at the back of his skull. White light spun across his vision, and he fell to his knees. His hands fumbled for his sword, but he only felt air. He'd left it with the lantern.

Another blow—a sharp punch to his temple—sent him sprawling onto his back.

A shadow loomed over him.

Blinking through the haze, Cole recognized the face. Drustan.

"Thanks for coming," Drustan said. "You saved me the trouble of having to find you."

Cole pushed up onto one elbow, his head swimming. "Where is Mistel?"

Drustan delivered a sharp kick to Cole's side. "Stay down," he growled. "You're not going anywhere."

Cole blinked against the pain. "The night watch is coming," he said. "Nash went after them."

Drustan laughed, cold and hollow. "Nash is a fool. I doubt he even knows where to find the watch. He still thinks he's my boss, but I've been working with Thusk for over a year now. Soon, everything Nash has will be mine."

Cole forced his next words out through clenched teeth. "He's your friend."

"I don't have friends." Drustan motioned to two guards who appeared from the shadows. "Lock him up. We'll send him out in the morning. I know just the master for him."

The guards seized Cole's arms and dragged him to his feet. He yanked one arm free, only to have a fist slam into his ribs and steal his breath. Cole went limp. His head fell forward, and the guards lugged him toward the center of the warehouse, his feet dragging uselessly behind him.

A cold, hollow ache settled in his chest as Mistel's face swam in his mind. She was out there somewhere, alone, and he was powerless to reach her.

Chapter Forty
Mistel

Mistel awoke to the muffled sounds of a struggle. She blinked at her dark, cramped surroundings. Two guards entered her line of sight, dragging a man toward her. They stopped right in front of her cage and unceremoniously dumped him on the floor like cargo. He groaned and rolled onto his side.

Her breath caught. Cole.

The dim light revealed blood streaking one cheek, closed eyes. As the guards opened the neighboring cage, her fingers tightened on the cold iron bars. Every instinct screamed at her to call out to Cole, to reach for him, but she held her tongue. Better that no one find out she knew him.

The guards dragged Cole upright. He came to life then, struggling against them with sudden energy. For a moment, Mistel thought he might break free, but before his resistance could amount to anything, they forced him inside the cage and slammed the door shut.

Cole thrashed in his cage, and Mistel's throat burned with the effort of holding her tongue. She waited, pulse thundering in her ears, until the guards disappeared between two rows of crates. Only when the echoes of their footsteps faded did she dare to whisper.

"Cole."

He groaned, his voice faint when he said, "Mistel."

Her heart squeezed. He sounded so dazed, so utterly vulnerable. Did he think he was dreaming? She tried again, louder this time. "Cole Tanniyn."

His limbs tensed, his eyes flashed open, and he sucked in a sharp breath. He pushed himself up, only to strike his head against the low roof of his cage.

"Ahh!" He winced and rubbed his head. Then, finally—*finally*—he turned his attention her way.

For a moment, confusion clouded his gaze, but then his expression shifted. Recognition. Relief. Something deeper. Oh, how she loved watching his face transform as he realized she wasn't a dream.

"You're okay," he breathed.

"Hello, my knightling," she said. "What are you doing here?"

He grinned, a shy look that sent warmth through her. "Rescuing you."

She twisted her lips and shot him a look. "Hmm . . . I'm confused. This is not the rescue I had in mind."

His brow furrowed, putting that little wrinkle between his brows that she found so endearing. "Don't worry. I'll think of something."

She laughed silently, unable to help herself. Even now, in the middle of this nightmare, his confidence—however misplaced—lifted her spirits. "Maybe *you* shouldn't worry." She reached into her pocket and pulled out the keys she'd swiped earlier. Letting them jangle softly, she tilted her head, watching his grin widen.

It was her favorite smile. The one that lit up his entire face.

"That's my girl," he said, his voice filled with admiration.

"We're spies, after all," she said. "And we stick together."

Cole eyed the guards in the distance. "I think this might be taking our alliance a little too far."

"Yes, well," she said, "what was your grand master plan to rescue me, anyway?"

His gaze flickered across the warehouse, scanning the rows of crates and cages, before settling on another set of guards near the far wall. "There are a lot of guards," he said. "Let's sneak out the way we came—downstairs and through the tunnel to the Black Boar."

Was that how she'd gotten here? "Don't tell me Kurtz is down there waiting," she said. "He's afraid of the dark."

"He went after my father."

"Oh." How unfortunate. They could use someone like Kurtz right about now.

Cole looked at her, his expression thoughtful. "You know, we're all afraid of something. But we can't let fear hold us captive."

She tilted her head. "That's very profound. Is it from a song?"

"No," Cole said, still staring at her. "I was just thinking... Kurtz is afraid of the dark, yet he's going to rescue my father anyway. True heroes do what they must, despite their fears. I made a promise to you, and I'm going to keep it."

Oh, this boy melted her heart more every day. Carefully, she unlocked her cage. Then she reached through the bars and passed him the keys. "Let's keep that promise together."

Cole made quick work of his lock, and as he eased himself out of his cage, Mistel was already waiting. She thought he'd start leading her out of this nightmare, but instead, he slid his hand up her jaw and into her hair, cradling her face in one hand.

His voice came low, almost reverent. "I love you."

Before she could process what he'd said, he kissed her.

Normally, such words would send her into a panic, but from Cole, they felt right. Perfect, even.

The kiss was brief—too brief—and when he pulled back, she could still feel the warmth of his lips. He turned to the flaxen-haired man in the next cage and handed him the keys through the bars. "Go with Arman," he said softly, then slid his hand into Mistel's.

Her pulse raced as he started through the maze of crates and cages, tugging her along.

"Wait!" the man behind them hissed.

Cole turned back. The man had already gotten out and, standing as he was, looked like a different person. Taller, strong and healthy. His features were striking: luminous blue eyes, golden waves of hair, and a knowing gaze that carried the weight of one who understood far more than he should.

"*Enayim lema'ala,*" he said, his voice resonant. "Take the teyvah to your king." He held out his hand, and in it was a small box, a timeworn piece of dark oak about the size of a whetstone. A faint crest shimmered on the top that looked like a circle of flying birds.

Cole took it. "Thank you, uh, what's your name?"

"Bahram Rakkel."

Cole's lips parted, and Mistel remembered this was the man who had shown Zanna the tunnel out of Ice Island.

"Where did you . . . ?"

But Cole didn't finish his question, because Bahram Rakkel began to fade away. His larger-than-life body grew vaporous until it vanished altogether.

Mistel could not stop staring at the place he'd been, her mouth gaping.

Cole tugged her hand until her arm went taut and she finally trailed after him, still looking over her shoulder at the place the man had been standing.

How?

When she lost sight of the cages, she turned her focus back to Cole. They slipped through the labyrinth of crates until they came to a sword propped beside a lantern nearly out of fuel. Cole threaded the sword into his belt, handed Mistel the lantern, took her hand, and they were off again.

Up ahead, Mistel spotted the stairs, but just before they reached it, a rotund figure stepped out of the shadows and blocked the way. He was bald, with a thin mustache and a smug grin that made her skin crawl. She'd seen him only once before, a day when they had played in the Dale.

Renshaw Thusk.

"Going somewhere?" he asked.

Chapter Forty-One
Zanna

BIG SURPRISE. KURTZ WAS LATE.

Zanna stood in the cold, damp bowels of Ice Island, just inside the heavy, ironbound door that led to the tunnel connecting the prison to the mainland. The silence was oppressive, broken only by the faint drip of water from the ceiling somewhere behind her.

He should have been here by now. Where was he?

She beat a fist against her thigh. He'd let her down again. The thought came unbidden, and it settled like a brick in her chest.

The door stood wide open behind her. Any moment, someone could stumble across her standing here like a fool with no reasonable excuse. The thought made her shift her weight from one foot to the other and punch her leg some more.

She was going to get caught, arrested, and thrown in a cell on the women's floor, all because Kurtz Chazir couldn't be trusted to keep a schedule.

She shoved the bitterness aside. She wasn't being fair. These past weeks, he'd proven himself reliable, shown his loyalty again and again.

And yet, how did she know he hadn't run off with some tavern wench? Fiora or Rilla? The idea burned in her chest. It was exactly the sort of thing the old Kurtz would have done. Pleasing himself without a thought of how it might affect those who counted on him. But he wasn't like that anymore. He'd said so, and she believed him. Didn't she?

She blew out a long breath, annoyed with her tendency to hold grudges.

The dark tunnel yawned ahead of her, swallowing what little light came from the single torch flickering on the landing halfway up the flight of stairs behind her.

Zanna's own words came to mind. How she'd asked Kurtz if he could handle the darkness. The way he'd snapped back had stung more than it should have. Kurtz had always been insufferably arrogant, but something in the tone of his denial had left her wondering.

What if the dark really had spooked him? Sure, Cole was with him, and the boy was more than capable of keeping Kurtz on task. But what if they needed her help?

She wedged a pebble into the doorframe, ensuring it wouldn't close and lock her out. It was a risk. A big one too. Someone might come along and shut the door fully, securing Crispen West's fate of being sold.

Zanna stepped into the suffocating blackness of the tunnel. She'd never been bothered by the dark—not even when Darkness had covered half of Er'Rets in its oppressive shroud—but for some reason, this darkness was so absolute it felt like a living thing, pressing against her skin and swallowing the sound of her footsteps. She counted each one, knowing the total distance was just over six hundred paces.

Even though she couldn't get lost, she still trailed one hand along the rough, damp wall to reassure herself. The cold seeped through the fingertips of her gloves, making her shiver. Each step felt tentative, and she strained to hear any sound.

By the time she reached three hundred sixty-two steps, a noise stopped her. Shallow, ragged breaths, straight ahead. Her heart jumped into her throat. Someone was there.

A scraping noise came next—boots scuffing against stone, perhaps?—then a dull thud as something struck the wall, followed by a muffled groan.

She shifted her feet, planting them firmly, wanting to be ready in case she needed to fight. Her boot caught on something, and whatever it was clattered ahead of her, sharp metal rolling over rock.

The breathing hitched and went quiet. For a moment, the only sound was the far-off *drip, drip, drip* of water.

A man's voice broke the stillness, hoarse and strained. "Who's there?"

Her shoulders eased, the weight falling away at the sound of that voice. "It's me."

"Zanna?" Kurtz rasped.

She exhaled. "What are you doing? Did something happen to Cole?"

"Mistel was taken."

Her heart lurched. "Taken? Where? By who?"

"Drustan. We think he took her through a secret passage under the Boar."

"Wait—Cole's alone? How could you leave him?"

"The king's with him," Kurtz said. "Came through the Veil. There wasn't time for me to linger."

"Yet here you are," she shot back.

A pause. "I told you I'd come." He spoke like he was gasping for air. "Blasted lantern ran out of oil."

She bit back a smile at how he'd misunderstood her criticism as surprise that he'd kept his word and come when she'd meant he was wasting time here in the middle of the tunnel. She decided to needle him in a way he could not mistake. "And you're afraid of the dark."

"I'm not afraid!" he snapped. "I'm fine."

His voice came from below her. Was he on the ground? "You're *not* fine. I could hear you unraveling. How long have you been here?" When he didn't answer, she softened her tone. "Breathe, Kurtz. Slowly in, slowly out." She crouched and reached out until she found his shoulder—he was sitting or kneeling. She placed both hands on his face. "Focus on me. On my breathing. Match it." She breathed in for three seconds and held it. Then exhaled for three.

Kurtz breathed with her, reached up and covered her gloved hand with his, drawing a shiver through her. They stayed like that a few seconds longer than they probably should have.

Quietly, tentatively, Kurtz said, "ZolZanna?"

He'd never said her full name before, and she liked it more than she cared to admit.

"You're going to have to trust me," she said.

When he spoke again, his voice was calmer. "I can do this. Just . . . lead the way, eh?"

Sure, *now* he was fine. His pride wouldn't let him admit otherwise. Zanna bit back a sigh. Typical Kurtz. Embarrassed at being caught broken, then annoyed about being embarrassed. Still, if pride was what kept him moving, she could work with that.

"Hold on to me." She stretched her arm down, her hand searching the air until it struck his forearm. His strong fingers closed around her wrist, the grip almost too tight, like a drowning man clinging to a lifeline.

With her free hand braced against the wall, Zanna started back toward the prison, towing Kurtz behind her like a ship dragging its anchor. His breathing steadied with every step, and despite herself, Zanna grinned.

This was going to be interesting.

Zanna pressed back against the damp stone wall, holding her breath as a pair of guards trudged past the entryway to the fifth floor. She glanced at Kurtz, who stood on the other side of the opening. Hand tight on the hilt of his dagger, he peeked out, then nodded.

Zanna went first, striding along the fifth-floor landing like she belonged on this level. Kurtz followed, their steps clicking in unison as they made their way past the cell doors on the right.

Over the waist-high rail on Zanna's left, the atrium yawned out, a vast diamond-shaped void plunging to the yard below. Railings curved around each floor in perfect symmetry, drawing the eye up and down the towering space. Every level mirrored the last—identical walkways, narrow cell doors. Distant voices and the faint clatter of chains were nearly swallowed by the sheer height of the space.

Crispen's cell was two from the end of a narrow corner, just before the walkway flipped around to the other side. A guard would be positioned there, would see them coming. Zanna only hoped he'd ask questions first before calling for help.

Sure enough, as they neared, a figure approached. A torch lit the guard's face just long enough for her to recognize Revik Tagg.

Her stomach twisted.

"You know him?" Kurtz asked from behind her.

"Unfortunately, yes," she whispered. "He's smaller than most guards, but has a crude fixation on me."

"Can we use that?"

The thought made it feel like worms were crawling over her body, but she swallowed hard and said, "I'll try."

"Then I'll hang back a bit," Kurtz said.

Wonderful. Tagg strode toward her, his gait casual, but his dark eyes gleamed in a way that made her cringe. She stopped and forced herself to hold still as his gaze roamed over her.

"Well, now, Anna Tankel, this ain't your floor." His grin was all teeth. "Decided to take me up on my offer at last?"

What would Mistel do? Zanna curled her lips into a playful smirk, pretending his very presence didn't turn her stomach. She traced a finger down the front of his uniform. "Couldn't stop thinking about it. But... maybe somewhere a little more private?"

His smirk widened. "Knew you'd come around." He leaned in, the stench of ale thick on his breath, and reached for her waist. "Couldn't resist me, huh?"

Kurtz cleared his throat.

Tagg stiffened, and Zanna stepped aside so the man could see Kurtz clearly.

His eyes narrowed. "Who's that?"

Kurtz moved before Tagg finished speaking. Quick and brutal, he drove his knee into Tagg's gut. As the guard doubled over, wheezing, Kurtz struck the back of his head with the pommel of his dagger.

Tagg crumpled.

Zanna wiped her damp palms against her tunic. It was over.

Kurtz nudged Tagg's unconscious form with his boot, then grinned at her. "Well done, eh? That was rather enchanting."

"Shut up and keep watch." Zanna knocked hard against his shoulder as she shoved past and yanked the keys off Tagg's belt. She found the fifth-floor master and shoved it into the lock. The bolt groaned as it slid back, and she opened the door.

Inside, a man slumped against the far wall, his wrists and ankles shackled, his face thin.

Crispen West.

His head lifted at the sound of the door, and he blinked as he took in Kurtz, dragging Tagg inside. "What—?"

"No time." Zanna crouched to unlock the chains around his wrists. "We're getting you out of here."

When she moved to his ankles, West rubbed the raw skin of his wrists. "Where are you taking me?"

"To Cole," Kurtz said, offering him a hand up.

The boy's name lit up West's eyes. "You're friends of my son?"

"Best friend he's got." Kurtz pulled West to his feet. "Now, stick close and keep quiet, eh?"

Kurtz led the way out, and Zanna shut the door behind them, leaving Tagg as the new occupant of the cell. Good riddance.

They moved quickly, back to the stairwell and down, their escape unhindered. Zanna fell a few paces behind, continuing to glance back to make sure they weren't seen.

Up ahead, a voice cut through the quiet. "Well, well."

Zanna froze and pressed herself against the wall at the bottom of the stairs. She carefully stole a glance around the corner. At the far end of the passage, Verdot Amal stood in the dim torchlight, arms crossed as if he'd been expecting them. Six guards flanked him, swords drawn and fixed on Kurtz and Crispen. Zanna held her breath, willing herself to remain unseen.

"This is disappointing, Chazir," Verdot said. "You'd think thirteen years in the Pit would have left you with more sense. But you always choose the wrong side, don't you?"

"The only disappointment here is you," Kurtz said. "Selling men like cattle? You won't get away with it."

"You'll think twice about that when you pledge your service to the Hamartano women as their newest eunuch."

"Never going to happen."

"You're a pawn, Chazir. You always have been. You think I didn't know you sent Fiora Lingel to me? You walked straight into a trap. Again."

"What do you mean, again?"

"I think you know."

Zanna wished she could see Kurtz's face. Though he faced away from her, she noticed him straighten and square his shoulders.

"You know what a maggot is, Verdot?" Kurtz asked. "It's a parasite. Born from filth. Lives off rotting flesh. Well, maggots turn into flies, they do. Buzz around, spreading filth wherever they land, thinking they're important. But in the end, they're just carriers of decay. That's what you are, buzzing about in the shadows, feeding off the ruin of others."

"Fancy words, but I'm not the one foolish enough to walk back into a prison."

"If you're going to kill me, get on with it, eh?"

Verdot tsked. "Considering what Jaelport is paying these days for eunuchs, that would be a waste." He gestured to the guards. "Take them."

Kurtz lashed out as the nearest man approached, landing a solid punch. West tried to fight as well, but in his weakened state, he barely got in a blow before being forced to his knees.

Zanna tensed and ground her teeth, wanting to run out and help them, but they were terribly outnumbered, and if she was going to do any good at all, she needed to be free and stay that way.

It took three men to force Kurtz to the floor and wrench his hands behind his back.

"Throw them in the holding cell," Verdot said. "They ship out in the morning."

"You think this ends with you selling me off?" Kurtz yelled.

Verdot walked away. "It ends when I say it does."

Zanna's heart pounded as the guards dragged Kurtz and Crispen away. Every muscle in her body screamed to act. She couldn't just let them be taken. Not like this. But what could she do?

Without a second thought, she turned and headed for the stairs leading to the underground tunnel.

She needed to get help.

Chapter Forty-Two
Cole

Cole shoved Mistel behind him and lifted his sword into first position. Kurtz's coaching came to mind. *Feet steady. Hands loose. Breathe.*

Thusk didn't carry himself like a trained fighter, which gave Cole a sliver of hope his odds might be better than he thought. In fact, the man wasn't even wearing a sword.

"We don't want any trouble," he said. "Just let us go."

Thusk's lip curled. "It's too late for that. The girl has already been sold."

A fiery surge swept over Cole. "You don't have the right to sell anyone."

"It's not about rights," Thusk said. "It's about opportunity. And I'm not letting a couple of minstrels get in my way." He gestured at them as if they were beneath notice. "Deal with this. Make it quick and quiet, and don't harm the girl. We've a schedule to keep." Thusk turned on his heel and walked toward the door. "The rest of you, we're moving out."

Cole eyed the clear path to the stairs. "Come on!" He grabbed

Mistel's hand and ran, only to slide to a stop when a man stepped into their path, sword in hand.

Drustan.

Cole's former stepbrother grinned that canine snarl that had haunted Cole's nightmares for so many years. "What's the matter, Coley? You scared?"

Cole's stomach twisted, but he met Drustan's gaze head-on. Arman had made him strong and courageous. Bold as a cham. More than a conqueror. "Not this time."

With a shout, Cole struck first. Drustan darted aside, laughing as he parried blow after blow with ease. Clashing steel rang out in the dark. Drustan's attacks came fast, calculated, and though Cole deflected them, each strike sent jolts up his arms.

Drustan was clearly stronger, but that didn't mean he was smarter.

The fight pressed on, fierce and unrelenting. Cole slashed across Drustan's arm, drawing blood, but a second later, Drustan's counterstrike nipped Cole's side. He grimaced at the searing pain but refused to falter. Not this time. Never again.

From the corner of his eye, he saw Mistel grab something from a crate and hurl it at Drustan. A clay pot smashed against his shoulder and scattered shards across the floor.

Drustan staggered, and his gaze snapped toward Mistel. Before he could go after her, Cole lunged forward and swung at his side. Drustan twisted, barely evading the blade, and countered with a vicious downward slash. Steel clanged against steel as Cole parried. Drustan's blade slid down Cole's until their hilts locked.

"You think you're a man now, Coley?" Drustan said. "You'll always be a sniveling baby."

Cole growled and shoved Drustan back. He struck again and again, driving him toward the crates. Drustan deflected each blow, wolfish grin steady.

Another pot sailed past Cole's shoulder, straight for Drustan's head. He ducked, and the clay shattered against the wall behind him.

Mistel was already reaching into the crate for another.

Drustan sprang toward her. Cole seized the opportunity and aimed a quick strike at Drustan's thigh. The blade sliced a shallow line through his trousers. Drustan hissed and swung wildly, forcing Cole to leap back.

A third pot caught Drustan squarely in the chest. He stumbled and coughed as shards and dust rained around him.

"You little wretch." He jabbed his sword at Cole, who shifted to block.

Drustan had been feinting, though, and while Cole overextended the reach of his block, Drustan spun toward Mistel.

"Get back!" Cole shouted, but it was too late.

Drustan drove his elbow against Mistel's temple, and she crumpled to the floor. A fourth clay pot slipped from her fingers and rolled toward her feet.

"Mistel!" Cole yelled.

Drustan chuckled as he stalked toward Cole, sword gripped at his side. "Don't worry, Coley. She'll wake up—eventually. Once I've cut you to pieces."

The sight of Mistel's crumpled body ignited a fire in Cole's chest. "You're not taking anyone else from me."

He charged, swinging his sword in a relentless barrage, each strike fueled by a mix of rage and desperation. Drustan barely managed to parry the onslaught, his grin faltering as Cole drove him back step by step. He was no longer a towering monster. He was a man who could bleed. And Cole would make him.

He gripped the sword with both hands and drove forward hard, jabbing at Drustan's chest, swiping for his feet. The clashing blades rang through the warehouse as their fight raged on, each blow louder than the last. Cole's muscles burned, but he refused to falter, repeating Kurtz's training in his mind.

Hold your ground. Don't retreat.

Drustan's sword flew from his hand and skidded behind a crate. He bolted toward it. Cole climbed over the crate and leaped down on the other side, landing between Drustan and his weapon.

"Yield," Cole said.

Drustan drew a dagger from his belt. "I'd rather not." He sprinted toward Mistel—who was now stirring—and slid on his knees beside her, dragging her up against him and pressing the blade to her throat.

She yelped, her hands flying to Drustan's forearm.

"Drop the sword, or I'll cut her," Drustan said.

Cole froze. Memories crashed over him. A small boy, powerless, watching as Drustan and his brother, Fen, pinned down Peat. Hearing the helpless puppy yelp as the knife did its work.

Worse, Cole recalled Kurtz saying, *"If a blade is at your skin, you're dead."*

"Maybe I'll give her scars to match the king." Drustan mimed a slash down Mistel's cheek. "Or I'll start with her ears, like I did with that mutt of yours." He shifted the dagger to hover over Mistel's ear.

Something inside Cole snapped. "If that blade so much as touches her, you will die."

"Ooh." Drustan chuckled darkly. "Threats don't sound much like threats coming from you, Coley."

Yet if Drustan had wanted to kill Mistel, he would have done so already. Thusk needed her alive, and while Cole didn't want to make the wrong choice when her life was at stake, all he could do was try and talk Drustan down.

"What's the matter, *brother?*" Cole asked. "Using the girl to sneak in a rest? If you're tired, just say so."

"I'm not tired."

"Then I guess you're just a coward if you need to hide behind Mistel. You've always been a coward, Drustan. Hurting anything smaller than you to try and prove you're strong. You want to fight me? Fight me like a man."

Drustan growled and shoved Mistel away so hard, she fell to the floor. Cole seized that moment to rush in and attack. His blade struck Drustan's dagger, then he swung around and thrust toward Drustan's belly. Drustan dodged, but not fast enough. Cole's sword nicked him. Teeth bared, Drustan jabbed his dagger at Cole, who parried easily, pushing Drustan back until his heels met the top edge of the stairs going down.

Drustan swung wildly. Cole blocked, and the force of his heavier blade against the smaller one broke the dagger in two. The tip clanged to the floor.

"Yield," Cole said.

Drustan's stare burned hot. "Never."

He lunged for Cole's waist. Cole whipped his sword in a brutal arc. The blade hit, jerking to a halt as it cleaved into Drustan's middle.

Drustan dropped to the floor. Blood quickly soaked the front of his tunic. He gasped for breath, eyes wide as blood pooled on the floor beneath him.

Cole looked down on him, hands trembling. "I should cut you to pieces," he said, "like you did to Peat."

Drustan's focus dimmed, and Cole waited, wanting to witness this man's final breath, wanting to see justice done, wanting to—

"Cole?"

Mistel's soft voice jerked him back from the abyss. He turned and met her gaze.

"Can we go?" she asked.

Cole glanced back at Drustan, whose lifeless eyes now stared at nothing. Cole wiped his sword clean on Drustan's pant leg, then threaded his sword through the loop on his belt.

He took a deep breath and nodded. "Let's get you back to Fat Vandy's."

"No," she said. "We're going to get your father. Kurtz and Zanna might need help."

He hoped they were already out and safe, but it would be good to make sure. Yet he didn't want to lead Mistel right back into danger.

"Hey." Mistel threaded her fingers with his and squeezed. "We'll be okay. I just saw you fight. You're amazing."

Cole felt a flicker of something that came so rarely, he almost didn't recognize it.

Worthiness.

Before he could dwell on it, Mistel slid her arms around his neck and kissed him.

The warmth of her lips seared through every layer of doubt he'd ever worn like armor. For a heartbeat, the world stilled. Not because they were safe—they weren't. Not because the mission was over—it wasn't. But because, in that moment, Cole realized he was strong enough to protect what mattered. He was someone Mistel believed in.

She released him. "Let's go find your father."

Yes. They'd go help Kurtz and Zanna to make sure they succeeded. "First, we need to get outside," he said. "The king is waiting."

He led her to the door, and they stepped out into a cold blizzard, snow up to their shins and swirling around them in the dark night.

Cole made sure his shields were lowered and his mind open. "Your Highness?" he called.

A distant voice answered. "Haven't seen him."

Cole's gaze snapped down the street to a man on horseback, holding a lantern. Lovell Dunn. Behind him, more riders approached, their dark silhouettes cutting through the snowy haze.

As the group gathered around them, Cole recognized Jol Quimby and five others: Torin Oxbow, Gunnar Gedmund, Lysander Thane, Thakkar Oruk and Alden Wroxton.

"Good to see you both on your feet and breathing," Quimby said.

"Renshaw Thusk is selling Ice Island prisoners as slaves," Cole said. "He and his men are around here somewhere."

"Aye," Dunn said. "We happened upon a few of them. No sign of Thusk, though."

You found her! Achan's voice burst between Cole's ears. *What took you so long? I was starting to worry.*

I ran into a few snags, Cole thought. *Any word from Kurtz?*

Not in some time, Achan voiced. *And you've been gone almost two hours.*

Two? Kurtz should have been back by now. *I'd like to see if they need help,* Cole thought.

Good idea, Achan voiced. *I'll go with you as far as I can. I'd tell you to take some of Lord Livna's men along, but even though they now know about Thusk, I'd still rather keep your involvement in the Mârad a secret, if I can.*

Cole heartily agreed. "Can someone give us a lift back to the Black Boar?" he asked Dunn. "We left our horses in the stables."

"There really an underground tunnel from here to there?" Dunn asked.

"Just follow the stairs down," Cole said. "You can't miss it."

Dunn dismounted. "Take Quimby's and my horses," he said. "Leave them in the stable at the Boar when you trade for yours. We'll explore that tunnel and get our horses on the other end."

Cole agreed, and before long, he and Mistel were riding Dunn's and Quimby's horses toward the Black Boar. Adrenaline had filled him with energy. He'd defeated Drustan and saved them both from being sold. Yet as they traded the horses for Cherix and Bart and rode toward Cliffwatch, Cole knew that their fight was far from over.

Chapter Forty-Three
Mistel

COLE LOVED HER.

The thought glimmered in Mistel's memory like candlelight on a blade: beautiful and a little terrifying. Her heart hadn't stopped racing since they'd escaped from that horrible warehouse. Sure, she'd stolen the guard's keys and would have gotten out of the cage on her own, but what could she have done against Drustan and his sword? If Cole hadn't come when he did...

But he *had* come. Her knightling had fought for her. Won for her.

Now, as they walked side by side through the tunnel beneath the frozen ocean, her limbs trembled, not just from the damp cold that had seeped deep into her bones, but from everything that had happened, including the vanishing of that man Cole said was Bahram Rakkel.

Mistel loved adventure, yes. But not the kind that rendered her helpless—she eyed the red stain on Cole's tunic—not the kind that ended with someone she cared about bleeding, sword in hand, standing between her and a monster.

She tugged her cloak tighter, grateful she still had it, grateful Cole was still with her. "How do runes stop bloodvoicing magic?" she asked, needing something to talk about, to distract her from what they'd just survived. "Shouldn't Arman's magic be unstoppable?"

Cole shot her a sideways glance. "Just because Arman created something doesn't mean people can't manipulate it. We're all free to make our own choices."

The logic of that settled over Mistel like an unbalanced yoke. Before she could respond, a noise rose ahead, soft but distinct—the scuff of boots on stone.

She stiffened. "Turn off the light."

"But we won't be able to—"

Mistel reached toward the lantern in Cole's hand and turned the damper until the flame snuffed out and plunged them into darkness. Silence stretched around them. She drew her cloak tighter around her shoulders and edged closer to Cole. Perhaps she should have listened to him.

A familiar voice cut through the darkness. "Cole?"

Mistel exhaled a long breath. "Zanna."

"We're here!" Cole called.

He found Mistel's hand and pulled her forward. She disliked moving blindly but trusted his sure steps to lead them safely.

Ahead, a faint stripe of golden light cut through the blackness. A door, cracked open and lit with distant torchlight. The door into Ice Island.

Zanna emerged from the shadows just outside the door. "It was a trap," she said. "They knew we were coming."

Mistel's stomach dropped.

"What happened to Kurtz?" Cole asked. "My father?"

"Captured," Zanna said. "Verdot plans to sell them both in the morning. They're in a cell on the ground floor."

"Then we get them out," Mistel said.

Cole gave her a sharp look. "Not without a plan."

"Don't get too close," Cole said, taking hold of Mistel's hand.

Warm, steady fingers. Arman help her, that hand had said *I love you* not so long ago, and now it wanted her to stay safe.

Two guards stood outside the door of the holding cell. Zanna had called the big one with warrior braids Nesson, and the other, all beard and attitude, Boreth.

"I'll be careful." Mistel kissed Cole's knuckles. Then she let go, squared her shoulders, and sauntered out into the corridor, voice rising into song.

> *"I don't belong here.*
> *Why do I try so hard to fit?*
> *I have so many feelings in a day.*
> *It's hard to know what to do or say."*

Nesson lifted his head. "What are you doing in here, poppet?"

"Do you remember me, Master Nesson?" Mistel asked, tilting her head just a bit.

"Should I?"

"The minstrels," Boreth said, stepping closer. "Sang out in the yard a few weeks back."

His belt jingled, and Mistel eyed the lovely, shiny keys hanging there. She beamed and stepped closer. "Did you enjoy our performance?"

"Sure, I did."

"You didn't say why you're here, miss," Nesson said. "And at this hour?"

Before she could spin a long tale, Zanna stormed down the corridor toward them, her expression so fierce, it almost scared Mistel. "You!" she yelled. "I told you not to leave the room."

Mistel darted behind Boreth and clutched his arm. "She just wants to spoil my fun."

"What's this about, Anna?" Boreth asked. His arm, raised between Zanna and Mistel, proved he'd bought Mistel's act.

"She needs to wait where the warden put her," Zanna said.

"It's so boring there." Mistel circled to Boreth's other side, keeping him between her and Zanna.

"I need her out of here," Zanna snapped.

"Why's she here so late, anyway?" Nesson asked.

"Wait a minute," Boreth said. "I say we hear her out."

While they argued, Mistel's fingers slipped the key ring free from Boreth's belt. Just a little tug, a shift of weight, and *behold*, they were in her pocket. She bit back a grin and whistled sharply.

Cole burst from the shadows and punched Nesson in the face. Zanna elbowed Boreth. The guards fought back. In the chaos, Mistel scrambled to the door, pulse hammering as she fumbled through a dozen keys.

Cole's shoulder slammed into her back, knocking her against the door.

She yelped.

"Sorry," he shouted, still swinging at Nesson.

Finally, a key turned, the lock clicked, and Mistel shoved the door open. There stood Kurtz, alive and bouncing on his toes. Crispen sat slumped against the wall.

Kurtz grinned so wide she could see both his dimples. "I should've known the key thief would come for us."

Mistel gestured out the door toward the brawl. "I think they could use your help."

"Happy to lend a hand."

Kurtz charged into the fray, and within moments, both guards were down. Zanna and Cole dragged Nesson into the cell, and Kurtz followed, hauling Boreth by the ankles.

"Son," Crispen said.

Cole helped his father stand. For a moment, neither moved. They just looked at each other. Then Cole briefly embraced Crispen. And just as Cole started to let go, his father pulled him into a fierce embrace. Mistel blinked away the sting in her eyes, smiling at the reunion. When they finally broke apart, everyone left the cell, and Mistel locked the guards inside.

As they raced back down the curling stairs, Kurtz swiped a torch from the wall.

"I much preferred my second, shorter stay on the island," he said. "But I'd rather not come back, eh?"

At the tunnel, they headed across the chilly darkness. Cole caught Mistel's hand as they ran. She felt happier than she had in weeks. Maybe forever. Love and success and hope made everything light. Surely there was a song in all this.

They eventually reached the stairs on the other end, climbed up, and exited the cave near Cliffwatch, where the acrid scent of smoke filled the night air.

"Something's on fire," Cole said.

Kurtz veered away from where they'd left the horses and followed the path toward the gatehouse.

Zanna called after him, "Where are you going?"

"To stop Verdot."

Of course he was.

Mistel followed with the others. The gatehouse was deserted, the gate open, and in the bailey, a wagon with two hitched horses stood empty.

Kurtz charged up the steps to Verdot's office, three at a time. The smoke grew thicker and stung Mistel's eyes.

At the top, Mistel paused in an open doorway and blinked through the haze into an office. A woman stood behind the desk, feeding scrolls into an iron brazier. Flames hungrily licked at the parchment.

Mistel gasped. "Rilla?"

Kurtz drew up sharply before the desk. "What are *you* doing here?"

Rilla, the barmaid from the Ivory Spit, glanced up. "It's not what it looks like."

"Well, I'm looking right at you, I am," Kurtz said, "and I have no idea what it looks like. What in blazes are you doing?"

"She's burning evidence," Cole said.

Kurtz vaulted over the desk and grabbed Rilla, who yelped but managed to toss another bundle of scrolls into the fire before Kurtz caught her wrists.

"Put that out!" he yelled.

Cole grabbed a water pitcher off the sideboard and doused the fire. Mistel snatched a cloak from a hook and threw it over the flames. The edges lit, but she folded the cloth in on itself, and the extra layers smothered the fire.

Footsteps pounded outside. "I've got the rest of what I left upstairs."

Verdot Amal.

Mistel's heart fluttered. This was it. They were going to catch the villain.

Zanna pushed Crispen behind the open door and drew her sword, every inch the fierce warrior.

Rilla stared at Zanna. "Don't hurt—"

Kurtz clamped a hand over her mouth and crouched with her, low and hidden by the desk. Cole wrapped his arm around Mistel's waist and tugged her against the sideboard with him. His touch steadied her. She eyed the cut on his side and wanted to say something, but the scrape of the door drew her attention.

Verdot entered, arms full of scrolls, and halted mid-stride. "Rilla?"

Zanna stepped away from the wall and slammed the door behind him. "I smelled smoke," she said coolly.

Mistel held her breath as Verdot looked Zanna up and down. "Miss Anna. Are you starting your shift? Or just coming off?"

"I'm finished with Ice Island."

Verdot chuckled nervously. "Ah, well, as you can see, it's very late. I'm just tidying up. Do have a good evening. If you need something, come back tomorrow when—"

"You won't be here tomorrow." Cole stepped out from behind the shelf, a fierceness in his gaze that stirred Mistel's heart.

"Master Tanniyn." A vein bulged in Verdot's forehead as he watched Cole cross the office. "The hour is quite late."

Cole edged past Verdot, opened the door, and stuck his head out.

"This is most irregular," Verdot said.

Cole turned, beaming as he stood just on the outside of the door. He spread his arms wide and said, "He's here."

Verdot frowned and peeked past Cole. "Who?"

"The king has a message for you. He says, 'Put to the test, you have failed to meet his standards.'"

Verdot blinked, his jaw working as he stammered, "Th-the k-king? Here?"

"Standing right beside me," Cole said, smirking. "Due to the runes, he can't see inside your office, but don't worry. I've told him everything."

Verdot's frown deepened as his gaze swept out the door.

Mistel looked too, biting back a grin at Cole, standing alone. Oh, but she loved a bit of drama. While she never wanted to return to the Veil, she wished she could see Achan right now.

"His Highness is in the Veil, Master Amal," Cole said.

Verdot's lips parted, but no sound came out. His gaze darted wildly around Cole, and as the weight of Cole's words settled, the color drained from his face. The scrolls he held slipped. He struggled to keep hold of them, but several tumbled to the floor.

He stepped back, using one foot to keep them from rolling, and bumped into Zanna. He jumped.

Mistel had to press her lips together to keep from laughing. Verdot Amal looked every inch the guilty villain.

Kurtz popped to his feet in one swift motion, hauling Rilla upright, one hand still clamped over her mouth. "I caught the arsonist," he said. "Shall we have her thrown in prison? It's just a quick dogsled ride away."

Verdot straightened his coat, sweat glistening on his brow. "Oh. Yes. Yes, of course." His gaze flicked from Rilla to the half-burnt scrolls and back again. Then the hunx turned on his partner in crime. "Woman, what are you doing in my office?"

Rilla wrenched free of Kurtz's hand. "Helping you destroy evidence, you fool. And don't think for a moment you'll pin all this on me. I know everything, and I'm happy to sell my secrets to the highest bidder."

From just outside the door, Cole chuckled. "The king has offered one rutah. Anyone care challenge him?"

Zanna crossed her arms.

Mistel tapped her chin. "I'd bid, but I left my coin purse with my other cloak."

"You won't get a penny out of me," Kurtz said flatly.

Cole shrugged. "Looks like the king wins. He says he's listening, Miss Vandy."

Verdot took a step toward the door, but Zanna blocked him, blade gleaming. "You'd best stay put."

Mistel caught the flicker of panic in his eyes just before Rilla latched onto her last weapon—her voice.

"You want the truth?" she spat at Kurtz. "You broke my heart when you ran off to join the Kingsguard, so when I saw you were back, I thought you'd come for me. But no. You rejected me again."

"I'm sorry," Kurtz said.

Rilla's voice cracked. "I wanted to hurt you back, so I listened.

Learned what I could. And when I realized you were sniffing around Verdot, I went to the man himself." Her smile turned brittle. "For a fee."

"She tried to extort me," Verdot said. "I've done nothing wrong."

"You lying snake," Rilla said. "When I found out Kurtz wanted to help Master West escape, I told Verdot, and we made a plan to capture them so he could sell them to the Ebens."

Mistel's stomach twisted. Sell them. To giants. She shot a quick glance at Cole. His jaw was tight.

"Shut up, fool woman!" Verdot yelled, his face blotchy. "You're digging both our graves."

Kurtz released Rilla and stepped around the desk. "What did Lord Nathak promise you?" he asked Verdot. "To get your help in the plot against King Axel."

Verdot's chin jerked up. "I don't have to tell you anything. In fact, you all need to leave my office immediately."

Cole lunged over the threshold and dragged Verdot outside the door.

"Unhand me! You have no authorityyy ee-ahh!" Verdot crumpled to his knees, dropping the remaining scrolls as he clutched his head and whimpered.

"His Highness would like a word." Cole's voice came calm and steady from outside the doorway. "He says he has authority here."

Verdot rocked on his knees and let out a choked whimper. "Yes, yes, of course, Your Highness," he said. "I-I only wanted a title. A title that should have been mine when my brother died with no male heirs. But the queen . . . she and Nitsa were friends. And the queen convinced the king to let women inherit and rule. If it had only been Nitsa, I could have waited. But the woman had five daughters. *Five.* I knew I would never get what was rightfully mine."

"The king demands to know your role in the assassination of his parents," Cole said.

Verdot let out a pitiful whine. "I forged letters," he admitted. "To Lord Agros. From Lord Agros. Between Kurtz and Eagan."

Kurtz sucked in a sharp breath. "I knew it, I did."

"What else?" Cole said.

Verdot wrung his hands. "Once the queen bloodvoiced the word *stray*, Nathak saw his opportunity to frame Eagan and Kurtz. He asked me to forge the letters. And once everything was set, I was to wake Gavin and pretend to help."

Kurtz's voice turned to iron. "Which is why you really refused to testify at the hearing."

Verdot nodded, shoulders sagging. "The bloodvoice mediators would have caught me otherwise. Nathak told me to pretend to be a coward. And I didn't mind. Not if it got me what I wanted. But it didn't. Nathak said since Duchess Amal was on the Council of Seven, we had to wait. He had me appointed warden here—*temporarily*—until he could get me placed over Carmine. But he lied. Repeatedly. I heard about his marriage proposals to the duchess and later to Lady Averella. He wanted Carm for himself. He was never going to give me what was mine."

"Then why continue helping him?" Zanna asked.

Verdot let out a hollow laugh. "I didn't. I helped myself. I helped the new king. I helped you and Eagan get out of Ice Island. I made up for my sins."

What a hunx. "Yet made a host of new ones, by the sound of it," Mistel said.

Kurtz crossed his arms. "Who else helped Nathak kill the king?"

Verdot's eyes darted around as if searching for an escape. "Kenton and his guards. And the Hadad. He spoke to us all."

"What about Careeanne?" Kurtz asked. "What about Falkson?"

Verdot shook his head frantically. "I don't know who else helped. I swear to you. Nathak kept most of his supporters separate back then. Said it was safer that way in case we were questioned."

Cole's gaze flicked to the brazier, where bits of charred

parchment still curled in the embers. "Why were you burning documents?"

"Rilla said Thusk was captured. I had to destroy anything that tied me to him."

Kurtz turned to Rilla. "And how did *you* know Thusk was captured?"

Rilla smirked. "I paid a man to follow you."

Mistel clicked her tongue. "Well, you should have demanded a refund, because Thusk's men were caught, but he wasn't."

"Yet," Kurtz murmured.

"In the name of King Gidon Hadar, you are both under arrest," Cole said, voice ringing firm from outside the door. "You will be held on Ice Island as you await your trial."

Verdot whimpered again, but Rilla just glared at Kurtz.

"This is your fault," she said.

"No," he said. "I'm done taking the blame for someone else's crimes."

"We'll put them in the Cliffwatch dungeon for tonight," Zanna said.

"I'll help." Kurtz grabbed Rilla's arm and dragged her toward the door. "We'll need Lord Livna to appoint a new warden first thing tomorrow."

"The king says he'll speak to Lord Livna," Cole said. "He thanks us for our service."

Mistel brushed ash from her sleeve and curtsied. "The pleasure was entirely ours."

"While we're gone," Kurtz said, "see what evidence you can salvage from that brazier."

As Kurtz and Zanna led Verdot and Rilla out of the office, Mistel's heart swelled. It was over. Truly over. They'd completed their mission.

She threw her arms around Cole and pressed a kiss to his jaw.

"We did it! The pieces of this twisted puzzle are finally falling into place."

He smiled, gaze warm and steady on hers. He slid his hands around her waist and pulled her close. "Wouldn't have been able to do it without you." He brushed a kiss to her lips. "I love you, Mistel Wepp."

She pulled back just enough to see the sincerity in his hazel eyes. "I love you too."

The words came so easily, it startled her, but the truth of them hummed through her bones like a chord. For so long, she'd chased adventure like it was the only thing that made her feel alive. But Cole, he was an adventure she'd never seen coming. The kind that anchored her instead of pulling her apart.

He loved her. And she loved him back. His wit and worry, his thoughtfulness and courage. And oh, that voice. She could listen to him sing forever.

"I suppose that makes the whole 'pretend cousin' thing a little awkward," she said, grinning up at him.

Cole laughed and kissed her again, this time slower, sweeter.

For once, Mistel didn't care what came next. The kingdom could wait. The world could wait. She had everything she needed, right here in his arms.

Chapter Forty-Four
Cole

Four months later

THE CHILLED WIND PUSHED AGAINST Cole's back as he stood at the bow of the *Zephyr*, a sturdy cog slicing through the waves, bound for Land's End. The rhythmic creak of the mast and the ever-present crash of the sea against the hull filled his ears, adding to the joy of the moment.

His father stood beside him.

Crispen West. Alive. Free.

Even after all this time, Cole still couldn't believe it.

Over the past months, he'd gotten to know the man a little. There had been much to do in Tsaftown. Prince Oren had wanted them to find Renshaw Thusk, and they'd tried to no avail. Though they had also followed his associates and Sir Fenris's remaining Howlers, and with the help of Nash Erlichman, found evidence to implicate dozens. This they passed along to Lord Livna who rounded up the villains and found them new accommodations in the Ice Island prison under the fair oversight of Tom Raven, the new warden.

During this time, Cole had rented a room at the Ivory Spit for his father. After a week of hot meals in his belly and sleep in a soft bed, Crispen West had recuperated, ceased stuttering, and began telling the most outlandish tales. And while he wasn't exactly a helpful investigator, he was good company and, having a decent baritone singing voice, had joined in on some of the Wandering Songweavers's performances.

While Crispen had never heard the term Mârad in conjunction with Cole, Kurtz, Mistel, and Zanna, Prince Oren had decided the man knew too much about their mission and had better stick with the group lest he stay behind to tell stories. Cole was grateful. He hadn't been ready to say goodbye to the man just yet.

"I met Nonda Fawst on a ship out of Armonguard," his father said, pulling Cole back to the present. "She was headed for Carmine on her way back to Mitspah. I was bound for Tsaftown."

"Did you really?" Cole asked.

"Aye. She nearly knocked me overboard, arguing with the captain about the lack of deck space. Had a parrot on her shoulder and a jar of leeches under one arm that she claimed were 'for emergencies.' Made me promise to seek her out the next time I passed through Mitspah, which I did."

Cole sifted the words for truth and decided he believed all but the parrot.

"I'm sorry Nonda sold you," Father said, shaking his head.

"It was a blessing." Cole glanced at the horizon, where endless blue stretched from east to west. "Drustan and Fen were horrible. Things would have gotten worse if I'd stayed. Maybe Nonda knew that. Maybe she was actually trying to help me."

Crispen snorted. "I doubt that very much, but you're a good sort to think the best of people." He shot Cole a sidelong glance. "How long were you with Lord Yarden?"

"Just shy of ten years," Cole said. "He gifted me to the then–Crown Prince as a cupbearer, but the prince wouldn't hear of it. Made me a stable hand instead."

Crispen arched a brow. "Sounds like a decent fellow, our new king."

Cole turned and leaned back against the rail. The cold wind gusted into his face now, but that didn't bother him like the wound in his side from the fight with Drustan. The small cut was taking forever to heal. "He's a good man. I wish you could have heard him bloodvoice all of Er'Rets."

"As do I," Crispen said. "They say it was a once-in-a-lifetime moment. We heard about it the next day when the shift changed. Prison guards burst in like messengers fresh from a miracle. 'Light has returned!' and 'The real prince pushed back Darkness!' One of the guards said the shadows peeled right off the walls, like they wanted to go outside and see the sun for themselves. I'm not saying I believed him, but it's not often the guards speak to prisoners, yet that day, they couldn't keep their mouths shut. For once, hope was thicker than the jam between my toes."

Cole chuckled at that last comment. "I take it you won't miss the place."

"Not for a moment. Didn't think I'd ever get out of there. I wouldn't have, if it weren't for you. Thank you, son." His brow sank, and his lips turned down at the corners. "I'm sorry I let you down when you were small. I hope we'll be able to make up for lost time."

Heat crept up the back of Cole's neck. He scuffed his boot against the wooden deck. "I look forward to it. Father."

Crispen pulled Cole into a firm embrace, squeezing tightly. Cole let himself sink into his father's arms and the strange, unfamiliar warmth of family.

A pinch at his temples, and a voice entered his mind. *Achan Cham.*

Cole stepped back from his father. "Excuse me. The king is bloodvoicing."

"By all means, speak with the king. I'll see you later." He clapped Cole's shoulder and walked away.

Cole gazed out at the sea and thought an answer to the silent call. *Hello, Your Highness.*

How do you fare, Cole? Made it out of Tsaftown?

Yes, sir. We're aboard the Zephyr, *headed south toward our next destination.*

Be careful there. Inko has gone missing, and that's made us all nervous.

We'll take care, sir. And we'll find out what happened to him. Cole hoped the stalwart old knight was all right.

What about Mistel? Will she be coming back to Armonguard?

No, Cole thought, never more certain of anything. *Mistel is staying with me.*

You sure about that?

Absolutely. We're a team, and I can't do this without her. Nor would he want to.

A flash of orange caught Cole's eye, bright and unmistakable. Mistel had just emerged onto the main deck, the wind tugging at her curls. She walked to the rail and grabbed hold of the worn wood with one hand. Her gaze panned the ship and found his.

She smiled.

Cole smiled back. *Here she is now*, he thought. *And so I'll leave you.*

Is that so?

Yes, Your Highness. Unless you have further need of me.

Achan chuckled. *No, Cole. I simply wanted to check in. But I can take a hint.*

As the connection with the king faded from Cole's mind, he had already descended the steps from the bow to the main deck. He wove between coiled ropes and stacked barrels.

The mission ahead was uncertain, but for the first time in Cole's life, he wasn't afraid. He was capable of filling this role.

And perhaps the best part was that Mistel had weaseled her way in. She was part of the team now, and they couldn't do without her.

Cole would never want to.

Chapter Forty-Five
Mistel

Mistel tried not to grin as Cole climbed down the stairs to the main deck, his gaze fixed on her like she was the only thing in the world worth looking at. It set her heart pounding, and for some reason, that made her want to sing.

> *"With the wind in my hair, the sun shining bright,*
> *We dance over the waves in golden sunlight.*
> *With my hand tucked in yours, that's where I will be,*
> *Sailing with you on the deep blue sea."*

Cole reached her then and rested his elbow on the rail beside her, his gaze steady, warm. "New song?"

"Yes." She tucked a loose curl behind her ear. "It's about a hero who rescued me."

A slow grin spread across Cole's face, freckles getting lost as his cheeks deepened a shade. "I'd like to hear the rest of it sometime."

"Oh, you will. People are going to love it. In fact, I think we're going to make a lot of money off it."

Cole laughed, a rich, carefree sound she'd grown to treasure. "With you singing, I have no doubt of that."

She bumped her shoulder against his. "And you playing."

"Yes, that too." He tipped his head, studying her. "Ready for our next adventure?"

She flicked her finger against his arm. "Why do you think I followed you from Armonguard? You need me."

He didn't argue. Just nodded, quiet for a breath, then said, "I do need you."

The words sent warmth curling through her stomach. She studied him: his tousled brown hair, the sharp cut of his jaw, the way the wind toyed with his cloak.

"You're looking a bit smug, my knightling," she said.

He turned slightly to face her, his elbow still propped on the rail. "Am I?"

"Mm-hmm." She smoothed a crease on his tunic. "What's got you so pleased?"

His voice softened. "Just thinking about how blessed I feel. And that I wouldn't want to do any of this without you."

Mistel hadn't expected that. Oh, this boy made her heart sing. She turned her head to face him. "Good. Because I wouldn't let you."

The *Zephyr* surged forward, slicing through the vast blue water, sails billowing in the wind. Ahead lay adventure, danger, and the unknown. And for the first time in a long time, Mistel knew exactly where she belonged.

Right here.

With him.

Chapter Forty-Six
Kurtz

"I haven't felt worse in all my days," Kressy said, "but out here in the air, it's not so bad. Least I can breathe without feeling like my insides are about to stage a mutiny. Don't know how sailors do it every day for so long."

Kurtz leaned against the mizzenmast as he grinned down on Lady Tara's maid. "Ah, but you've got it all wrong, you do. See, sailors aren't immune to seasickness. They've just learned to stagger around like drunkards so no one can tell the difference."

Kressy laughed at this, which gave Kurtz a little thrill he hadn't felt in quite some time. The maid had a pretty laugh—high and lilting—the kind that made a man feel clever even when he wasn't. Not that *he* wasn't.

Kressy twirled a loose thread on her apron. "Still, standing too long makes me feel like I've got wobbly legs and a belly full of sloshing porridge."

"Well, if your legs give out, just make sure to fall my way, eh?" Kurtz said. "I'd hate to see good porridge go to waste."

Kressy giggled again, and Kurtz let his grin widen just a little.

He caught sight of Zanna across the deck, watching him, arms folded, eyes sharp.

Oh, that was too good to ignore.

So he leaned in, tilting his head just so, his voice dropping into that low, easy drawl women liked. "If you need to steady those wobbly legs, you could hold onto me, you could. Fair warning, though. Pretty lass like you, I might take that as an invitation to dance."

Kressy's cheeks pinked, but before Kurtz could lay it on any thicker, she smoothed her skirts and stepped back. "I should check on m'lady. Good day, Master Chazir."

"Duty calls." He winked.

Kressy hurried toward the cabins, and as soon as she was gone, Kurtz turned back to Zanna, half expecting her to still be glaring at him.

But she wasn't.

She had that knowing look instead. The one that struck him harder than it should and made his chest feel tight.

Memories of the tunnel slammed into him. The dark swallowing him whole. The way the walls had closed in once his lamp had sputtered out. The sick, despairing thought that maybe this time he wouldn't make it out.

And then . . . The feel of her hand on his skin, the calmness it had brought, steadying his breath.

If Zanna hadn't come looking for him . . . he might still be there.

Yet looking at her now made him nervous and a little out of control. He shoved off the mizzenmast and crossed the deck toward her. Just to clear the air. Nothing more.

"You didn't have to come with us, you know," he said when he reached her.

"Now that Prince Oren knows what happened to the prisoners and there's a new warden, my job there is done. He sent me with you. I'm here. Better get used to it."

Eben's breath, she was touchy.

"About what happened in that tunnel . . ." He exhaled sharply. "I'd appreciate it if you kept that to yourself."

Zanna arched a brow. "You think I'm going to tell everyone how you lost yourself?"

Those words stung. "I didn't lose myself. I was just . . . resting."

"You were in a ball on the ground, *crying*."

Now, just a minute. "I was *not* crying." His voice pitched too high, and he winced. "I don't cry."

She smirked. "You were in a fit of hysteria, Kurtz. If I hadn't come along, you'd probably still be lying there in the dark."

Bah. It was one thing for *him* to think that. Quite another for *her* to say it out loud.

Then she launched the killing blow. "You needed me. Admit it. You *needed* me."

Oh, but the way she said that lit him on fire, and not the good kind. "I didn't need you then, and I don't need you now." He stabbed a finger toward the deck. "You stay on your side of the ship, and I'll stay on mine, eh?"

With that, he turned on his heel and stalked toward the bow.

Why was he so rotting stubborn when it came to that woman? She brought out the worst in him.

And why did Prince Oren insist on shackling him with ZolZan the Barbarian? Surely she could be more useful *anywhere else*.

But no. Here she was. Part of his team.

The weight of leadership pulled on his shoulders, a burden he wasn't sure he wanted but had no choice but to carry. He was responsible for these people now. For getting the answers they needed. For keeping them all alive.

Including Zanna.

He huffed. She probably thought *she* was in charge.

The *Zephyr* creaked through the waves, the coast looming in the distance. The real danger lay ahead, and like it or not, he and Zanna had to figure out how to work together.

Even if it killed them.

Or drove him mad.

Or worse—

Made him *like* her.

Bonus Epilogue

Thank you for reading *Shadow of Ice Island*. We hope you loved the story. Find out what happens next with our Bonus Epilogue, a special gift, available only to our newsletter subscribers.

This Bonus Epilogue will not be released on any retailer platform, so scan our QR code to get your free gift. You acknowledge you are becoming a Sunrise Publishing and Jill Williamson subscriber. Unsubscribe from any of the newsletters at any time.

THANK YOU

Thank you again for reading *Shadow of Ice Island.* We hope you enjoyed the story. If you did, would you be willing to do us a favor and leave a review? It doesn't have to be long—just a few words to help other readers know what they're getting. (But no spoilers! We don't want to wreck the fun!) Thank you again for reading!

We'd love to hear from you—not only about this story, but about any characters or stories you'd like to read in the future. Contact us at www.sunrisepublishing.com/contact.

We also have regular updates that contain sneak peeks, reviews, upcoming releases, and fun stuff for our reader friends. Sign up at www.sunrisepublishing.com or scan our QR code.

COMING NEXT IN THE KING'S SPIES: SCOUNDREL OF CLAYMORE KEEP

Thirteen years in prison for a crime he didn't commit left Kurtz Chasir bitter, broken, and hungry for revenge. Now serving as the king's spy, he's hunting the woman who framed him—until his mission forces him to work alongside Zanna tan Quelle, a fierce warrior who challenges everything he thought he knew about trust, forgiveness, and love.

When they uncover a sinister conspiracy threatening to plunge the kingdom into eternal darkness, Kurtz faces an impossible choice: cling to vengeance or embrace the redemption Zanna—and his faith—offer him.

Can a man haunted by betrayal learn to trust again? Or will his quest for justice cost him everything—including his chance at love?

An enemies-to-lovers Christian fantasy romance full of espionage, adventure, and swoon-worthy moments.

Chapter One
Kurtz

Control was rarely offered. It was seized. Kurtz Chazir hadn't officially been handed the reins of this mission, but he knew what had to be done and didn't ask permission. Five lives depended on him to lead them through the sweltering desert to Barth, capital of Barth Duchy. It was their second mission as spies of the king, masquerading as a minstrel band called the Wandering Songweavers, a name that made them sound perpetually lost.

They weren't. Kurtz knew exactly where he was as he led their group along a dusty mountain path winding east through the Cela Mountain, a rolling sea of tawny hills dotted with sagebrush and twisted trees that stretched endlessly before them. Slower than the main road, but safer. And it cut a more direct path, it did, to the ruin where his contact would be waiting. If Kurtz missed that meeting, the trail to Careeanne might vanish along with any hope of proving who else had conspired with Lord Nathak to kill King Axel.

One might call Kurtz mad for chasing leads on a thirteen-year-old crime, but he had spent thirteen of the last fourteen years in prison, falsely accused of conspiracy in the murder of King Axel Hadar, a man he'd loved and respected. Now free, Kurtz meant to track down and hold accountable everyone who'd played a part in the king's assassination. At the top of that list was Careeanne Nariel, the woman who'd not only betrayed his trust years ago but framed him, then twisted the truth and testified against him. She'd all but put him and Eagan in prison herself.

While Prince Oren and Achan—Axel's son and Er'Rets' current king—did not begrudge Kurtz this side quest, it was not the current mission. That was twofold. First, to find Inko son of Mopti, the king's land warden, who'd vanished in Barth while cultivating crops. Kurtz wanted him found too. Inko was a respected Kingsguard Knight, retired from combat but still wise and capable. A friend, of sorts.

And second, to track down the Ice Island prisoners who'd been trafficked to Barth.

Two missions at once. No problem, eh? Kurtz could juggle both, he could.

What he wasn't used to was this heat. Raised in the North, he'd been content in Tsaftown's snowy winter and blissful in their first spring after the curse of Darkness had lifted. But after sailing south and crossing this blistering expanse, he understood why so many villains came from the southwest. Barth and its deserts were the cracked heel of Er'Rets: calloused, ugly, and dry as bone. The perfect place to hide if you were breaking the law or hiding from it.

The humid air pressed against Kurtz's lungs as he held his brisk pace—too brisk judging by the steady burn of Zanna tan Quelle's glare on his back. The half-giant female soldier rode behind him with Cole's father, Crispen West, who prattled on about how to know the time of day from the height of a cactus.

Cracked as desert clay, that one.

"They're nature's sundials," West said, "unless it's windy. Or they're shy."

Kurtz glanced back. Zanna's expression was flat as a blade. Hard to say what irked her more: West's nonsense or Kurtz's relentless pace.

Trailing at the back of the line, Cole Tanniyn and Mistel Wepp rode side by side, paying little attention to their surroundings. Lost in each other's company. Again.

Kurtz had trained Cole better. And while the cold the lad had caught on the ship explained some of his sluggishness, the greater problem was the ginger-haired songstress riding beside him—her figure could make even a travel-stained dress indecent. As useful as the girl had been on their last mission, the longer she and Cole spent in each other's company, the dimmer the lad became.

Still, the pair had helped Zanna rescue him and West from Ice Island. They were capable of heroics, though they hardly looked it. Not that Kurtz was one to talk. He'd made more blunders than the four of them combined.

Achan Cham.

The king's telepathic bloodvoice brought a smile to Kurtz's face. That the lad used his informal name with Kurtz pleased him. More than that, it soothed the deep-seated guilt he carried over King Axel's death. A death Kurtz should have prevented had he not been so smitten with Careeanne, the two-faced viper.

He lowered the shields around his mind and thought, *Yes, sir?*

How far are you from Barth? the young king bloodvoiced. *From the city, I mean?*

Day and a half, Kurtz thought.

Cortland does not answer me. I'm concerned.

The hairs on Kurtz's neck prickled. Cortland Agros had been sent to Barth with Inko to secretly audit Duke Falkson's books. *Could someone have discovered his true purpose? What does Jax say?*

There's some kind of darkness there that Jax doesn't understand, the king said. *I cannot see the city. It's similar to the runes hiding Ice Island or the smoke that covered the Chartom camp just outside Armonguard.*

That statement dumped ice water down Kurtz's spine. *Someone doesn't want bloodvoicers to see what's going on in Barth, eh?*

That was my first thought, the king voiced. *I don't like Magonian magery, and I like it even less in Barth. Cela and Barth combined...*

Would make a powerful force, they would. Did Jax find clues in the safe house? Signs of a struggle?

Sorry to confuse you, the king said. *Jax isn't in Barth. He chased a lead south and is in Armonguard at the moment. Cortland was fine when he left. Jax thinks the darkness is interfering with my magic.*

Logical, that is. Perhaps it's a fog spell like the Chartom mages used.

Yes, well, be on guard, Achan said, *but get there as quickly as you can. If Cortland is well, your goal hasn't changed. Get the band hired at a tavern, start listening, find Inko. And learn why so many Ice Island prisoners were trafficked there.*

Yes, sir.

Message me as soon as you can about Cortland, even if you must ride back outside the affected area.

Will do, sir.

The connection ended. Magonian magery in Barth? Kurtz recalled Yagil Hamartano's paranoia when they'd met in Ice Island. The convicted duke had warned him that the mages and black knights were in league. He'd also been certain someone meant to kill him. Then a few weeks before Kurtz left Tsaftown, Yagil had died—poisoned the coroner had said. If the man had been right about his own murder, was he also right about the mages and black knights working together?

Arman, let it not be.

The hot wind rose thick in Kurtz's ears, pelting him with

sand. He pushed Smoke harder up the path. Behind him, Zanna muttered.

"What was that?" Kurtz called over his shoulder.

"I said, what's your hurry? You're pushing these animals like we're outrunning a fire."

The woman could find fault in a sunrise. "If you want to stroll, find another escort."

"That's not an answer," she sang.

"Wasn't meant to be," he muttered.

She exhaled hard, like a bull ready to charge. A moment later, she rode up beside him, long legs astride her horse in worn canvas trousers: practical, improper, and maddeningly hard not to notice. She sat tall in the saddle, the afternoon sunlight glinting off her skin and that infernal braid swinging down her back like a whip.

"You do realize you're not the only one with orders," she said. "Some of the Ice Island women were taken to Meneton. That's where I should be headed."

"Then why aren't you?" he asked.

Her dark eyes narrowed, but she didn't answer.

He knew why. The king's command outweighed Prince Oren's. Achan wanted her to keep Mistel in check. Mistel wanted to be with Cole. And Cole was working with Kurtz. By logistics alone, Zanna answered to him, even if she loathed it.

Zanna fell back in line, letting Kurtz breathe easier.

At least for the time being.

He didn't speak again until he pulled them off the path just as twilight began to swallow the dusty hills. He dismounted and scanned the scrubland until he caught sight of a weathered stone arch—half collapsed and tangled in thorny brush—jutting from the slope overhead. His contact had been clear: camp within sight of the "broken gate."

"Let's make camp." Kurtz pointed to a patch of uneven ground some twenty paces from the gate. "There."

Zanna frowned, nodding over Kurtz's shoulder. "There's a cactus cluster up ahead. I could knot together—"

"We've gone far enough," Kurtz said.

She folded her arms. "I could knot together Mistel's scarves, make a sand shield. Less grit in that pretty smile of yours."

Kurtz sought out the cacti. She wasn't wrong, but it was too far from the gate. "Don't need you dressing up our campsite. I need you to make a fire."

"It's not decorative. It's functional. And I can do both."

"You look like you're doing nothing to me," Kurtz muttered, already moving up the slope.

Zanna swung down from her horse and yanked her gear from the saddle.

Before she could question his authority again, Kurtz repeated his orders. "Mistel, West—kindling. Cole—horses. Zanna—fire."

While they got to work, Kurtz climbed to the arch, scaring a pale desert skink into a cleft between two rocks. Up close, the leaning stones looked drunk. Half the stone wall behind the gate had collapsed into a gully. Long ago, mountain giants had built stone rings to mark sacred grounds where they communed with ancestors. Now it was but a remnant of a people who had vanished over time. Most travelers avoided such places, afraid curses clung to the stones. Kurtz didn't believe such long tales, but he welcomed the superstition. It kept prying eyes away.

A pebble rolled behind him. West appeared, stick in hand. Too thin from years on Ice Island, his clothes hung loose over bony shoulders. He whistled low, shading his eyes in the fading sunset, his freckled face an echo of his son's. "Old traders used to stack stones like that to mark where they buried their treasure. Bet there's silver under there."

Downhill, Mistel snorted, cradling a bundle of kindling against her hip. "You just made that up."

"I did not!" West said. "My great-uncle told me about it."

Zanna pulled her sword off her back and climbed closer, frowning up at the dark arch. "That's no trader's marker. It's a blood gate. Old as anything you'll find in these hills. Giants built them. We shouldn't be anywhere near it."

"Sounds ominous," croaked Cole as he fitted a nose sack to his horse, Cherix. His cold had sapped what little voice he had.

"Brilliant," Mistel muttered. "We're sleeping beside the entrance to the Lowerworld."

"That would make a fine song," Cole rasped.

"Enough, eh?" Kurtz snapped. "Horses. Kindling. Fire. I want it going before dark."

All but Zanna scattered. She stood her ground, hip cocked, arms crossed.

He fought back a grin. "Think you can handle that?"

She dug her heel into the ground and stalked toward the horses, grumbling about peacocks.

Kurtz chuckled under his breath. Maker help him, he liked getting under that woman's skin far too much for his own good.

Soon enough, a small fire crackled in the clearing, casting a soft glow against the rising dark. Cole was still off brushing one of the horses. West lay blessedly quiet on his bedroll. Mistel sat by the fire, humming as she fed small sticks to the flames. Zanna sat cross-legged opposite, sharpening her sword, her eyes tracking Kurtz's every move as he paced.

"I'll take first watch," he said.

"You need rest," Zanna said. "You've been riding like a madman all day."

"I'm fine."

"Fine is what people say when they're not fine."

He exhaled loud enough to be sure she heard it. "You sound like Sir Gavin. Back when he was my *nursemaid*."

"The Great Whitewolf is a genius."

"He's my cousin. Relentless, he was."

She stilled her sharpening stone. "What's the point of having a team if you won't let us pull our weight?"

Kurtz hated when she made good points. Relinquishing control made his skin itch. As much as he didn't want to admit it, Zanna was smart, strong, and more than capable of taking first watch.

"I'll take second watch," he said.

Her eyebrows arched high on her forehead. "*And* first watch?"

"You take first," he said.

She nodded and returned her attention to her blade.

"Don't make me regret it." He strode away from the fire. "I'm going for a walk."

"To do what?" Zanna called.

Blazes, that woman was nosy. "Still not my nursemaid," he called back.

Her satisfied chuckle drifted after him. "Try not to get lost in your own ego. I doubt any of us could find you."

He paused and glanced back. "Don't you have a post to watch?"

Her eyes glinted in the firelight. "Already am."

Cheeky female. Kurtz left before she could see the grin tugging at his mouth.

His contact had told him to meet the Hare after dark. Yet as Kurtz neared the gate, nothing stirred. Better to keep the ruin between his meeting and his team, so he circled wide, boots crunching softly over loose stones and brittle weeds. The last threads of twilight bled into the charcoal sky. He kept his hand near his sword, listening to every whisper of wind against the ancient stones.

No movement. No glint steel. No scent of another man's sweat. Yet the silence convinced him that someone was watching. He hoped the man would show before it got too dark.

Kurtz didn't like the not knowing. He couldn't afford a single mistake, not with Inko and half the prisoners from Ice Island still unaccounted for. He hadn't seen a watcher since the night he'd kissed Rilla Vandy at the Ivory Spit. The celestial creatures had appeared to warn him—because he'd been about to make a mistake he wouldn't have been able to take back. He still couldn't believe Rilla had conspired with Verdot Amal just to wound him for rejecting her, that his refusal had cut her that deep.

The same watcher had shown himself to Zanna, and later to Cole and Mistel, to help them. But for Kurtz, he only ever appeared when he was on the edge of disaster. By that logic, he should be glad he hadn't seen him lately. No watcher meant no grave errors. No traps he couldn't see coming.

The existence of watchers, also called *malakim*, should comfort him, proof that Arman had an eye on things. But all it did was remind him how little control he had. If the watchers were silent, he was on his own. And that, more than anything, made him feel small.

He slipped along the backside of the arch, about to give up when a low voice cut through the stillness.

"Kurtz Chazir."

He jerked a half step to the right, hand on his hilt. A shadow peeled away from the dark, lean and ragged as a waif. Perrin Vance—better known as the Hare—smirked as he raised a hand in mock surrender.

"You're late," he said.

"Traveling with others." Kurtz jerked his chin toward camp. "Came as fast as I could, I did."

"Got the money?"

"If you've got the information, eh?"

"At least let me see it," Vance said.

Jaw tight, Kurtz pulled two golds from his pocket. Costly, this meeting, but if it helped him find Careeanne, it would be worth it.

He held up the coins, and Perrin's grin widened.

"Garran and Delia Nariel disowned their daughter the year 512."

Kurtz's pulse quickened. "Because of the trial?"

"Because of what she confessed under oath. Her testimony disgraced her family. Such conduct could not be overlooked, even by her own parents."

No surprise there. Kurtz pictured her walking into his tent alone, bold as a harlot. He'd never imagined a nobleman's daughter would behave in such a way. Had foolishly thought Yobatha, the goddess of pleasure, had been smiling on him when in truth, Careeanne Nariel had been setting the snare to frame him.

"What happened after?" Kurtz asked.

"She stayed with friends for a time," Perrin said, "but scandals burn everyone they touch. They asked her to leave. She moved to Meneton, opened up a dress shop. The Gilded Seam. Looks prosperous."

A flutter ran through Kurtz's stomach. "She lives in Meneton?"

"That I don't know, but the woman running the shop says she rarely comes in."

Kurtz muttered an oath. Careeanne, so close, in the very city Zanna wanted to reach. Maddening.

"She changed her name," Perrin added. "Goes by Caris Narel now. Close enough to remember, different enough to hide."

No wonder she'd eluded Kurtz. "Anything else?"

"Whispers that she keeps strange company. Smugglers, gamblers, worse. She never married, has no children, avoids society. No one's seen her in months. That's all there is." Perrin held out his hand.

Kurtz passed over the coins. "I'm a bloodvoicer. If I have any further questions or need to hire you, can I contact you directly?"

"Of course—if you pay."

Kurtz thought of something else. "Hear anything of Dovev Falkson?"

"The Duke of Barth?" Perrin tipped his head. "Not much. Keeps to his estate. Avoids common folk. The uncommon ones too."

"That sounds like him," Kurtz said. "What about strange magic? A cloud or some kind of fog?"

"There's always strange magic in Barth," Perrin said. "I stay away from that place. But a merchant recently told me he was turned from the gates. They're getting pickier about who they let inside."

Kurtz didn't like the sound of that. "Guess I'll find out soon enough."

"Barth is where you're headed?"

"That's where." He gave the man a quick nod. "Appreciate your help."

"Anytime." Perrin shifted the coins between his thumb and first two fingers so they scraped together. "Always glad to work for a man who pays."

When Kurtz returned, Zanna was waiting at the edge of camp, arms crossed, sword belted at her side. The firelight traced her silhouette, softening the steel in her stance. "You're sneaking off now?"

He stopped, not in the mood for more verbal sparring. "I told you. I went for a walk."

"Alone in the dark. You? Who were you talking to?"

"Myself."

"I heard two voices."

"Maybe my echo is as relentless as you are."

"Then maybe if I listen hard enough, it will tell me what you're hiding."

"Stop acting like I owe you an explanation."

Her jaw tightened. "Someone has to look out for you."

"I've been looking out for myself for a long time."

"Do I need to remind you who dragged you out of that Ice

Island tunnel?" she shot back. "Or how your little barmaid dalliance gave Verdot Amal a spy at the Ivory Spit."

He took a step closer and held her gaze. Her eyes were black velvet in the dark. "You think you know me?"

"I know if you keep taking off alone like that, it's going to get you killed."

His chin dropped. "Better me than one of you."

"Don't you dare decide that for us." Her hand twitched at her side, not quite reaching for her sword but close. "We're on this mission together, like it or not."

"Not." Kurtz pushed past her and dropped to his bedroll.

Zanna, thankfully, said no more. Kurtz kicked off his boots and stretched out, the fire crackling like his nerves. The air felt heavy with Zanna's accusations and the ghost of Careeanne. Maddening, that she might be so close. He'd already told Zanna they weren't going to Meneton, so he couldn't very well turn around now, especially not with the king eager for word about Cortland. No, he had to go to Barth, fulfill the mission, *then* go to Meneton, if it wasn't too late.

A soft gust of wind swept through the camp, brushing sand across his face. He shut his eyes as grains stung his cheeks. For lands' sake, Zanna had been right about building a sand shield. Maybe the desert was punishing him for ignoring her, or for letting her get under his armor in the first place.

The woman breathed steadily just a few feet away. How was he going to uncover anything with her breathing down his neck? And how could he focus on the Barth mission knowing Careeanne Nariel might be the opposite direction? Sleep stayed stubbornly out of reach, driven off by duty and the women he couldn't seem to escape.

Acknowledgements

It is only by God's grace that I was able to find the time to write this story. There were many years when I was able to write full-time, but that is not the case today. I teach fifth grade during the school year, and that full-time job makes writing a challenge. So I am beyond grateful to have made it to the acknowledgments section of this book.

Thanks to Susan May Warren for helping me brainstorm this story. No one brainstorms like Susie, and I pinch myself over and over that she blocked out time on her calendar to help me.

A shout-out to the amazing team at Sunrise Publishing who work hard to solve our problems of what to read next. Thanks for all you do, Susan, Rel, Sarah, Katie, Caroline, Kristyn, and Tari! And thanks to cover designer Emilie Haney and line editor Megan Gerig for their fantastic work as well. ♥

Big hugs to Andrew Swearingen, Kelly Fernlake, Niki Florica, and Megan Gerig for helping me when I get stuck and for writing stories in the land of Er'Rets. I'm so grateful for you all.

Huge thanks to Bobbi Mash for beta-reading this story and for adding some excellent romance edits. No one knows romance novels like Bobbi, and I was completely spoiled to have her help on this story. I also got some assistance from my bestie, Kim Titus, who gave feedback on the Kurtz and Zanna scenes before she started reading the next King's Spies book. Thank you, Kim!

A very special thank you to Carissa Barrows for allowing me to publish her lyrics to "Woe to the Five," a song she wrote that was inspired by my novel, King's Folly. I thought it would be fun if Cole and Mistel made the song part of their act. Carissa performed this song on her YouTube channel, and you can listen to it by searching: "Woe to the Five (Original Ballad)" on YouTube.

As always, a gigantic THANK YOU to my Patrons, whose kind generosity allows me to create. I am so grateful for you all: Philip Schmidt, Bethany Baldwin, Carissa Barrows, Connie Hendryx, Emily Hutnyak, Paul James, Marie Lynch, Jenni McKinney, Deena Peterson, Linda Samuels, Stephen Swanson, Madi Trandahl, Jennie Webb, Kay Freeland Chang, Jessica Dowell, Danielle Birney, Tracie Heskett, Darrin Hutnyak, and Rachelle Sperling.

And finally, to you, dear readers. I am so honored that you take the time to read the stories I write. Thank you.

Jill Williamson is a multi-passionate creative who loves the arts. She's written over two dozen books for readers of all ages and is best known for her Blood of Kings fantasy series, two of which won Christy Awards and made VOYA magazine's Best Science Fiction, Fantasy, and Horror list. She produces films with her husband and teaches about writing at conferences.

Visit her at www.jillwilliamson.com.

BLOOD OF KINGS: LEGENDS

  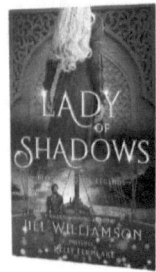 

Award-winning author
JILL WILLIAMSON
with Andrew Swearingen,
Kelly Fernlake, & Niki Florica

Return to the world of Er'Rets in an epic fantasy series brimming with richly woven tales of loyalty, love, and sacrifice...

We solve the problem of what to read next.

Jody Hedlund's
BRIDE SHIPS ⚓ NEW VOYAGES

BOOK ONE

A new world. A new hope. An unexpected love. What life awaits these brides?

We solve the problem of what to read next.

HEROES OF RENEGADE

Another epic series created by
SUSAN MAY WARREN
and LISA PHILLIPS

We solve the problem of what to read next.

YOU MAY ALSO LIKE...

When a blizzard strikes Deep Haven and Megan is overrun with catastrophes, it takes a former Ranger to step in and help. But the more he comes to her rescue, the sooner she'll move out... Come home to Deep Haven in this magical tale about the one who got away... and came back.

Still the One by **Susan May Warren and Rachel D. Russell**

Grace Howell leaves her life as a ballerina and returns to Heritage, Michigan, to heal. Teaching dance is just a temporary gig, until she finds herself unexpectedly charmed by small-town life and her growing attachment to Seth Warner, a man from her past with a troubled history of his own.

You're the Reason by **Tari Faris**

Dani Sullivan is determined to revive Jonathon Island's fading charm and reunite her fractured family. Her plan? Reopen the Grand Sullivan Hotel. But without the funds to restore the hotel, Dani's forced to accept help from Liam Stone—a big-city hotel developer whose sleek, modern vision is everything she's trying to avoid.

Meet Me at the Grand by **Lindsay Harrel**

We solve the problem of what to read next.

WHERE EVERY STORY IS A FRIEND, AND EVERY CHAPTER IS A NEW JOURNEY...

 Subscribe to our newsletter for a free book, the latest news, weekly giveaways, exclusive author interviews, and more!

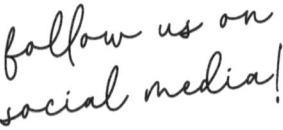

 @sunrisemediagroup

 @sunrisepublish

 @sunrisepublishing

Shop paperbacks, ebooks, audiobooks, and more at
SUNRISEPUBLISHING.MYSHOPIFY.COM

www.ingramcontent.com/pod-product-compliance
Lightning Source LLC
LaVergne TN
LVHW040038080526
838202LV00045B/3392